THE LINE UNBROKEN

THE LINE UNBROKEN

BIRTH OF MAGIC™ BOOK ONE

ND ROBERTS

MICHAEL ANDERLE

DISRUPTIVE IMAGINATION

LMBPN Publishing
PMB 196, 2540 South Maryland Pkwy
Las Vegas, NV 89109

First US edition, May, 2020
Version 1.02, April 2022
eBook ISBN: 978-1-64202-909-3
Print ISBN: 978-1-64202-910-9

THE LINE UNBROKEN TEAM

Thanks to our Beta Readers:
Larry Omans, Jim Caplan, Micky Cocker, Rachel Beckford,
John Ashmore, Kelly O'Donnell, Mary Morris

Thanks to the JIT Readers

Veronica Stephan-Miller
Diane L. Smith
Dorothy Lloyd
Dave Hicks
Peter Manis
James Caplan
Misty Roa
Deb Mader
Jeff Goode
Micky Cocker
Kerry Mortimer
Angel LaVey

If I've missed anyone, please let me know!

Editor
Lynne Stiegler

DEDICATION

For Lynne, who saved this book at least four times

— Nat

*To Family, Friends and
Those Who Love
To Read.
May We All Enjoy Grace
To Live The Life We Are
Called.*

—Michael

PROLOGUE

Beringia-Canada Border, WWDE+210

A new light burst into being over the land bridge, painting the sky a rich red that washed out the rising sun on the horizon.

A solitary arctic fox trotted through the snow, weaving to keep to the lighter drifts where the trees crept onto the ice. Startled by the sudden flash, she darted for cover, the kill clamped between her jaws, leaving a scarlet trail in the pristine snow. She poked her nose out into the wind and sniffed. Satisfied there was no immediate danger, she settled into the crevice between two boulders to eat her meal out of the cold, turning her back as she drew farther into the lee of her shelter to avoid the biting teeth of the wind.

The wind didn't care about the cold. It only cared to play.

Great, wild gusts lifted the snowflakes, flurrying them at the moment before they settled on the waste. One stole a feather from the fox's ptarmigan and set it to dance in the updrafts around the boulder formation. The feather rose in a whirling spiral, buffeted by invisible paws. It drifted a little way across the uneven ground, almost indiscernible in the whiteout.

The skeleton of a tree offered brief shelter until the wind captured it again, tossing the feather onto one of the small rises crowding the hoary wasteland around the rocks. The snow blanketing the rise shivered when the feather landed with the lightest touch.

The fox paused in her meal when another flash of light lit the dawn.

This one did not come from the sky.

The trembling ground was enough to convince her that it would be better to return to her den. She abandoned her meal and set off, careful to avoid the sources of the rotten meat smell that had arrived in her territory some moons ago.

That meat was contaminated. Not for consumption. Dying at the hands of a two-legs was to be avoided at all costs. The fox had witnessed her mate learning *that* lesson the hard way, but a vixen had to eat, and food was plentiful on the tundra for those hungry enough to take the risk.

Delicate steps took her to the edge of the forest, where she knew she would find safety. The bad smell was stronger here, but no large predator came far into the close-growing pines where the bears lived, not even the two-legs. Lulled by her proximity to sanctuary, the fox did not see the red glow beneath the snow until it was too late.

A decomposing two-legs erupted arms first from the

heavy drift that had built on top of its corpse, eliciting a panicked scream from the fox.

She snapped at the hands that grabbed her, to no effect. The two-legs was larger, stronger. It didn't react to the pain of being bitten.

Still, she fought capture, screaming in anger as she scored the two-legs' rotting flesh with her claws. It bit her tail, and she took its eye with a desperate swipe.

The two-legs fumbled, giving the fox the chance she needed to escape into the forest. This forest had never been a place for the two-legged. The fox was queen here, as long as she avoided the bears. Nevertheless, the two-legs crashed after her, hurtling through the undergrowth with no regard for the injuries the branches caused it. The two-legs tore after the fox, but she was faster.

Just.

The fox was momentarily confused by the unexpected continuation of the pursuit. Her clever mind raced as her heart beat fit to burst with the exertion of running for her life. A risk was no risk at all when the other prospect was certain death. Decision made, she switched her course and ran on, endlessly pursued by the red-eyed two-legs.

She paused to catch her breath and sniff out her path, lapping a few cooling mouthfuls from a stream that wasn't completely iced over. The two-legs almost caught her when it leapt recklessly from the embankment.

It missed her, landing half out of the water, just out of reach.

The fox darted across the creek and into the trees on the other side, the two-legs a hair's breadth behind her the whole time with its grasping hands and snapping teeth.

All thought was gone except the drive to escape. She pelted through a break in the trees and skidded into a clearing, banking sharply to avoid the twin bear cubs frolicking in the melt.

Her only goal now was to hide. She darted under a fallen log before the mother spotted her, knowing the penalty for disturbing a mother bear and her cubs would be every bit as painful as an end at the hands of the two-legs.

Her pursuer stumbled into the clearing and forgot all about the fox when it saw two much larger meals play-fighting. It salivated, its remaining eye glowing brighter in the shade of the pines.

Then it growled, and the mother bear awoke.

The fox cowered in her hideaway, instinct pinning her to the spot. She tasted her heart in her mouth as the mother bear reared up.

The two-legs was too focused on its prey to see the eight-foot grizzly bear behind it.

The mother roared her displeasure and removed the two-legs' head with a well-aimed swipe of her enormous paw. She nosed her cubs when they ambled over to investigate, their curiosity tweaked by the strange beast their mother had just dispatched.

The fox shrank back under the log as the mother herded her cubs out of the clearing.

Danger gone, the fox was suddenly starving. Her stomach complained bitterly about the abandoned ptarmigan the whole time she was putting distance between her and the larger predators. She loped through the undergrowth in the opposite direction from the bears, her mind fixed on finding food to ease the gnawing in her stomach.

There were rabbits aplenty deeper in the forest.

CHAPTER ONE

Salem, MA, Samhain Night

Midwinter chill bit the air inside the tent, one of many scattered across Salem Common that night. The meager heat cast by the camp stove did little to comfort the two women inside, although the warmth from the food and drink they'd consumed at the Samhain feast earlier that night lingered.

Sarah Jennifer Walton, granddaughter of the long-forgotten Terry Henry and Charumati, sat cross-legged on her bedroll, cupping a mug of honeyed tea in both hands.

"Ten months," Esme remarked, lifting her mug to Sarah Jennifer.

"Ten months since you tricked me into thinking you needed my help," Sarah Jennifer replied. She'd been in this part of Massachusetts since coming across Esme and sticking around to help the old woman make it through winter.

The memory of their first meeting made her smile.

Little had she known at the time, Esme was far from a

frail old woman in need of help. She was indeed a witch, or something like one, and it had been Sarah Jennifer who was in need of help. Help mending her broken soul.

Almost a year of assisting Esme in her role as the forest community's caretaker, wisewoman, midwife, doctor, and general busybody had done much to remind Sarah Jennifer that the universe did not, in fact, revolve around her grief, and that she could continue to wander and that would be just fine, *if* she could live with knowing she was shirking her responsibility to humanity, whether unenhanced, Were, vampire, or witch.

Sarah Jennifer's time with this woman she called friend had revealed a new side to the UnknownWorld—one filled with wonder.

She hadn't known Esme was anything other than an ordinary human at first. Then, as time went by, she had noticed odd things happened around her. But it wasn't until tonight that Sarah Jennifer's suspicions had been confirmed, when they had arrived in Salem, and she had been included in the town's Samhain celebrations.

She had been made welcome, and had shared good food and admittedly confusing conversation with the townspeople.

Then the ghosts had arrived.

Sarah Jennifer hadn't been visited by any of her departed, and she'd been grateful for it. The fire ritual she had taken part in after the feast that night had been the completion of her journey to catharsis. She was ready to rejoin the world, even if that meant opening herself up to being hurt by it again. Still, learning about the Were pack terrorizing the area gave her a reason to stick around a little longer before she started on figuring that out, and she had the mystery of Esme's magic to unravel.

Esme clicked her tongue, breaking her reverie. "You've got that look on your face I can't tell if you're thinking hard or you've got gas."

"Like you're not reading my mind." Sarah Jennifer fixed her friend with a firm look. "Tell me how you got your magic, Esme. Because there's another explanation for what I've seen tonight. The rest of the UnknownWorld doesn't know about this town or any magic. I would have heard about it."

Esme's eyes crinkled. "You're a sharp one, Duckie. I'll give you that. Salem today is not the same Salem as it was pre-WWDE. It's a smidge to the north and closer to the coast than both of the towns you'll find marked on any map." She smiled. "This valley, these hills, the standing stones on the ridge where you met Annie tonight—none of that existed before Salem was founded. We shaped the land to hide from the world."

Sarah Jennifer stared at Esme, seeing her friend for who she was at long last. This unassuming, sharp-tongued, salt-of-the-earth woman with an iron will and pragmatic determination had the ability to recreate reality. She kept her true power hidden and used it to take care of people.

She knew Esme was on the side of right. Still, she needed to hear her friend say the three little words that explained why she had abilities a vampire would be jealous of. "*How?*"

Esme "Would you believe technology over superstition?" She scrutinized Sarah Jennifer for any hint of understanding.

"Every time, and especially after everything I've seen over the last few months." Sarah Jennifer sighed internally. It would be just her luck to run into yet another of Esme's verbal knots and come out none the wiser.

Not this time. This time she was Alexander, and the knot would come apart under the blade of her desire for the truth. "I come from a family of Weres and vampires. You know that already because I didn't hold back about who I am. You said Samhain is about dropping the barriers. Truth, Esme. You have nanocytes, don't you?"

It was Esme's turn to be surprised. "What do you know about nanocytes?" Her hoarse laughter rebounded off the canvas. "Looks like we've both been holding back. Maybe we end Samhain night with a conversation."

Sarah Jennifer smiled. "Never a bad thing. I want to hear your story. Where are you from? How did you get your power?"

"Now, *that* is too long a story for one night." Esme shivered. "I'll be glad to get home. It's colder than a witch's tit in February."

Sarah Jennifer wrinkled her nose when a gust of icy wind intruded, throwing open the tent flap where it had worked loose. "Yeah, it's not just the witches who are suffering."

She put her tea down and got up to tie the loose flap off, being careful not to bang her head on the poles and bring their shelter down on their heads.

Esme pulled her blankets tighter around her body. "Throw another chunk on the stove, there's a dear." She snuggled into her pallet and waited for Sarah Jennifer to get into her bedroll.

Sarah Jennifer looked across the tent at Esme. "Start with magic. How do you explain it? I've seen the supernatural, and I've seen high technology. I've *never* seen anyone bring back the dead."

"Like you guessed, Duckie. It's not magic." Esme scowled. "But you already know the truth, or some of it, anyway. I have nanocytes, yes."

"But you call yourself a witch?" Sarah Jennifer pressed. "Why?"

Esme started to answer one way, then changed her mind. "It's easier," she admitted. "Too much time has passed, and people have short memories. They have forgotten the power of our Queen. Besides, there are those on the council who would insist they are witches even if you showed them proof."

Sarah Jennifer wasn't surprised to hear that. The apparent connection between Esme and Bethany Anne explained enough to satisfy her overstimulated mind for the moment. "It didn't take long for them to forget about my grandparents or the FDG, either. So, the ghosts at the feast tonight. They weren't real?"

Esme waved a hand. "Who's to judge what's real? The shades were constructed from the memories of those present; that's real enough as far as I'm concerned. But that's not what you want to know."

"No." Sarah Jennifer wasn't entirely certain *what* she wanted to know. Everything, of course, but what was relevant right now? Her brain was mush, too overtired to give her any answer. She opened her mouth to speak, but all that came out was a huge yawn.

"Looks like you're done with the conversating for

tonight," Esme teased, poking her friend's knee with her foot.

Sarah Jennifer stretched in her bedroll, drowsiness stealing her words. "Between the feast and the fight, I'm beat."

Esme chuckled. "Sleep, Duckie. Plenty of time to talk on the way home."

***

Early the next morning, Sarah Jennifer left the tent and stretched to work the kinks out of her spine. The commons was empty in the predawn, except for the tents.

The street beyond was just starting to show signs of life. Sarah Jennifer smelled bread somewhere, which was the smell of humanity, as far as she was concerned. Meat could be hunted. Bread was only found in civilized places where it was safe to work the land and produce grain for the flour.

Breakfast would wait.

She took a moment to enjoy the crunch of her feet on the frost-tipped grass, then set off for the town boundary at a creaky sprint. Her first objective for the day was the rapid attendance to her body's needs.

Her knee hurt like a bitch, as always. Activity usually took care of the stiffness from her old injury, which in turn lessened the aching reminder to be humble that her grandfather had given her lifetimes ago. Sarah Jennifer often wondered why it had never fully healed, despite her natural enhancement giving her an almost instant healing ability. Sylvia's claims of her holding onto it to punish herself were laughable. Who wanted to live in pain?

She pushed on into the forest.

A brisk five-mile run and a lingering shower under an ice-cold waterfall later, Sarah Jennifer felt almost human again. The faintly throbbing reminder of the mead she'd consumed at last night's feast had faded completely by the time she got back into Salem, leaving plenty of room for all the questions she had about witches and magic and the asshole Weres living in the forest of Lynnwood.

Sarah Jennifer headed for Salem common at a brisk jog, waving to the people she'd met at the feast the night before as she passed through the town.

She had a theory about the Weres, and they would wait for a moment, too.

This area hadn't turned out to be the worst place to settle for a while. The people of Salem and the surrounding area were good-hearted and worked hard for each other. Still, Sarah Jennifer much preferred the quiet of the cottage she shared with Esme, two days' journey from the town by horse and cart. She'd gotten so used to being away from the bustle of centralized living during her years wandering that she couldn't have seen herself staying for very long if it weren't for their secluded idyll.

Sarah Jennifer diverted to the bakery on her way back to the tent. Home was calling her.

The tent was no longer there when she arrived. The horses were hitched to the cart, and Esme was engrossed in conversation with Annie, the witch Sarah Jennifer had rescued from the aforementioned asshole Weres the night before.

Sarah Jennifer slowed to a walk when she saw the cart. She gave the horses an apple each, taking a moment to rub Cordy's neck while her bum knee made its usual complaint about the sudden change of pace. "You could have waited, Esme. I would have taken care of all of this."

Esme turned from her conversation and waved Sarah Jennifer over somewhat impatiently. "C'mon, Duckie. When have you known me to wait around? You've been gone half the morning already. We need to see to the defenses before we leave."

Sarah Jennifer raised an eyebrow as she climbed onto the cart. "The sun rose less than an hour ago, and I stopped for pastries." She dangled the bag out of Esme's reach.

"Then I suppose I can forgive you, just this once." Esme flashed her wizened grin at Sarah Jennifer, and caught Annie's sleeve as she turned to leave. "You be sure and stay inside the town until I get the boundary hex charged."

Annie nodded solemnly. "I'm not going to risk it after last night. If your apprentice hadn't been there to drive those mangy Weres away, goddess knows what they would have done to me." She lifted her head to smile at Sarah Jennifer. "Merry met. Don't be a stranger here now, okay?"

Sarah Jennifer wasn't sure what she'd done to earn the warm welcome she'd received from the people of Salem, or why both Annie and her daughter had assumed she was Esme's new protégé, or similar. Confusion appeared to be the order of this year so far, but she nodded her thanks all the same. "I'll be sure to visit when I'm over this way next. You have a wolf problem I need to take care of."

Annie's smile was a reward all by itself. "We'll be grateful for it."

Esme clucked for the horses to move, calling back to Annie as the cart rumbled on its way, "Remember. Don't go wandering until you can feel that the boundary is recharged."

"Apprentice, huh?" Sarah Jennifer remarked as they set off. "My psychic powers tell me that the chances of me doing magic are…let me see…zero."

Esme gave her a pointed look and turned her attention to her hands in her lap. She didn't speak until they reached the pair of standing rocks either side of the turnoff to the North Road. "Stop here."

Sarah Jennifer drew the horses to a halt and eased herself down from the cart. She walked over and examined the carved stones with interest. "These are…what?"

Esme lifted her hands in apology. "A lot of nonsense, but it's necessary nonsense." She frowned in amusement at the crude penis scratched into the ancient stone. "We were talking about magic and technology. Time to pick that up again."

Sarah Jennifer leaned in to look at the graffiti and nodded at Esme skeptically. "The magic penis rock is important, *riiight.*"

Esme waved Sarah Jennifer away with her staff, then raised her hands and face to the sky. "The stones are the marker that the people need. They believe there is magic in the stones that keeps them safe. In reality, their belief is what powers the barrier that repels people with invader nanocytes."

"'Invader nanocytes?' That's a good one." Sarah Jennifer waited for an explanation, but none was forthcoming. She leaned against one of the stones with her arms folded. "I don't know much about nanocytes, but I'm pretty sure that *all* of the UnknownWorld is the result of an invasion."

"You've a sharp mouth on you today," Esme muttered grimly. She opened her eyes and pointed her walking staff vaguely in Sarah Jennifer's direction. "You know what I mean. It's science viewed through the lens of the fantastic. There are different types of nanocytes. They're usually reprogrammable, in my experience, which means they can be taught to avoid Salem. The unenhanced can't even see the turnoff because the hex blocks it from their minds."

"What do they see?" Sarah Jennifer asked with curiosity.

Esme shrugged. "Just trees. Stand back or get your ass bitten."

Sarah Jennifer jumped away from the standing stone when the energy she'd felt last night on the common poured from nowhere and everywhere all at once. The air shimmered briefly, forming a rippling golden wave that extended in a dome over the town before vanishing from sight. "So, the magic penis rock is important after all. Are you doing that?"

Esme lowered her arms and turned to go back to the cart. "It's the only way to keep Salem safe. I recharge it every Samhain when the people are most open to their belief."

Soft golden light shone in her eyes, its glow muted compared to the bright flashes of red, purple, blue, or yellow Sarah Jennifer was used to seeing.

"Meaning, you can tap their energy. I get it. The feast. The ritual and the focus on lowering the barriers." Sarah Jennifer wasn't in agreement with the charade, but if the people weren't harming anyone, it wasn't her place to pass judgment. "I have a different question. Why aren't your eyes red?"

Esme's gaze flashed ruby before settling back to their gentle shine. "I don't *want* them to be red." She dropped her hands, done with her task. "We should get going. We've got another stop before we get home."

She climbed back onto the cart, leaving her protégé by the barrier.

Sarah Jennifer probed the barrier. She was able to pass her hand through it with no more than a tingle along her skin.

"Are you going to stand there dancing like a scatter-brained nomad all day?" Esme called sharply. "We won't make camp at this rate."

Sarah Jennifer climbed into the cart and closed her eyes, settling in to think about the first leg of the return journey to the cottage. The last three days had been an education about the woman she'd thought she knew.

She wondered what other revelations were to come.

CHAPTER TWO

<u>Salem University, MA</u>

Sarah Jennifer sat cross-legged on her bedroll by the campfire they'd made in the former reading room of the university library. The wind whistled through the gaps in the walls, but the roof was intact, which was a blessing since it had started snowing again.

"There are different kinds of nanocytes. I get that. We have a mix in my family of Weres, superhumans like me, vampires, and a couple we have no idea about. My mom— her eyes glow blue, and I never saw that anywhere. Or met anyone else who could heal people."

Esme stirred the pot and sniffed. "I'd say that's about done. What color did you get?"

Sarah Jennifer waved a finger at her eyes and shrugged. "What you see is what you get. I'm a no-glow zone."

"Hmmm." Esme craned her neck to look into the pot while she scooped them each a bowlful of stew. "That remains to be seen."

Sarah Jennifer accepted the rustic wooden bowl and

inhaled the aroma of turkey, sage, and onions with gratitude. "You always find the right accompaniment for the meat."

Esme winked. "It's the least I can do to provide a fitting send-off for the animal who gave its life so we could eat."

Sarah Jennifer raised her eyebrows as she lifted her spoon to her mouth. "Oh, so you *do* subscribe to all the hippy-dippy stuff." She ate her bite, smirking at Esme as she chewed.

"Do you think your recent success with hunting is entirely down to your skills?" Esme asked. "The air around us is saturated with nanocytes. They are in the earth and the water. The flora and fauna."

She pointed her spoon at Sarah Jennifer. "They're everywhere, especially in humans, and they can be used—*if* your will is strong enough."

Sarah Jennifer didn't see how wanting something made it happen.

Esme didn't see why Sarah Jennifer couldn't stop broadcasting her thoughts so loudly.

She returned her attention to her meal. "I'm not asking you to pretend it's magic. I'm telling you that we can use preconception and ritual as a focusing tool for our will. Did you come into this life as a soldier? No. You had to train your skills. What's different about using the trappings of religion and the like to train the technology inside your body?"

Sarah Jennifer felt her face make her skepticism clear despite her efforts to show respect for Esme's knowledge. "It's technology that I have no way to affect. What do I do, sit here and imagine I can transform into a wolf?"

"You could start by fixing your knee instead of complaining about it." Esme smiled as she put her empty bowl to the side. "I don't expect you to get it straight away."

She settled into a more comfortable position. "Annie, her job is to keep the crops thriving year-round. She has control over nature because she believes in her ability as a witch."

"How does belief have anything to do with it?" Sarah Jennifer's mind ran free with memories of her and Sylvia's attempts to turn wolf. "This is alien technology, as far as I understand it. We don't have control over what it does to our bodies." She waved her hand vaguely at the forest in the distance. "Like these Weres who have been bothering the town. My guess is that they don't have an Alpha worth a damn. All they need is someone to take charge and instill some discipline. It's not magic."

Esme wondered if Sarah Jennifer's potential would be limited by her inability to imagine the fantastic. "It doesn't matter what it is, as long as it works. For all our knowledge, and as far as the people of Salem are concerned, there were natural witches long before WWDE. Who are we to say which myths are based on truth?"

She poked Sarah Jennifer's knee. "This is as good a start as any."

The younger woman shook her head. "It's not as easy as that. Otherwise you'd still be young."

Esme laughed, a long, deep belly laugh. "That's your standpoint, eh? Hold my staff." She thrust her walking stick at Sarah Jennifer and covered her face with her hands. She pushed her hair back, revealing a face forty years younger and hair that was thick and glossy and chestnut in color. "Things aren't always what they appear to be."

Sarah Jennifer gaped as Esme shook her hair and released the form. "Then why on earth do you… Oh, because it would freak people out if you didn't age."

"Got it in one," Esme confirmed. "Now, your knee. How are you going to take control of that pack if you have such an obvious weakness?"

"Not a weakness," Sarah Jennifer retorted. "I fight just fine, injury or no injury."

Esme nodded, giving Sarah Jennifer a skeptical look. "Prove it."

It was Sarah Jennifer's turn to look skeptical. "You want me to fight you? Esme. I'm not going to do that. You'll get hurt."

"Nonsense," Esme called over her shoulder as she stalked out of the building.

Sarah Jennifer followed her out into the snow. The horses snickered in recognition. "Esme. Come on. There's no need for—"

Esme swung her staff and took Sarah Jennifer out at the knee. "Told you."

Sarah Jennifer pushed herself up from the floor, furious that Esme had made her eat her words, along with a mouthful of snow. She got to her feet and took her fighting stance. "Fine. It's on."

She dodged Esme's staff and darted in to restrain her, ignoring the grinding in her knee.

Esme wasn't there to be captured. "Nice try, Duckie. No cookie."

Sarah Jennifer spun to see that Esme had somehow

gotten behind her and let out a growl of frustration when a tree root burst from the ground and snagged her feet. She hit the ground again.

She hauled herself up and wiped the slush from her face, glaring at Esme the whole time. "Stop cheating! You can't have the *ground* attack me!"

Esme blew on the tip of her finger and smirked as the creeping roots receded. "You've got nanocytes. You can do the same if you want it badly enough." She crossed the space between them faster than a little old lady ought to be able to and tapped Sarah Jennifer's bad knee with her walking staff. "Now. Heal that."

"OW! How the f—" Sara Jennifer drew a breath before she lost her temper completely and embarrassed herself with poor language. "I don't *have* any conscious healing abilities. I told you, that's my mother's skill. I'm faster, a bit stronger, and I don't age or injure easily. That's all I've got, besides heightened senses."

Esme shook her head. "This is hopeless. You need a history lesson."

Sarah Jennifer sighed, bending to massage her throbbing knee. "What is it I'm not getting?"

Esme held her hand out and pulled Etheric energy into her palm to create a small swirling golden cloud. "You're blocking yourself. Believe you can heal your knee. Believe with utter certainty that you have the power to fix the damage to your cartilage. More than that, *know* it."

Sarah Jennifer found the idea ridiculous. "This is worse than training with my grandparents. At least I had a chance of meeting their expectations."

Esme sent the energy to ease the swelling in Sarah

Jennifer's knee. "Yes, because they were limited in their knowledge of the gift they'd been given, most likely. I have had more than two lifetimes to reach my potential and an education to help me figure it out."

Sarah Jennifer let out a sharp laugh as her pain faded. "I don't think anyone knew anything. They were too busy holding humanity together."

"Noble work," Esme told her. "But it all came to nothing in the end. We have to take care of our own. If you're determined to do something about those Weres, you'd better be prepared. Come on. We have a long journey ahead tomorrow. We'll work on your knee another time."

Sarah Jennifer returned to their camp and settled in, pissed off. What Esme was telling her made no sense. She needed to get an understanding of the technology inside her body. Esme was right about her impediment. Hell, if she was fighting herself, the first thing she'd go for was her knee.

She curled into her bedroll, her tumbled thoughts churning as she willed sleep to come. She couldn't afford weakness if she was to help the people of Salem.

Esme woke Sarah Jennifer the next morning with a prod of her staff. "You sure like to lie in," she remarked dryly. "You're certain you were in the military?"

"Not for a long time." Sarah Jennifer sat up and rubbed her eyes, then glanced at the faint line of light touching the horizon. "It's still night."

"Says you," Esme told her gruffly. "Some of us have been

up and working for hours." She took the blanket filled with books outside and put them on the cart.

Sarah Jennifer joined her, stretching her joints in the dawn light. The encroaching forest was misty. "Leftovers for breakfast, or strike camp and eat when we get home?"

Esme smiled at Sarah Jennifer, pointing into the trees. "I'll get breakfast on. You'll find a stream that way to fetch water."

"Suits me." Sarah Jennifer yawned and went to fill their water skins.

They struck camp immediately after eating. The miles passed unnoticed for the most part. Sarah Jennifer tried everything she could think of to produce energy like Esme had, hoping against hope that she could fix her knee and become the formidable fighting machine she'd been raised to be.

Nothing she did made a difference, and Esme's intervention soon wore off, leaving her to contemplate her failure as the familiar throbbing returned.

"There's too much to process," Sarah Jennifer complained, breaking the silence. "Magic, the Weres. Why didn't you tell me about any of this before?"

Esme grasped the reins. The horses plodded on, Dusty leading Cordy along straight ruts worn into the overgrown north road by decades of use. "There's a lot I've kept back from you," she admitted. "Can you understand that it's difficult to open up after keeping secrets for so long for the good of everyone? Baby steps, Duckie. I swear you'll know everything soon enough, and when you do, you will probably wish you didn't."

Sarah Jennifer continued, unperturbed by Esme's

attempt to divert her. "Okay, so, there's obviously some bigger picture I'm not getting. Help me understand, Esme. Tell me what you can. How do you know about Bethany Anne?"

Esme yawned. "That's an easy one to answer. I worked for her before she left Earth behind."

Sarah Jennifer gestured for the reins. "You rest and talk. I'll drive. What work did you do for her?"

"Not that the horses need telling where to go." Esme appraised Sarah Jennifer for a moment before passing her the reins. "Let's see. I know you know what a computer is. Do you understand what they do?"

"I've used them," Sarah Jennifer replied. "Can't say much of it stuck. I prefer action to sitting around thinking."

Esme chuckled. "You don't say. I was a research assistant at a TQB facility in Europe. I handled data for the scientists there, analyzing test results for the most part, although my boss wasn't averse to pulling me in to cover when she was between assistants. That was before the struggle to steal TQB technology began."

That piqued Sarah Jennifer's curiosity. "There was a struggle?"

Esme nodded, a sly smile sneaking out. "For the people trying to steal the Empress' technology, yes. There were some casualties while Bethany Anne was in the process of closing down her activity here on Earth. The facility I worked at in Scotland was one of them. Most everyone was killed, and I was taken to a ship and healed with the other survivors."

Sarah Jennifer fixed Esme with a hard stare. There was

only one way she knew of to get nanocytes you weren't born with. "You drank vamp blood? Tell me you didn't."

Esme burst out laughing, startling the horses into picking up their pace. "Are you *mad*? I'll drink vamp blood the day I want red eyes and a sudden liking for claret. A nanocyte solution was injected into my vein. The nanocytes were programmed to repair damage."

She held out her hand, and a ball of golden light appeared over her palm. "It wasn't until much later that I understood the side effects of introducing additional nanocytes to someone who was born with them. Useful side-effects, to be sure, but unexpected. That's enough for now, Duckie. I'm tired."

Sarah Jennifer watched in amazement as the golden ball floated up to light their way in the falling dusk. "The day went so fast."

"It's all that thinking you keep doing," Esme deadpanned. "You know it's going to do you good. Keep it up." With that, Esme folded her hands on her stomach and closed her eyes. "Wake me when we get home."

CHAPTER THREE

Esme opened her eyes again when Sarah Jennifer turned the cart into the yard at the cottage. "You see to the horses. I'll shake out the cobwebs and put the kettle on."

Sarah Jennifer waved Esme into the cottage and began unhitching Cordy and Dusty, her thoughts turning to the more normal concern of the mutt pack she had to take care of. The attack on Samhain night aside, the Lynnwood pack —known as the Wolf-kin to the people of Salem—lived by raiding up and down the coast. There was no way she was going to allow that to continue.

Likely Esme had more to say on the matter. However, Sarah Jennifer had her heart set on finishing the conversation they had been having for the last two days. The canny glint in her friend's eye as they'd left the ruins of the university had been almost too hard to ignore. The bits and pieces of information Esme had revealed since had only added to the air of mystery surrounding the old woman.

"Less of the old!" Esme crowed indignantly from the kitchen window. "I'm offended by the thought!"

Sarah Jennifer rolled her eyes as she walked over to look in on Esme. "Stay out of my thoughts and you won't get offended, huh? Is there no privacy around here?"

Esme cackled, turning back to the kitchen as the kettle began to hiss. "Privacy! Now that's a myth from old times, I tell you. Kids today. You don't know you're born."

Sarah Jennifer leaned in at the window, smiling at the memory Esme's grumbling brought her. "You sound just like my grandfather. So, you were around before the World's Worst Day Ever. Tell me about it. It was a golden age, right?"

Esme cast a glance her way. "You mean, before the whole world went batshit-crazy and blew itself to kingdom come? I wouldn't call it a golden age. As far as I can remember, the majority lacked food, shelter, health-care, education, or some combination of the four. The people who had the power to do something about it were too busy arguing among themselves over arbitrary issues, and the people who might have done something about it were all too busy taking photos of their food to give a shit. WWDE couldn't have happened to a nicer species."

She nodded toward the door, ignoring Sarah Jennifer's confusion. "Come on in, Duckie. Tea's ready."

With a window or two open to let out the musty air, and the appearance of Esme's stew pot over the roaring fire in the grate, the sitting room was soon just the way Sarah Jennifer remembered it from her first night back in spring.

She sat down in her overstuffed chair with her legs

curled under her body and accepted the hand-thrown mug from Esme. "I've been looking forward to this."

"Being home? Or figuring out what I've been trying to teach you?"

"Both. I couldn't fix my knee no matter how hard I tried."

"There is no try," Esme told her. "Only do."

Sarah Jennifer scowled over the rim of her mug. "There you go, sounding like my grandfather again."

"Are you angry with him for the damage he caused you?" Esme asked.

Sarah Jennifer almost spat out her tea. "Well, yeah. Wouldn't you be angry if someone who was supposed to care for you took away your ability to fend for yourself?" She sighed. "I was cocky. He taught me a lesson I don't ever want to forget."

Esme shrugged. "Seems to me like he did you a favor. You never struck me as the thoughtful type. More the type to rush in and get yourself killed."

"What's that got to do with healing my injury?" Sarah Jennifer demanded, feeling more than a little bit called out.

Esme dipped her head. "Maybe you're holding onto that bad knee because you're afraid of your own arrogance."

Now Sarah Jennifer did feel attacked. "You sound like my sister. What do you know?"

Esme smiled. "I know you're self-healing, and that you haven't healed that knee. Just saying."

"Yeah, well, don't," Sarah Jennifer shot back, getting to her feet. Her knee twinged as if to prove Esme's point.

Esme gave her a pointed look. "Suit yourself."

Sarah Jennifer sighed and sat down again. "I'm sorry. I didn't mean to snap at you."

"Snap away," Esme told her. "Just don't complain when I bite back. You're the one who's determined to deal with the pack. I'm just trying to help."

Sarah Jennifer didn't know what to say to that. She stared into her mug as though the tea might hold the answers she was looking for. The fire crackled, soothing her with its sound. "Maybe I am holding on to some bad feeling about TH taking me down. I don't see how that's preventing me from healing, though."

Esme smiled softly. "You'll work it out when you're ready. Now, where were we in my story?"

"WWDE," Sarah Jennifer reminded her. "You were going to tell me what happened in Scotland when it went down."

Esme got up to stir the pot. "Ah, yes. Scotland was beyond me by then. I'd been healed three, no, four? Maybe it was five years before that. Time runs together when you've been around as long as I have."

"You're only a few decades older than me," Sarah Jennifer reminded her.

"I'm twice your age, at least," Esme countered. "Live another hundred years, and tell me if you can place every event you lived through. Anyway. I came here to America before WWDE. Before Bethany Anne left." Her expression grew distant as she worked to recall the time before civilization collapsed. "I kept to myself. After the attack, isolation seemed like the only thing to do. Then, when I stopped getting any older, I knew I had to find out what had happened to me."

"Did you meet Bethany Anne?" Sarah Jennifer asked. "Did she teach you how to control your nanocytes?"

Esme shook her head. "No. Not directly. She was gone by then. I learned the hard way—years of study, and gaining the trust of others who held different parts of the puzzle."

"More witches?" Sarah Jennifer inquired.

Esme shook her head. "Again, no. There was a vampire I knew. Before her, other humans, and the odd Were who had a link back to before WWDE. Your grandmother. Now, she was something in her youth."

Sarah Jennifer's mouth fell open. "You met my grandmother?"

Esme nodded. "In her Navy days."

"My grandmother was in the Navy?" Sarah Jennifer searched for her next question but found herself stuck on the thought of the Alpha of Alphas obeying anyone else's orders.

"Who do you think inspired me to change my eye color?" Esme teased, fighting off a yawn. "We're getting off-track, and it's late. My bed is calling."

Esme got to her feet and headed for her bedroom. "You need to concentrate on how you're going to take over the pack."

Sarah Jennifer resolved to get the whole story another time. Esme wasn't the only one ready for some serious pillow time.

Sarah Jennifer awoke the next morning feeling determined to prepare herself for a showdown with the pack. For once, she was up before Esme. If the soft snores from the other bedroom were anything to go by, her friend had overtaxed herself in the last few days and would be dead to the world for hours yet.

She grabbed a quick breakfast of leftovers from the pot after nursing the fire back to life and headed out to feed the horses with wolves on her mind.

Having met—and beaten the crap out of—two of the pack, she didn't see that they were such a menace. Then again, she'd grown up with Weres as part of her family and didn't find any but her grandmother to be the least bit intimidating.

She released Cordy and Dusty into the paddock, smiling when her mare nosed her hand in search of another apple.

"Not a chance," Sarah Jennifer told her good-naturedly. "You've already eaten more than your share."

She thought long and hard about how she was going to conduct this mission. Esme rose sometime after midday, and the two of them spent the remainder of the day taking care of chores around the cottage and discussing what Esme knew about the pack. There wasn't much to tell, other than a repeat of what she'd learned. Around twenty years ago, the Weres had deserted the city, and this pack had settled in Lynwood after the Alpha killed a man in Salem.

Sarah Jennifer was itching to get moving. Still, she was never one to turn away a tactical advantage, even if it meant sitting around with her thumb up her ass while she absorbed Esme's advice about navigating the Lynnwood forest in preparation for scouting the pack's territory.

There was only the fight, and it lived in her heart, just like it did the Colonel's.

Her parents had despaired when they'd first realized her soul was the mirror image of her grandfather's, eventually calling TH and Char back from their fifty-year vacation to train some sense into her. She had been incredibly grateful for every single moment of that training.

Her years of wandering had given her the advantage of knowing where the centers of population were holding on, even thriving in some cases. Not here. Her grandfather's belief that the enhanced had a duty to humanity was also hers, but civilization had all but fallen here.

The UnknownWorld was fractured all along the east coast, and the North American Pack Council was nowhere to be seen to take care of the shambles. It wasn't just the east coast, but all of America that had to be unified if they were to regain what they had lost. But how? She was one woman. Well, two women, since she doubted Esme would let her go it alone.

Sarah Jennifer gave herself a mental shake. Bethany Anne had been one woman as well. One woman with unlimited wealth and access to pre-WWDE technology, but so what? People had done more with less, and there were a surprising number of Weres scattered around the country—if you knew where to look.

Was this the bigger picture her friend had hinted at? Rebuilding?

Sarah Jennifer knew at that moment what she had to do. The UnknownWorld would have to come to terms with her way or deal with the consequences. She would have to drag civilization back up by the bootstraps if necessary, starting with the Lynwood pack. If she had to kill the Alpha to get the pack's obedience, she would do it without hesitation.

She was going to save every one of them whether they wanted it or not, asshole wolves and all.

CHAPTER FOUR

<u>Lynnwood Forest, MA (one week later)</u>

Sarah Jennifer tried and failed to breathe without gagging on the smell.

She was crouched in a pile of shit underneath another pile of shit, smelling like, yeah, *shit*. Just like the good old days in the Force De Guerre, but without the hot chow to look forward to.

Stellar.

Salem felt like home. Not because of the magic and Weres, but because they had taken her in and treated her as one of their own. The pack's home brought back a whole different set of memories.

She was hidden less than fifty feet from the center of a rough ring of stone-and-wood houses and within spitting distance of the well the pack used. The predominant combination of unwashed male Were and rotten garbage hovering around the settlement was without a doubt the worst stench Sarah Jennifer had ever been subjected to, proving that unique wasn't always special.

Unfortunately, she couldn't skip due diligence on her recon because the nasty Weres smelled bad. She had to identify the Alpha. She found herself wanting to smack some basic hygiene into him as much as she wanted to take his pack.

The Weres were lucky they had nanocytes to protect them from disease. Who was stupid enough to dump their garbage this close to their living space? It was wedged between the walls, filling the gap between two abandoned homes.

No wonder the people of Salem didn't want them; the dregs of the UnknownWorld all seemed to have washed up here, "washed" being a stretch. Sarah Jennifer thought they might be allergic to water.

They lived like pigs, just like Esme had told her. Sarah Jennifer couldn't wait to get out of there. Esme's tale of adults who should know better had struck a nerve. She supposed some would have pity on the pack, but not her. Civilization was what you made of it.

People had a choice, and in her experience, they chose according to their nature. She had encountered innumerable small settlements during the years she'd wandered and met people on both sides. This pack lived by raiding. They made no effort to integrate with successful communities. That was exactly the kind of bullshit she was here to put a stop to.

There would be no more raiding once the pack was hers, but first, she needed to know if they were redeemable. If only she hadn't had to smear herself in garbage to get to a perfect vantage point.

Sarah Jennifer settled in, resigned to the wait.

Her mind wandered over other times she'd been on hurry-up-and-wait assignments, resting briefly on Portland, her first major battle. That was when she had learned to assess the situation instead of running in half-cocked.

As the night passed, she examined each hut, her enhanced vision adjusting with the fall and rise of the light. The settlement spoke to her of sadness. There was no decoration anywhere to indicate the pack cared for their homes. They were scruffy and non-uniform, and all seemed equally run down.

The evidence was overwhelming.

Sarah Jennifer repressed the urge to leave then and there. She really didn't *want* a pack. She'd had a pack, and they'd left Earth without her. She'd had a mate, and he'd left her emotionally. She'd almost had a child, a life too fragile to meet her in this world.

There were too many parts of life Sarah Jennifer would rather die than experience again, and every one of them played in her memory during the long night. As always, it came down to one thing: she'd been running from loss, and she wanted to keep running.

She'd spent all those years wandering the wilds, avoiding any kind of human connection beyond the conversation required to make trades, only to find herself back where she started. A pack was an instant family, a responsibility that turned her cold. Who wanted to love? That was an invitation to pain.

But still.

The path through life turned many times upon itself, especially for the long-lived. People were bound to find themselves retracing their steps one way or another. If she ran now, she would always regret leaving these people to their fate. Who else could help them, and by helping them, help the people of Salem?

A thin golden line crept onto the horizon, telling Sarah Jennifer that dawn had arrived to banish her dark thoughts.

Shortly after that, she heard the sounds of people waking up.

A human woman emerged from the huts, followed by the pack. They mooched around until the woman called them for breakfast, then got set to lounge around some more.

Sarah Jennifer observed the pack's morning routine with growing dismay. No wonder their place was a shit-hole. Where was the Alpha?

She noted that all of the women she saw were human. The men were all Weres, as she'd been told, but they were young like the ones she'd come across on Samhain night.

Sarah Jennifer was less than delighted when the night's chamber pots were emptied on the trash heap. However, none of the Weres picked up her scent as they went about their morning business.

She continued to observe until late evening, then crept away after the settlement quieted down.

Sarah Jennifer made it back to her camp and sat down after a long soak in the nearby stream to consider the things she'd learned during her observation of the pack.

It was small, the hierarchy unclear. There were clearly

two factions, although neither asserted themselves over the other. That was dangerous, she knew. Given that no one strong personality asserted themselves over the whole, no wonder the pack was directionless.

All of the people, Were and human alike, looked like they could do with a good meal.

She hadn't detected any signs of an Alpha, although she'd heard his name mentioned. Brutus had to be a fake name, though. Nobody would be cruel enough to saddle their child with something so ridiculous. Right?

It gave her something to consider. She'd return in a couple of days to see if things had changed.

The stench of the settlement clung to Sarah Jennifer's skin, putting her off eating anything despite the change of clothes and the immediate dunking she'd given herself on arriving at her camp.

She had too much to think about to sleep. The pack looked to be completely miserable, and she couldn't figure out why they lived so appallingly. Even without an Alpha, they should have some order to their lives.

A man spoke, dragging her from her thoughts.

"Well, well, well, what's this then? A pretty little thing like you all alone in the woods. C'mere, let me see you, sweet thing."

Dammit, she needed to get her situational awareness under control!

Not every bad guy announced himself. Although, to be fair, she'd been traveling for a while now, and most of them did. She couldn't think why since it just gave her a chance to kick their balls into their throat before they had a chance to finish their creepy monologue.

She sprang up from the log she was using as a seat, facing the intruder in a ready stance. "What the hell do you want?" she spat, in no mood for the interruption. She wrinkled her nose, catching his familiar reek. He was one of the stinkers from the village, although not one she'd seen when she did her recon.

"I'm gonna take you home with me, that's what," the Were informed her, then leered. "Brutus won't be happy, but I don't care." His eyes crawled proprietarily over Sarah Jennifer's body, making her mentally throw up. "Linus will back me up."

"Ugh, I don't think so, Stinky," she replied. This Were *was* a lead, finally, however malodorous. Time to get the damsel act out. "But I can see that I'm outmatched, so I'll come with you. Tell me about Brutus and Linus?" she asked, dropping her voice to one of sweetness. She knew exactly who Brutus was, but she had to act dumb for now. "Who are they, your bosses, or something?"

The Were's leer dropped away, replaced by a look of bruised pride. "You don't need to worry about them. You're gonna be my bride. You can cook for me, and give me some sons."

He wants a bride? Sarah Jennifer thought. *Not in this lifetime. Providing a reason for a funeral I can maybe see my way to helping with.*

Sarah Jennifer hid her disgust and smiled at the Were. "Okay, but it doesn't sound like you have the last say on what you can and can't do."

The Were considered that for a moment. "You're right. Brutus might decide to keep you instead, and his women never last long. He takes them into the forest, and they don't come back."

Like she was property to be handed around and dumped for worm food when they were done. Classy. Sarah Jennifer thought quickly. This guy was going to blow her cover either way, so she needed to make sure she was prepared to confront the pack. Becoming worm food was *not* on her list of objectives. "Can I be honest?" she asked, lying blatantly. "I know I'm not getting out of this. Give me a few minutes to pack my things, and I'll come with you willingly. I can see you're the safest choice."

Sarah Jennifer could almost hear the cogs turning in his brain. She wondered if he was smart enough to take the opportunity. While she was prepared to take out every Were in the forest if necessary, she had to hold out hope that they were just suffering from an extreme case of ignorance, since that could be cured.

"Okay," he agreed. "But don't try anything stupid."

Sarah Jennifer gathered her belongings, making sure to keep her weapons hidden from the Were. "What's your name?" she asked as she tied her bedroll onto her backpack.

"Lucifer," he replied too quickly.

Sarah Jennifer gave him a knowing look. "Really?"

He looked away. "It's Rory."

Sarah Jennifer lifted her pack. "Well, Rory. I'm ready to go."

They set off in the direction of the settlement.

"It won't be a bad life," Rory told Sarah Jennifer. "Safer than wandering around in the forest by yourself. I'll be good to you, and you'll take care of me. Make the house someplace to look forward to coming home to."

That wasn't what Sarah Jennifer had expected. "It sounds more like you want a mom than a wife."

The village was busier, and if possible, stinkier than the previous day. The pack was gathered in the center of the huts around a group of Weres Sarah Jennifer hadn't yet seen. She assumed she was looking at the Alpha and his inner circle, judging by the size of them and the way the Weres deferred to them while they stared at the spoils of the latest raid.

Rory proudly marched her over to the largest Were of the bunch.

Sarah Jennifer winced. Damn subterfuge; she actually felt sorry for Rory, not that she had a choice. She was on her own and had to play it sneaky.

The huge Were turned away from the ass-kicking he was giving another Were almost as large when Rory called for his attention. Was this Brutus or Linus?

"Brutus, you're back. I have a request."

Sarah Jennifer saw that the Were on the ground was one of the two who had attempted to kidnap Annie last night.

Sarah Jennifer had to work hard to keep her face straight when she saw Brutus up close. Something was familiar about him, but she couldn't put her finger on it.

Brutus' eyes burned into her as she shook herself free of Rory's grip.

"Do I know you?" Sarah Jennifer asked.

"No," he replied, looking her up and down. His eyes

stopped on hers again, recognition lighting his face. "But I know who you are, cousin. Sylvia Walton?"

"Sarah Jennifer," she corrected. That smirk—how could she have missed it? "You're a Timmons."

"And you're a Walton," he repeated, beginning the dance. "Have you come to kill us? I hope you brought backup." He flexed his chest as he spoke, showing off his size.

Sarah Jennifer wasn't intimidated. She had grown up sparring with werebears, and her "cousin" wasn't anywhere near the size of Bogdan. His ego, however, was clearly twice the size of that of anyone else she'd ever met. His confidence in himself was supreme. It would be his downfall.

She circled him slowly, never taking her eyes from his as she began needling him. "I should kill you before I take your pack. You clearly aren't caring for them. What Alpha lets their pack live in squalor like this?" She indicated the shabby village, the skinny pack members, the garbage dump in plain sight. "Your pack is hungry, *cousin*. It would be a mercy for me to take them since you clearly can't provide for them."

The Weres drew a collective breath when Brutus bristled at her insults.

The Alpha's face darkened as he moved to stay opposite her, unsure of her intentions. "What do you know? Where was the Pack Council to look out for us? Where was Charumati? Nobody gives a shit, so we live as free Weres."

Sarah Jennifer fixed Brutus with a cold look. *The* Look. He balked under her glare, understanding at a visceral level what that look meant when it came from a Walton. She knew she had him at that moment. He tried to hide the flinch from the pack, but it was too late.

"Free to keep the people around here living in fear?" Sarah Jennifer accused, coming to a final decision. "This pack is breaking every law of the UnknownWorld. Not anymore, Timmons. Cousin or not, I'm shutting you down. This pack is mine now."

The pack sensed the inevitable fight and made room. Nobody wanted to get in the way of a battle for dominance.

Brutus growled. "Not fucking likely."

He took a swing at her, testing. Sarah Jennifer hopped out of the way easily, grabbing his arm and twisting it to force him to the ground. He didn't give in to the pressure on his elbow. He kicked out at Sarah Jennifer and caught her shin.

It hurt like a bitch, making Sarah Jennifer angry. At least, that was what she *wanted* him to think.

Brutus smirked again, until she wiped it off his face with a ringing bitch-slap.

"*I challenge you, Brutus,*" Sarah Jennifer roared, goading him further.

The pack fell back at this, edging into the spaces between the huts to clear the entire circle at the center of the village. They knew the rules of a challenge insofar as they applied to them, and their only role was to get the hell out of the way.

Sarah Jennifer grabbed Brutus as he lunged at her, dropping them both into a roll and tucking her feet into his stomach. She pushed hard with her feet as she reached the point she'd calculated would be most effective to her strategy, sending him flying fifty feet into the garbage dump.

That was a move she'd learned from her mother, and it got the reaction she wanted, which was to drive Brutus further into his rage. Her smaller size wasn't an issue as long as she was in control of the fight, and she didn't want to drag this out any longer than she had to. It was all tactics.

Sarah Jennifer continued to taunt him as he pulled himself out of the shit-pile, applying psychological pressure. In her experience, it was just as effective as pain as a motivator. "I will take your pack, *cousin*. I will show them what it means to be part of the UnknownWorld. What it means to have an Alpha who deserves their loyalty and trust, instead of one who would bring a death sentence on their heads from his actions rather than do an honest day's work."

Her tactics worked like a charm. Brutus moved like the wind, his bulk belying his speed. He wasn't expecting Sarah Jennifer to be faster. Her punch connected, while his missed.

Then, he ruined the fight.

Sarah Jennifer's knee twinged, revealing her weakness. She saw Brutus react to the fraction of a second her timing slipped, but he went for her face again. Sarah Jennifer didn't allow the incongruity to put her on the back foot.

There was more going on than met the eye with this pack, and she would get to the bottom of it as soon as she was in control of them.

The whole pack cringed at the resounding crack as Sarah Jennifer broke their Alpha's jaw. Brutus' head wobbled with the force of the impact and he fell to his knees, helped by a kick in the sternum as he went down.

Brutus glared at her hatefully as he knelt in the muck, breathing heavily, waiting for his cracked bones to heal.

Sarah Jennifer noticed a few of the Weres were less than bothered by her treatment of him. She wondered briefly which one of them was Linus. "Is there anyone here who wants to challenge me?"

Brutus' shifting gaze gave her the answer she wanted.

It would wait. For the moment.

She flicked an imaginary piece of dirt from her shoulder and offered Brutus a hard smile as she held a hand out for him to take. It was all for show, to establish her dominance over the pack. Her breathing was even.

She wasn't even sweating, and the pack noticed.

They fell to their knees, foreheads touching the stinking muck as they gave their obeisance to their new Alpha. It warmed Sarah Jennifer to see them submit to her since it would make the job of civilizing them easier. "Get up out of the mud. You are not slaves."

Brutus groaned.

"Are we done, *cousin*?" Sarah Jennifer asked, taking her anger out on him. "I could do this all day, but you're looking a bit the worse for wear. You don't have to die; just submit to me and swear you'll live right from now on. The family way."

"Fuck you!" Brutus grunted, holding his ribs. "I am not submitting to a human, family or not."

She replied to his outburst with another kick, this one to his head. "It's going to suck to be you then, 'cuz. I'd hate to have your headache when you wake up."

She focused her attention on the pack as Brutus collapsed from his half-sitting position into a heap. *"Who is your Alpha?"* she demanded.

The pack replied, subservient to a one. "You are, Mistress!"

Sarah Jennifer wrinkled her nose in distaste at the title. "You will call me Major Walton." It was self-promotion, but hell, nobody else was here to do it. That was part one of her plan half-done.

"Get up," she told the pack. "There are going to be a lot of changes around here. If any of you remember what the FDG was, then you'll have an idea of what I intend for you. Who was Brutus' second?"

A Were who was mostly made of shoulders raised his hand hesitantly.

"Name?" she barked at him.

"Bruiser, Major Walton."

Respectful—she could work with that. "Follow me, Bruiser. You are my new sergeant. The rest of you had better start getting this shithole cleaned up. When it's livable, go take a bath or something. Don't you know you all stink?"

The Weres got busy, unsure of this strange woman who had arrived and turned their lives upside down but certain that not obeying would be detrimental to their health.

Sarah Jennifer stalked over to the largest house, correctly assuming it was Brutus' home. Not anymore. It was hers now. She hoped that one day she could tell her grandfather about the time his Wildflower took over an entire pack in only three moves.

"Your Alphaness?" Bruiser's tentative voice came from

the door as Sarah Jennifer looked around the house with disgust. She was shocked to see a trio of young women hiding in the back room. They were much younger than she'd assumed when she did her recon, but they weren't injured.

"Wait in here," she told them. "I'll be back to speak to you soon."

The three women nodded in silence and Sarah Jennifer strode back outside again, deciding the smell was better out there and that she didn't really want the house, anyway. If she had to stay, she'd build her own.

"Major is fine," Sarah Jennifer informed Bruiser. "What's the problem?"

The Were was beginning to look confused. "What should we do with Brutus? He's still alive."

"Is he conscious yet?" she asked.

Bruiser looked at Brutus. "No, Major, ma'am."

"Then he can stay where he is," Sarah Jennifer told him. "Now, these human women. Are they here of their own free will?"

Bruiser looked at the floor. "Mostly. Tamara and Sofie are with the Ace brothers. The new girl was taken by Linus, and Brutus fought him for her and won."

"As I suspected." Sarah Jennifer switched to her parade voice, which was loud enough to be heard across the settlement and beyond. "I will personally break my boot off in the ass of any Were who so much as breathes in the direction of those women. Do I make myself clear?"

Sarah Jennifer called the women to the door, wanting to make sure she was getting the truth from Bruiser. "Do you want to leave?" she asked gently.

Tamara and Sofie shook their heads. "We were just taking care of Missy until Brutus got back."

Missy nodded mutely, not believing the new Alpha was for real.

Sarah Jennifer smiled. "It's okay. Go gather your belongings. We leave as soon as I'm done here. I need to make sure my pack is on the right track before we leave this shithole."

The woman who'd made breakfast stepped forward and put her arms around the woman. "I'll take her, but I'm not leaving my boys."

Sarah Jennifer scrutinized the blue-eyed, blonde-haired woman and the two Weres who stood nearby who bore the same striking features. "Fair enough. Do you know how to get to Salem?"

The woman snorted softly. "Considering that's where I was born and raised, I'm going to say yeah."

Sarah Jennifer nodded at the young woman who wanted to leave. "Why are you still standing here? Go. Pack."

The young woman rushed off before Sarah Jennifer changed her mind.

Sarah Jennifer noticed everyone in the pack making an effort to look busy. She turned her attention to them. "Pack meeting," she told them. "Now."

CHAPTER FIVE

The Weres gathered around the front of Brutus' house, shuffling anxiously under the steel glare of Sarah Jennifer. She did a quick headcount—twenty-four. Twenty-five if she counted Brutus, who was still sleeping like a baby while his nanocytes healed the damage she'd done to his skull.

The pack seemed nervous and no one was able to meet her eyes. They were all pretty young. She didn't think any of them were older than fifty or sixty. They reminded her of sulky teenagers. A few skulked in the back, whispering among themselves. Any other pack would have fought to the last Were for their Alpha. What was wrong with them? Did they even know what it was to be Weres?

Sarah Jennifer couldn't afford to feel too sorry for them. An Alpha needed to show strength, or they'd lose control of the pack. What would her family do? Her grandmother would beat the mouthy ones senseless, but none of those had shown themselves yet. She chose to refrain from beating up any of them except for Brutus because none had openly spoken against her. Her mother would make a friend of each and every one of them, showing them the error of their ways through her pure goodness.

What was her way? She didn't want to be a disciplinarian, but she knew they needed it. This was rock-bottom living, so the only way they had to go was up. Hard but not harsh was the direction her instinct was telling her to go. Her grandfather had told her that strength came in many forms. That it took a strong person to take a life, but a stronger person to save one.

By that logic, these Weres were going to make her indestructible.

She spoke to her pack. "Why do you live like this?"

Bruiser raised his head. "It's what we've got. Salem won't have us, and it's not safe for Weres in the city."

Sarah Jennifer raised an eyebrow. "They won't have you in Salem because you raid and steal, Bruiser. Don't try pulling that shit when Rory attempted to kidnap me less than two hours ago. Why isn't it safe in the city? Truth, now!"

The pack cringed. Another Were spoke up. "The leeches. They'll drain us and sell our blood to the highest bidder!"

That was news to Sarah Jennifer. However, it did explain what Esme had told her about Weres leaving the cities. She'd thought the blood traders had been driven out, along with the pirates. She'd encountered enough of them on her journey east. If the trade was starting up again, she would have to add taking them out to her to-do list. It was a good thing she had her very own tac-team now.

She just had to train them first—no biggie. The first

step was going to be the hardest. She had to give them something to live for without scaring the shit out of them.

"Not on my watch," Sarah Jennifer stated acidly. "This pack is under my protection now, but things are going to change around here. I know you aren't evil. You've had bad leadership, and I'm here to put that right. The question is this: do you want the opportunity to change? To live right? To do good? This is your chance to take the first step on that path."

Most looked skeptical at her speech. Maybe a view of the stick would make the carrot more attractive to them.

"Put it like this. I can help *you* make *your* life one to be proud of. Or, I can wash my hands of you all and burn this place to the ground with everyone in it. Do you like hurting innocent people? Stealing their livelihoods and leaving them to starve? Or would you rather save that for those who deserve it, like the leeches?"

That fired them up.

The pack babbled their disbelief.

"We can't fight the leeches!"

"They have guns!"

"Shock rods!"

"Silver!"

Sarah Jennifer dropped her hands to her hips and silenced them with a look. "You have something they don't —a Walton on your side. By the time I'm done with you lot, you'll be as hard as a woodpecker's lips."

A few were intrigued by the prospect, she could tell. Brutus had begun moving. He was coming to from the probable skull fracture she'd given him to go with the broken ribs and jaw, which should have healed up by now.

She breathed a sigh of relief that she hadn't killed the closest thing she had to a relative in this area and put a hand to her mouth as her stomach protested at the attack on her senses.

Sarah Jennifer pointed at the trash heap. "First things first. Every breath I take is a new assault on my patience. Seriously. Get the shovels out, or get wolfy. Whatever you need to do, I don't care. Just get digging and get that shit-heap moved away from the settlement. It had better not be here when I get back. It's time you took some pride in yourselves and in your home. We will talk more about how I'm going to run things around here tonight."

The pack rushed to do her bidding.

"Where're you going, Major?" Bruiser asked.

"I need a word with the previous incumbent," Sarah Jennifer told him. She stalked past and grabbed the semi-conscious Brutus by the shirt, dragging him behind her as she strode out of the village and back into the forest. "Make sure this place is clean when I get back."

Brutus struggled against Sarah Jennifer's iron grip as she dragged him toward her camp. He was fully conscious now and furious at his predicament.

He snarled and twisted, his shirt's seams popping with the effort. "Put me down, you bitch!"

Sarah Jennifer dropped Brutus, then turned and punched him in the jaw again, stunning him before he could attack. "You know, you could try asking nicely," she told him, planting a boot between his shoulders to keep him on his belly. "I'd much rather you walked by yourself, but it's obvious I'm dealing with a petulant child here."

She grabbed his wrists and used his flannel shirt to bind

his arms behind his back, then she pulled him to his feet and gave him a little shove to get him going. "Get in front, and no funny business."

He dug his heels in. "Fuck you!"

"I warned you," she told him, encouraging him to start moving by applying her foot to his ass. "Move it or lose it."

Sarah Jennifer trussed Brutus to a tree trunk when they reached her camp, winding the good rope from her pack around his neck and tying it off so he couldn't shift to his wolf form without cutting off his air supply.

When she was done, she took a seat on the log she'd been using earlier and faced him. "That's better. Now, we might not be blood cousins, but I'm doing my best not to just end your sorry existence. You can help make my wish a reality by not giving me any more shit. I am your Alpha and your better. I will *take* your respect from you if you don't give it freely." She'd heard her grandmother dressing the pack down enough times to know how these things went.

Brutus was furious, his face red and his eyes bulging as he choked himself, trying to snap the rope. *"You're not my Alpha!* I don't know what the fuck you are! You haven't even got a fucking wolf!" Brutus spat, missing her and hitting the ground instead.

Sarah Jennifer stared him down, her eyes hard and cold. Brutus looked away first. "I didn't *need* a wolf to kick your ass, did I?" Her smile didn't touch her eyes. "Let me explain how pack hierarchy works. Your Supreme Alpha, Charumati, is my grandmother. You, dear cousin, are a no-good asshole *mutt*. That means that I outrank you in pack position, in strength, and in skill, wolf or no wolf. You should be glad I need every wolf in the pack to face the leeches, or I'd have sanctioned you there and then."

He ignored her, and kept struggling against the clove hitch she'd secured him with. It just bound him tighter to the tree, the more he pulled. His face turned red, then purple. Sarah Jennifer wondered if she really did need him. Probably not, if he was going to fight her the whole way, but she wanted to give him a chance.

She tugged on the rope in her hand, making sure he gave her his full attention. "Listen up, Brutus. I'm being pretty decent here. Any other member of our family would have put a silver round in your brain and slept soundly that night by now. Hell, I watched my grandparents shoot your father three times just for talking back. I'm not as touchy, so you lucked out. I'd rather not kill you, but I will if you keep fighting me. You get one chance and one chance only not to screw this up. Tell me about the blood trade around here. Where are the leeches based?"

He stopped struggling and looked at Sarah Jennifer, assessing her uncertainly. "What do you know about leeches?"

Sarah Jennifer's lip curled. "Enough that I'm not going to allow them to stay in business. It's one thing to find Weres selling their blood willingly, however disgusting I think it is, but I will *not* stand for them having it taken against their will or being murdered for it. Nobody should have to live in fear of being drained." She fought off the memory of Joseph and Petricia, broken after their encounter with blood traders. "I've seen what they did to vampires. 'Leeches' is the right word for them."

Brutus' face changed, his aggression disappearing in a

mixture of disbelief and something she couldn't place. Sarah Jennifer felt like she was seeing him for the first time as he shuffled into a more comfortable position against the tree.

"What are you gonna do about it?" Brutus demanded, his distrust reappearing. "You're just one person, whatever your weird-ass abilities are."

Sarah Jennifer grinned. "That's where my new pack comes in."

Brutus snorted with laughter. "Those useless assholes?" He stopped laughing when she slapped him.

"How are they supposed to want better from themselves when their leader talks down to them?" Sarah Jennifer asked. "I don't want to hear that kind of negativity from you anymore."

Brutus sobered. "I'll take that, but you've got no chance. All they're good for is causing a distraction while I fight and steal to get what we need to survive. That's without Linus, Dinny, and Reg, and all the shit *they* cause."

Sarah Jennifer noted the valuable nugget. Brutus looked unsure, out of his depth. It was becoming clear that he did care about the pack, but it didn't change that he'd done a piss-poor job of leading them. "Why are they useless, Brutus?" she asked, going heavy on the snark. "Could it be because their Alpha has let them live like degenerates instead of demanding better from them?"

She paused for a minute. Was she looking at this wrong? "Do you even know *how* to lead? Tell me how you came to be the Alpha."

Brutus sneered. "Why should I? Untie me, and maybe I'll talk."

Sarah Jennifer pressed her lips together. She was getting through, she could see that he wanted to talk. But she would keep the upper hand for now. "That's not how it works. I don't trust you yet, and until I have a reason to untie you, you're staying right there. The first step to trust is communication, so get to talking."

Brutus spluttered, trying to come to terms with Sarah Jennifer's demands. Finally he sighed, gave up his attempts to get free, and asked what she wanted to know.

"Start with where you were born," she instructed. "Who raised you? Do you keep in touch with your brothers and sisters? I remember meeting your dad, sort of. He was an asshole by all accounts."

Brutus looked pained. "I wouldn't know. By the time I was born, Joshua was dead, and I've never met any of my siblings. We were shunned by the NAPC after what he did. My mom didn't know what to do with a teenage Were, so I left her behind in New York to make it by myself." He scowled at the softening of Sarah Jennifer's face. "I don't want your pity. I found my own way. Okay? I left New York for Boston when it got too dangerous to stay there, then the leeches took control of Boston, and our Alpha brought the pack out here. I took over when Katia died, and that's that."

Sarah Jennifer couldn't help but feel sorry for him. She guessed there was a lot more to the story, but trauma didn't excuse bad behavior from the victim. Her mercy would come in the form of teaching him self-discipline and some damned respect for himself and others. He would learn that the hard way wasn't so hard when you slept with a clear conscience.

She pinned him with a sharp look. "What do you mean, 'that's that?' You have a responsibility to provide structure and discipline for your pack."

Brutus scowled. "The pack don't give a shit about how they live, just that they get to keep doing it. Why should I try if they won't? Katia used to kick the shit out of them if they didn't listen, but I hate doing that. I was only disciplining Dinny and Reg because I had to go rescue them from some witch in Salem who nearly killed the pair of them. I've told them to stay away from there many times, but they don't listen. It's like they *want* to get killed."

"Quit whining," Sarah Jennifer told him. "You did your duty. Besides, it wasn't a witch who kicked their asses. It was me, and I have no intention of killing anyone unless I have to. How old are you, anyway?"

"Nearing sixty," Brutus replied. "I'm not a kid."

Dammit. He *was* a child, in Were years anyway, and he'd raised himself for the most part. Sarah Jennifer's heart broke for him. She couldn't imagine what she'd be like today without the guidance of her family. Their strength was her strength, passed down through the generations. Even though they were millions of miles away, their lessons still guided her every single day. "Did anyone ever care about you?" she asked softly.

He nodded, the story spilling out of him in a hot rush. "My mom loved me. She just couldn't handle the wolf in me." He shrugged. "That's why I left her. I wasn't easy, and she was only human. Like I said, I made my way to Boston, and Katia took me in. Treated me good, you know? Like a younger brother. It was great for a while, even after we left the city."

"So, what happened to make the witches reject you?" Sarah Jennifer interjected.

"Katia took exception to the council's demands and killed the guy trying to enforce them. I guess after that, the council didn't like the idea of a bunch of wild Weres in their town." Brutus sighed. "I thought things could be different, you know? I could be part of something better. Shortly after we set up out here, Katia was killed, and it all fell to shit without her to keep the pack in line."

"How was Katia killed?" Sarah Jennifer asked gently.

Brutus shrugged. "We don't know. She went on a hunt alone, and never came back. I went to look for her and found her blood. Whatever killed her took her body." He met Sarah Jennifer's eyes, his flat gaze devoid of all emotion. "Listen. There's no point in striving when there's nothing to strive for. When nobody else gives a shit. You try to build something good, and some fucker comes to kick it down again. I'd rather be the one breaking shit than the one getting their shit broke."

Sarah Jennifer tried to understand. She knew Brutus wasn't lying. His heart rate had remained steady as he revealed his past to her. She remembered herself at that age—full of spit and vinegar, ready to take on the world if it looked at her in the wrong way. She'd had her training to knock it out of her, a structured upbringing. Brutus had experienced nothing but loss and disappointment. "That's not true anymore. I'm here. I will protect you all as long as you follow my orders and stop being part of the problem."

"Why are you doing this?" Brutus asked. "Why take my pack and leave me alive? I thought those witch-bitches sent you to assassinate us. Stuck-up fuckers in their nice safe town, enjoying the high life while we all starve out here." He sighed. "It hurts me to steal, to take food from people's mouths, but I have to take care of my own."

Sarah Jennifer found herself torn. It wasn't like Esme to be judgmental, but in this instance, she thought her friend might be wearing blinkers. Everyone here was "trying to take care of their own," not realizing that as part of the UnknownWorld, "their own" extended beyond their doorstep.

"The witches aren't the bad guys here," she told Brutus. She ran a hand through her hair and sighed heavily. "I don't think there *are* any bad guys, just two sets of people at cross purposes."

"Tell that to my pack!" Brutus cried. "I might be a shitty Alpha, but I'm all they've got. The pack is rough, yeah, but that's because the witches have made damned sure we don't have a community to rely on when times are hard."

Sarah Jennifer was going to have a serious talk with Esme when she got back to the cottage. The witches had painted Brutus and the pack in an entirely different light than the one she'd found the Weres wallowing in. She'd seen this Us and Them attitude before, and it got nobody anywhere. Could either side accept that they were equally to blame?

Salem was the only safe harbor in the area for the UnknownWorld, as far as she could see. Both groups needed to work together if they were to survive and rebuild society.

"What?" Brutus asked, filling the silence Sarah Jennifer let drag out while she put her thoughts into an actionable plan.

The way forward was clear. It wasn't going to be easy, but she could handle the pressure. After all, she was nothing if not professional. TH always told her that amateurs talked tactics, but professionals were all about the logistics. If everyone was too short-sighted to see past their misconceptions, she would have to start banging heads together until the council and the pack quit fighting each other.

"I'm taking the pack to Salem," she told Brutus, making her decision.

"Fuck! *What?*" It was Brutus' turn to be shocked.

"I will vouch for the pack, and I will control them." She unsheathed her knife. "You are welcome to join us, as long as you stay in line."

Brutus pressed himself against the tree trunk. "What if I won't? What's the knife for?"

His heartbeat rose as she approached slowly and deliberately and crouched next to him. She ran the razor-sharp edge lightly along his face from his temple to his chin. It sizzled where it touched, creating the smell of cooked meat as the silvered blade did its work. When she was done, a thin scar was left behind. Brutus touched it gingerly.

"That's what the knife is for," Sarah Jennifer told him. "To permanently remind you of what happens if you fuck up. If I have to take my knife to you again, it'll be because I'm removing your heart. Consider yourself warned. Now, do you submit to me?"

The fire did not leave his eyes, but there must have been some of her Uncle Timmons' brains in him because Brutus nodded.

"I submit," Brutus agreed. "You are my Alpha."

Sarah Jennifer wasn't done. "And you will support me in everything?"

Brutus met her eyes. He was humbled, accepting her as his superior in every way. If he'd been in wolf form, she suspected he would have been showing her his belly.

He nodded. "Yes, I swear. Now can you untie me? We need to get back before Linus gets ideas about Missy."

"Relax, I've got you." Sarah Jennifer undid the rope from Brutus' throat and helped him up, remaining at the ready in case he tried any funny business when she released his wrists.

He didn't. His whole demeanor had changed, his deference to her obvious in his lack of posturing.

"Are you for real?" Brutus asked, rubbing his scar gingerly. "Like, really for real? You're not going to leave us?" The relief in his voice was tangible.

Sarah Jennifer's heart constricted as the responsibility she'd taken on hit her like a ton of bricks. She was a loner, a solitary soul, and she'd just adopted twenty-five unruly kids. It had been her choice to leave the military life behind, but how else could she teach them to live right? She suddenly understood why her grandfather had such a potty mouth.

This was full circle for her. It hurt to discover the price of her childish wish. She was the best of the best, but she had been all alone. In a way, she understood that fate had brought her to this juncture to save her from herself.

She put a hand on Brutus' shoulder, trying not to read too much into the minute flinch as she touched him. "I'm not going anywhere, I promise. You are mine to take care of now—and mine to kick into shape." She lifted her head as the scent of deer wafted past. "But first, let me show you why you don't need to steal when nature will provide everything but the coffee."

Brutus sighed. "Coffee. I *wish*."

Sarah Jennifer looked off to the right, hearing the movement of deer nearby. "Let's start with some fresh meat."

CHAPTER SIX

They left the forest at dusk, carrying a deer apiece.

Sarah Jennifer considered the hunt successful in more ways than providing the pack's meal that night. Brutus had proven to be every bit the natural hunter once she'd reminded him of the basics, and she had to admit that he wasn't so bad to be around once he'd dropped the attitude. She'd learned a little about the pack from him, and shared some of her plan for instilling structure into the pack's lives.

An angry shout cut their easy banter short as they neared the settlement. They looked at each other and started running. Sarah Jennifer sprinted ahead, Brutus following hard on her heels as she dashed toward the source of the shout. She got a view of the center of the settlement a moment later.

Sarah Jennifer was pleased to see that the trash heap had shrunk considerably in the time she'd been gone, which meant that most of the pack had obeyed her and gotten straight to work.

However, they were not working now.

Sarah Jennifer understood why they had left their task when she saw one of the human women standing in front of Brutus' house, waving a cast iron skillet at a group of Weres. It was the mother of the blue-eyed Weres who had offered to take Missy back to Salem.

The pack hung about, watching uncomfortably as three of the Weres did their best to persuade her to let them into Brutus' former home. They were in wolf form, taking turns nipping at the legs of the woman with the pan.

"Linus," Brutus growled, his eyes flashing yellow with anger. "That sneaky fucksack! Sarah, you have to stop him. Help Maria." He explained quickly how Linus occasionally got it into his head to claim a human bride, and that he'd always taken the women into the forest and sent them in the direction of Salem.

Sarah Jennifer was relieved to hear that Brutus hadn't been killing the women, as Rory believed. "My name is Sarah Jennifer, don't shorten it." She handed her deer to Brutus and pushed through the pack, wincing at the clang produced by the skillet hitting Linus' skull when the woman scored a hit. That forced the wolf to change back into human form.

The woman continued to rage at the other two Weres trying to get through the door. Bruiser and the woman's sons hung about to the side, clearly wanting to intervene but not daring to.

"You'll not touch them, none of you!" the woman scolded. She was resolute, using her body to prevent the Weres from entering the hut. "The new Alpha said Missy was to go free, and I mean to make sure she gets to Salem safely!" The tiny woman was fierce, in full-on Mama Llama mode. There was blood running down her calves, but her injuries weren't holding her back from her defense.

Sarah Jennifer thought her determination was admirable. The woman was impressive.

"The Alpha isn't here, Maria." Linus sneered, stalking her as his cronies, also back in human form, egged him on.

"Oh, but the Alpha *is* here, Linus," Brutus called. "You're in the shit now."

Sarah Jennifer caught his tone. It was the same one Sylvie had always had when she'd been mean and their mother had seen it. She noted the power struggle between Brutus and Linus as her next obstacle to remove, easily done by making it clear to the pack where her favor lay.

"What the hell is going on?" Sarah Jennifer demanded, grabbing Linus by the scruff of his neck and giving him a shake. She checked the women to see if they were unharmed. She pointed at Bruiser and Maria's sons. "You three, restrain Reg and Dinny."

Bruiser launched into action when he had an order to follow. He grabbed one of the two attackers and forced him to the ground, while the younger Weres took an arm each and forced the other to join him in the dirt. He wasn't called Bruiser for nothing, apparently.

"Maria, is it?" Sarah Jennifer inquired.

The woman nodded. Her blue eyes blazed with anger, and she kept her gaze firmly on the Weres. She didn't lower the skillet for a second. "Damn bastards thought they'd help themselves to the girl."

Sarah Jennifer shook Linus again. "It's okay, Maria. You

can stand down, I'm here now." She wasn't surprised when the young woman rushed to Brutus, hiding behind him.

"You're serious about helping her get out of here?" Brutus asked Sarah Jennifer.

She nodded. "You got a problem with that?"

"No, none at all." Brutus smiled, another weight falling visibly from his shoulders. "I didn't want Missy here in the first place. I only claimed her to stop Linus from forcing her to mate with him."

"You swear you didn't take any women?" Sarah Jennifer turned her attention to the other human women, her stern tone tempered with a kind expression. "Who took you from your homes? Was Brutus involved? Be honest, please. I need to get to the bottom of this so I can punish the appropriate people."

One by one, they shook their heads.

"We chose to stay," Sofie told Sarah Jennifer on behalf of herself and Tamara. "We didn't have any people, and it's not so bad here as long as you avoid Linus."

"That's right," Maria interjected. "It's always them!" She pointed at Linus and the other two Weres, who were doing their best to look innocent. The rest of the pack had drifted closer to see what was going to happen. "They've been nothing but trouble since Katia was taken from us."

"Just these three?" Sarah Jennifer asked.

Everyone but the three Weres in question agreed that they were to blame. They were the ones who had earned the pack's reputation, doing more than was necessary on the raids, damaging property and attacking those who fought back.

Sarah Jennifer pried the story out of the pack over the

next twenty minutes, cutting off any Were who wasn't giving her the essential information she was looking for.

She heard more about the pack's history as the discussion went on. Katia had been a true Alpha, gathering the orphan Weres left behind when the disappearances began and keeping them safe from the blood traders. They had lived in Boston after the leeches drove the people of the UnknownWorld underground. Tired of living like rats in the sewers, Katia had led them into the forest with the promise of a better life.

Katia's skills and strength as a leader had carried the pack through the first months of living in the forest. Then she was killed, leaving the pack bereft, and Brutus had been in contention with Linus ever since. Sarah Jennifer didn't have to be a genius to understand Katia's death had shattered the pack into factions, each blaming the other for their failure to thrive.

They admitted to raiding. They'd raided because they had no survival skills. They were city wolves, driven out in fear of their lives and struggling to survive in these hard times. They knew no other way. Street kids stealing to survive was a cliché for a reason. Sarah Jennifer could admit she had no problem with it up until the point where there was a choice.

There was no excuse.

"Apologize to the ladies," she told them, kicking Linus' knee out to make him kneel. Reg and Dinny apologized.

Linus mumbled under his breath, not knowing Sarah Jennifer could hear the string of profanity he was directing at her. The other two found his insults hilarious until Brutus stepped forward and slammed a fist into his temple.

"Show some fucking respect," he snarled, yellow-eyed. His scar twisted as he bared his teeth, transforming his handsome face into something far more sinister.

Linus snarled right back, unafraid. "I told you before, and I'll tell you again. No beta is running my life, and no little bitch will, either!"

Sarah Jennifer's mind turned, weighing every nuance of the exchange. She was beginning to understand the dynamics of this pack. Linus was clearly the troublemaker, but she'd needed to see it with her own eyes before applying the lesson of why it was a bad idea to annoy your Alpha. She had hoped that she wouldn't need to make an example of any more of the pack after Brutus. She was aware that there were too few of them for her future needs.

Still, needs must.

She drew the handgun hidden in the holster on her belt and shot the mouthy Were in the knee.

Linus dropped to the ground, screaming as his knee gave way and the silver round burned him from the inside.

"The next one goes into your head," Sarah Jennifer informed him in an even tone. "Submit, or die. Choose now. I'm not going to keep wasting good silver on kneecaps."

Linus sobbed with pain, apologizing to her and to the women through his tears.

"Good. It's a start." Sarah Jennifer turned her attention to Reg and Dinny. "You two can help him now."

Dinny and Reg rushed to get the silver out of Linus' knee before it was ruined for good.

Sarah Jennifer raised her voice so all could hear. "I told you things were changing around here. Let this be a warning to you. It is the only one you get. *I will not tolerate behavior like this.* You are not animals. From now on, you will be held to a higher standard. There are two ways: my way, and the hard way. The result will be the same, so I suggest you think about that before acting out of line."

Bruiser raised his hand. "What does that mean? What do you want from us?"

Brutus made a motion to silence him, but Sarah Jennifer stopped him. "It's okay to ask questions. I want you to be something to be proud of instead of a mutt pack I have to exterminate. The only way I know how to make that happen is the military way, so that's what I'm going to use."

She didn't elaborate, letting the idea sink in. She was going to have a hard enough time building their confidence to the point where they could deal with the blood trade in the city. "This pack is messed up. It's like you don't know what it is to be Were. Luckily, I know two things: how to lead a successful pack, and the military way."

"Military?" Maria interjected. "Like the FDG? 'Cause we all know they're not around anymore."

Sarah Jennifer lifted her chin. "Lady, I *am* the FDG." She paused as the memory of her last visit to Chicago surfaced. "Well, what's left of it. This pack will train, and together we will stamp out the leeches. But first, you need to make amends. Lesson one. Things have to change between the pack and the people of Salem."

The pack murmured uneasily.

"Come around to the idea," Sarah Jennifer instructed. "It's happening."

Maria frowned in consideration. "I guess I'll wait to

take Missy," she told Sarah Jennifer. "Better to have the pack for protection in case we run into any nomads on the way."

Sarah Jennifer nodded her agreement. "Then it will be a little longer before Missy gets back. I have some attitude adjustments to make before I can trust my pack around others."

A little longer turned out to be three weeks, during which time she got to know the young men she was now responsible for.

That first day she had them finish cleaning up the settlement, supervising while she drilled the new hierarchy into them. There were no free rides on her bus.

Sarah Jennifer knew from experience that it wouldn't take more than a couple of nights with an empty belly for any of them to learn that lesson. She had to teach them responsibility for each other, something many of them would be resistant to until they realized that the benefit of contributing daily to the well-being of the pack was getting a share of whatever food Sarah Jennifer provided. She had faith that the skills they learned would teach them to bond as well as to face adversity with dignity.

Everyone was subdued that evening despite the hearty meal they made from the deer Sarah Jennifer and Brutus had brought back from the hunt. She didn't find that too extraordinary. They'd had their world turned upside down by her arrival, and she wasn't done with them by a long shot.

Once she had them behaving like a pack instead of acting like a herd of cats, she intended to make a proper assessment of their potential roles. For now, she paid attention to how they conducted themselves during the cleanup and renovation of the settlement. The six youngest tended to stick together and showed promise with their curiosity. Bruiser continued to stand out as sergeant material. He was most at home filling the role of Brutus' enforcer, but he was malleable, as was his friend Ozzie.

Sarah Jennifer decided to test the pack's progress on the first day of week two. She woke them before dawn and praised them for their efforts, glad to be able to breathe and smell only nature. "Here's the reward. We're going fishing. Everyone grab what you need and bundle it. Don't bring more than half of what you can carry in your wolf form.

"Where are we going, Major?" Rory piped up.

"There's a lake around fifty kilometers north of here. It's cut off from the main waterways during winter, so it's pretty much guaranteed to be stocked if you don't mind breaking through the ice." Sarah Jennifer held up her pack. "I have everything we need to make a good catch. You all need warm clothing since even with your enhancement, it's going to be bitter."

"What about you, Major?" a younger Were by the name of Geordie asked. "You're not a wolf. How will you keep up with us?"

Sarah Jennifer grinned, shouldering her pack. "I might not have a wolf, but I'll eat my boots if any of you can catch me when I'm trying." She clapped her hands. "Why are you all still standing around? Get a move on! We leave in thirty minutes."

The pack obeyed eagerly, packing warm clothing into bundles that they tied around their bodies. Sarah Jennifer indicated Brutus join her before he shifted. "I'm going to cut ahead of the pack and have them track me to the fishing spot. Choose two others to play tail-end Charlie with you."

"Huh?" Brutus shook his head. "Look, the military talk? I don't get it. Just tell me what you want."

Sarah Jennifer folded her arms. "You'll get used to it." She sighed when Brutus continued to wait for clarification. "You take the position at the rear of the pack and make sure none of them gets into any trouble."

"And you couldn't just say that because…" Brutus' expression was respectful enough. It was the twinkle in his eye that gave away his teasing.

Sarah Jennifer wondered if Brutus was a gift from Saint Payback for the crap she'd given her grandfather. "Would you prefer to miss out on the run?"

Brutus shifted and gave her a pointed look before bounding off to snap playfully at the heels of the Weres he'd chosen. Sarah Jennifer wasn't surprised to see he'd gone for Bruiser and Ozzie.

The three of them took their positions and Sarah Jennifer set off running. She kept to the head of the pack to start, then opened up her pace after a few miles once she was comfortable the pack was focused on the route. She led them out of Lynnwood and up the old highway a short way, sticking to the verges to avoid long-abandoned vehicles choked with growth. The next turn took them into a younger forest, where the trees were spaced farther apart and the undergrowth less dense, making their progress smooth.

Sarah Jennifer smelled water and whooped. "Nearly

there, boys! Catch me if you can!" She stopped holding back and gave herself to the wind.

The pack yipped when Sarah Jennifer vanished from view. She wasn't as fast as a vampire, but it was close enough from the Weres' perspectives. Brutus howled, driving the pack on faster.

They found her at the edge of the lake, where she'd gathered a number of branches that she was in the process of stripping with her field knife.

Sarah Jennifer waved them over once they were done getting dressed. "Lesson two. There is food everywhere you look in nature. We're going to set lines, then you're going to watch and wait to catch the fish while I find some deer. Take a knee." She sighed when they looked at her in confusion and waved her knife at the ground in front of her. "Here. Kneel. Pay attention."

The pack gathered around as Sarah Jennifer laid out the items she pulled from her knapsack. "These are fishing hooks made from whatever I found lying around. We also have fishing line. How to make it is a lesson for another day." She showed them how to make a tripod from sticks lashed together with bark, then how to set the line from it after punching a hole in the ice to feed it into.

When they were done, she selected Geordie and Carver to accompany her, leaving Brutus in charge of the fishing effort while she tracked down the promised deer.

"Why are we hunting so far from home?" Carver inquired as they walked into the forest.

"To avoid thinning the deer population close to the settlement," Sarah Jennifer replied. What she didn't add was she wanted to know how much headway she'd made with getting the pack to trust her orders. She located a herd within a few miles of the lake and had Geordie and Carver carry the two they caught back to the rest.

The boys, as she was starting to think of them, left the fishing holes when they emerged from the trees with the deer.

"How many fish do we have?" Sarah Jennifer asked. She grinned as those who'd made catches proudly held up their haul. "Not bad. Okay, boys. I'm going to parcel the meat out for us to carry back to the settlement."

She noted the gleam in Linus' eye. "I hope I don't need to emphasize that anyone who decides to stop for a snack on the way home will find themselves on a vegetarian diet for the next month."

Sarah Jennifer walked through the settlement after dinner, listening to the pack talk through the events of the day with hope in her heart. They were adjusting to her leadership with a minimum of upset, for the most part because they'd been crying out for a strong hand since Katia's death. With the security of regular meals and the absence of the tension at the top, they were showing signs of the pack bonds Sarah Jennifer had despaired to see lacking in them when she'd arrived.

Brutus approached as she passed the well. "Hey. I'm going to keep bunking with Bruiser. We'll build you a place to call your own when we get back from Salem."

Sarah Jennifer nodded, not wanting to tell him that she didn't anticipate them returning to Lynnwood for a long time. "Thanks." She smiled at Brutus, allowing him to see her softer side. "I know it's been a lot for you. You're handling it pretty well, considering."

Brutus snorted softly. "Yeah, sure. I'm glad you're here, SJ."

Sarah Jennifer hit him in the shoulder. "SJ? That's not going to fly."

Brutus rubbed his shoulder, a mischievous grin on his face. "Yeah? I like it. Suits you."

Sarah Jennifer offered him a middle-finger salute as she walked toward his house. "That's no way to address your Alpha."

"Yeah, but it's perfect for my pain-in-the-ass cousin," he called after her.

Sarah Jennifer closed the door. She went straight into the bedroom, stripped the bed, and laid her bedroll out, yawning as she bundled the discarded sheets onto a chair in the corner of the room.

She would have a talk with Brutus about the importance of following rank structure tomorrow. It would involve him doing laps of the settlement. Lots and lots of laps.

CHAPTER SEVEN

Sarah Jennifer was running on four paws while the world burned and magic crackled all around her.

The acrid odor stung her sensitive wolf nose as she tore through the forest toward Salem, but she felt more alive than she'd ever been. The hot wind caused by the fire spurred her to ever-greater speeds. Her paws flew along the ground, and the pack was right on her heels.

They howled as they pressed harder, opening up the gap between them and the legions of the dead closing in behind them.

There was danger all around. Despite it, Sarah Jennifer's heart soared to be back on the sharp edge. She dodged a collapsing tree. The disturbance caused by the heavy trunk hitting the forest floor threw up embers to catch her fur coat, but she ignored the pain. The necessity of getting the pack to the town ahead of the dead behind them overrode her needs.

The pack needed her, and the people of Salem needed her pack.

The scene shifted as the road to Salem came into view. The fire and the pack melted away, leaving the twin stones at the barrier hex. She was still in wolf form. Her canine nose picked up a curious scent as she entered the clearing.

A woman stood at the center of the circle, suffused in golden light. She was both there and not there. Sarah Jennifer yelped with fear when she saw that the woman was her in human form. She growled at the interloper.

"Peace, Sarah Jennifer Walton," the doppelganger told her softly, stilling her anger with a wave of pure love. "I am not you, but neither can you comprehend me as anything but a reflection of yourself. I am not of this Earth. I am Kurtherian."

Sarah Jennifer growled. This is the enemy Bethany Anne had gone to the stars to fight, she thought, unable to speak.

A flood of warmth and peace washed over the clearing. "I am not the enemy," the Kurtherian told her, reading her mind. "The magic-workers of Salem have named me Gaia, but my name is Lilith.

Sarah Jennifer recalled hearing that name at the Samhain feast. Gaia was the witches' deity, but the witches' power came from Kurtherian technology. Her immediate thought was that Lilith could have set herself up as the witches' ruler, but everything she'd heard about "Gaia" pointed to Lilith being a benevolent guide.

Lilith dipped her head. "Your reasoning is good. I was sworn to Earth's protection by Bethany Anne."

Bethany Anne wouldn't leave Earth in the hands of an enemy, Sarah Jennifer's brain imparted. She padded over and lay at Lilith's feet, no longer threatened by the apparition. She wished she could speak in her present form. She had a lot of questions for this Kurtherian.

"Welcome, my champion," Lilith told Sarah Jennifer, passing a hand over her head. "We have much to discuss."

Suddenly she was able to speak. "Your champion?"

Lilith's mouth turned upwards in a beatific smile. "Yes, my child. The Earth is in need of a defender, and you will be my sword and shield. See."

The road dissolved around them as Lilith showed her the path ahead. Weres imprisoned behind bars in Boston, crying out for a savior. Her pack by her side, working as one to free them.

"Your warriors await you," Lilith told her. "But the people need you most of all. See."

Sarah Jennifer's view panned out, showing the world at large. It was worse than the apocalypse. WWDE was a ripple on a duck pond compared to this tsunami of horror.

There was no sense or reason to what she was seeing. Red-eyed men, women, and children, driven insane by hunger and compelled to roam in search of a satisfaction they could never find. She saw the fall of the cities, the world in flames as the army of the dead spilled across the land.

Lilith spoke over the chaos of the vision. "They are not dead, they are broken. They will not die but instead will lose their reason. They will cannibalize their fellow men and live to pass the malady on. You are the shield between the Mad and the rest of humanity until Bethany Anne's gift can be given to all. Do you accept, Sarah Jennifer Walton?"

"Yes." Sarah Jennifer agreed immediately. Her path was clear to her, everything Esme had been holding back, the need to bring the UnknownWorld together. She knew deep in her heart that this was the real reason she had stayed when her family left to fight among the stars.

Someone had to stay behind. Her fight had always been here, at the end of the world. Everything else had been insignificant up until this moment. "What's the deal? Why not gift it now, before the Madness begins?"

Lilith's grief was tangible. "I cannot give magic to the world yet, and the Madness has already taken over Europe. I have a plan, but until it comes to fruition, you are humanity's only hope of survival."

Sarah Jennifer would fight for humanity or die trying. "Where do I start?"

Lilith shook her head. "Our time together is too short, and I have something important to say. The Mad will come to you, my champion. Be stout of heart when they arrive, for your pain will cause you to slip from the path if you do not acknowledge it.

"I have a gift for you," she continued in a dreamy voice. "The wolf you have carried in your heart for all your life is yours to command."

Sarah Jennifer was awake in the next moment, every detail of her dream crystal-clear in her mind. She didn't know whether it had been a dream or a vision until she opened her eyes and everything in the room looked wrong.

She scrambled to her feet. Her *four* feet.

Her clothes were shredded around her, and her bedroll was ruined. *Shit.* It *was* real. She was in wolf form.

Sarah Jennifer had larger concerns than the bedroll. How did she change back?

The next second she was human again, her will being enough to enact the switch.

Sarah Jennifer looked at her hands. "Huh, what do you know? Esme was right; it's all about wanting it."

She switched back and forth a few times, testing her new form, then tried to heal her knee without success before dressing and leaving the house in search of Brutus.

Maria pointed her to the western edge of the settlement, where she found him preparing to leave for a hunt with Bruiser and Ozzie.

"Mornin', Major!" Bruiser called brightly when he spotted her.

Brutus' nose wrinkled as she joined the group.

"What's going on here?" Sarah Jennifer asked, knowing full well. She also knew how to keep them on their toes.

Brutus frowned, while the other two suddenly found their feet very interesting.

"We were going to hunt," Bruiser explained.

"Told you we should have asked her first," Bruiser's companion muttered sourly.

"Yes, you should definitely report that the only three officers I have are planning to go hunting and leave the pack to take care of themselves," Sarah Jennifer replied sagely. "Smart wolf."

"Sorry, Major." Ozzie attempted a salute, the beating she'd given Brutus still fresh in his mind. "We did tell Big Ace to keep an eye on them."

Sarah Jennifer folded her arms. "Well, that makes it okay, then."

Bruiser frowned. "It does?"

"No, dumbass." Brutus slapped him on the back of the head. "Do we have permission to go hunt?"

Sarah Jennifer patted Ozzie and Bruiser firmly on their backs, making them stumble as they walked. "Go on ahead and find some breakfast bacon for us all, and I might forget you didn't ask first."

They shifted and loped noisily into the forest before Sarah Jennifer could change her mind and call them back.

"They're not going to find anything, making that much noise," she commented to Brutus, shaking her head with a grin.

Brutus' nose twitched. "You smell different. What gives?"

Sarah Jennifer laughed in his face. She quickly stripped, relishing his outright shock when she changed form. She pranced around Brutus on four paws, shaking her golden fur before switching back and giving him a smug look.

"What the fuck?" Brutus exclaimed. "You didn't have a wolf yesterday!"

"Must be this place, rubbing off on me," she joked, bundling her clothing and weapons into a backpack and tying it on. "Are we going to go hunting, or do you want to stand here chatting while those noisy A-holes scare all the food away? Can you smell that?" She sniffed the air, her enhanced senses picking up the scent and sounds of a wild pig herd in the near distance.

"Heel, boy!" she called to Brutus before switching back to wolf form and bounding silently into the forest at an angle that would put the pigs between the two pairs of hunters.

An hour later, they returned to the settlement with four fat wild pigs slung on long branches held between them, cleaned, dressed, and ready to butcher.

Sarah Jennifer had assessed the three Weres throughout the hunt, feeling growing satisfaction that the pack was becoming capable of feeding themselves without resorting to raiding nearby communities. They still had a lot to learn. Brutus had done the best, but without her, they would have lost one of the pigs. The others had gained in stealth and learned the basics of woodcraft, although they still had little to no situational awareness.

It was a wonder they'd survived this long without Katia. Sarah Jennifer directed Brutus, Bruiser, and Ozzie to erect frames to hang the pigs on and called the pack to gather around and take a knee. "Lesson three. Waste not, want not."

"Are we gonna have bacon?" Little Ace piped up hopefully.

Everyone's ears pricked at the mention of bacon. Sarah Jennifer jumped on the teachable moment. "Sure, once we've cured the meat."

"Why bother with that, Major?" he asked, brow furrowed.

Sarah Jennifer knew hot chow was a great motivator, and she used it regularly. It was almost time to move on, and she wanted everyone ready when the day rolled around.

The pack scuttled off, everyone doing their part. She expected no shenanigans, but kept her eye on Linus and his buddies. Brutus directed the younger Weres. "We need a table to cut the meat on," she told him. "Where do you usually process big scores like this?"

Brutus shook his head. "Little Ace wasn't lying. We've only ever managed to catch rabbits and squirrels, and not too many of them, either. We just went and raided the farms when we got hungry."

Sarah Jennifer sighed with exasperation. "Go grab a sharp knife. Your education begins now, along with everyone else's. Do we have salt?"

Brutus nodded.

Sarah Jennifer thanked the stars for small mercies. "Good, go get that too. Pork will go bad if you don't process it properly." She pointed at an empty shack. "Rory, Geordie, Big Ace, get that cleared out so we can use it as a smokehouse."

Brutus took Bruiser and Ozzie with him, returning from Maria's house a few minutes later with a table, two knives, and a sack of coarse sea salt. A short time later, Sarah Jennifer had one of the pigs turning on a spit over the fire pit she'd had Geordie and Carver dig and prepare.

As the day progressed, the smell and sizzle of the pigs kept drawing the pack to the firepit in hopes of a morsel. Sarah Jennifer sent each one away with a new task, never pausing in the task of teaching Brutus, Bruiser and Ozzie the art of butchery and how to preserve meat using the second pig.

By the time night had fallen, the settlement was a new place. Leaving Brutus to guard the meat, Sarah Jennifer took Bruiser with her and made an inspection of the common areas. She found that the pack had worked a lot harder than she'd expected. They had followed her orders to the letter. In the center of the village stood a new trestle table made by Ace and the rest of the younger Weres. It was set with a mish-mash of plates, mess tins, and bowls. Nothing matched, but it was all clean—including the pack, who'd all managed to bathe and smelled much better.

Sarah Jennifer graced her people with a smile. "This is

the standard I want to see every day, no matter where we are. Sergeant Bruiser, it is your responsibility to ensure I am not disappointed."

"Yes, Major," Bruiser replied. "I don't know why we didn't do this before. It feels good to have worked for our comforts."

Sarah Jennifer dipped her head in understanding. "Because it didn't occur to you. What do you say to some dinner?"

Bruiser was all for that suggestion. Sarah Jennifer called the pack to the table, the rush reminding her of chowtime with the FDG reserves who had helped her grandfather's tac teams train. They had always been ready for a meal too.

The pack was ravenous after the first day's hard work they had experienced in a long time. Sarah Jennifer hoped it didn't take them too long to get used to the pace since she'd be expecting more of them every day from now on.

Even the human women had participated. She appreciated their efforts to bring some cheer to the table with the wreaths they'd spent the day weaving. Maria had baked fresh bread rolls and made apple butter. Sarah Jennifer tried not to think too hard about where the ingredients had come from.

Before the pack ate, they thanked her, Brutus, and the others for providing a feast. Sarah Jennifer was almost sad to bring their exuberance crashing down, but she had news for them that was best faced on a full stomach.

As the last bites were swallowed, she stood, drawing the pack's attention. They'd had their liberty; now it was time to focus on tomorrow's objective. She'd break them in gently.

"Well done today, all of you. Seeing you all work together gives me hope that this pack can pull back from disaster. And look what you achieved!" She waved her hand around the settlement. "This place looks amazing. *This* is the power of the pack in action. This is the life! A worthy cause, a job well done, and hot chow at the end of it. What do you say?"

They cheered. Not usually her thing, but the Weres at the table had a long way to go before they were capable of bearing praise with the stoicism of Marines.

Sarah Jennifer held up a hand to stay their enthusiasm. "There will be time for that. Today, you helped yourselves and each other. It's a new day tomorrow. We're going to pack up and leave for Salem."

Shocked gasps went around the table.

Sarah Jennifer dispelled them with her hand. "It is time to make amends for your crimes. Make the reputation of this pack something to be proud of. This is not a discussion, and if I wanted your opinions on the matter, I'd have asked for them. If you have objections, they can be lodged with Sergeant Bruiser or our newest sergeant, Ozzie."

She indicated the Were in question, promoting the smart wolf officially. Ozzie blushed, waving off the good-natured ribbing of the others.

"Rest assured, the sergeants will pass them up the chain of command to Lieutenant Brutus, who will ignore them because I don't give a crap about hurt feelings when we have a goal to reach." Her tone made her resolve clear. "This pack belongs to me. Your debt to society is my debt, and I sure as hell don't want a debt on my hands. I am responsible for every single one of you, and you will obey me to the letter, or suffer the consequences. You will find me hard but fair. I take no bullshit excuses, and I will demand the very best from each of you. No matter what lies ahead, I will be here, watching over every one of you. There will be days and even years where you wish I'd never come here, but you will obey me. You will learn that you can depend on me, and I will fulfill my role as Alpha."

Sarah Jennifer stood to make sure she had the attention of everybody at the table, meeting the eyes of her pack as she looked around at them. The next words she had to say were the most important. She made the vow to herself as much as to the pack hanging on her every word.

"*Honor. Courage. Commitment.* Those are what I promise you, and those are what I expect in return. Lieutenant Brutus, Sergeants Bruiser, Ozzie, and Maria. You four stick around, please. The rest of you hit the sack. We've got a big day ahead of us tomorrow, starting at dawn."

CHAPTER EIGHT

There was another holdup at the rear of the line.

Sarah Jennifer had made it clear that those stalls and interruptions needed to be nipped in the bud immediately by the sergeants. They had a schedule to keep and were already two hours behind to reach the cottage before nightfall. She'd set a brisk pace for the pack, choosing "volunteers" to carry the humans piggyback-style and swapping them out every hour.

The village had been stripped of anything useful, each person carrying as much as they were capable of. She wanted to reach Salem before nightfall on the second day to avoid an extra night spent sleeping in the snow. Esme's cottage was less than ten kilometers away, and Sarah Jennifer relished the thought of seeing her closest friend again.

She halted the line until the stragglers caught up, then continued leading everyone through the undergrowth surrounding the various pines that dominated the area.

When they arrived mid-afternoon, Esme was waiting at

the gate with a wide grin and open arms for Sarah Jennifer, who returned the hug with enthusiasm.

"Good to have you back, Duckie. Who are these strapping young men and women?" She swept the pack with a piercing look, making them squirm under her inspection.

"These are my pack, Esme." Sarah Jennifer told her with a wink and a smile. "They've turned over a new leaf, I promise. Is it okay if we use the meadow to camp out tonight?" She turned to glare at the pack, intending to remind them of their manners. To her shock, they were all showing the utmost respect to Esme as they waited quietly in the road.

"See?" Sarah Jennifer told Esme. "Brutus, you're in command until I'm done catching up with my friend. Get camp set up. I'll be there in a while."

Brutus led the pack farther down the road to the meadow. They had talked more as they walked, and she was beginning to think he had potential if she could knock that chip off his shoulder. In any other pack, he would have grown to be a fine Alpha given time, but he was her beta now and would remain so for as long as they both lived.

"Putting quite a ticket on yourself there, Duckie," Esme commented dryly, disturbing her thoughts. "Hope you can live up to it."

Sarah Jennifer looked askance at Esme and laughed, seeing the complete lack of malice in her remark. "Me too. I'd better go and check they're not trashing the meadow. I don't want to leave them unsupervised just yet. Join us for dinner?"

Esme's eyes crinkled at the corners. "You don't have to

ask me twice. See to your people. I'll be along when you're set up."

They hugged again, and Sarah Jennifer proceeded to the meadow. She had a full afternoon of chores planned for the pack, partly to keep the rowdy Weres out of trouble, and partly to spend some more time getting to know them before they got to Salem. She spotted the pack making themselves comfortable on the meadow wall, draining the last of the water in the canteens and chatting among themselves.

She strode into the meadow, gaining their attention with a barked order. "Get off your lazy asses! There's no time for lounging around. We have a guest for dinner, and we're going to provide a pleasant meal and a relaxing environment to serve it in."

As they jumped down from the wall, Sarah Jennifer counted them off into teams. "If you're a one, you're on firewood with Sergeant Bruiser. Do not leave the immediate area, do not approach any locals. Twos, you're on water duty with Sergeant Ozzie, and the same goes for you. Three and Four, tents." She was interrupted by Big Ace, waving a hand over in group three. "Yes?"

"We don't got any tents, Major," he told her.

Sarah Jennifer pursed her lips. "We don't *have* any tents. Three and Four, you are on inventory. I want to know what we have and what we need. Five, you are on fire duty, get it started and keep it going, do it safely. Six, you are our sous-chefs for the evening. Report to Maria and obey her every word as though it came from my mouth. Brutus, Linus, you're with me."

The pack went about their tasks as Sarah Jennifer

located the containers with the parcels of smoked pork and selected a decent piece of belly with a thick layer of salt-and-herb-crusted fat, wrapped in clean leaves to preserve it. She stood to leave, motioning to Brutus and Linus to follow.

Esme met them halfway up the road, struggling under a double-armload of folded canvas.

Sarah Jennifer took the canvas sheets from her, offloading them onto Brutus and Linus. "Take those ahead. Our talk will wait for now."

"We were going to have a talk?" Linus asked.

Brutus shoved him. "Just do what you're told. Come on."

Sarah Jennifer noted the strain on Esme from carrying the heavy load and linked arms with her to lend her some support under the guise of closeness. Esme would never be seen to need help, and she would never insult her friend by offering.

"You're a godsend, Esme." She didn't bother to ask how her friend had known what they needed. Esme always knew when and where she was needed, and the canvases were perfect for tents. "I have a gift for you, too."

Esme's face wrinkled in delight, her eyes reminding Sarah Jennifer of two currants in a bun as she unwrapped the pork belly piece Sarah Jennifer had chosen for her.

"It's been a while since I had a nice bit of crackling!" Esme pulled a piece off and set to crunching it while she took the rest to her larder. She returned a moment later with her enormous carpet bag. Sarah Jennifer took it, ignoring Esme's protests as she heaved it onto her shoulder.

When they returned to the meadow, preparations for camp were well underway. The first and fifth team had the fire crackling merrily, and teams three and four were almost finished with the inventory. Maria was having the time of her life in command of team six, and if her ears didn't deceive her, she heard Ozzie's team returning with the pack's now-filled canteens.

Esme took her bag and headed straight for the cooking station, stopping here and there to chat as she went. Sarah Jennifer watched her go, feeling a weight lift. Now that they had the canvas, there was less worry about the fragile humans getting sick from sleeping outdoors in the snow.

Sarah Jennifer called Little Ace over. "What do we have in the way of knives? Do we have a machete?"

The young Were called back to his team, "Tyson, bring the blades!"

Tyson picked up one of the bags the teams had used to organize the inventory. "Whose idea was that?" Sarah Jennifer asked Little Ace.

Little Ace pointed at a slightly older, bulkier version of himself. "My bro, Big Ace. He's good at thinking of things and keeping them in order."

Sarah Jennifer shouted to the older brother as she took the bag from Tyson, "Hey, Big Ace! Get over here." She glanced into the bag, cataloging the contents and noticing all the blades had been cleaned and oiled.

He looked at her with a "who, me?" expression.

Sarah Jennifer gave him a sharp look. *"Now!"*

The Were hurried at her command.

"Private Big Ace. Without checking, tell me what is in

this bag." She held it up so he could see the faded logo on the side.

Big Ace rattled off a list. "Sixteen bowie knives, four machetes, sixteen eating knives, one large axe, an augur, and three blades I don't know the name of. Also, a whetstone, cloth, and a jar of oil, ma'am."

Sarah Jennifer nodded. "Very good. The three you couldn't identify are rigging knives, for sailing. Are the rest of our supplies organized as well as this bag?"

Big Ace nodded. "Yes, ma'am. I like to organize things."

Little Ace chipped in with a laugh, "Hell yeah, he does!"

Their Alpha nodded. "Congratulations, Big Ace. I'm promoting you to Quartermaster. You are now responsible for inventory and requisitions. Your job is to know what we have and keep it under lock and key. Nobody gets anything without running it by you first."

Big Ace's eyes widened at being given the responsibility. "What, even you, Major?"

She nodded. "Even me, Quartermaster. I can override your decision at any point, so don't let the power go to your head. You have a duty, passed down through the ages from one military outfit to the next, to prevent waste and pull miracles out of your ass. Do you know how to keep a ledger?"

Her new QM nodded eagerly, running off to his knapsack to fetch something.

"Oh, shit. You got him started now." Little Ace's laughter had continued unabated. "I hope you know you just created a monster!"

Big Ace returned, proffering a tatty notebook to Sarah Jennifer. She took it and thumbed through it, being careful not to pull it apart as she turned the delicate pages. Every line was filled with tiny script and numbers detailing the exploits of the pack: places visited, items stolen, property damaged.

"This is exactly what I needed. Thank you, Quartermaster Ace. You may resume your duties. Here, this will help." Sarah Jennifer unslung her pack and dug deep before pulling out an unused notebook she had found in an abandoned store some time back. She had briefly considered trying her hand at poetry when she found it. The idea was cast aside, but she had kept the notebook. Paper was too rare to leave behind.

Big Ace could hardly contain his excitement at receiving the gift. "For me? Really? It's so clean, I can't write in this." He turned the notebook over in his hands and opened it reverently.

Sarah Jennifer couldn't help but smile. She had only been with the pack for a few weeks, but already she felt like she was making good progress with them. They were responding to her brand of leadership, not just because they feared her but because she was showing them that there was another way. "You keep your records like you always have and report back to me at the end of each day. Everything that comes into the pack, everything that leaves, and who it leaves with."

The Ace brothers scurried off toward the cooking station, engrossed in the notebook's hard cover and the ribbon bookmark.

Sarah Jennifer found that Esme had wandered back over. "They aren't rotten," she told her friend. "Just bruised from poor handling."

Esme sighed with regret. "I'll admit we might have been hasty in rejecting them. You appear to have, what did you say? Ach, yes, 'kicked them into shape' nicely."

Sarah Jennifer smirked. "I'll tell you all about it over dinner tonight, but I didn't have to do much kicking. I'll wager Linus has a limp for a while, though. They haven't done themselves any favors in the past, but I understand how they got into this mess. They're just a bunch of lost children in need of a firm hand."

Esme laughed along with her. "They've got that in you, Duckie. I don't think you'll have any more problems. I checked them all out, and they're mostly harmless. Grateful even. That Maria woman is a riot. I believe she is the mother of the Ace boys?"

"Yeah," Sarah Jennifer confirmed.

"What about the others?" Esme inquired.

Another thing Sarah Jennifer didn't know about her pack. She had to get to work on that. "Maria doesn't want to leave the pack when the rest of the human women go home. Same with Tamara and Sofie. The five of them are a family within the pack. Besides, Maria will tell you that she wasn't kidnapped in the first place. I've got some stuff to do, but you're welcome to stay with her if you like? Dinner will be a few hours yet, and I have an afternoon's instruction planned for the pack."

Esme clucked. "No need to worry, Duckie. I'll be happy to keep Maria company. Have fun, and I'll see you at dinner."

Sarah Jennifer watched Esme leave, then turned her attention to the pack. "Listen up! My next lesson is how to create a shelter with nothing but the blade in your hand and the good brain you were born with."

"But your witch friend brought us the canvas!" Reg complained.

Sarah Jennifer singled him out with a sharp look. "That's for the ladies' tent. We won't always have canvas. How many times have you been caught out at night and had a hard time of it?"

The pack nodded reluctantly. They had all been forced to huddle together in wolf form at night before they founded the settlement, just to keep warm. Brutus had told her more about the pack's escape from Boston on the hike to Esme's land, giving her an idea of where they were lacking in skills and common sense.

She resumed her lesson, selecting a group of mature pines that would do the job, grabbing the big axe and heading for them. It was hot work even in the wintry air, but the axe made short work of the trunks.

Sarah Jennifer instructed the Weres to drag the trees to one side and strip the branches after she felled them.

"Quartermaster Ace, Sergeants, stand by. The rest of you, back in your teams," she ordered once they were done. "The officers will give each team an equal share of the resources. Each team will work together to build the shelter they will be sleeping in tonight, so make sure you put your best effort in. If you're struggling, ask for help. I will be walking around, as will Lieutenant Brutus and the sergeants."

She clapped her hands to get the pack moving. "Let's go, we're burning daylight!"

CHAPTER NINE

It was just like the old days, Sarah Jennifer thought. She held a Were easily in each hand by the scruff of the neck, their hind paws dangling a foot off the ground. She gave each a shake, the rattling of their skulls putting a stop to them snarling at each other.

"Reg, Linus, change back, now!" she commanded.

The wolves became surly young men, and she dropped them without ceremony. "Now tell me, what is so important that you two need to duke it out instead of building your shelter? Do you want to sleep in the snow tonight? You too, Dinny. Start talking."

The shelter in question bore a strong resemblance to the pile of firewood on the other side of camp. She gave all three of them a stern look. "*Well*?"

"It keeps collapsing, and it's *his* fault!" Dinny whined, pointing at Linus.

Linus snarled again. "It's not my fault you're a dumb-as-shit, inbred asshole!"

"*Enough!*" Sarah Jennifer bellowed, her patience worn

thin. It wasn't good management to put your subordinates down, but these three were irritating the shit out of her, as well as ruining the pack unity vibe the other teams had going on. "You're all dumbasses. In fact, Team Dumbass will be your team's designation until you earn something better. Why am I not surprised that you three were the only ones not paying attention to the instructions? Look around you. What do you see?"

She indicated the other five teams, who were all engrossed in the challenge. The shelters were taking shape. A circle of tepees made from pine branches surrounded the campfire.

"Shelters," Linus admitted.

She'd had the pack take a knee while she showed them how to peel the bark in strips from the tree trunks, running them through a series of easy, durable knots they could use to lash the boughs together to make frames that would hold layers of foliage.

Sarah Jennifer sighed. Just because they were dumbasses, it didn't mean she'd leave them to freeze. They were her dumbasses, after all. "Show me where you went wrong."

Twenty minutes later, Team Dumbass had the beginnings of a workable shelter. Sarah Jennifer left to take on a challenge of her own, leaving Brutus to supervise the teams.

She chose a stand of more mature trees and took the axe to three red pines, making sure to leave the oaks alone. They were sacred to these parts, and now that she had met "Gaia," aka Lilith, she did not want to give any disrespect by felling the trees associated with her in case it went down poorly when they reached Salem.

It was a few minutes' work to drag the first and largest tree behind her to the space she'd claimed in the meadow, but it was going to be tricky work to make straight planks with the tools she had.

On her way around the camp area, she almost tripped, stubbing her toe hard enough to make it tingle through her boot. She realized the thing she'd tripped on was a nice chunk of oak, perfect for what she had in mind.

"Gaia" provides indeed, Sarah Jennifer thought with humor, scooping the oak up and readjusting her grip on the pine.

She worked to strip the branches and bark from the thick pine, putting aside thoughts of the Kurtherian who had visited in her dream for a moment of peace.

The pack gravitated to her one by one, having finished with their shelters and been released by Brutus to come watch. She ignored them and moved on to carving wedges from the oak with her knife.

"Whatcha doin' there, Major?" Carver called into the enraptured silence.

Sarah Jennifer had taken care to learn all their names by now. Since not far in the future, the pack would fight and maybe even die under her command, it was the least she could do, even if she decided to keep them at a distance like she'd seen her grandparents do with the FDG reserves who used to assist the tac teams with training back in the day.

She didn't think she would enjoy being that kind of leader. She took too much joy from being hands-on and involved. Being a pack leader wasn't much different from being an officer, she considered. She was their teacher, their disciplinarian, and their example. She could see how every interaction was a teaching opportunity she could use to build her pack, and it looked to be lesson time again.

"Good question, Carver. Okay, pack, eyes on me. Lesson five. If you haven't got it, make it." Sarah Jennifer proceeded to explain the method of splitting wood using the low-tech method of wedges and a hammer. "If we had the correct tools, we could do this in one stroke. It is usually done with a maul, or at least a hammer and chisel, but we have neither at this moment. As it is, our enhanced strength is a bonus when it comes time to applying force. Watch this."

She took one of the wedges and lined it up with the marks she'd scored down the center of the pine. "Oak is one of the hardest woods, while pine is reasonably soft in comparison. We use one to split the other." She drove the oak wedge in using just the heel of her hand, which bled for a second before healing without a scar. "Who would like to try? Don't hold back; we've got three trees and enough wedges to go around."

Little Ace and his buddies were first to volunteer. Sarah Jennifer had noticed from the start that they were usually quick to lend a hand to their mother and the other human women.

Sarah Jennifer handed them the wedges with a smile. "Looks like we have some willing sacrifices. Just do exactly as I did, and we'll have the resources we need for the next part of the task."

The boys had paid close attention, and soon the three

trees had been split and split again, until they were reduced to a pile of wobbly boards that would serve nicely for the purpose she had in mind.

"Great job!" Sarah Jennifer exclaimed after inspecting the work. "I think you've earned a rest. Go get a drink and get cleaned up for dinner. It smells like it's nearly chow time."

"Aye, that it is," Maria called from the camp kitchen. "But don't call my food chow, Major, or you won't be getting any."

They all laughed as they went about it.

Sarah Jennifer needed one more thing before the next part of her project could go ahead. Wheels. She didn't know if there was a wheelwright in the area, but she knew someone who would know.

"Why don't you rebuild the cart, Duckie?" Esme offered after hearing Sarah Jennifer's plan. "It's falling apart anyway, but the wheels are sturdy. Jim Johnson made them with good iron. You can use that canvas I gave you to build a cover."

It was just like her grandfather always said—none of them were as smart as all of them. Esme had just proven that again. She smiled. "Thank you."

Sarah Jennifer called Brutus over and sent him to fetch the cart from Esme's barn. "Just don't spook the horses, or you'll be pulling the new cart to Salem by yourself," she told him as he set off for the road.

He returned with Cordy and Dusty harnessed to the cart just as Maria called the pack for dinner.

Maria had continued to shelter the young women beneath her wing, giving them jobs to do and scowling fiercely at any Were who approached them with anything but good intentions. Sarah Jennifer didn't miss the skillet that was never out of the motherly woman's reach. Missy was much less afraid than she had been when she'd found her in Brutus' house, although she still gave her kidnappers a wide berth.

Team Dumbass would be fetching their own dinner for the foreseeable future.

She thought the couples, Big Ace and Tamara, and Little Ace and Sofie, were doing a lot to help Missy feel settled. The women fussed over her, and the Ace brothers, who were teenagers in Were years but had the appearance of good-looking twenty-something-year-olds, did their best to assure her they would take care of her like a sister. It made Sarah Jennifer chuckle to see how Missy blushed under the attention.

Then she remembered Brutus, who had turned the horses loose to graze and was standing still by the cart, watching her observe the pack. "Come on, we've still got work to do." She began dismantling the cart bed, Brutus looking wistfully at the rest of the pack eating around the campfire.

"We eat last," she told him. "Get this done, and then you can fill your belly. We need to check the frame and see if we can get away with fitting a bigger bed to it."

"What're you thinking?" he asked, scrutinizing the partially-exposed wheelbase.

Sarah Jennifer paused in her work. "I'm thinking we extend the wheelbase and convert it to a covered wagon the women can sleep and travel in. It'll cut down the time spent on the road, and we can load all our inventory in as well. Only thing is, I don't think Dusty is up to the job. We're going to have to take turns pulling it."

Brutus grinned. "That's better than us all carrying everything on our backs. I can't say I'm looking forward to reaching Salem, but it's no fun living out here. The sooner we get there, the better."

Sarah Jennifer clapped him on the back. "That's the spirit. Let's go scrounge up some tools from Quartermaster Ace."

"Yeah, I wanted to talk to you about that." Brutus ran a hand through his hair. "You keep giving us military titles. We're no army."

"Establishing the hierarchal structure gives the pack a system they can rely on," Sarah Jennifer told him. "You know I was raised by the military side of our family. It served me well, even if I wouldn't admit it at the time."

Brutus stopped. "So why did you stay?"

Sarah Jennifer shrugged. "I learned early in life that it wasn't going to serve me to rebel. No one could have given me a better start than I had."

"I get it," Brutus murmured. "I guess that's how I felt when Katia was in charge. Like as long as I knuckled down and did what she told me, things would turn out okay. But still, why not just establish your dominance and go with traditional pack structure? Like I said, we're no military."

Sarah Jennifer looked him in the eye and recognized his fear. "Not yet, you're not. But you will be, and then we're going to rescue all the Weres in the city."

Brutus was incredulous. "You want us to go back to Boston? No. Fucking. Way. We only just got out of there alive. What makes you think any of us would go back there?"

She reassured him with a brief hand on his shoulder. "I know you'll go. You'll do it because there are Weres being drained of their blood—over and over and over again. I've seen them, Brutus. I know where they are. I am going to turn this pack into a finely-honed fighting machine, and then we're going to hit the leeches where it hurts and rescue every single one of the Weres."

Brutus remained silent while she requisitioned what she could to help the job along from Big Ace, who she was pleased to see was taking his promotion very seriously.

"What do you need all of that for, Major?" Big Ace clutched the stub of his pencil tightly between a thumb and finger, poised over the notebook held lovingly in his other arm.

Sarah Jennifer stamped her foot impatiently. "Construction, now hand over the tools. I'd like to eat sometime tonight."

"Maybe you should eat first since you're cranky," Esme commented from behind her. Brutus wasted no time in agreeing, and the pair of them gently nudged Sarah Jennifer toward the makeshift table where Maria had placed their dinner.

"Oh, fine," she capitulated half-heartedly. It did smell good, and she was satisfied that the pack had eaten and were turning in for the night under the direction of Bruiser and Ozzie, who joined them after the pack had all disappeared into their shelters.

Sarah Jennifer looked around the table at the people who were becoming her adopted family. Every one of them had been chosen for her, just like a real family. And just like a real family, there were bridges to build if she wanted those relationships to thrive. She finished the last mouthful of her dinner, wiped the last smears of gravy up with the crust of her bread, and considered the logistics of what she was trying to achieve.

It would have been nice to find a well-trained pack, but she saw the benefit of starting from scratch. There was only one possible direction to go from rock bottom. They had no bad habits to unlearn, and most were eager to learn and responded to praise and encouragement. The more she got to know them, the more she believed they might just have a chance to survive the horror Lilith had shown her.

Brutus brooded over his food. He paid little attention to the table-talk, instead getting lost deep in his thoughts as the two sergeants bantered with Maria and Esme.

"What's on your mind?" Sarah Jennifer asked him quietly, disturbing his introspection. He started to say something, then stopped, tried again, and failed.

Sarah Jennifer bumped him with her shoulder. "Take your time."

Brutus drew a deep breath and let it out slowly. "I'm trying to get my head around everything that's happened. Everything that's *going* to happen. You don't fuck around. All these changes, and wanting to turn us into some kind of fighting force."

"Force for defense," she corrected.

"Whatever." Brutus sighed. "This is our reality now, I accept that. How do you know about the Weres in Boston?" This drew the attention of the rest of the group.

Sarah Jennifer kept her voice low, not wanting any of the pack to overhear. "Same way I got my wolf."

"Tell us!" Bruiser and Ozzie chorused *sotto voce*.

Sarah Jennifer had decided it wasn't wise to talk about her vision without Esme to back up her veracity, although the appearance of her wolf had been the subject of much speculation among the lower-ranking pack members.

This was as good a time as any to reveal some, but not all, of what she had been shown by the Kurtherian in her dream. There was no sense in scaring them to death. By the time she was ready to tell the pack about the Madness, they would be ready to face it. She meant to make sure of it.

Sarah Jennifer paused as she worked out the easiest route through the story, "I was visited psychically by a being from the stars by the name of Lilith. She's known to the witches as Gaia, the Earth Mother. Lilith showed me the locations of the Weres in Boston and unlocked whatever it was that stopped me from becoming a wolf."

"Earth Mother? What are you talking about, the witch goddess?" Brutus asked dubiously. "What's that mumbo-jumbo got to do with us? Those witches are a taco short of a combo plate if you ask me."

"Nobody did ask you," Sarah Jennifer told him. "Keep making statements like that, and you'll be on the team with the rest of the dumbasses. Gaia might be a legend made up by the people, but Lilith is real. Esme will confirm what I'm telling you."

Esme nodded. "It's true. Sarah Jennifer has been chosen to bring the UnknownWorld back together. You should be grateful. It was only her intervention that saved your sorry hides."

Sarah Jennifer moved the conversation away from chosen ones and interventions to focus on an equally important, and less contentious, topic. "You have tacos out here? Why did nobody tell me?" Her mouth watered at the memory of the taste of her favorite childhood meal, despite just having eaten.

That was a reason to visit Boston all by itself.

CHAPTER TEN

Mid-morning came around and passed. Sarah Jennifer and Brutus stood back from the road, admiring their work. They had stayed up working until the early hours, and the covered wagon was ready to roll.

Sarah Jennifer tested the strength of their alterations by having the pack get in one after another until she was certain it would hold weight without coming apart.

"It's rough, but it'll do the job," she murmured to Brutus. "Looks like we're about ready to move out."

The pack had all but finished removing the signs of their stay under the watchful eyes of the sergeants and Big Ace. Little Ace, Carver, and Geordie had taken some time to carve a crude wolf's head on the siding of the wagon. Sarah Jennifer had allowed it on the condition their two teams took the first shift pulling. Piles of belongings lay neatly next to the wagon in the order they would be loaded.

Sarah Jennifer jumped up onto the driver's bench and

let out a piercing whistle. "Okay, we're good to go, people! What do you think of our ride?"

The pack wolf-whistled and catcalled, pleased with the effort she and Brutus had put into making the journey to Salem easier for them all.

Sarah Jennifer grinned, energized by the reaction. "Glad you like her. Now get your asses moving and get her loaded. Quartermaster Ace, they're all yours."

Once Big Ace had directed the loading of all the pack's belongings evenly along the floor of the wagon, it was time to get the passengers aboard. Esme shuffled over, leading Maria and the young women behind her. They climbed up onto the wagon carrying bundles of blankets for the splintery benches. Sarah Jennifer held out a hand to help Esme up.

"Thank you for this," she told Esme. "We'll build you a new cart when we get settled in at Salem, then you can come home."

Esme raised an eyebrow. "What do you mean? I live in Salem. I thought you knew the cottage wasn't my home."

Suddenly, Tom's words at the Samhain feast made sense. "Did you lure me here and have me fix the place up just so I could...I don't know what. Feel better about myself? Why?"

"It wasn't just feeling better about yourself, Duckie. This pack wasn't the only broken thing." Esme clucked in that motherly way she sometimes adopted. "You had to accept who *you* are before you could accept them." With that, she climbed into the wagon. Sarah Jennifer was called over to help attach six wolves to modified harnesses found in Esme's tack shed, forestalling her from thinking too hard about the woman's statement.

An hour later, Sarah Jennifer sat astride Cordy at the rear of the procession as they made their way out of Lynnwood and set off up the north road. She couldn't help marveling at the sight of a wagon pulled by wolves, surrounded by more wolves. What would it be like to see them from a distance?

The wagon was too wide for the backroads. Sarah Jennifer would have preferred to keep out of the way of prying eyes along the north road, but taking the highway instead of trying to force their way through the forest roads would cut a significant amount of ass-ache out of the journey. She'd gone through the rotation schedule with the teams before they left. The teams would take one hour pulling, followed by an hour's rest on the wagon. The other two teams would keep guard in wolf form since they couldn't fight for shit in human form yet, surrounding the wagon at all times. She would stand guard over her charges whatever came.

"How are we doing up front?" she called to the teams.

A chorus of howls filled the air. The guard teams frolicked around the wagon, full of the joy of the upcoming run. Maria poked her head out and gave Sarah Jennifer a thumbs-up.

She rode around to check on the two teams set to pull first, noting they were securely harnessed and that the collars the women had made from the stable tack were doing their job. She recognized Little Ace in his wolf form by the diamond-shaped flash on his fur that gave both brothers their name. He and Carver were the leads,

Geordie and Bard had the middle. Sarah Jennifer couldn't tell which of the other two was Rory and which was his brother Rider. The twins were identical in both forms, and she wasn't willing to sniff out the difference while they were exerting themselves.

Sarah Jennifer reined Cordy in as she began to prance. "Keep up the good work! And don't push too hard. If you need to swap out, just howl, okay?"

The teams yipped, throwing themselves into the collars to get the wagon rolling.

Satisfied, she circled back around to her position as tail-end Charlie.

The pack made good progress throughout the day, reaching the planned camp a short time after dark. The campsite was the empty ruin of an old town set back from the grassy highway. The buildings were long gone, and grass grew over the stubby foundations that prevented the trees from moving in.

Sarah Jennifer directed the guard teams to check the area and went to help the women down from the wagon when they returned to tell her it was clear.

"Oh, but that's *good!*" Maria exclaimed, joints popping and cracking as she stepped down and stretched her cramped back. "Those benches are not easy on a mature woman's back!"

She was followed by the rest of the women, and then Esme, who hopped down with no complaint.

"You ought to try being stuck on a dirigible for two weeks, girls. This is nothing! I'm going for a walk. Want to join me, Duckie?"

"That sounds like a great idea," Sarah Jennifer agreed,

feeling a little bit saddle-sore. "I'll get Cordy rubbed down and be with you shortly."

Esme winked. "Well, don't take too long. I can sense a herd of deer not too far from here, but they're on the move."

Brutus held out a hand for Cordy's reins. "I'll take care of her for you. You go get us a nice fat deer or two."

Sarah Jennifer handed the reins to him gratefully. "Sounds good, thank you. Looks like we're going hunting, Esme."

"Can you see okay?" Sarah Jennifer whispered a short time later as they crept through the trees.

Esme's whispered reply was acerbic. "Of course I can, there's a moon above us. What do you take me for?"

Sarah Jennifer snickered. "You're crabbier than usual, so I assumed you were feeling your age or something. I can carry you if you want. Nobody can see us."

The night became brighter as Esme began to glow. "Duckie, I don't need help. I've managed to get by for over two centuries without being carried about like a babe, and I certainly don't need it now!"

"Two hundred years. I can't imagine what you've seen." Sarah Jennifer was astounded by the beauty of her surroundings. "I wish I'd pumped you for more information about pre-WWDE Earth before I went to take control of my pack. What else don't I know about you?"

Esme smiled secretively. "That's for me to know, and you to find out—if I choose to tell you. Hush now, you'll scare them away." She pointed ahead of them to where the herd of whitetail deer moved quietly through the moonlit forest, pausing here and there to crop at the vegetation.

"It's a shame to ruin this," Sarah Jennifer whispered. "We can't take them all." She left the rest unspoken.

"Look closer," Esme replied, barely audible.

Sarah Jennifer did as Esme instructed. There were twelve deer in the herd. Most of the does were pregnant. On closer inspection, she saw that one of the bucks had a lame leg, and two of the does were elderly, struggling to feed in the frost.

Esme patted Sarah Jennifer's shoulder. "Those three won't last the winter. It's a mercy that we take them to nourish ourselves. No need to make them suffer, though. Have you got your knife?"

"Here," Sarah Jennifer patted her belt.

"Good. Hold on." Esme pushed her sleeves up and held her hands palms up. She began to glow again as she spoke. "Gaia, help us shepherd your Earth. Let us bring peace to your creatures in these, their final moments."

Sarah Jennifer glanced away as Esme gave her blessing. She wondered how her friend could continue with the trappings of religion when she knew her deity was an alien and her magic came from technology.

For once, Esme didn't hear her thoughts. Sarah Jennifer put them away with all the rest for later, grateful for the reprieve. However it was that Esme's magic worked, it did work. The deer ceased their cropping, lying down one by one until the whole herd was sleeping peacefully.

Esme waved Sarah Jennifer over as she set off toward them. "Come on, Duckie. Our three will remain asleep, but we haven't got long before the rest of them wake up. I'll get the small doe, and you get the other two."

"We don't want you overexerting yourself," Sarah

Jennifer bitched good-naturedly as she hoisted the buck and one of the does, balancing the weight evenly across her shoulders. Esme's thoughtful glance told Sarah Jennifer that she might not have gotten away with her mind-fart after all. "Let's get them out of here and take care of the messy part before the rest of the herd wakes up."

They walked a short way, Esme leading them to a stream. She eased the deer into a pool of moonlight on the pebbled bank and turned her body to look at Sarah Jennifer. "Let's talk about Lilith."

Sarah Jennifer let her two deer slide to the ground. "I don't know enough to talk about her," she replied, bending to let the stream water run over her hands. She drew her knife and got to work processing the deer.

"Start with how an alien worked herself into your head," Esme suggested, her attention on her own deer. "Because your psychic ability is negligible, I can tell you. We'll get to my involvement with her later."

Sarah Jennifer cursed her mental overload for allowing that connection to slip by. Of course, Esme was involved with Lilith. "You can guess how freaked out I was when I had the dream where I met her."

"Not to mention your wolf," Esme put in.

Sarah Jennifer looked up from her task. "Yeah. That, too. Do you know about the Madness?"

Esme shook her head. "I know that the living dead are coming. That was all Lilith cared to share with me. That, and that you were the one who was going to stop it. I tried telling the council, but most of them wouldn't hear it."

Sarah Jennifer frowned. "That's not exactly it. She said I'm humanity's shield. Me and my Weres. Lilith told me

Bethany Anne wanted to give everyone magic." She paused while she worked her knife's edge through a delicate part. "Not that it's magic."

"We'll have to agree to disagree on that," Esme told her. "I stand by what I said. Names have power, and the only name as comes to mind when I think to describe my abilities is magic, whether I'm aware it's created by the technology inside me or not."

"But you *are* aware," Sarah Jennifer argued. "I can't see how people can fool themselves into believing in superstition over fact."

Esme shrugged. "People fool themselves into believing all sorts of things," she replied. "How's your knee?"

Sarah Jennifer glowered at Esme and remained silent for the duration of their task. She stewed over the dichotomy Esme represented as they walked back to camp. How was it possible to *believe* something into reality? It wasn't logical. But as a rational person, how could she dispute the evidence she'd witnessed her entire life?

The fantastic existed, she couldn't deny it. What other connections had she missed? Sarah Jennifer's mind circled all the way back to camp, where she had to let it all go again.

The pack was overjoyed when they returned to the meadow with the deer. Brutus had organized them well; the fire crackled merrily, and the shelters were built for the night's sleep. Maria had the camp kitchen fully staffed with the Weres from team six, who she had adopted as her own. They soon had venison cooking in strips.

Sarah Jennifer strolled around after dinner, checking in with each member of the pack. There was no sign of any of

Team Dumbass anywhere. She made her way back to the fire, where most of the pack were picking through the remains of the deer.

"Has anyone seen Linus, Dinny, or Reg?" she asked the pack.

The Weres around the fire shook their heads. Their ways had been unpopular, but without an Alpha around, the pack had been too afraid to put them in their place. The majority of them had been shunning the three miscreants since Sarah Jennifer came along.

Brutus appeared beside her, hearing her voice. "Maybe they left."

"I don't fucking *think* so." She cursed against her better nature, angry beyond reason that they'd decided to take the coward's route. "Those three have a lot of making amends to do. They're not slinking off and getting away with it." She called the pack in. "Who was the last person to see Team Dumbass?"

Kalder raised his hand. "I saw them when we were on firewood duty. They were heading off to find water."

He was interrupted by Bard. "No, my team was on water duty. Team Dumbass was on latrine duty."

"Where's the latrine?" Sarah Jennifer asked.

"Dunno, Major," Bard replied with a shrug. "They were supposed to dig it out of the way so's we don't smell it."

"I'll go check," Brutus offered.

Sarah Jennifer nodded. "Take Kalder and Bard with you in case they're being difficult. Rider, too."

Brutus nodded curtly. "Yes, Major. Come on, you three."

They headed out of the meadow, vanishing into the dark as they entered the trees.

"*Major!*" Brutus screamed a few minutes later.

Sarah Jennifer ran in the direction they'd gone, followed swiftly by the rest of the pack. She passed the half-dug latrine, seeing signs of a struggle but no sign of Brutus or the missing Weres.

"Where are you?" she shouted.

"Over here," Brutus' tremulous reply came from the trees beyond the ruins.

When they found Brutus, he was kneeling by Dinny's prostrate body. "I think he's dead."

Sarah Jennifer was there in a flash, feeling for Dinny's pulse. It was weak and unsteady. She caught a whiff of burnt hair. "We need to turn him over," she told Brutus calmly. "Be gentle."

The pack looked on in fear. Nobody liked Dinny, but that didn't mean they weren't affected by him being attacked by an outsider.

Brutus and Ozzie gently turned Dinny so he was lying on his side, and Sarah Jennifer's suspicions were confirmed. "He's been hit with an arc rod." She scooped Dinny up, careful not to aggravate the burn on the Were's neck. "He'll be okay, but we need to get him warmed up and fed so he can heal from it. Back to camp, everyone."

She placed Dinny inside the wagon on a pile of blankets, wrapping him securely before going back outside to address the pack. They were afraid, huddling together for comfort. They all knew there was only one group who used the electric shock weapon that had been used on Dinny.

Sarah Jennifer moved among them, passing comfort with her touch. "Stay here, stay together. Do not even go for a shit without your team. No exceptions. I'm going back to look for the others."

"I'll come with you, Duckie," Esme offered.

They went back to the place where they'd found Dinny and Sarah Jennifer searched for evidence as to where Linus and Reg had been taken, and by how many assailants.

The moon burned coldly overhead, highlighting the disturbed ground and throwing the attackers' escape route into sharp relief.

"There were four of them," she told Esme, indicating the prints in the churned-up slush. "Look. They came in here, there was a scuffle here. This is where they overpowered Linus and Reg. The prints get deeper here where they picked them both up and carried them off. What's that way?"

"Boston, "Esme replied sadly. "That way is Boston. They're not coming back, Duckie."

CHAPTER ELEVEN

Linus lay next to an equally silent Reg. They had given up resisting when their captors made it clear they had no issues with using their arc rods on the two Weres.

He had come round from the first shock to find himself being carried hand and foot through the forest by two of the militiamen who had attacked them while they were digging the latrine. He'd seen Dinny die before he passed out from the arc rod the soldier had jammed into his ribs. At least for Dinny, it was a quick end.

Reg trembled next to him, noiseless tears falling as he pleaded with his eyes for Linus to do something. What he wanted him to do, Linus didn't know. The soldiers had fitted them both with shock collars, hogtied them, and thrown them into a vehicle. Linus didn't know which direction they were going, but he had a good idea of what was going to happen to the two of them when they got there. They both did.

The leeches had taken them, and now they were going

to be drained. They were doomed.

Stark imaginings of being hung upside-down for his throat to be cut went around in Linus' mind until the vehicle stopped. The doors opened, and they were roughly pulled out by the soldiers and dumped on gurneys.

Linus squinted through swollen eyes to see where Reg was being taken, just in time to see him get shocked by one of the evil bastards.

"Leave him!" he cried weakly, earning himself another shock. He struggled against his bonds. "Let him be!" Everything went black when the soldier shocked him again without a word.

He woke up in a strange room. A strip light assaulted his eyes as soon as he opened them. He was lying in a bed with bars on the side.

"Linus," a voice hissed from beside him. A battered face he hardly recognized stared at him from the next bed. He panicked when he saw the tube running from his arm to a container between the beds.

"Linus," Reg hissed again, a little louder this time. "Wake up!"

Linus blinked. "Reg?" He registered the IV line running from his arm, and their situation became clear. All his worst nightmares had come true, and further, it looked like they would be coming true for a long time to come. He tried to get up but was jerked back by the restraints around his neck, waist, and limbs. No matter. He tried to shift and was rewarded with a shock.

"Uh-uh," a new voice jeered. "I wouldn't try that again… Linus, is it?" The voice belonged to a white-masked face that appeared over Linus' bed. It was a sharp face, with cold eyes. He couldn't tell whether it belonged to a male or a female, just that the leech behind the mask was devoid of empathy. "Now be a good dog and lie down. It'll all be over soon."

Reg sobbed, and the fight went out of Linus. "Just get it over with," he whispered, looking away. There was nothing he could do.

The leech laughed. "Come now, it's not all that bad. Just a couple of pints, and then if you've been a good doggy, the nice guards will give you din-din."

Linus felt the leech fiddle with the tube on his arm. A few seconds later, the clear tube turned red. By the time it reached the container, Reg had the same happening to him. The younger Were's sobs increased, and then Linus smelled fresh urine. His fire returned.

He struggled against the restraints again, his rage canceling the pain from the shock that ripped through him from his collar. He called, "Reg, Reg! It's okay. Look at me. *Look at me!* I'm right here, bro."

"So dramatic," the leech interrupted. "Calm down, it's only blood. Guards! I'm done with these two for today. Throw them in the kennels with the other dogs."

They were wheeled out of the room without ceremony into a featureless corridor. Linus tried to get a sense of the building they were in as they were moved, but the strip lighting burned his eyes, and he was exhausted from shock and blood loss.

The gurney stopped. Linus was unstrapped by one guard while another held an arc rod to his temple. They left the collar on him. Too weak to stand, he was thrown onto a cot in a concrete cell.

They were in a prison.

"On your bed, dog," one of the guards spat. He slammed the door, leaving Linus in darkness.

Linus heard another door slam—Reg getting locked into the next cell. As his eyes adjusted to the darkness, Linus became aware of a sliver of moonlight illuminating the narrow window in the wall above his head.

He struggled to his feet and stretched painfully. He hoped Reg was handling it in there. He sniffed, turning a slow circle around his cell. There was a toilet and sink attached to the wall along with the cot, and a desk with a pile of clothing on it. This cell had held many Weres before him.

The overlaying scents of despair and anguish weren't strong enough to make Linus miss the tray of food behind the pile of clothing on the desk. He attacked the food hungrily, not caring what it was. He just needed nourishment for his body. He was surprised to find the tray held a generous portion of good meat in gravy, a pile of greens, a portion of mixed beans, and a crusty roll. There was also a large plastic bottle of water.

After he was done eating, he examined the clothing that had been left for him. It was an all-in-one suit, faded orange in color. Under that was some gray underwear, a pair of open-toed sandals, and a stiff, scratchy towel. Linus wrinkled his nose and discarded the orange suit. He yawned, his brain convinced by the meal that the danger was over for now. He climbed back onto the cot, curled up, and fell asleep.

A clang woke him up. The tiny window let a single ray of the morning sun into the cell. Before Linus could scramble to his feet, the door was thrown open, and two guards holding arc rods muscled into the cell. He kept his eyes on the floor, not wanting to give the guards a reason to shock him.

"Get up, you lazy dog," the first ordered. "Get your shit on and get out here." He picked the orange suit up and flung it at Linus, who grabbed it and made for the door.

"All your shit, dumbass," the other guard mocked. "And no bullshit or I'll introduce you to Buzz here." He thrust his inert arc rod toward Linus a couple of times, sniggering when Linus cowered away from the weapon.

Linus realized with crushing sadness that he didn't mind being called "Dumbass" by the major. When she'd called him that, she'd always had a touch of warmth in her voice—like an exasperated parent who knew their kid could do better. It hit him that she cared about the whole pack, himself, Reg, and Dinny included. These guys didn't give a shit. He gathered his things and left the cell. The cell next door was open. They must have already taken Reg.

The guards prodded him, forcing him to walk ahead until they reached a barred gate bisecting the corridor further on. He was made to wait while another guard opened the gate, and then they made him hurry up the corridor to the next gate. That happened twice more, then the final gate opened, and he was in the biggest bathroom he'd ever seen.

Showers lined the walls, and there were three rows of slatted benches.

"Go on then, you filthy mutt. Get in there and get the stink off you." The guard gave Linus a shove, causing him to skid a little on the tiled floor. They laughed at him as they left to stand outside.

Linus wished he could shift and tear their throats out, but that wasn't a possibility with the band of metal fused around his throat. Head down, he slumped toward the farthest shower.

He stripped and stepped under the running water, feeling vulnerable as he turned to get some soap from the dispenser on the wall between the showerheads. As he rubbed the astringent soap into his hair and skin, he allowed himself to cry for the first time since their abduction.

He began to wallow in his hopelessness, thinking about how he should have done things differently. It was *his* behavior that had isolated the three of them from the pack. Reg and Dinny had followed him, wearing blinkers of hero-worship. Before Katia had taken them in, he'd looked out for them all, his hustling on the streets of Boston just barely getting them by.

Katia took no shit from him. She had protected them but had never given them an inch. He thought bitterly that part of the reason they'd had such a hard time after she was taken was because she did everything for them without teaching them to do it for themselves. The major was different. She wanted them to be independent, to take care of themselves. Shit, she was even going to teach them to fight. All of that was gone now.

He left the shower, dried, and dressed as quickly as he could. The guards escorted him down another corridor through more manned gates. Linus could smell a large number of Weres up ahead, including Reg—which was a relief. How many Weres were these bastards holding prisoner?

The guards deposited him on the other side of the final set of gates. "In you go, fresh meat," the gate guard ordered nastily. Linus took a quick look around the room. The guard slapped his behind, making him jump. "What're ya waitin' for? Chow time, mutt. You ain't got all day, get in there!"

He walked to the food line, careful not to make eye contact with any of the other prisoners. There were over a hundred Weres in here, easy. Linus was shocked to see the female prisoners far outnumbered the males. A sharp scent struck his nose—a number of the females were pregnant.

They spoke in whispers as they ate, too cowed and broken to make more noise. Nevertheless, Linus could sense the power in the room. He was a small fish lost in the ocean.

He took a tray from the pile and waited his turn silently. The man behind the counter plopped three ladlefuls of food and a bread roll onto his tray. It was the exact meal he'd eaten last night. Still, it was freshly cooked, and he was still feeling a little fuzzy from having his blood taken. He finally lifted his head, looking for Reg.

He saw his friend across the room and made his way to the table. Reg sat with his back to him, talking to the Were next to him. He turned as Linus approached, the relieved smile on his face saying a thousand things neither of them knew how to express. He made a small gesture to the Were he'd been talking to.

"Linus, look who it is!" Reg kept his voice low, but he couldn't keep the joy out of it.

The Were woman turned, and Linus almost dropped his tray.

"Katia!"

North Road, MA

Sarah Jennifer sat vigil through the night. Esme and Maria tended Dinny's burns while he lay unconscious in the wagon. Occasionally they were visited by pack members who wanted to know how Dinny was healing. Morale was low. Nobody had liked Linus or Reg much, but they were still pack, and the loss had hit them deeply.

Dinny woke just before dawn, startling the birds with his screams.

The pack piled out of their shelters in wolf form, ready to tear the throats out of whatever threatened them. When they realized it was Dinny making all the noise, they slunk back inside.

Sarah Jennifer hopped into the bed of the wagon, seeing Esme calming the traumatized Were with her magic.

"Hush now," Esme soothed, a soft golden glow emanating from the palm stroking his head. "I won't let anything else bad happen to you." She met Sarah Jennifer's eyes with an imperceptible nod. "He's almost recovered."

Sarah Jennifer left them to it. Esme had everything in hand, and the pack needed her at this moment. They'd emerged from their shelters once more, in human form now that they weren't expecting danger.

Sarah Jennifer adjusted her assessment of the pack's morale as they gathered around the remains of the campfire. It wasn't just low. They were shaken to the core by the attack and kidnapping of their own, her included. Now she understood her grandfather's pain at losing someone under his command. She felt it had been a failure on her part to protect those she had sworn to keep safe. But she had also learned from the colonel's actions that you didn't quit, didn't stop striving to create a better world.

The loss of Linus and Reg was a valuable lesson. Her pack needed to be able to defend themselves and sooner rather than later. Her experience told her that a busy mind and body didn't have time to dwell on fear. It was her duty as Alpha to break the desultory mood they were in.

"Eyes on me!" Their heads snapped around at her sudden shout. "We have been violated; two of our own have been stolen from us. What are we going to do about it?" She expected at least one of the Weres to offer a snarky comment. It was a testament to their distress that nobody said a word. "I'll tell you what we're going to do. We will serve Justice on the leeches and the wastes of oxygen who enable them."

She burned with heated fury. Her eyes blazed with red light that washed the wan dawn away as a sense of certainty settled over her. That was new—a side effect of Lilith's gift, maybe. She wasn't complaining. She'd always loved the way her mother's eyes glowed blue. She had, however, expected they'd glow yellow.

Little Ace looked for permission to speak. "How're we gonna do that, Major? The leeches have soldiers and arc rods. We can't even fight. We have no weapons except our teeth and claws, and we know how effective *they* are against the shocks." His eyes were blank, his dejection clear.

Sarah Jennifer lifted her chin. "I'll tell you how. Your training starts today." She was interrupted by Esme exiting the wagon. "Go get something to eat and then start striking the camp. We leave as soon as possible." She patted a few of them on the arm, noting who was afraid and who was angry. Who would fight, and who would be around to rebuild afterward.

Esme waited until Sarah Jennifer was done before speaking. "Dinny will recover. They fair kicked the shite out of him, though. It'll be a few days before he's back to full strength, but he'll be all right."

Sarah Jennifer smiled in relief. "That's good to hear. I just wish I could have saved Linus and Reg."

"I wouldn't worry about them for now." Esme's eyes twinkled. "Lilith came to me last night and told me they're alive and that they'll wait for you in the place she showed you." She patted Sarah Jennifer's back lightly and shuffled back to the wagon.

That gave Sarah Jennifer something to hold on to. She hadn't lost Linus and Reg forever. They were being held with the other Weres she'd seen in her vision. The invisible weight on her shoulders lifted a fraction.

Camp was being struck as fast as she'd yet seen the pack do it. Nobody wanted to linger for a moment longer than necessary.

Sarah Jennifer called for everybody's attention. "We will go to Salem as planned. When we get there, we will train, and train, until we are ready to get our packmates back and stamp those festering bloodsuckers into the ground!" Her eyes glowed again, bathing the pack in their light. She felt the mood shift completely, giving way to a fierce determination that burned in her pack's hearts as well as her own.

At that moment, Sarah Jennifer felt a connection to them all in her mind. In her soul. They were one with each other. A single intent, a solitary emotion.

They were *pack,* and they were *hers.*

A short time later, Sarah Jennifer looked down on the wagon from the top of a nearby ridge. It was loaded and ready to go. Ozzie and Bruiser were harnessed at the front, leading the two teams who would pull today to speed the journey up. None of them wanted to be on the road any longer than necessary. They had a goal to reach. A purpose to fulfill.

Sarah Jennifer had a perfect vantage point. The top of the ridge gave her a view of the road for miles both ways. They had a full day's travel ahead of them even with the extra wolf power on the wagon, and she intended to make the most of it. She'd split the pack into teams. This time Brutus and the sergeants had helped her decide who was going into which team, and they would be the permanent tac teams she had planned on creating. Each team would be trained slightly differently, depending on what she had in mind for them, but all of them would have the same basic training, and all of them were going to learn hand-to-hand combat FDG-style.

Later today, she would take her own turn in the harness, along with Brutus, but first she had a lesson in mind. The pack was physically fit, but their mental and psychological fitness left a lot to be desired. It was time to get them thinking smart, Brutus included.

Tac teams One and Two stood in a loose arc around

her. Team One consisted of Little Ace, Carver, Geordie, Bard, and Tyson. These five were the brightest and most willing, the Weres who asked questions of her in their eagerness to learn. They were angry, not afraid. They would be her knife-hand, the surgical strike force who could think on their toes in the middle of a shitstorm—get in, complete the objective, and get out. They would be the scourge of the blood trade, the rumor the leeches feared.

Team Two had the spirits of protectors. In the short time she'd been with the pack, she'd seen Kalder, Patrick, Tim, Rider, and Tucker go out of their way to make life a little easier for their packmates. They volunteered for the heavy work, so she would charge them with the heaviest work of all. They would be led by Brutus and strike fear into the hearts of any who threatened the pack. They would protect others, no matter the cost.

Sarah Jennifer had to admit they had a long way to go, but they were ripe for training. They were all hormonal rage and no direction, something she remembered feeling all too clearly. It was why her parents had called the colonel and Char back from their tropical getaway—to train some respect and humility into her and Sylvia, her especially. Today she would begin grinding them against the whetstone.

Sarah Jennifer addressed Teams One and Two in a no-nonsense tone. "Today you will learn observation and how to protect a moving group. Our pack is small right now, but when we leave Boston, it's going to be a hell of a lot bigger. Many of your new packmates will be vulnerable. Many will be injured or frightened. They will be relying on us as much as everyone down there is right now."

The teams grimaced and growled, eager to be the Weres they saw in their Alpha's eyes.

"Welcome to the sharp edge," she told them with a smile. "Orders. Tac Team Two, make with the wolves. You will keep the wagon surrounded at all times. Do not allow *anything* to come between your team and our people."

Their clothing already tied in the traditional bundle, Brutus and his team bounded off on four paws a few seconds later. Sarah Jennifer turned to her future all-stars with a grin. She lived for the objective, she couldn't deny it. Her team was the same, their five faces shining bright with longing for the action to begin.

"Tac Team One. Today we are acting as overwatch. It is our job to make sure any potential threats to the pack and to Salem are spotted and neutralized before they become a problem."

"How do we do that, Major?" Little Ace was first with a question, as always.

Sarah Jennifer admired the kid's thirst for knowledge. "Easy now, Private Ace. We keep to the high ground, we keep eyes on the wagon, and we use our enhanced senses to sniff out any trouble. Or dinner, but no tearing off into the woods without permission. You check in with me every twenty minutes, and you stay with your buddy. Got it?"

"Yes, Major!" The earnest reply from the team warmed Sarah Jennifer. She shooed them off to change into their wolves while she did the same, then five gray-brown streaks and one golden one flew across the landscape as the wagon rattled down the north road.

CHAPTER TWELVE

A howl alerted Sarah Jennifer to danger. She yipped the stop signal, and the teams began to slow. They were two miles or so from the outskirts of Salem with the end in sight, and one of her overwatch sentries had seen something to howl about.

The wagon grumbled to a stop, and the women jumped down to release the teams from their harness collars. If there was danger approaching, they would need every fighter available.

Sarah Jennifer shifted to human form the instant she was freed, taking the clothing Maria held out and quickly dressing before jumping on Cordy's back and riding to meet her scouts. A pair of wolves approached, shifting to human form with their last few steps so they could share their information.

"There's a roadblock up ahead. They've got fire." Rider panted heavily, having put everything into reaching her.

"Good work, Private." Sarah Jennifer told him. She let

out a long, piercing whistle, the signal for the pack to close in.

The horses stamped nervously as Esme halted Dusty by Sarah Jennifer. "What's the fuss?" she asked.

Sarah Jennifer nodded at the road ahead. "There's a blockade at the boundary hex. Would the council allow that?"

Esme shook her head. "No clue, Duckie. Best we go check, eh? Come on, we'll ride ahead. It'll be right as rain, you'll see."

A few minutes later, the other seven Weres from Tac Teams One and Two bounded in from various points in the forest. They helped Teams Three and Four into the harnesses, keeping the best fighters free.

Sarah Jennifer ordered the advance, cautious in the face of the unknown. Gone were her days of rushing in without a thought. Experience and the weight of her responsibility to her pack moderated her impulses. The survival of the pack was utmost.

The wagon crawled toward Salem, with Sarah Jennifer and Esme leading on the horses and the guard teams hugging the wagon. The blockade came into sight, trees felled and stacked to shoulder height to cut off the road.

"What's the meaning of this?" Esme demanded in a strong, clear voice. "Come out here now and show yourselves!"

A curly head popped up over the top of the uppermost tree trunk and disappeared the next second. Sarah Jennifer recognized that red-going-to-gray hair.

So did Esme. "Magnus! What are you playing at? Get

your skinny ass down here and tell me why the road is blocked. Does your mother know you're doing this?"

Annie's son popped his head up again. "It doesn't matter what my mother thinks. We know what you're up to, and we're not having those filthy Weres in our town!"

"We" appeared to be the council members who had been absent from the Samhain night festival, Sarah Jennifer realized, unable to understand their motive for hating so strongly. Had that only been four weeks ago? So much had changed in that short time.

Esme wasn't waiting for answers. She swept a glowing golden hand in front of her body and the barrier collapsed with a crash, the trees spilling haphazardly into the road.

The pack bristled, ready to attack.

"Stay back," Sarah Jennifer commanded. Cordy danced beneath her, startled by the commotion. Sarah Jennifer patted the mare's neck to calm her.

Magnus emerged from the wreckage, his face burning with anger. The others stayed behind the collapsed roadblock. "No, Esme. Not this time. You brought *her* into our town with your talk of visions. Now you're back with a pack of wolves. We won't have this! You'll have to get through me first!"

Magnus' hands began to glow, although they didn't match Esme's in brilliance.

Esme was furious. "Magnus Edwin Anderson! If you take one more step, I'm going to whup your behind so hard you won't be able to sit 'til next Solstice! Come away from there and let the wagon through. Gaia wills it!"

Sarah Jennifer saw Magnus twitch. It was enough for her. She leapt between the two groups, holding her hands up. "Stop this! Magnus, I will vouch for the good behavior of my pack."

"Your pack?" He sneered. "Those fleabags have no leader, no *morals*! I will keep them out of my town if I have to die doing it!" He raised his hand.

"*I said, STOP!*" Sarah Jennifer's eyes flashed red, stronger than Magnus's glow, and almost brighter than Esme's. She felt a pulse of energy leave her.

The energy washed over Magnus and his eyes became unfocused for a few seconds. When he recovered from his daze, he looked at Sarah Jennifer with a mixture of awe and fear.

The glow left him, and he stared at Sarah Jennifer with dawning realization. "It's all true, isn't it? The dead are coming, and Gaia has charged you with our protection. I didn't want it to be true! Oh, what have I done?" He rounded on the other council members, full of rage. He had a horrified expression on his face. "Everything you said was a lie! We almost died for your lies!" He pointed at one of his former allies. "This is your doing, Darren! You, and...and those *friends* of yours!" He turned and ran toward town, sobbing wildly as the shock of what he'd almost done set in.

"What have you been doing?" Esme growled, stalking toward the remaining six council members. A glow came from the spot where they all crouched. "Oh, you think to attack me, do you? Gaia gave you that magic. She gave it out of love, so *you* might give that love to others. Too long have I stood by and watched men like you take what they want, and may I be cast from grace if I stand by and allow it again!"

Sarah Jennifer stayed close behind, certain of Esme's magical prowess but also aware of what cornered men were capable of. She needn't have worried.

Esme swept a hand at the men's hiding place and the wood erupted, scattering in all directions and leaving the council members exposed. They stood close together for support.

Sarah Jennifer thought they looked terrified, and with good cause.

Esme was standing taller, and the glow had spread until it looked to be pouring from her entire body. She raised her arms the same way she had when she'd summoned the ancestors on Samhain. "You are all relieved of your positions and banished from this town."

To Sarah Jennifer's surprise, the six men were slammed by the air and thrown over the wagon and the bewildered pack. They hit the ground on the other side of the barrier hex with a thud.

They scrambled to their feet, outraged by Esme turning the town's protection on them.

One came closer, his hands glowing dully. "I'll get you for this, Esme Proctor! The barrier hex is only as strong as the witches maintaining it, and you won't be able to sustain it with just the five of you!"

Esme gave him a tight, grim smile. "I can sustain the hex all by myself."

"Not if you're dead!" The man threw his hand up, sending the ball of light at high speed toward Esme.

Time slowed for Sarah Jennifer. Her first reaction was to dive toward Esme and take the hit herself, but she couldn't move.

Esme stretched a hand out to Sarah Jennifer, using magic to prevent her from interfering. On the other hand, she held a single finger toward the approaching ball of magic. The ball stopped in midair, floating between the two groups.

She gave Sarah Jennifer a reassuring nod before turning her attention to the man who had thrown it. "That could have killed someone. You shouldn't have done that, Darren. Rule One is not to be ignored. It's a sorry thing that's coming next for you."

"Rule One?" Sarah Jennifer asked.

"Belief in action," Esme replied. "Lilith might believe in the goodness of mankind, but I'm a tad more practical. Just watch."

Darren sneered, but when he opened his mouth to speak, his words failed him. The dull glow from his hands suddenly flashed, then winked out. It reappeared some way above his head, hovering. It was joined by the ball he'd sent at Esme.

The two balls merged, creating a much larger concentration of magic. Darren's demeanor changed. All of his aggression vanished, replaced by fear.

His cronies beat a hasty retreat as the magic fell from the sky, whistling as the ball picked up speed.

Darren moaned weakly and made a break for it, running into the forest. The ball of light changed course to follow him, crackling as it flew through the trees in pursuit. A minute later, there was a flash of light, a scream, and then nothing.

Esme dropped her arms, turning to Sarah Jennifer with

the same grim smile as the five men fled. "Get the wagon rolling, Duckie. We'll have no more trouble from them."

There were no more surprises on the way into Salem. The wagon pulled by wolves drew attention from everyone they passed, but the sight of Esme perched at the front with Sarah Jennifer sated their curiosity.

Annie, Sarai, and Lenore waited outside the town hall for them. They extricated themselves from the people lined up around the block and made their way over to the cart, glancing warily at the wolves.

"Welcome back," Lenore began. When she saw Esme's fury, she backed off, turning her attention to the women getting down from the wagon instead.

"Some welcome!" Esme didn't even wait for the wagon to come to a complete stop before jumping down to castigate Annie. "Where's that damned son of yours?"

Annie was resolute for the first time since Sarah Jennifer had met her. "Now, look here, Esme!"

"Look *nothing*, Annie!" Esme thundered. "Where is Magnus?"

People had begun to gather at the spectacle. Annie's face grew redder as Esme's voice grew louder. "Him and his buddies had the town road blocked off. He was about to use magic on me! You know what'll happen to him if he does that. The rules are very clear about what happens to those using the gift for evil. Now, where is he?"

"He's with Tom," Annie conceded. "He came back all worked up a little while ago. You're right, we shouldn't have let him run with those assholes. Just... Just don't hurt him, will you? He's only mortal, Esme. He can't help how he feels. Imagine how you'd feel if you aged and your twin didn't."

Magnus and Sarai were twins? That was news to Sarah Jennifer. When she'd met them at the Samhain feast, she'd assumed they were born at least twenty years apart. She was no stranger to the problems caused by age gaps. She'd failed in her marriage because of the aging issue. She told the pack to follow Sarai, who was waiting on the steps to take them into the temporary sleeping quarters being set up in the main hall.

Sarah Jennifer kept an eye on the situation while she helped unload the wagon. Big Ace was checking off each bag as the unloading went along, barking orders at the younger Weres. She felt like she'd made a good choice putting him in a position he could flourish in. The young women had already left with Lenore, who had promised them all a hot bath and a good meal.

The argument between Esme and Annie was still going on. "I've given him leeway for twenty years because you asked me to. This is his last chance, Annie. The pack is here to stay. They need this town as much as we need them."

Annie sighed. "I know. I'm sorry it came to this, Esme. I should never have put you in this position. I'll have a word, a real one this time. If he doesn't change, we'll have to bind his magic." She sighed again and left to find her son. As she turned to go, she patted Sarah Jennifer on the arm. "I'm sorry, child. He's not a hateful person, my Magnus. Just easily led. He'll make amends for what he's done. We need to work together to face what's coming."

Brutus' ears pricked up at this. He'd surreptitiously placed his furry head under Sarah Jennifer's hand. She'd been scratching his ears absentmindedly throughout the whole exchange. "Ew, Brutus! Get inside with the rest of them, and get some clothes on!"

She could have sworn he was sashaying as he padded off with his tail high.

Esme chuckled, coming to stand beside her as she watched him go. "He's a child."

Sarah Jennifer shook her head fondly. "Aw, he's not too bad. Kind of reminds me of his grandfather, my Uncle Timmons. Good heart, impertinent as hell. I'll have him and the others at their potential soon enough. We have a town to fortify, and I need my tac teams ready to break the rest of my pack out of the place they're being held."

"The rest of your pack?" Esme inquired.

"You heard right," Sarah Jennifer told her. "Did I ever tell you the tale of my grandmother's reluctant rise to Supreme Alpha? When I said I was getting back to my roots, I didn't just mean my FDG ones. I will take every Were I find into my pack and protect them. In return, they will protect humanity from the Madness. We will survive this, Esme. I'm going to make damn sure of it, or my name isn't Sarah Jennifer Walton!"

The conviction she felt caused her eyes to glow briefly. Her determination to see this through was absolute. She would fill the role as required, would bleed and fight and die to ensure humanity made it to the other side of the horror. "I'm going to need the use of the park. If anyone from the town wants to train, they are welcome to join us. The more defenders we have, the better."

"Defenders. That's a good name," Esme concurred. "I know of a few in town who would rather die trying to do the right thing than run. You need some training of your own."

Sarah Jennifer frowned. "I do? In what?"

"Your magic," Esme replied. "You have it, now you need to learn to control it."

Sarah Jennifer considered that for a moment. "I don't believe in magic. I always had the potential to turn wolf from my mother's side of the family. That's not magic, it's technology."

Esme set her chin at an obstinate angle. "Ignoring magic just because you don't believe in it is foolish and vain. You're going to ignore a tactical advantage? Is that what your grandfather taught you to do?"

Sarah Jennifer sighed, knowing Esme had her. "No."

"Then it's settled." Esme folded her arms. "You will train, and that is that."

Sarah Jennifer was suitably chastised. Whatever she had done to scare Magnus was definitely not part of her usual ability set. "Yes, Esme. I'll train."

"Good girl. Now, I've got things to tend to. I'll see you at the park tomorrow." Esme shuffled off in the direction Lenore had led the women earlier.

Sarah Jennifer scolded herself. Esme was right, as always. Damn her hubris! Lilith had unlocked her wolf form, and the glow from her eyes appeared to have an inspirational effect on others. Magnus had been inspired to leave off his delusions, at any rate.

Whether she had scared him or forced him to obey, to dismiss the value of such an ability would be stupidity itself.

"You ought to put yourself on Team Dumbass if you

keep thinking like that," she scolded herself out loud. She shook her head and headed for the town hall.

The moment Sarah Jennifer entered the building, Brutus approached and pulled her off to the side out of hearing. He was thankfully in human form and wearing clothing. He had trouble meeting her eyes, his insecurity showing as he hugged himself. "They don't want us here. I don't think they ever will."

Sarah Jennifer wrapped an arm around his shoulder. "It will work out okay. Trust me, they need us."

He looked up. "What do you mean? I heard your witch friend say the same."

Sarah Jennifer wasn't ready to burden the pack with what she knew. They needed to be built up, not terrified with tales of what was coming. Nevertheless, Brutus was her second and her family. She owed it to him to be straight. Soon, she promised herself. "Do you trust me?"

Brutus nodded. "You've done right by us, defended us, and showed us the error of our ways. I trust you, cousin."

Sarah Jennifer appreciated the sentiment. "Then I need you to take my word for it when I say that we have enough to deal with in our immediate future. We need to get our people back. We need to rescue all of the Weres being used like cattle. To do that, the pack needs to be sharp, efficient, and deadly. Then we can think about the bigger picture."

Brutus mulled it over for a minute. "Okay, but as soon as we get Linus and Reg back, you'll tell me all about it. Deal?"

She shook his outstretched hand. "Deal. Now let's get everyone settled for the night. Training begins at dawn, and they're going to need their rest."

"Don't count on a rest just yet," Esme cautioned as she returned from the main hall.

Sarah Jennifer tilted her head. "Why not?"

Esme indicated the main hall with a gnarled hand. "We'll be spending the evening helping out."

CHAPTER THIRTEEN

Sarah Jennifer followed Esme into the hall, skirting the lines of people winding around the room. Esme marched past the people, not stopping for more than cursory greetings as she ushered Sarah Jennifer to the head of the lines, where the council members bustled around clusters of tables set around the back of the meeting hall.

"What are we helping with?" she asked as Esme shuffled over to the empty table at the side of the paneled room. In this section of the hall, the tables had a row of privacy screens behind them. Sarah Jennifer peered behind the one at their table and saw it was hiding a cushioned table with a step stool.

"This is the day we look to others, and provide succor to those in need," Esme told her. "It's getting to the end of the day now, so there shouldn't be too many more people to see. We will be healing those who can't heal themselves. You see Magnus, Lenore, and David? They will be dealing with disputes and matters of law."

Sarah Jennifer looked at the other side of the room, where the council members were poring through scrolls and books from the shelves along that wall. The Hall seemed to serve as a function room, library, and anything else a small town needed.

"It's been a hospital a fair few times," Esme told her. "Even a war room at one point."

Sarah Jennifer sulked. "Will you quit reading my mind?"

Esme just laughed. "Believe me, Duckie, if you weren't broadcasting so loudly, I wouldn't."

Before Sarah Jennifer could complain further, the doors were opened, and more of the people who lived outside of Salem and the surrounding areas flooded in. It was a shock to Sarah Jennifer. She hadn't been in a crowd like this since Samhain night. It was deafening compared to the feast night because the hall was smaller than the pavilion they'd gathered in. How could they help all these people in one evening?

"Magic," Esme told her.

Sarah Jennifer gave up telling Esme to stay out of her head.

The evening passed in a blur of sick children, home remedies gone wrong, farming accidents, and illnesses. One of the injured people was Jim Johnson, the town's blacksmith.

Sarah Jennifer waved him over to their table. "What happened?" she asked, peering at the towel wrapped around his forearm.

Jim unwrapped the towel and revealed a nasty burn. "Experiment," he grumbled as if that explained everything.

Sarah Jennifer had an idea he'd been playing with fire and come in second best. "What happened?"

Jim grinned. "You're going to be pleased, Major. I was thinking to have you come out to the forge and see my pride and joy, but then I got a bit carried away."

His grin turned to a sharp hiss when Esme eased the towel from where it had stuck to the wound. "Dammit, are you trying to rip my skin open?"

"Hush, now," Esme told him as she wet the dried area with a damp cloth and continued unwrapping his burn. "You don't want me to heal it all together."

Jim settled when Esme paused to apply her magic. His pained expression melted away as the golden glow from Esme's hands left his skin unmarred. "You're a wonder, Esme," he praised, flexing his hand. "No pain whatsoever."

"I'll be at the forge as soon as I get some time," Sarah Jennifer told him.

Jim waved over his shoulder as he left. "I'll look forward to it, ma'am."

"Ma'am?" Sarah Jennifer echoed as the next patient took Jim's place.

Sarah Jennifer and Esme fell into a practiced rhythm until Tom and Sarai came around with baskets full of sandwiches and cakes.

Annie's husband and daughter worked their way around the tables, pressing a bundle into each worker's hand with a flask of coffee as they passed. They sat with Annie for a brief time until the organized chaos resumed around them.

Before Sarah Jennifer knew it, it was full dark outside,

and the last of the people had left the town hall. The weary councilors retired to one of the back rooms leading off from the main hall at Annie's direction.

Tom and Sarai were waiting for them as they filed in and took their seats around the long table. The meeting table had been set and decorated with holly and ivy, and the gaslights were set to emit a warm glow. A large tureen sat on a cart, filling the room with a rich aroma when Tom lifted the lid and began serving stew.

"Get some of that down you," Tom told Sarah Jennifer warmly as he filled her bowl. Sarai followed behind her father, handing out crusty bread rolls from her basket with a pair of tongs.

"You're not eating with us?" Sarah Jennifer asked them.

"I'll rest when everyone is fed," Tom replied.

Sarah Jennifer smiled in approval and tucked in.

Annie gave her husband a loving look and a pinch on the derriere as he moved on. "That's my love," she told him proudly. "Always putting others first."

"You'll come and eat with us, Tom," Esme demanded, pointing her spoon at a couple of empty seats between Sarah Jennifer and Annie. "You've worked as hard as any of us. Besides, this is a meeting. Your presence is required."

"You don't have to tell me twice, Esme," Sarai called, plonking her ample rear into the chair next to Sarah Jennifer and pulling a bowl toward her. "What are we meeting about?"

Annie spoke up as Tom took the seat next to her. "The army of the dead."

Esme cut in, "The time to defend against them is getting

closer. Fortunately, Sarah Jennifer has arrived, just as Gaia promised."

Sarah Jennifer looked up from her food. "I know her as Lilith," she told the group. She is an alien entity, not a goddess."

Everyone but Esme found somewhere else to look.

"I told you they don't want to hear it." Esme clucked with a chiding look that told Sarah Jennifer not to rock the boat. "Time to get some things out in the open, don't you think? Where's that cousin of yours?"

It was Sarah Jennifer's turn to look aside. "He's not ready to hear this yet. Wait, I thought none of you believed in the Madness and the army of the dead?"

A mumble of embarrassment came from the councilors.

"I don't know why you insist on this," the bearded man Esme had identified as David earlier objected. "Sarai could have just eaten the wrong kind of mushroom. She never had any visions before. None of us have, except for you women."

Sarah Jennifer scowled at him, thinking his sour outlook wasn't going to do anyone any good.

Annie got to her feet and leaned over the table to stick her finger in his face. "Now listen here, David."

Sarai put her hand on her mother's arm. "It's okay, Mom. I know what I experienced was real." She offered a small smile in return for Sarah Jennifer's inquisitive glance. "Last Samhain, I was given a vision by Gaia. I saw the dead, an army of them coming to Salem. I saw my family and friends die, only to rise red-eyed and starving for flesh and blood. I saw everything we've worked for razed to the ground. And then I saw you. Gaia showed you to me for a reason, Sarah Jennifer. She showed me that you are the only one who can stop the dead from taking us and making us like them!" Sarai was passionate at this point.

She spoke clearly and defiantly despite her obvious fear of the fate she'd been shown. Sarah Jennifer believed every word she said. Then again, she had Lilith's "visit" to compare it to.

Annie continued, "When Sarai came to the council with what she'd seen, we petitioned Gaia for visions of our own. You asked me on Samhain night why I didn't just 'blast' the Weres who attacked me? I saw you, leading them into battle against the dead."

Tom gripped Annie's hand. "You were brave."

"I still don't like it," David complained. "How can we trust the word of a stranger and just get along with the pack like they haven't been a thorn in the side of the peace we have here?"

There was a rumble of agreement from the councilors.

Sarah Jennifer was speechless for a moment, thrown by the selfishness she was witnessing. Lilith wasn't giving her a lot to work with. Even Butch and Skippy would have been preferable to these cowards in a battle against the dead. She pushed down the pain of their loss even as she recalled how their deaths had affected the family. Her grandfather had been stoical as usual, but a bit of the sparkle had left her grandmother's eyes that night.

"I've already started training the pack to rescue the Weres in Boston." Sarah Jennifer began to understand the mountain she had to climb. "I'm going to talk to them about the Madness soon. I need you to understand that what's coming is far worse than the dead rising. We could figure a way to wipe zombies out by the million if that was the case, at no risk to ourselves. What Sarai and Annie have seen are living people who have been corrupted by broken technology."

She changed tack, seeing her words weren't sinking in. "They have a sickness," she relented. "It gets into their blood and drives them to commit atrocities, but they are still *alive*, and they can be cured. I don't want to kill them, although I'll do my duty by the uninfected if it comes down to it."

"What duty is that?" David inquired with genuine curiosity that nevertheless held a hint of humoring the crazy woman.

"To protect humanity until the cure is found." Sarah Jennifer got to her feet and leaned on the table to meet his gaze with a frown. "I have to build and train an army capable of protecting the uninfected once the Madness hits these shores. Where do you think it's more likely to land than this coastline? Dumbasses who ignore history—I'm beginning to think the world is mostly populated by them."

"We're all doomed if that is true!" David exclaimed.

Sarah Jennifer lifted a hand to cut off David's blustering. "Doomed or not, we have to try. My duty is to get as many people through what's coming as I can. Stick your head in the sand all you like. What I don't have to waste is time spent knocking sense into those who can't get their heads around people's differences being key to surviving an extinction event."

She lowered her voice, realizing she was barking at David. She returned to her chair and spoke from her heart. "I'm not going to apologize for taking this seriously.

Everyone here needs to harden up if you want your children's children to see the other side. My grandparents lived through the World's Worst Day Ever and spent the years afterward rebuilding civilization until they left to defend Earth from space. I am the sum of their success, so trust me when I tell you I know what I'm talking about. We're about to enter the Dark Ages times a *hundred*. Trade will cease, and the roads will be abandoned as people cut themselves off to protect their families from the Madness. Others will be displaced in their thousands, taking the infection with them."

There were gasps as the reality of Sarah Jennifer's description set in.

"What can we do?" Magnus asked in a near-whisper. "We aren't strong enough to protect the whole world."

"No, but you can protect Salem." Sarah Jennifer told him. "And from here, the Unknown World will protect humanity. This town is the perfect stronghold. The barrier hex will keep out the Mad, right, Esme?"

Esme lifted a shoulder. "It remains to be seen. I'm going out there tomorrow with Annie and Lenore to bolster the physical defenses."

"I'm going, too," Sarai put in. "It's time I put my gifts to better use than coaxing food from the ground."

Annie smiled. "Don't dismiss your gifts," she told her daughter. "There will be a time when everyone here will be grateful for your control of nature."

Sarai nodded. "Oh, I know. I was thinking we could put up more defenses. I had an idea that a wall of thorns would work." She smiled at Annie. "You know, like in that story you always told me when I was small, about the princess asleep in the tower."

"This is exactly the kind of thinking we need," Sarah Jennifer told Sarai. She turned her attention back to the rest of the council. "In this situation, only one thing is clear. Everyone who knows what's coming must do everything they can to help humanity to survive, so put your grown-up pants on and get settled in for the ride or get the hell out of this meeting room and make room for someone who is willing to give what it's going to take to pull through."

"I'm willing to do my part," David assured her. "But I'm no soldier."

Magnus agreed.

Sarah Jennifer looked hard at the witches around the table. "The people will need administration and organization as much as they'll need food and shelter. Will you do your part and take care of the people we save?"

"We will fight to our last breath to see people safe," Esme stated flatly, giving the grumblers a look that *dared* them to argue. No one did. "How can we help you get prepared?"

Sarah Jennifer had no idea. Nine magic users and a barely housetrained wolf pack weren't a lot to stand against the destruction of the human race, but it was what she had to build on. The colonel had done much more with much less, a sentiment she was going to have to adopt as her personal mantra.

"Spread the word. I'm calling a town meeting. I want everyone in the park at dawn." Sarah Jennifer folded her hands on the table. "The first thing we have to do is get everyone working together, so they're ready to handle the growth in our ranks. Then I'm taking a road trip to Boston.

Brutus managed to get control of himself just in time to avoid knocking a fancy vase off the skinny-legged table by the meeting room door. He steadied the vase with shaky hands, trying in vain to convince himself that he'd misheard Sarah Jennifer.

However, Brutus was too experienced a survivor to lie to himself. There were too many things about his cousin's behavior that made perfect sense. The world was about to go to shit worse than ever.

He backed away from the door and made his silent way to the roof of the building, following the instinct that the only way he'd be able to process the enormity of Sarah Jennifer's undertaking was if he had the stars to give him perspective.

Brutus was relieved to find the roof was unoccupied. He made his way to a plywood structure that served as a sometime guard post and peered inside, counting his blessings when he discovered there was a chair and a table with a full oil lantern. He was distracted by the rare sight of an intact book on the table.

His mother had taught him to read from the mismatched library that had been her prized possession. Brutus recalled many an evening spent in the company of Jim Hawkins and Long John Silver. The way his mother did the voices gave him a shiver up his spine whenever it was the captain's turn to speak.

He sank gratefully onto the chair and lit the lamp before picking up the paperback, holding it out of reach while he fiddled with the lamp and worked out how to turn it up enough to read by.

Brutus cradled the book in his hands and read the title. The cover showed a city in flames, which brought reality crashing back down.

The fate of the world in his hands wasn't a situation Brutus ever expected to find himself in, even indirectly. Neither did he miss the irony of him and Sarah Jennifer being thrown together to be the saviors of humanity. His branch of the family'd had little contact with hers, despite the North American pack's allegiance to Charumati.

Brutus remembered the story Sarah Jennifer had told him of the time his father mouthed off to the purple-eyed Queen of the Weres and received a chestful of lead for his disrespect. There was nothing wrong with exerting authority when the situation called for it.

He smirked, the pull on the scar tissue on his face a sensation that was rapidly becoming a reminder of Sarah Jennifer's gruff attempts of showing care instead of her reaction to his initial tantrum at her arrival.

If anyone was equal to the task of taming the Weres, it was that unshakeable woman. He thought about what she'd told the pack when she was teaching them how to build shelters. No obstacle was insurmountable. There was no goal that wasn't achievable if it was broken into smaller parts.

For the first time, he found himself truly grateful for her rigid insistence on structure. Where Sarah Jennifer went, he would follow. She had chosen her path, a path

Brutus had resolved to follow when he submitted to her as his Alpha.

Brutus relaxed, the privilege of not being the one in command giving him comfort.

Sarah Jennifer would tell him when it was time to worry about the monsters.

CHAPTER FOURTEEN

Sarah Jennifer's breath made clouds in the chilly predawn air. Her position on the bandstand gave her a view of the whole park. She listened to the conversations of the people arriving, wanting a good read on their mood.

"You feeling nervous?" Brutus asked, leaving his place at the wooden rail.

Sarah Jennifer looked away and ran a hand through her hair as the throwaway comment reminded her that this was another point of no return for her. Once she took responsibility for the town, she was obligated to stick by them to the end. "If I say yes and no, would you get it?"

Brutus shuffled nervously, taking hold of the rail. "Yeah... So, I... I overheard you all in the meeting last night. I know what's coming."

"Yet you're still here," Sarah Jennifer commented. "You're not afraid?"

"Afraid?" Brutus snorted. "I'd be stupid if I wasn't, but I've got your back. I don't know how I'd feel in your shoes. That's some heavy shit you're dealing with."

Sarah Jennifer scrutinized Brutus for a long moment. "One of these days, you're going to be a good enough fighter to make that mean something." She grinned when his face got caught somewhere between disbelief and outrage.

"You won *one* time," Brutus shot back with an identical grin. "You should count yourself lucky I'm not stupid enough to prove my point. I'd hate to get stuck with the responsibility of saving the world just because I kicked your ass."

Brutus sidestepped when she moved to punch him in the arm. "You know I'm not letting you go to Boston on your own, right?"

Sarah Jennifer smirked when he blocked her feint and took his balance with a swipe of her foot, grabbing the back of his coat to stop him from falling. "I think what you mean is, 'thank you for offering to take me with you on this invaluable training opportunity, Major.'"

Brutus regained his feet and whirled around. He bowed to Sarah Jennifer, still grinning mischievously. "That too, SJ."

Sarah Jennifer dissolved into laughter. "You're an ass, Brutus."

The council had been true to their word. By the time the sun licked the horizon, the men and women of Salem had all gathered at the bandstand to hear her speak.

The chatter was mixed. Some were feeling positive, others confused and negative. They didn't know Sarah Jennifer. She wasn't from Salem. Why were things changing so suddenly? Sarah Jennifer had thought about the best way to approach the townsfolk long into the night and come to the decision that upsetting their belief system wasn't the way to go.

She cleared her throat when she had silence. "Merry meet to you all. For those of you who don't know me, my name is Major Sarah Jennifer Walton. I am a former FDG officer, and the granddaughter of Colonel Terry Henry Walton. The Weres among you might know of my grandmother Charumati."

Sarah Jennifer made her eyes glow, drawing gasps from the crowd. "Most importantly, I have been charged by the being known to you as Gaia to protect humanity." She pointed to where the pack was situated, set apart from the townsfolk. "This is my pack. All the things they've done in the past will be atoned for as we defend the town during the hard times ahead. I am creating something new, a defense force to face the dangers that are coming to our shores. But right now, the UnknownWorld is being hunted to extinction. People are dying at the hands of leeches."

"You mean, the *Weres* are dying," someone objected from the middle of the crowd.

Sarah Jennifer had expected some resistance. "Yes, the Weres, and before them, it was the vampires. How long until they expand to the magic users? How many of you will be safe then? How many of you come from the cities, how many fled the violence there? Let Salem be a beacon of hope to anyone from the UnknownWorld who wishes to live without fear."

A ripple of murmurs ran through the crowd, and a Were called, "The barrier hex protects us from the leeches. Why would we risk them learning our location?"

Esme interrupted. "Aye, but six of the Council have

been banished for betraying us." She made no apology. "Darren and his faction tried to drive wedges between us all. Who knows what they intended, but it wasn't the good of our community. Hard times are coming. You all know it as well as I do. We have been weakened, but we have also gained strength with the coming of Major Walton and her pack."

"The same pack who terrorized everyone for miles around?" a woman called.

Sarah Jennifer raised her voice, so there was no mistaking her words. "The pack is under my control. All Weres will answer to me, including those who live here in Salem. Anyone who has an issue with submitting is free to challenge me, but I'd rather we saved time than me beat compliance into anyone and everyone who wants to argue. I claimed the title of Alpha of North America by right of bloodline, and I will demand the allegiance of every Were on this continent with the same determination I intend to defend their lives."

Esme took over from Sarah Jennifer. "I thought better of you all. We are all part of the UnknownWorld. There are Weres in captivity, human beings who are suffering while we live a good life. Does it sit well with you all to have lived in peace and safety when it was in our power to end such cruelty?"

The people murmured uneasily.

"Nobody is being asked to give more than they are able to," Sarah Jennifer assured them. "But I want you to think about how you received my pack twenty years ago, and how that behavior contributed to the way they've been living since. They came to you as frightened youths, and you turned them away. This is your chance to make amends and do better by yourselves and the rest of the UnknownWorld."

One woman asked Sarah Jennifer, her tone lacking the argumentative note of the previous speakers, "Can you help us learn to defend ourselves against the leeches? There's no question they're going to find us. I want to be ready when they come."

Sarah Jennifer grinned. "Lady, nothing would make me happier. Let's get started. Break yourselves into groups. Magic users over here with Esme—you will go to the practice area. All Weres, go introduce yourselves to Lieutenant Brutus. You will be learning how to work together as one pack."

The group split, most heading for Esme, Annie, and Lenore. Sarah Jennifer saw Magnus standing behind his mother. She couldn't help feeling sorry for him. It was bad luck for him that he hadn't inherited the longevity his twin had. He'd appeared to be contrite enough after the encounter at the hex boundary. Humbled by his mother, no doubt.

There were a few people still hanging around the base of the bandstand, a woman and two men. Sarah Jennifer descended the steps to meet them. "What's the problem?"

The woman was the same one who had asked if she would teach them to fight. She answered Sarah Jennifer, "Miss, I ain't got no magic, nor can I turn into a wolf. But I'm strong, and I can swing an axe. Will you still have me in your defense force?"

The other two had similar requests. One was Jim, Salem's blacksmith.

She looked the three of them over. They were all well-muscled from a lifetime of honest labor and eager to contribute. "I can't see why not, but let me be very clear. You do exactly as you're told. I don't want you training with the pack since you could get killed accidentally." The pack might have been weak compared to her family, but they still outmatched any unenhanced human.

"I was thinking I could do something more suited to my skills," Jim admitted.

Sarah Jennifer nodded. "Sounds good to me, but I have a question. What do you know about engines? Specifically, the kind that power vehicles."

Jim's eyes lit up. "What don't I know? There's been no call for motorized transport here, but a man needs a hobby, you know?"

Sarah Jennifer smiled as she figured out the cause of the blacksmith's injury yesterday. "You've got a car. That's how you got burned, right?"

Jim nodded. "Homemade fuel is tricky, Major. I figured I'd come here to find you when word went out about the meeting." He grinned sheepishly. "Fuel is the issue, but I have an idea about that, too."

Sarah Jennifer liked this man's easy honesty and eager attitude. "Then welcome to the Defense Force, Lieutenant Johnson. You just made chief engineer."

Jim blushed. "I don't know about all that fancy stuff. I can show you my vehicles whenever you're ready. Just swing by the forge when you get time."

He departed with a spring in his step, leaving Sarah Jennifer with the young woman and her companion.

"What job do you have for me, Major?" the young woman asked.

"You'll see," Sarah Jennifer promised, thinking a home guard to keep order once the town began to grow would be a good idea. "Just as soon as I figure out where your talents are best placed. What's your name?"

"Izzy, miss. *Oh!* I mean, Major," she replied.

"That's Private Izzy, now. Are there any other regular humans who want to fight?" Izzy nodded. "Good, gather them, and we'll meet back here tomorrow. I'll come up with a schedule to get you all battle-ready. For now, you're dismissed."

Izzy grinned. "Aye, Major. Thanks."

Sarah Jennifer returned the grin with a warm smile. "Enjoy your last day of freedom. Tomorrow your work begins."

She watched Izzy and her companion leave, laughing and joking. That was good. She'd seen war, and they would all need the memory of moments like this to remind them what they fought for. She set off running to catch up with Jim.

"Wait up," Sarah Jennifer requested when he slowed down. "I'd better see those vehicles. One moment." She glanced at the area where the Weres were grouped around Brutus and searched. She located the two faces she was looking for and summoned them with a whistle and a nod.

Geordie and Carver obeyed instantly, breaking off from the pack and sprinting to Sarah Jennifer's side.

"I have something in mind for you two," Sarah Jennifer informed them. "Follow us."

She and Jim strode ahead with the two young men

hurrying to keep up. Jim went ahead once they cut out of the town and turned onto a dirt track. "Not far," he promised after they'd been walking for a few minutes.

Sarah Jennifer heard running water, then the hills parted as the track took a corner and they were delivered into a tree-dotted valley.

Jim opened his arms as they approached the long L-shaped log cabin nestled between a thicket of pines and a stream.

He dashed ahead. "Give me a few minutes to disable the security measures."

"Why are we here?" Carver asked, watching Jim hurry inside the cabin. "Did he join us?"

Sarah Jennifer nodded. "This man could be our greatest weapon."

Geordie frowned at a clang from inside the cabin. "What, he's going to fight with us? But he's just a human. He'll get killed."

"Humans are not defenseless," Sarah Jennifer told them. "This man has an engineer's mind, which we are sorely going to need. Unless you want to pull that cart forever?"

Both Weres assured her that wolfpower was not their preferred way of traveling long distances.

"Then sharpen up, Sergeants," Sarah Jennifer instructed, smiling at their surprise at being promoted. "You two are going to pay attention to everything Lieutenant Johnson tells you about building and maintaining vehicles. It's a sideways promotion, but out of everyone in the pack, you two are the best choice for the job."

Carver and Geordie thanked her profusely.

"Don't thank me. Just work hard," Sarah Jennifer told

them. She walked away, giving them space to discuss the change while they waited for Jim. She admired the cabin as she strolled through the trees, and found herself lingering over her inspection of the jetty. The thick posts were chained by frozen wavelets for the winter, as was the skiff moored at the end. She knew that achieving this level of craftsmanship required natural talent to go with learned skill.

"You like the water?" Jim asked as he returned, ending the moment.

Sarah Jennifer smiled. "I like eating the fish that live there. It's a beautiful home you've got," she told him. "I'd be glad to take a tour after we've seen the vehicles."

Jim waved them around the back of the cabin. "It'll take a few minutes for it to heat up inside, anyway. The barn is this way."

Geordie and Carver exchanged excited glances, which didn't go unnoticed by Sarah Jennifer. She set off after Jim, shooing the Weres as she went.

Jim stopped outside the barn door and pulled a square fob from his pocket. "You mind me and keep your fingers clear of the machinery," he told Geordie and Carver as he pushed the button on the fob.

Sarah Jennifer couldn't help but chuckle at their nervous agreements. There was the whine of a motor as the barn door retracted into the wall, and Jim's workspace was revealed.

The first thing she noticed was three large, boxy items covered with dust sheets between ordered workbenches, followed by the heat. "Have you got your forge back here?" she asked.

Jim pointed at one of the two open doors on the far side of the barn. "It's through there. But that's not what you came to see." He went around and pulled the dust cover off the first vehicle. "What do you think?"

Sarah Jennifer's hopes soared at the sight of diplomatic plates and tinted glass. She dashed over to the black SUV and opened the door on leather and polished wood inlays. "Where in hell did you find this?" she asked in astonishment.

Jim chuckled. "Wait, I'm not done."

Sarah Jennifer turned to look at him, her eyebrows rising as her sense of disbelief grew. "You can't beat this, surely?"

Jim pointed at the next vehicle. "Would you care to do the honors?"

Sarah Jennifer grinned. "Would I!" She teased the cover off, revealing the heavily modified ATV beneath. The exposed engine had been covered with thick, perforated grating that gave protection while still allowing airflow to the 1000cc engine.

"Hello, my pretty," she murmured appreciatively, trailing her fingers over the body as she walked around the ATV. She sucked in a breath at the siding Jim had constructed from the same grating, set between the ribs of the roll cage.

"This one here's my favorite," Jim told them, uncovering the third vehicle, an average-looking black pickup truck with a faded sticker on the rear window. "She's not going to win any prizes for beauty, but she's the only one that ran without work when I found her."

"They run?" Sarah Jennifer asked.

"Major! Check this out!" Geordie's voice traveled from somewhere beyond the side door, forestalling Jim's reply.

Jim clapped with delight. "Looks like the boys found old Bluebird. This way."

He guided Sarah Jennifer through the organized chaos to the covered patio outside, where Geordie and Carver stood gazing at a big, yellow bus with its hood propped up.

Sarah Jennifer was lost for words. People like Jim were rare. He was exactly what they needed, someone who knew how to make the world *run*. "I want to hear all about the restoration process, but that will have to wait for a long night's watch and a bottle of something warming. Where did you get these vehicles?" she asked, making a mental calculation of how many of the pack she could spare to join Carver and Geordie in getting some education from this quiet genius.

"I rescued them from the old municipal depot," Jim told her. "Bluebird here was in good condition when I found her. I don't know, something spoke to me when I walked into the depot and saw her looking out of place there with the excavators and such."

Sarah Jennifer made a mental note to visit this depot as she got on her hands and knees and shuffled underneath to peer at the chassis. "What fuel are you running them on?"

Jim pressed a hand to the small of his back as he bent over to watch Sarah Jennifer's inspection. "Well, that's the thing, Major. They ran on diesel, which is somewhat scarce —meaning there's no damned diesel."

"I know you didn't burn yourself hauling water," Sarah Jennifer commented as she pulled herself out from under the bus. She got to her feet and wiped her hands on the clean bandana Jim offered.

Jim pulled a second bandana from another pocket and tied it around his head to keep his hair out of the way. He motioned for Sarah Jennifer to follow him back into the barn, where he crossed to the door to the forge.

"I learned engines from the manuals Esme gave me," he told her, pointing out a cubby that held shelves packed with books and notebooks. The aforementioned manuals filled most of the space. "I have books on chemistry, as well. It's how I learned enough about converting plant oils into fuel to regularly set myself on fire."

"I hope you're not going to blow up your new apprentices," Sarah Jennifer told him, only half-joking.

Jim put his hands on his belly and laughed. "No fear of that, Major. The first thing I'm going to have them learn is how to make a shortwave radio. I know the Defense Force needs them."

"And then some." Sarah Jennifer smiled as they passed through the forge into a single room with concrete walls and a metal door. She noted the equipment set up on the stone-topped cabinets lining the walls as she joined Jim at the engine he had out on a block of blackened iron in the center of the room. "This is where you make the fuel?"

"You've got it," Jim told her as he opened one of the airtight cabinets and showed her the trio of mismatched gas cans inside. "You're looking at my whole supply. Twenty gallons, more or less. That'll get you just over eight hundred miles in the ATV."

Sarah Jennifer cradled her chin as she converted the miles to kilometers. It was almost a thousand miles from here to Chicago, the nearest place she could acquire replacements for the combustion engines currently in the vehicles and power packs that stored Etheric energy to run them on. Her thoughtful look turned into a frown when she factored in the obstacles along the way. "That's not enough."

"It's not a lack of fuel that's the issue. It's winter." He pointed out a rectangular box in the engine. "I tweaked the engines to take plant oils, which I get from Annie. The new fuel took care of the problem, but it's a two-part process to make it. The burn was from messing up the preparation. I can't make any more until spring."

Sarah Jennifer wasn't so sure that Jim would find success before blowing himself up. She put a hand on his elbow and steered him back to the bus, sighing internally at the delay to the rescue plans. "I need all four vehicles to run on power packs. Can you do the work to convert them?"

Jim's lip curled. "Why would you want me to do that? Solar batteries aren't worth a damn unless you live in the desert."

Sarah Jennifer chuckled and patted Jim's back. "Did you hear me mention anything about solar power? These power packs will run indefinitely without needing to be recharged. I have access to that technology, or I hope I still do. I'm going to go to Chicago to pick up a bunch of power packs that will run at more than—what were you getting out of that oil? Forty miles to the gallon?"

"Thirty-six," he admitted, his eyes glazing over at the possibility of *real* power. "I'd better get started on figuring out how to do the conversion. I'll have to go to the university library…" His voice trailed off as he made plans.

"You have a few days to figure it out, maybe two weeks," Sarah Jennifer assured him. "I'll have to go to Chicago on foot, and I have to make sure the Defense Force training is in place before I can leave."

She grinned at the look of amazement from Jim. "Don't check out on me just yet. I have a list of other modifications for the bus. Don't get me wrong, Bluebird is a solid ride, but she's a long way from being a tactical assault vehicle."

Jim nodded, stunned by the ease Sarah Jennifer talked about traveling a thousand miles and back. "I'll do what I can."

Sarah Jennifer smiled. "I just bet you will. Listen up, this is what I need…"

CHAPTER FIFTEEN

<u>Salem, MA (four weeks later)</u>

The pack stood to attention as Sarah Jennifer walked along the ranks, giving every single Were the hairy eyeball. They were scratched and bleeding from wounds in various stages of healing. She was glad the cold didn't affect any of them because they'd ripped their clothing attempting to scale the old university building.

She removed her flannel shirt to wipe the mud from her hands. "Let's start with the positives. This concludes your first month of tactical assault training, and nobody was seriously injured. That's good. You made mistakes, and next week you'll make fewer. What did you all learn today?"

Little Ace raised his hand. "A variation on the same thing we've been learning all week. We suck. Why do we even need to know how to climb a building? It's damn hard, and it keeps going to shit. Major, how are we supposed to rescue people for real if we can't even get the practice right?"

The rest of the Weres grumbled their agreement.

Sarah Jennifer laughed good-naturedly. "Do you think I was born with the ability to scale a building? I had to learn, just like you are. This is why we practice, Private Ace. It will come, you just need to train. You've only been at this for a few weeks. Why are you being so hard on yourselves?"

Little Ace grimaced, his hands clenching into fists. "I want to be ready *now*. I can't stand the thought of everyone locked up in that prison."

Sarah Jennifer remembered that compulsion all too well. It was the one that had driven her to be the best at everything in her youth, and the same one that had her thinking she could skip off to Chicago after a few days of prep. Well, she knew better now. She had pushed the forty-two Weres hard this last four weeks, just as Esme had pushed the magic users, and both arms of her Defense Force were coming together.

"I'm proud of how far you've come already," she told Little Ace. She patted him on the shoulder and looked around for her lieutenant. "Come on, get packed up. We're going back to town. Brutus, the pack can take liberty for the night. I want you all back fresh as daisies at first light, understood?"

"Yes, ma'am!" Brutus replied smartly.

She swatted him with a grin. "Less of that. Go have fun, but not too much, you get me? Trust me when I say it won't go down well if anyone misbehaves."

The magic users had been working just as hard as the Weres. Sarah Jennifer summoned the two branches of the nascent defense force that evening to discuss the day's training around the communal dinner arranged by Maria and the young women, who had decided to stay and become part of the Salem community.

Appetite satisfied, Sarah Jennifer left the training ground after dinner and crossed the commons as a shortcut to the town hall. The hall had become the official Defense Force HQ, just another use for which the building had been made, Esme assured Sarah Jennifer.

Sarah Jennifer entered her office. She'd had her eye on a smaller office off the main corridor, but had been forced to adjust her expectations when the line outside her door during her "open" hours on the first morning began to disrupt the normal town business. There had to be *some* perks to being chained to a desk. Now she was situated at the back of the town hall in a cozy suite comprising a small bedroom, a bathroom, and a study leading off from her office with its cast iron stove and a well-stocked drinks cabinet tucked between the bookshelves.

She took a seat in one of the soft chairs by the stove and threw in another log to warm up the study for Esme, who she expected to arrive soon. She poured two whiskeys and sat back to wait.

Her mind wandered in the quiet. She swirled the drink around the glass, allowing a small smile of satisfaction to touch the corner of her mouth. All that time spent denying her roots, her very nature even. It had been a waste. She had never felt as alive as she did right now. Her childish definition of what it meant to be the best was laughable in the face of everything she had learned in the last year.

It was about more than victory over her opponent, more than knowing every technique there was to learn. It was about using the advantages she had to build a better world. To protect those who had no advantage of their own, to give *them* a chance to flourish and be free.

She was building more than an army. More than a force for war. They were defenders, every one. The Salem Weres had fit into the pack, and the magic users had turned out to be reasonable. The regular humans of the town were a blessing. She was forging bonds between the factions of the UnknownWorld. She would scourge the leeches, hold back the Madness; whatever it took to keep humanity going until Lilith's mysterious plan came about, and she would love every moment of it.

The Force now boasted cooks, a father and son tracker-trapper team, a host of people who worked together to make clothing and other everyday items, and Izzy and her two sisters were working with Quartermaster Ace on the logistics side of things. More than any of those, Sarah Jennifer was glad they had Jim Johnson. His skills were invaluable, and Geordie and Carver, the young Weres with the big imaginations, were flourishing under his guidance. Committing resources to the brain trust was always a smart move, but she sure as hell wished she had access to a mind like Ted's.

She sensed Esme before she heard or smelled her. She knew on an instinctive level that she was sensing the well of Etheric energy deep within her friend. Looking within, Sarah Jennifer tried to see her own "magic."

"That's a good start, Duckie," Esme commended, distracting Sarah Jennifer from her soul-searching as she entered the office. "It never hurts to look inside. That's where our strength comes from, you know."

Sarah Jennifer shrugged. "It's like you said, any ability I can develop is a tool in my arsenal. Whether I'm comfortable with it or not is irrelevant. What I want to know is how you got your magic, how you can hear Lilith. You promised."

Esme drained her glass and sat down. "Well, I suppose now's as good a time as any. Pour me another finger or three of that, would you? David was beyond tiresome today."

Sarah Jennifer complied, topping up the glass with a generous splash.

Esme took a deep swig. "Ah, that hit the spot. Where do I start..."

"The beginning!" Sarah Jennifer exclaimed. She was impatient for Esme to reveal her deep past. "Where were you born?"

"That one's easy, I was born and raised by my gran in a little village in Scotland. It was beautiful there, but no place for anyone who stood out. Not even at the turn of the century. Gran always told me that it was no different for her growing up in England, except if she was caught, it would've been hanging for maleficium instead of being burnt for heresy like they did in her gran's day."

"So, your whole family had magic then?" Sarah Jennifer hung on Esme's every word.

Esme lifted a shoulder. "Of a more...subtle kind. I doubt you'd see it as magic."

"I don't see what you can do now as magic," Sarah Jennifer reminded her.

"Well, we'll just have to agree to disagree," Esme replied with some bite. "We practiced what you would call paganism or Wicca, and we gave our thanks to Mother Earth for our blessings. It's a practice I keep to this day. But I digress. It wasn't until long after I came to America that Lilith was able to speak directly to me."

She got up from her chair and threw another log onto the stove. "Brrr, it's cold tonight, Duckie. Where was I? Oh, yes. The first years after WWDE were shaky, to say the least. The meek did not inherit the Earth, except in exceptional places where the leaders' might defended right. Mostly, the ones holding the power took what they wanted and damn the rest. I set up home outside of New York with Annie and Lenore, and more women joined us as time went by, looking for a better life than they had going from one man's protection to another. It didn't last."

Sarah Jennifer wondered how that had gone down with the men who those women had run from. "What happened?"

"It was destroyed when we were attacked by a bunch of ne'er-do-wells who thought we would swoon gratefully when they marched in swinging their dicks." Esme's lip curled. "They died disappointed, and I can't say I'm sorry. Those men were the type to take what they like and damn the consequences to anybody else. We had other things to worry about."

"What?" Sarah Jennifer asked, fascinated by the look into the past.

"A town full of women in those days was a magnet for every asshole male who thought he could waltz in and make himself a harem. We allowed those who proved they were decent to stay, and we drove the rest out. But fear is a funny thing. When the same men who were happy for us to tend their wives in childbirth noticed we weren't getting any older, the accusations of witchcraft began. We left quietly and made our way to Salem."

"That's when you founded the town?" Sarah Jennifer needed to know. Esme still hadn't gotten to the part about Lilith, but she didn't care. She was hearing history first-hand. If only her grandfather were here. He would love hearing Esme's story.

Esme nodded. "Salem is historically entwined with witchcraft. It made sense to me that those who knew might gravitate there, so we altered the land to make the town defensible and built from there. It was the battle of New York that made it possible to find people belonging to the UnknownWorld and gather them in safety."

"I know about that battle from my grandparents," Sarah Jennifer told her. "The one against the first leeches."

"Were they there?" Esme asked.

Sarah Jennifer shook her head. "No, it was a tactical lesson they found appropriate to pass on about the real history of the world."

Esme shrugged. "No matter. We'd been assisting the New Yorkers in any way we could—without anyone knowing, of course. It was beyond anything I'd experienced." She pulled her shirt collar aside to show Sarah Jennifer a puckered scar in the hollow of her shoulder. "Not least because of this."

"You were shot?" Sarah Jennifer's mouth dropped open in shock.

"Aye, Duckie. Don't interrupt! I'm getting to the good

part. There was a man. More than a man, he commanded the very skies. I was hit getting some children to safety. I should have died, but he was there by my side in an instant. I couldn't even see him move, he was so fast! He forced me to drink from his wrist, and I heard Lilith speak for the first time. Before I could thank the man, he vanished into thin air, and I never saw him again."

Sarah Jennifer was astounded. She knew exactly who Esme's silent savior had been. "I hate to be the one to tell you this, but you drank vamp blood. You met the Dark Messiah, Michael Nacht. The massacre was the turning point in the war. So what happened next?"

"Messiah, eh?" Esme asked, absorbing the information.

Sarah Jennifer nodded. "The first vampire, no less."

"I can see how he got the name." Esme tilted her head. "Guess I still have some things to learn. Anyway, we managed to get out of the city and back to Salem, and things started to get back to normal. But my connection with the earth grew stronger, and my small abilities with medicine and nature became something different. We were afraid, not understanding the changes that were happening to me. We cast our circle and called out for guidance, and Gaia—Lilith—answered our petition. She taught me to accept my gifts and how to share them for the benefit of all."

Sarah Jennifer turned it all over in her mind. "How does this help me in the upcoming war? I saw what happened to Darren when he used magic as a weapon. I'm no good to anyone if I get turned into a ball of red mist unless I'm standing in the middle of them when it happens and I take them out with me. As a plan, it's not my favorite, Esme."

"There you go again, attacking head-on without a thought." Esme sighed disapprovingly. "What have you learned?"

She took a moment before answering. "That there are other ways to solve a problem that don't involve kicking the crap out of it. To think around it instead. You know, my family has a saying, 'None of us are as smart as all of us.' Us Waltons have a stubborn streak a mile wide, but we always need reminding of it. Thanks, Esme. You always come along at exactly the moment I need you."

"It's a gift," she replied dryly, putting the empty glass on the table and getting up to leave. "It's late, Duckie. I'll see you soon. Mind me now, keep looking within."

"I will," Sarah Jennifer promised. "Bye, Esme."

She lay in bed that night, bone-weary but too full of questions to sleep. She hadn't listened much to what she'd been told about the nanocytes in her body, but she remembered enough to work out that the magic came from Michael. How, she had no idea. Maybe the women's beliefs had a lot to do with the flavor of enhancement they'd received? But then, she'd seen Lilith. How did the Kurtherian factor into it?

There was only one way to find out.

Sarah Jennifer closed her eyes and concentrated on clearing her mind. Her brow furrowed as her dismissal of her daily routine gave the thoughts at the back of her mind room to play. She pushed those away with the reminder of Samhain, which brought a pang of bittersweetness as she released the fleeting memory.

Sarah Jennifer smiled and shook her head as her mind

attempted to circle back to her to-do. She focused on her breathing and searched for the silence within.

When she found it, she also found that she wasn't the only occupant. Her inner vision was lit by a soft golden glow that felt occupied.

"Lilith?" Sarah Jennifer's voice wavered as she breathed the name. She was taken aback by the sudden appearance of Lilith in her mindspace. This time the Kurtherian wore her own face, which while completely alien, was worn with lines of care.

Lilith smiled and opened her arms, the mandibles that formed her top lip curling up. "Welcome, Sarah Jennifer. I am glad you have found me. I hope you find my appearance less disconcerting this time?"

"You're in my mind?" Sarah Jennifer cursed her inability to keep her inner thoughts to herself. However, there was something to be said for not watching her body moving with someone else's mannerisms. "How can you do this?"

"With difficulty," Lilith informed her. "It wouldn't be possible if you didn't have a natural ability to communicate mentally. It's a lot easier while you're conscious."

Sarah Jennifer sighed. "So Esme keeps telling me. But that doesn't explain why I can see you."

Lilith scrutinized Sarah Jennifer for a long moment. "The important thing is that we can talk. I'm trapped beneath a mountain in Siberia."

The name was familiar to Sarah Jennifer. "I've got family there. But you already know that, right?"

"Yes. I know what you know," Lilith explained. "I just wish it was easier to share what I know with you."

"So talk, tell me what you know." Sarah Jennifer listened in silence while Lilith told her story. Betrayed by her lover and imprisoned inside a computer. Her short time with Bethany Anne, ADAM, and TOM. Her rising panic when she stumbled upon the perfect storm that was about to hit the Earth, and her dogged attempts to warn humanity that had gone in vain until she'd connected with an old woman in North America.

"Esme," Sarah Jennifer interrupted. "You said you had a plan that hinged on me?"

"It's a long shot," Lilith told her. "We need to locate a person."

Sarah Jennifer didn't think that would be too difficult with the right transport.

Lilith shook her head, reading Sarah Jennifer's thoughts. "This person may not have been born yet."

Sarah Jennifer's mind jerked on the incongruity. "You're losing me. That doesn't make sense. How can you be so confident that this supposed child is going to be born at all? And you still haven't told me why they're so important."

"I can't tell you if you're going to be reactionary," Lilith told Sarah Jennifer. Her voice took on an underwater quality. "You were trained better than that. Concentrate, or we will lose the connection."

Sarah Jennifer latched onto the truth in Lilith's command. She wanted answers too much to allow the discomfort she felt in the shifting of her world to drive her emotions. She sat up in her bed and breathed out her anger before Lilith's flickering form vanished.

"You have it in you to bear this," Lilith told her as she

reformed in Sarah Jennifer's mind. "You have borne much worse and come out stronger. Life is pain, we both know that. You were forged in the fire of grief and emerged unbreakable."

Sarah Jennifer shook her head. "All I had was nothing left to lose and time on my own to contemplate the meaning of life without a single person to care for. That all changed on my first night in Salem. You were there on the beach that night somehow, weren't you?"

"I was there through Esme." Lilith's face was full of empathy. "But I heard your song long before you offered it to me as Gaia. I saw you hiding from yourself. Your pain was so great that I heard it from the other side of the world. I felt your heart breaking, and I called you to me."

"The day in the yard, I felt something…extra." A tear rolled down her cheek. She let it be.

Lilith surrounded Sarah Jennifer with comforting energy. She would regret the cost to her reserves later on, but she deemed it necessary at the moment to make the expenditure in the name of healing Sarah Jennifer further. "I saw something else besides your heartbreak. I saw who you had the potential to be, who you were *meant* to be. The Madness has been spreading out from Europe for over a decade. My calculations say humanity will be extinct within another seventy years unless you evolve."

"You can't calculate for humans. We're adaptable, but not *that* adaptable." Sarah Jennifer laughed at the idea of the next generation being born with the ability to fight off zombie hordes. "Don't get me wrong, pockets of people will survive. Some will be immune, and others will be smart enough to make it through relatively unscathed. We got through nuclear Armageddon. We'll come back from this."

Then something she had said without thinking clicked. "Oh, you're counting on the immunes, right?"

"That's exactly what I'm counting on," Lilith answered fervently. "What you're not aware of is that nanocyte saturation is complete across the Earth. I believe we can trigger the evolution you are talking about. We just need to find *one* immune person."

Sarah Jennifer had a sinking feeling she had a long mission ahead of her. "It sounds like you want me to chase my ass around the world looking for people with immunity to this Madness."

"Not the world," Lilith told her. "Europe, the epicenter of the Madness. Finding any immunes who have survived is the only hope, Sarah Jennifer. There's a laboratory in Switzerland where we can upload the code from the clean nanocytes of the immune humans to a system that will overwrite the corrupted code in the nanocytes of those afflicted with the Madness."

Lilith flourished a hand, and a globe of golden light appeared in the space between them. "This is the world," she told Sarah Jennifer as the details firmed, revealing the continents as Sarah Jennifer recognized them from the globe on her office desk. "Pay attention because I can't manifest this for long. These are the places where I read the highest concentrations of Etheric energy."

"Meaning those are the places where the Weres and everyone else in the UnknownWorld are located." Sarah Jennifer seared the map into her memory before it dissipated, noting especially the marker that wasn't too far from Boston.

"We will talk again soon," Lilith promised as she began to fade.

"Next time, you can tell me more about this Madness," Sarah Jennifer stated, but Lilith was gone.

Sarah Jennifer opened her eyes and lit her lamp, holding the image Lilith had shown her in her inner vision as she got out of bed and went into her office.

She grabbed the globe on her desk and pushed pins into the places Lilith had marked. "Siberia is pretty busy, she murmured. "Mainland Europe looks like a riot." She assumed that was because it was overrun by the Mad, who ran on Etheric energy the same as everyone else with nanocytes.

The mark that interested her most was on a town around fifty miles west and slightly north of Boston, near what had been Harvard pre-WWDE. Sarah Jennifer recalled that many of the university buildings were still standing, but what about farther outside of the town? She pulled the appropriate ledger from the bookcase and flipped through it until she came to the records for that area. The only outstanding feature in the area was a maximum-security prison from before WWDE. Further research in the town archives scored her a mildewed newspaper clipping that matched what she remembered from her vision. The high walls and barred windows all but screamed "Were containment facility."

Sarah Jennifer returned the globe to its place, blew out the lamp, and went back into her bedroom. At least she had an idea of what they were up against. It made persuading the people of Salem to do their part a lot easier now that she knew what she was asking. At least, she hoped it would. These days, she was thinking about her grandfather a great deal more. Unlike TH, she had to make the decisions alone.

Would she make the right ones?

CHAPTER SIXTEEN

Brutus found Sarah Jennifer in the rooms leading off her office. He frowned upon seeing she had her ops bag open on the bed. "I thought we weren't leaving for Boston yet?"

"Change of plans," Sarah Jennifer told him around the knife hilt in her mouth. She finished digging around in the bag and pulled out her wolf harness, which Sarai had modified to remove the rein clips and replace them with expanding pockets. "Bingo."

She slipped the blade into the sheath on her harness and turned to the dresser to grab the firelighter she'd left there. "I have to go to Chicago, but I'll get a vehicle while I'm there. I'll be back in ten days, two weeks tops."

"What do you mean, 'change of plans?'" Brutus moaned. "Again? Can't we just make a plan and stick to it for more than five fucking minutes?"

Sarah Jennifer picked up her boots and tied one onto each side of the harness. "Quit whining. I have to go to Chicago. It's the closest place I know where we can get access to gravitic technology without a fight. With the power packs, we have four working vehicles."

Brutus leaned against the wall with his arms folded. "I don't see why you have to go all that way just for a few batteries."

"Not batteries," Sarah Jennifer corrected. "Power packs holding Etheric energy have a longer life than any other power source on this planet, and they are *reliable*." She gave him a pointed look and returned to packing her harness. "We need that technology to power our vehicles. Besides, I need to see my sister. Why are you making such a big deal out of it?"

Brutus bit down on his retort and sighed. "Because I don't like you leaving me here where I can't watch your back. I already lost one Alpha that way. I can't take that."

Sarah Jennifer shook her head, feeling sorry for him in his little-boy-lost moment. "There's no way I can take you with me," she told him. "I need you to lead the pack and make sure preparations for the prison rescue don't drop off in my absence. Besides, do you really want to get stuck in the middle of my and Sylvia's argument?"

"Why are you two feuding?" Brutus asked, deciding to come at it from another angle. "Maybe it'd be easier to see her again if I was there to diffuse the tension."

Sarah Jennifer's face hardened. "I don't want to talk about it."

Brutus winced and held his hands up. "Sorry I asked. Didn't mean to poke a sore subject."

Sarah Jennifer sighed and dropped the harness onto the bed. "No, I'm sorry. It is a sore subject, but you trusted me with your past. I won't keep you in the dark. I was married to a human and we were going to have a baby, but it wasn't to be. I stayed with my husband for a long time after, but it wasn't the same, and eventually I left. Sylvia was there for me, but I needed to be on my own, so I left her, too."

Brutus listened with growing sadness for the hurt his cousin had suffered as she told him about her years of wandering. "There's only one way to go from bottom," he reassured her. "We've all been there in one way or another. I didn't understand how much shit I'd gotten the pack into until you kicked my ass and showed me differently."

Sarah Jennifer handed the harness to Brutus, chuckling softly. "If only an ass-kicking was the solution. Sylvie is going to be pissed when she sees me. While a twenty-year sabbatical isn't unheard of in my family, I've been gone a while longer than that."

She grinned, nostalgic for her twin's sharp tongue. They were both stubborn enough to keep the most minor disagreement going forever and a day. She would just apologize. "Wait here a minute. You can give me a hand with this."

She dashed into the bathroom and came out in wolf form a few moments later.

Brutus helped Sarah Jennifer into the harness and walked with her to the boundary stones, talking over his plans to grow the scavenging crews as they went.

"Be careful out there," he told her in a soft tone.

Sarah Jennifer nodded and wagged her tail to show him she understood. With that, she set off at a steady run, her golden fur standing out against the snow.

. . .

Pittsburgh, PA

Sarah Jennifer held herself still in the culvert, resisting the urge to shake off the meltwater soaking into her belly fur until the band of humans bumbling by on the street above had passed.

They weren't the first to have pursued Sarah Jennifer for her pelt since she'd left Salem six days ago, but they *were* the first who were feral enough to decide to eat her as well. While mildly amusing, it was almost enough to put her off barbeque.

Almost.

She wouldn't turn down a nice, slow-cooked deer haunch right now. Or even a half-cooked one, since she'd been in wolf form for a couple of days and her fur was attracting too much attention from the humans for her to have hunted effectively while traveling.

Sarah Jennifer continued to actively ignore the trickle of the wash and focused on tracking the band of would-be hunters as they moved down the street. As the sound of the mob receded into the distance, the thought occurred to her that if Esme could change her appearance, maybe she could do the same.

She rested her nose on her paws and concentrated on clearing her mind of everything except her desire to be invisible to the human eye.

Her paws remained golden blonde.

Sarah Jennifer sniffed in annoyance and got up to shake the water off. She left the culvert and padded cautiously along the wash. When she was confident she was out of sight, she picked up speed again, keeping her ears pricked for both the sound of rushing water and nearby humans as she ran.

Sylvia's house was another hour away from the edge of the city. Sarah Jennifer arrived in the quiet, tree-shaded area somewhat bedraggled, and still in wolf form. She skulked past a trio of houses that hadn't been there the last time she'd visited and scratched at the door, hoping her idea of breaking the ice didn't get her shot before Sylvie realized who she was.

Sylvia opened her door and looked at the wolf sitting on the stoop.

Sarah Jennifer stared at Sylvia with her head tilted and her paw up, just like Clovis used to do at the table.

Sylvia scowled and held the door open. "Come in, then. But don't think for a moment that turning into a wolf is any excuse for the amount of time you've been gone without a single word to tell me you were alive."

Sarah Jennifer shrugged off her harness and transformed. "Sorry."

Sylvia narrowed her eyes as she stood aside. "Get inside before my neighbors see you and think I've taken to nudism." She grabbed a long patchwork cardigan from the hooks by the door and thrust it at Sarah Jennifer as she entered the hallway. "My bedroom is upstairs to the right. You'll find warm clothes up there."

Sarah Jennifer nodded, chastened. She went upstairs and returned a moment later with a pair of jeans and a white tank top to go under the cardigan bundled in her arms. "It's good to see you, Sylvie."

"You too," Sylvia replied warmly. She pointed at a door

at the end of the hall. "Bathroom is there. Get cleaned up. I don't want mud all over the house."

"Through here," Sylvia called when Sarah Jennifer emerged from the shower.

She followed the sound of splashing water to the kitchen, where Sylvia had gone back to washing her dishes.

She leaned on the doorframe and folded her arms. "How did you know it was me?"

Sylvia looked over her shoulder. "Like I wouldn't know your eyes anywhere. Do you remember the time we got caught stealing cookies, and Felicity chased us all the way around the house?"

Sarah Jennifer laughed, remembering how they'd run to hide in the attic, suppressing their giggles as they'd looked at each other through the gaps in their hiding places. "I thought she was going to whup our asses for sure."

Sylvia looked up at the curse. "I see the wolf isn't the only change you've made."

Sarah Jennifer shrugged. "I realized I'd be able to run a lot faster without the stick up my ass." She looked away, murmuring her next words. "Plus, I have a pack now, and they drive me insane."

"You have a what? Sit down," Sylvia urged, drying her hands before indicating Sarah Jennifer join her at the breakfast bar by the window. "You've been gone for so long, Sarah. I have something to tell you."

Sarah Jennifer wilted when Sylvia met her curiosity with a sad shake of her head. "Who died?" she asked, dreading the answer.

Sylvia reached across the breakfast bar for Sarah Jennifer's hand. "It was Dad," she told her quietly. "He died a hero, fighting to free some slaves from an evil AI. Mom came to tell us, but you were nowhere to be found."

Sarah Jennifer's eyes stung. "I guess I knew that not everyone who went with Bethany Anne would survive. Still, Dad? He never wanted to fight."

"He did it to be with Mom," Sylvia reminded her. She stared at Sarah Jennifer with curiosity. "Where have you been all these years?"

"Wandering," Sarah Jennifer replied, looking down at their entwined hands while she absorbed the news that her father was dead. "Searching for my purpose."

Sylvia did her best to keep the pity off her face. She'd come to terms with her sister's nature in the first decade after she'd left and was just grateful to have Sarah Jennifer sitting across from her. "Did you find what you were looking for?"

Sarah Jennifer snorted softly. "I found a fight."

Sylvia rolled her eyes. "Not a difficult thing in this world."

"What would you do if you found out the apocalypse was going to hit? " Sarah Jennifer asked, pulling her hands free. "Sit back and let it happen?"

"Another one?" Sylvia scoffed. "I'd do the same thing I did every other time the world went to shit around me. Dig in and wait it out. Help who I can."

Sarah Jennifer held no judgment for her sister's choices. "You know I can't just watch humanity go extinct when I have the ability to do something about it. Remember I told you something was changing about my nanocytes?"

Sylvia nodded. "I figured that's how you got the wolf."

Sarah Jennifer shrugged off the comment. "That's actually a recent development. The first change was my ability to talk mind to mind."

Sylvia shot up on her stool, her jaw dropping. "You're shitting me? We always wanted psychic twin abilities!" She screwed up her face as she concentrated. "What am I thinking right now?"

"I don't know," Sarah Jennifer admitted. "So far, the most I've done with it is embarrass myself." She hesitated a moment. "I'm not kidding about the apocalypse, Sylvie. Everything on Earth has nanocytes now. They're in the air, the dirt, the water, and in every living being. But something has gone wrong. Instead of making people smarter or giving them extra abilities, the nanocytes are turning people into mindless killers. I have to stop it."

Sylvia's face creased at the magnitude of what Sarah Jennifer was telling her. "That's... It's above *everyone's* pay grade. Shit, Sarah." Her expression changed as her mind threw up a defense against the shock. "What am I doing? I haven't even offered you anything to eat."

She got up from the breakfast bar and started taking ingredients out of the cupboard next to the sink, needing physical activity to occupy her hands while her mind worked to process the bombshell. "I won't bother to ask if you're hungry. You have a Were's appetite to appease."

Sarah Jennifer went with it. "I could eat. You still refusing a balanced diet?"

Sylvia smirked. "Yes, I'm still vegetarian. You can indulge your murderous habits when you leave my house."

"Bet you didn't make Mom eat rabbit food when she visited," Sarah Jennifer grumbled, regretting her choice of words when she realized it would likely be rabbit stew in Esme's pot today.

"I did not," Sylvia confirmed. "But you are not my mother, so you'll respect my wishes in my home."

Sarah Jennifer folded her arms on the breakfast bar and settled her head on them to watch Sylvia make bread.

Strangely, her sister's reaction made her feel less numb to the task ahead. She'd felt no shock or fear when she'd learned about magic, the blood trade, Lilith, and the Madness. While the horror of the situation appalled her, there was no part of her that wanted to run and hide from what was coming. Her indignation that humanity should fall to a technical error after surviving the nuclear apocalypse rose with every passing day, strengthening her resolve to do something about it.

She was not one person alone battling against the oncoming slide into chaos. The world was suffering and would continue to do so until they found Lilith's immune, but there were others like her who refused to give in.

After ten minutes of muttered curses, Sylvia looked up from her studied pummeling of the dough. "I can't see how you can do anything about the nanocytes failing. Please don't take this on, Sarah."

Sarah Jennifer smiled. "I love you, too. But I'm not on my own. I have a bunch of witches on my side, and my pack is growing every day." She broke into a chuckle. "That's why I'm heading to Chicago. I need the technology to get my people mobile. There are hundreds of Weres being held in a prison by blood traders. It's my intention to free them and take them into my pack before I go to Europe to stop the Madness."

Sylvia stared at Sarah Jennifer, her hands sinking unnoticed into the dough. "Witches? You're batshit crazy, just like our grandfather."

Sarah Jennifer laughed, holding up her hands in surrender. "You got me. What can I say? The thrill of an impossible challenge speaks to my Walton nature."

Sylvia wasn't fooled by Sarah Jennifer's joke. She pointed a floury finger at her. "You're stubborn, you mean. We don't *all* have the urge to be the unstoppable force meeting the immovable object. Tell me how you got dragged into this, and maybe I'll help instead of knocking you over the head and locking you in the root cellar until you see sense like I clearly should."

Sarah Jennifer scowled through her laughter. "Okay, okay."

CHAPTER SEVENTEEN

Over the next hour, Sarah Jennifer told Sylvia about the journey that had resulted in her meeting Esme and everything that had happened in the year since.

Sylvia peppered Sarah Jennifer with questions about the twist on Kurtherian technology that had resulted in witches and teased her mercilessly about their connection to Brutus and her experiences of being a pack leader.

She listened with amazement to Sarah Jennifer's description of Lilith while they ate the fresh-baked bread with apple butter. "I feel a lot better about your chances, knowing you're not doing this alone. An alien trapped inside a mountain, huh? That's something."

Sarah Jennifer grinned. "You don't say. Oh, and I can do this…"

Sylvia made the appropriate noises of amazement when Sarah Jennifer made her eyes glow. "They're different than Mom's," she remarked, which led to more catching up on what Sylvia knew about their family.

Sarah Jennifer was surprised to hear that Kailin had

chosen to go to space. "What about Chicago?" she asked with growing concern. "I'm counting on not having to go all the way to the Alameda shipyard. I need the equipment to convert four vehicles on power packs, for a start. And a whole bunch of power packs. Some decent weaponry wouldn't go amiss either if it can be sourced."

Sylvia sighed, seeing their grandfather's determination in Sarah Jennifer's scowl. "You're set on this, aren't you?"

Sarah Jennifer nodded solemnly. "I am. Who else would be stubborn enough to step up and force the Unknown-World to unite? Without me, it's bye-bye, humanity. If the Weres and the witches go back to feuding, the leeches will continue to deplete the world of the only people who can defend the people from the Madness until a fix is found."

Sylvia went to the cupboard beneath the stairs and brought out a briefcase. She opened it and showed Sarah Jennifer the screen and keyboard inside. "I think you need this more than I do."

Sarah Jennifer looked at the device with curiosity. "What is it?"

"It's an interstellar communicator," Sylvia told her. "Uncle Ted built it. I'm thinking maybe the right thing to do is call our grandparents and have them fix this."

Sarah Jennifer closed the briefcase, shaking her head resolutely. "They have their own war to fight. It's our responsibility to make sure they have a home to come back to when they're done saving it from whatever's out there. I'll call them when this is over."

Sylvia dropped her head back and grunted with annoyance. "Ugh! Why do you have to be so damn noble all the time?" She gave Sarah Jennifer a put-upon look and flounced out of the kitchen. "Come on, then, if you're so determined to be the hero."

"Where are you going?" Sarah Jennifer called.

Sylvia paused at the door. "Forget Chicago," she told Sarah Jennifer with a scowl. "I have what you need. When I found out that Kailin had been run out of his own business, I got a touch of that righteous determination you and the colonel are so fond of. I went to Alameda and blew the shit out of the factory."

Sarah Jennifer did a double-take. "You did *what*?"

Sylvia shrugged. "It was personal. Our family built that place from nothing, and those scumbags took it by force. I haven't forgotten my training, even if I live a more peaceful life these days." She grinned at Sarah Jennifer's open-mouthed disbelief. "What? I can't get annoyed?"

She told Sarah Jennifer about the raid while she led the way to the rear of her property. "I didn't just barge in there, thinking to break my foot off in someone's ass. I moved there, got myself a job in the factory, and worked out the lay of things before I made a plan. I didn't blow it up until I'd had the opportunity to steal everything that wasn't nailed down."

Sarah Jennifer was impressed. "Fair enough. It's what they deserved."

Sylvia produced a key and ducked between the trunks of a stand of pine trees to the outbuilding nestled out of sight behind them. "This is where I stored everything."

Sarah Jennifer drew in a breath as Sylvia opened the outbuilding door and ushered her into a room stacked with crates of varying sizes. "How long did you spend sneaking this stuff out?"

Sylvia grinned, leaning against a crate with her arms folded. "I triggered a spillage that was lethal to the humans, which gave me the time. I got most of this stuff out over the space of a week." Her grin morphed into a scowl. "I would have had longer if they hadn't been so damned keen to get the factory up and running again."

"The nerve!" Sarah Jennifer sympathized dryly.

Sylvia shot her a grin. "I know, right? Come on, let's get you equipped to take on the world."

Sarah Jennifer let Sylvia's snark slide off. There was a time when her sister's flair for the dramatic would have driven her to snap back, but she found that time had made what was once unbearable feel comforting. "I thought you weren't on board with this?"

Sylvia snorted. "I'm on board with you *surviving* this. You might be humanity's golden hope, but I don't have to like it."

"That's good enough for me," Sarah Jennifer conceded. She indicated the treasure trove with a hand. "This is beyond anything I could have expected. Thank you, Sylvie."

"You're going to need help getting this stuff back," Sylvia told her shortly. "Stack what you're taking with you outside the door while I bring the truck around. I don't need it until late spring, and it's sitting idle."

"Will you come with me to Salem?" Sarah Jennifer asked.

"No." Sylvia smiled. "You can send that cousin of ours to bring it back once you've freed the prisoners."

"Are you sure?" Sarah Jennifer asked, knowing her sister would refuse the offer. She had to try. "It's going to get hairy once I take down the blood trade. Worse if the Madness gets to America before I can stop it."

Sylvia shook her head, smiling while she held back tears of pride. "My home is here. Go, save the world. I'll be here to throw you a party when you're done."

"I hate parties," Sarah Jennifer retorted.

Sylvia grinned. "I know. That's exactly why I'm going to throw one for you." She hugged Sarah Jennifer. "I have something else for you, so you don't forget us while you're saving the world."

Sarah Jennifer followed her back into the house. "You're not exactly forgettable. I just have to look in a mirror, and there you are."

Sylvia hunted through the coat stand, ignoring her sister's teasing. "I mean all of us," she clarified, pulling out a camo jacket.

Sarah Jennifer's mouth fell open. "Is that TH's jacket?"

Sylvia nodded. "Mom was wearing it when she visited. She forgot about it, I guess. Their alien friend hurt himself jumping out of their ship, and she was pretty wrapped up in healing him."

She held it out. "Try it on."

Sarah Jennifer nodded and slipped her arms into fabric that had been softened by time. She laughed softly. "I'm an idiot."

"Well, yeah, but why are *you* saying it?" Sylvia asked.

Sarah Jennifer stroked the jacket. "Would you laugh at me if I told you I've been getting through this on autopilot? Reach goal X to make goal Y possible, rinse, repeat, without allowing myself to remember how it affected TH when we lost someone. I never saw myself as a leader. Or so I thought."

"Are you kidding? Sylvia contended. "You were made for this. Why do you think he pushed you so hard?"

"Training is one thing," Sarah Jennifer told her. "Putting it into practice is agonizing. I'm taking my people's lives into my hands and pitting them against the worst thing this world has ever seen. It might not be the zombie apocalypse, but it's going to look a hell of a lot like it." She threw her arms around Sylvia and squeezed tightly. "Thank you. You've given me the strength I need to remember that we can survive loss."

Sylvia returned Sarah Jennifer's hug with feeling. "We can survive anything. We're Waltons, dammit!"

Sarah Jennifer swallowed the lump in her throat. "You're right. This connection to TH means so much. He always knew I could do more, and I'm ready to prove I'm worthy of his belief in me. I want to call him, but I won't. Not until I can tell him I'm everything he ever hoped I'd be. But first, I'm getting my dumbasses back."

Sylvia raised an eyebrow. "No Were left behind, huh?"

Sarah Jennifer shook her head. "Not on my watch."

Canada-Maine Border

Shelley Babcock skipped along the road with her foraging basket swinging in time to her song. Her mama was going to be *so* happy about the nuts she'd found in a squirrel hole in the trees beneath the mountain. They were frozen, of course, but the freeze had come quickly this year, preserving the tasty treats instead of causing them to rot.

She felt bad for the squirrel that had worked to gather the nuts, but Mama had told her the squirrels had so many hidey-holes that they often forgot about them. They needed the food. Their goat herd had shrunk considerably this winter.

Shelley wondered if Brad would be around to play when she got home. She liked Brad. They were the only children in the town who were too young to go on the hunt with the adults, so they'd formed a strong bond over the years. She saw her mama smiling at them sometimes, a strange smile that she thought was as sad as it was happy. Who knew what went through grown-ups' minds?

She left the forest and made her way into the open area the people in her town had cleared around their homes. Still skipping, still singing, she was unaware of the other person sharing her space.

A rustle made her look around. Shelley smiled when she saw it was Brad. There were wolves, bears, and even the occasional big cat in the forest. Her friend was a sight for sore eyes.

Shelley waited for Brad to catch up. "Are you hurt?" she asked when he got closer, seeing he was walking with a lurch. "I'll get your parents."

She hesitated when Brad didn't reply. "Brad?"

Brad continued his odd gait, getting closer to Shelley. He let out a moan.

Shelley didn't like the shiver that ran down her spine. "Brad, stop it! You're scaring me." Her instinct told her to run, but this was her friend.

Brad came within arm's reach, and Shelley saw his eyes. His *glowing red* eyes.

Brad let out another moan, and the foliage around the tree line shivered.

Shelly's eyes darted between Brad and the rabbits that emerged from the forest. "Brad, what's happening?" she cried, letting out a shocked screamlet as she stumbled away from the red-eyed rabbits. "Brad? What happened to you? Brad! Talk to me!"

Brad grabbed her arms and leaned in as if to whisper.

Shelley's next scream was choked by the blood that gushed from her neck when Brad bit her. She fought his grip, but he was stronger than Shelley's daddy, and she couldn't escape.

She kicked Brad away and ran for home, feeling dizzier with every step. She was almost in sight of her house when she fell to the ground, weak from blood loss.

Shelly tried to call for her mama, but all that came out was a gurgling whisper. She forced herself to keep moving, crawling up the street. Where was everybody?

She remembered as if from a distance. The hunt.

Shelley was tired. So tired. Perhaps if she rested here…

She jerked awake as something brushed her face.

"Mama?" She blinked, not understanding the patchwork of furry bodies in her blurry vision.

Shelly's heart mercifully stalled as the rabbits surrounded her. Her final sensation was of being covered by a soft blanket as she breathed her last.

The town's adults returned from their hunt to find Shelley's body five meters from her front door. The cause of death was quickly confirmed as a rabbit attack.

Fearing rabies, the town's leaders decided the only way to deal with it was a cull of the local rabbit population. Meanwhile, Shelley's family took her body home, and her father and brother took their shovels out to the town's cemetery.

Shelley's mother cried herself to sleep that night, knowing the men wouldn't return until they'd cut through the frozen ground. She awoke in the dark, hearing someone moving around in the kitchen. "Ned, is that you?"

She went to investigate, calling her husband's name again. Deciding it must be an animal gotten in, she grabbed the broom as she entered the kitchen. The pantry was open.

Grasping her broom, she marched over to the pantry door, intending to scare the animal out before it devoured what little food they had stored.

She dropped her broom when she saw her daughter— her deceased daughter—sitting cross-legged on the stone floor, gnawing on a joint of raw venison. "Shelley?"

Shelley's head jerked up at the sound of her name, her eyes fixing on her mother. She smiled, blood running down her chin to match the glow in her eyes.

Shelley's mother screamed.

<h1 style="text-align:center">CHAPTER EIGHTEEN</h1>

<u>Salem, MA</u>

Sarah Jennifer drove into Salem midmorning with her mood lifted by her time with Sylvia. She was met at the boundary hex by Esme and Brutus.

"You two want a ride?" she called out the window as she pulled up at the standing stones.

"Don't get comfortable," she told Brutus when he jumped into the back of the truck with the crates. "We're heading straight out as soon as I've dropped this load off for Jim and requisitioned what we need to live off the land for a week."

Esme got in beside Sarah Jennifer. "You could take a day to rest up before heading out again."

Sarah Jennifer adjusted her grip on the wheel and put her foot down. "World's not going to save itself. I want those vehicles operational, the Weres out of the prison, and a ride to Europe. Not too much to ask, is it?"

Esme chuckled. "One step at a time. We're not going in the direction of the forge."

Sarah Jennifer shook her head. "No, we're heading to Requisitions first. I don't want to leave every piece of space-age technology we have in the hands of anyone except Big Ace. He'll inventory everything and give Jim what he needs."

Esme and Brutus headed in separate directions when Sarah Jennifer let them out in front of the town hall. She drove around to the Stores entrance and located Big Ace, who was only too happy to personally pull the list of supplies Sarah Jennifer gave him while his brother supervised the unloading of the truck.

"I'm not exactly sure what's here," she told him. "Not all of the crates are labeled. Get Jim down here to help you identify everything for the inventory."

Big Ace breathed a sigh of relief. "I appreciate that, Major."

Sarah Jennifer grinned. "Hey, this stuff is based on alien technology, okay? Jim might not know what he's dealing with either, but he's the engineer, so we go with what he can figure out. He has free rein until my bus is ready."

Big Ace nodded firmly. "If you say so, Major."

Sarah Jennifer stayed for a few more minutes to check in with them. Both brothers flashed wide grins at her inquiry as to how they were settling into Salem.

"I like it here," Little Ace told her. "I've been talking to this historian guy who thinks he knows where we can find a pre-WWDE weapons stash."

Sarah Jennifer patted his shoulder. "Sounds like something worth investigating even if it turns out to be a shot in the dark. Keep up the good work."

Little Ace nodded. "I will. It feels good to be an active

part of something instead of doing nothing but hide in the forest, wondering what bad thing is going to happen next. You've given us structure and a code to live by."

"I like not worrying about Mom," Big Ace supplied. "Did you know we have family here? Humans, but still blood. She's staying with them."

His attention was caught by one of the privates walking past with a pistol shoved in the back of her belt. "Excuse me, Major," he told Sarah Jennifer. "I need to educate Green on why carrying her weapon safely is conducive to her continued ability to claim she has two ass cheeks. I'll send someone to look for you when we're done."

Sarah Jennifer waved the offer away with a smile. "That's okay. I'll be back." She took a crate of power packs and left them to their tasks. It would be a few hours before she and Brutus could depart, so she headed over to Jim Johnson's in the truck to see how he was getting on with the bus.

The property looked empty when she arrived, but the ringing of a hammer on metal assured her otherwise. She went around the cabin and into the barn that served as Jim's workshop, leaving the mid-sized crate on the only bench with enough clear space to hold it.

Sarah Jennifer found Jim at his forge, working on a long piece of metal with total concentration while Carver assisted him. She leaned against the doorframe and waited until he broke to quench the object before waving to catch his attention.

Jim lifted a hand to return her greeting. "Major, you're back."

Ignoring his statement of the obvious, Sarah Jennifer

indicated the workshop with a finger. "I brought the power packs."

Jim's eyes widened. "Give me a few minutes." He joined Sarah Jennifer after putting his tools down and giving Carver instructions to eat and rest. "You want to see how the bus is coming along?"

Sarah Jennifer led the way back through the workshop to the covered patio, pausing to grab the crate as they went. She tried to see the finished bus in the skeletal frame and the panels and assortment of parts organized on the ground around it. "Jim?"

Jim laughed at her skeptical look. "It looks like this until the last day of the build, then…" He made the sound of an explosion, assisting the effect with a flourish of his hands. "She's a beast. See all those spikes? They're part of the armor, which I have the pack coming over to help me fit tomorrow."

Sarah Jennifer decided to wait for the final result before passing judgment. She placed her case on a workbench made from two stepladders and a length of wood and opened it. "I brought you twenty power packs."

Jim plucked one of the power packs from the crate and inspected the smooth metallic tablet from all angles. "How does it connect to the engines?"

Sarah Jennifer took him out to Sylvia's truck and showed him the engine. "It doesn't connect to the current engine," she told him. "You'll have to convert it. If you put off the pack to visit with Big Ace, he has all the components you need to build a new engine in the crates I brought back from my sister's, along with weapons and other useful stuff."

Jim put the power pack back in the crate and scratched his chin in consideration. "For a start, the replacements are motors, not engines." Seeing Sarah Jennifer wasn't bothered by the distinction, he rolled his eyes. "Maybe this isn't the best use for something so valuable. Maybe these packs would be better used to power the expansion of the town."

Sarah Jennifer grinned. "I brought back at least six cases of them. Trust me, I'll be speaking to the council about the coming expansion. This rescue is the priority."

Jim nodded. "I'm not suggesting otherwise, but wouldn't you rather I put my effort into making as much biofuel as I can before you leave instead of risking the lives of those people on the chance I don't mess this up?"

Sarah Jennifer frowned. "I don't want to hear that kind of talk from you, Jim Johnson. Who taught you everything you know about mechanics?"

Jim hesitated. "Well, I learned from books. From tinkering and the mistakes I made."

Sarah Jennifer folded her arms, increasing the intensity of the hairy eyeball she was giving him. "So, what makes you think you can't figure this out?"

Jim wilted, unable to decide why he found her scowl so adorable. "You're a good girl, Major."

Sarah Jennifer raised an eyebrow. "Lieutenant, I'm at least twice your age."

Jim lifted his hands. "What can I say? You're cute as a button when you're angry, and you have a heart of solid gold."

Sarah Jennifer dropped her hands to her hips and started tapping her foot, wishing she had her grandfather's stoicism when she started chuckling along. "I hope not. It'd be a solid pain in the ass to carry around. Jim, you can do this. I know you can. There's no point expanding the town if everyone dies in that prison."

Jim held his hands up in defeat, his laughter coming to an abrupt halt. "Okay, I give. I'm guessing you had a plan in mind when you brought all this space-age tech to me."

Sarah Jennifer nodded to indicate the path to the front of the cabin, and they set off walking. "Sylvia's truck was converted with a custom power pack, but I'm hoping that seeing how it was fitted to the truck will be enough to help you figure a way to fix the bus so she gives us what we need."

"Can you leave it with me so I can take a look in detail?" Jim asked hopefully. "I might have to figure ways to fabricate the components we don't have."

Sarah Jennifer hesitated since the truck wasn't hers to leave, especially not with a man she knew full well was going to dismantle every component of it. "Lieutenant, do I have your promise that it will be put back together again when you're done? Because this is my sister's truck. Trust me when I say that she'll *never* let me forget it if I don't return it in the same condition I borrowed it."

Jim's raucous laugh bubbled up from the bottom of his boots and exploded in peals. "You got me there, Major," he admitted, slapping his leg to try to get himself under control. "If you don't mind me asking, is your sister scarier than you?"

"It depends on your perspective," Sarah Jennifer told him. "Put it this way: if it was a choice between swimming naked in a leech-infested pool every morning for the rest of my life or waking up to Sylvia's patented 'I disapprove but it's not my place to comment' stare every day, I know which I'd choose."

That didn't help Jim one bit. "Major, you're killing me here," he managed between continued outbreaks of chuckles. "I had an aunt just like that, except on family occasions, she'd always overindulge and comment on everything she'd saved up all year."

Sarah Jennifer folded her arms, smiling. "Well, I don't want to kill my only engineer. The pack leaves for Boston in a week, and I'm pretty sure you're still working on our assault vehicle."

Jim glanced at Sarah Jennifer to see if she was joking. Her face confirmed she was not. "A week?"

Sarah Jennifer shrugged without apologizing. "We go as soon as you're done. I'm leaving with Lieutenant Timmons in a couple of hours to do some recon, so that's your week. When we return, it will be with the information we need to storm the prison."

All the humor was gone from Jim's demeanor. He pulled a notebook from his pocket and scribbled a note. "I understand, Major. Bluebird will be ready. I may need as many hands as the pack has over the next few days. That okay by you?"

Sarah Jennifer nodded. "I'll leave a message for the sergeants to expect you. I have to run now." She glanced at the truck. "Keep working on the bus. I'm expecting great things when I get back."

Jim's smile returned, although it was muted, compared to his usual sunny grin. "Before you go. I have something for you." He retrieved a sandalwood case from his "office" and presented it to Sarah Jennifer with the same solemn smile. "These have been in my family for generations. I've maintained them, as did my father and his before him. You get the point."

Sarah Jennifer took the case and opened it carefully. She looked at the matched half-barrel shotguns inside, her heart skipping a beat at the intricate inlays in the grips. They were the most beautiful killing machines she'd seen in her life, but she wasn't doing this for personal gain. "Thank you, Jim, but I can't accept these. They're an heirloom, so they should go to someone in your family."

She bemoaned her refusal internally, her only solace that it was the right thing to do. Her grandfather would approve of the great personal sacrifice she'd just made.

Jim's face firmed as he shook his head. "I haven't got a family. Too long playing in my workshop, and I never settled down and had children. They're yours, Major. I know you'll use them with honor."

Sarah Jennifer allowed herself one more look before closing the case. "I don't know what to say, except thank you."

His voice was gruff as he held out a leather gun belt and a heavy pouch for her to take. "Here. I hope you don't mind that it won't fit when you get wolfy."

Sarah Jennifer took the belt and tried it on, recognizing Sarai's work as she fastened the buckle. "It's a perfect fit." She gave the pouch a little shake. "Ammo?"

Jim nodded and picked up the crate. "Oh, yeah. It's my variation on the scattershot my great-grandpa used to keep the predators away. It's a mix of steel shavings and silver dust. Now get out of here. I can't get the engine stripped out if you're going to stand here jawing for half the day."

Sarah Jennifer chuckled. "You got it. Thank you again, Jim."

She left for town, stopping by the training field to check in with the pack before meeting Brutus at the town hall.

Her cousin was pacing outside the store's entrance when she got there. Brutus hefted two heavy packs, thrusting one at Sarah Jennifer when she arrived. "I thought you said we were in a hurry? I've been waiting here for an hour."

Sarah Jennifer took the pack and slipped her arm through one strap without pausing. "I was with the pack. An Alpha has to keep in touch, you know. I've been gone, so I haven't had the time I would have liked with them."

Brutus chuckled. "Considering your idea of quality time consists of teachable moments strung together with painful reminders of how not to fuck up, they're probably okay with that."

Sarah Jennifer looked over her shoulder as she set off for her office. "Becoming the best doesn't come without a price. I have one more thing to take care of, and then we're good to go."

Brutus followed her through the town hall corridors, grumbling under his breath about Sarah Jennifer always having "one last thing" to do before she was ready as they entered the office.

He dropped onto the chair behind her desk and studied the open map while Sarah Jennifer put the case and the pouch she was carrying down and dashed into the living area.

She returned a minute later with her wolf harness and

her coat. She dropped her coat onto the table and adjusted the straps of the harness to fit her human shape before putting it on and holstering her pistol under her left arm. "So we'll take a straight route until we get to Lowell. Then we cut into the forest, staying close to the road and out of sight until we get to Harvard."

"Nice belt," Brutus commented as she made more adjustments to her harness to get her weapons sitting comfortably against her body. "What's in the case?"

Sarah Jennifer opened the case and lifted the shotguns out. "A gift from Jim Johnson." She handed one shotgun to Brutus while she holstered the other and filled the pockets of her belt, harness, and coat with shells. "Not that I'm going to waste the ammo he gave me. Silver—"

"Is too valuable to waste," Brutus finished with a grin. "I remember." He examined the modified shotgun with care, unable to resist running his fingers over the inlays in the polished wood of the shortened butt. He peered into the barrels and let out a low whistle. "This is a hell of a gift."

Sarah Jennifer nodded, satisfied that she had everything. "Jim is a good man. He's working tirelessly to get the bus ready." She punched Brutus lightly in the shoulder as she accepted her gun back. "You look nervous all of a sudden."

Brutus turned to pick the map up. "Me, nervous? No way. We have a foolproof plan, right?" he grinned as he folded the map and stashed it in the pocket of his utility vest

Sarah Jennifer laughed. "We sure do."

They had gotten no more than five steps from the office when Sarah Jennifer remembered she'd left her garotte in the bathroom. She held up a finger with an apologetic smile as she ran back in. "One *last* last thing."

Brutus laughed. "You want to bring everything you own? I'm all for waiting until you're so weighed down we have to take a vehicle."

Sarah Jennifer and Brutus left Salem in plenty of time to reach the campsite she'd chosen in the forest surrounding Lowell. They had a twelve-hour walk ahead of them, untaxing for the enhanced. Their easy conversation was interspersed sporadically with periods of comfortable silence brought on by the beauty of the land.

"I've never been this far west," Brutus admitted as they followed the ghost of a road enclosed by hundred-year-old pines. He kicked at the carpet of needles. "I thought where we lived was a forest. *This* is a forest."

Sarah Jennifer pointed out the signs of a civilization long gone, thinking that there was a lot to be said for a long walk over a quick car journey. She got to appreciate the land and how it told its story. "This all used to be occupied. The trees didn't waste any time in recovering their space without people to hold them back."

Brutus left the road to examine the ruins up close. "It's hard to believe. The coast and the city are all I've ever known. The old world managed to hang on better there. You said there's likely still an occupied town near the prison?"

Sarah Jennifer nodded. "Yeah, there will be somewhere that the guards and their families live. Chances are it will be near the prison, but far enough out that the guards' families aren't the first victims if there's a breakout.

Harvard was still mostly intact the last time I passed through, we'll start there."

Brutus folded the map and sighed as he returned it to his pocket. "The world is an ugly place. How can anyone go to work at that place all day, then come home at night and kiss their wife and kids goodnight?"

Sarah Jennifer grabbed his arm. "The world is what people make of it. Ugly things are happening, yeah, but we're acting to put a stop to them. Now get your head in the game. We have a job to do."

Brutus nodded. There would be time to figure it out after they'd found out what level of resistance the pack was going to face when they attacked the prison. "I'm ready. How do you want to do this?"

Sarah Jennifer pointed to the pocket on Brutus' vest. "We work our way around the towns on that map until we find the one that's still got people in it. Then we watch from a distance."

CHAPTER NINETEEN

<u>**Harvard, MA (two days later)**</u>

Sarah Jennifer crouched motionless in the shadows of the side street, her body clock ticking patiently through the third hour she'd spent waiting for Brutus to appear.

She was soaked to her skin by the steady sleet, her knee ached like a godforsaken bitch in the windchill, and the last thing her stomach had seen was the remainder of the dried deer meat they'd shared in the ruins of the apartment building they'd slept in last night.

In short, she was cold, wet, as stiff as the two shots of Esme's homebrew she wanted, and hot chow was the *very* last thing she could expect to round the day out. Never mind the lack of progress she and Brutus had made by sticking together on their first day in the town.

None of that was relevant because Brutus was so damned *late*. She didn't know why she'd listened to his idea to split up today. She didn't think he'd be stupid enough to confront any leeches he came across directly, but she was beginning to wonder if he'd fallen prey to a trap.

A movement to Sarah Jennifer's left distracted her from the rabbit hole she was on the brink of falling into. Two teens entered the side street, a girl and a boy. The whites of their eyes were all that showed in the unlit street, but Sarah Jennifer picked out their outlines easily against the glow of the lights in the street beyond.

The girl kept the boy close while they crept between chunks of concrete and rubble piles. Her arm was a frail shield against the night. Nevertheless, her encouragement gave the smaller boy the comfort he needed to keep going.

Sarah Jennifer sniffed the air. Her newfound ability to transform into a wolf gave her senses that were every bit as sharp as the queen of the werewolves'. There was no mistaking that smell. The two children approaching her position were Weres.

She noted their continuous nervous glances and the care they took to make no noise as they placed their steps on the rubble-strewn ground. They clearly knew they were risking everything by being out in the city at night. Shit, everyone from the UnknownWorld knew it wasn't safe to be out in the light of day, never mind after dark.

Sarah Jennifer wanted to know who let their kids be out here at all? If she was a mother…

She pushed the thought away before its barb tore out her heart.

The boy, who Sarah Jennifer noted was very young now she could see him better, stumbled on the swollen asphalt. He dropped his scavenged cans of food, and they clanked along the ground as he landed hard on his hands and knees in the broken street with a sharp cry of frustration and pain.

The girl rushed to silence him, but it was too late.

A menacing chuckle came from nearby.

Sarah Jennifer left the wall, reaching for her guns as she slipped out of the shadows and moved to stand between the children and the three looming silhouettes that appeared in the street behind them.

The children gaped in fear for a split second at the sudden appearance of Sarah Jennifer, then turned to run. They froze again at the sight of the three partially-armored leeches. The boy threw his arms around the girl's waist and began to cry, caught between the strange woman and certain death.

The leeches advanced with their arc-rods spitting electricity at the children.

Sarah Jennifer stalked toward the three men, her coat flying out behind her as she drew the matched set of short-barrel shotguns given to her by Jim. She thought that he'd approve of the first use she'd found for them.

"Hide," she told the children as she strode past them.

She didn't wait to see if they obeyed.

The leader waved his arc-rod at Sarah Jennifer. "Get outta the way, lady. The kid's bleeding money onto the street here."

Sarah Jennifer's objective changed at that moment from saving the children to saving the children and ensuring these three stains on humanity ceased breathing.

She treated the asshole to an inside view of her shotgun barrels in reply.

"Well, well, well." He sneered. "Looks like we have ourselves a concerned citizen, boys." The other two snickered.

"You must be new around here," the leader told Sarah Jennifer. "We run this town, and those kids are nothing but income waiting to be processed with the rest of the dogs."

"They are *people*." Sarah Jennifer's eyes flared red with rage. She fired her left gun, having no patience for further conversation.

Jim's homemade shot fragmented into sharp slivers on impact. The leeches' arc-rods clattered to the ground as they fell, their screams cutting the night.

"Keep it down, will you?" Sarah Jennifer muttered, reloading as she sidestepped to avoid a pile of smashed bricks. "People are trying to sleep, dammit."

The three men apparently had a problem hearing her. Sarah Jennifer remedied the noise pollution problem by emptying her right barrel into the leader's chest. She shook her head at the efforts of the surviving leeches to crawl away while she reloaded.

"You don't threaten children and get to live," she told the survivors as she picked her way through the rubble. This had gone on too long already. She fired point-blank into both their faces while the leader gurgled his last.

She stepped over their steaming corpses and went to look for the children. "Assholes. Suddenly, the stories about Bethany Anne's tendency to foul language make sense."

Where the hell was Brutus?

The scuffs the children had left in the rime of dirty snow coating the sidewalk were easy enough to track. The sleet began to come down harder as Sarah Jennifer took a left out of the side street on the children's trail. She looked around, hoping she caught up with them before the sleet erased their tracks.

A spot of blood at an intersection led her deeper into the ruined part of the town. She hadn't come this far to be put off by a challenge. Another blood spot on a rusted mailbox confirmed she was still on the trail a few blocks later. She spied a fresh print in the slushy dirt as she passed an abandoned strip mall and noted the change in direction the children had taken. A glance across the overgrown former parking lot gave her the choice of a convenience store, a nail salon, a gas station, and a glass-fronted office building.

Her eye was drawn by a glint of yellow light inside the single-story office building.

"Got you," Sarah Jennifer murmured.

"Got who?" Brutus asked.

Sarah Jennifer wheeled around, annoyed that she hadn't heard him approach. "Brutus! Where have you been?"

Brutus pointed at a building on the other side of the parking lot. "There was a couple of leeches—"

"Never mind." Sarah Jennifer started in the direction of the office building. "I stopped a trio of leeches from attacking some kids. That's who I've found. Come on."

Without waiting for a reply, she set off at a contained run for the door where she'd seen Were eyes glowing. It was hanging off its hinges, making it no challenge to enter the abandoned building.

Brutus sighed and followed her inside. "That's what I was trying to tell you," he whispered as they walked through the unlit hall. "I'm late because—"

Sarah Jennifer turned and glared at him. "Your excuses for keeping me waiting for almost four hours can wait. There are children in danger."

Brutus narrowed his eyes, annoyed at being cut off twice in as many minutes. He half-bowed with a flourish of his hand toward the office building. "Fine. Lead the way, O Mighty Alpha."

Sarah Jennifer had more important things on her mind than Brutus' hurt feelings. She *had* to find those children. "Stay alert. They're around here somewhere."

They moved silently through the offices while Sarah Jennifer searched for the children. Brutus ambled along behind her, wondering how long he should let her search this place before he told her that he knew exactly where the kids were.

Sarah Jennifer reached the back of the building and went out the door. She frowned when all she found was a tatty fence separating the building from the alley out back.

Brutus came to stand beside her and folded his arms. "You done?"

Sarah Jennifer ducked into the alley and looked both ways before turning to Brutus with her shoulders slumped. "Yeah, I guess so. I just can't stand the thought of children out there, alone and afraid. You didn't see them, Brutus. Where are their parents?"

"In the prison," Brutus replied to Sarah Jennifer's complete confusion.

Sarah Jennifer looked at him skeptically. "How can you possibly know that?"

"Because I saved a kid from a couple of leeches and she

took me to meet the others," Brutus informed her with a smug grin. "That's what you get for being an ass. Are you ready to listen to where I've been all day?"

Sarah Jennifer shrugged. "Sure, go ahead. But I'm not staying in this trashy alley with my stomach complaining that my throat's been cut. Let's go and find somewhere warm and dry where we can get something to eat."

Brutus nodded. "Sounds like a plan, and I know just the place." He set off for the end of the alley, pausing to look back when he realized Sarah Jennifer hadn't moved. "Well, do you want to meet those kids or not?"

He led Sarah Jennifer a couple of blocks before taking a right into a dead-end street. "This way," he told her, bending to lift a grate.

They dropped into the dry concrete tunnel below, and Brutus indicated the right-hand path with a nod. "The kids followed their parents here after their town was raided by the leeches," he explained as they made their way through the tunnel system. "They realized pretty soon that not only were they not going to be able to free the adults, but they'd also put themselves at risk of being caught and locked up with them if they tried. They stumbled on these maintenance tunnels while looking for somewhere to hide and have been here since."

Sarah Jennifer absorbed the information without taking her attention off their environment. The tunnel system was dry, at least. It had power, as evidenced by the lights and the clean air coming from the vents. It wasn't even that cold down here. Still, it wasn't anyplace kids should be living.

Brutus halted at a locked door. He looked at the camera set into the wall above and waved. "Lucy, kids? It's me, Brutus. I brought my Alpha to help like I said I would."

Sarah Jennifer smiled and made her eyes glow for the camera.

The door clunked and clicked, then opened, revealing four boys no older than fifteen standing there with metal bars gripped ready to use if they were being tricked.

"What kind of Were has red eyes?" one of the boys demanded, clutching his weapon.

Sarah Jennifer found it difficult to maintain her exterior calm in the face of the children's bravery. "The one who's going to get your parents back," she swore, her heart breaking for these children who lived ready to die.

They needed a savior. All she could offer them was a home and the means to save themselves.

She sidestepped Brutus and gave the boys her most honest smile. It was not the warmest, she knew. The fire never completely left her eyes, but her smile told the recipient that she cared despite not being anyone to mess with. "Good to meet you all. My name is Major Sarah Jennifer Walton. Who do I have the pleasure of talking to?"

The boys stared at her in awe, their Were instincts telling them that this woman was to be obeyed. They mumbled their names, dropping their guards as Sarah Jennifer shook each of their hands in turn.

Sarah Jennifer repeated their names to sear them into her memory. "Jake, Luke, Benjamin, and Tyler, huh? Brutus tells me that your parents were taken by the leeches."

Benjamin was the only one who wasn't rendered

speechless by the pretty lady with the aura of a warrior. "Brutus told *us* that you're the leader of his pack, and you're going to break into the prison and get everyone out."

"That's why we're here," Sarah Jennifer confirmed. "To gather information that will help us succeed."

Luke leaned in to whisper to Jake, who nodded and spoke up. "We should do this in the den. We'll only have to repeat it all for the others."

Benjamin and Tyler agreed, and they led Sarah Jennifer and Brutus into their inner sanctum. Far from the miserable hovel Sarah Jennifer had expected from children left alone, the tunnel opened into a large, bright space hung with thick fabric and artwork in fancy frames. The children were dressed in rags, but artfully so. She heard laughter, and none of them looked malnourished.

The boys scattered to spread the news of their arrival. Brutus excused himself to go check on the child he'd saved earlier, leaving Sarah Jennifer with Benjamin.

Benjamin grinned and waved for Sarah Jennifer to follow him. "Let me show you around."

Everywhere Sarah Jennifer looked, there were children busy working on things necessary for the improvement of their living situation. Benjamin guided her through a part of the room where a few of the younger children were being taught how to weave winter blankets by a girl of around thirteen.

"How long have you been here?" she asked Benjamin.

"I don't know. A couple of years?" he replied casually. "We do okay as long as we avoid the people in the town.

These tunnels let out in a few different places. It's not hard to get food at night when everyone is asleep."

Sarah Jennifer stopped to stare at a group of statues placed aesthetically in front of the dividing wall, which was made of yet more fabric. "I see you've been picking up more than food."

Benjamin grinned. "There's a ton of abandoned buildings in this town. Treasure-hunting gives us something to do besides looking for food and taking care of the little ones."

Sarah Jennifer chuckled. "I like it as a pastime. You kids have a certain style."

Brutus returned with three children in tow. "Major, I'd like you to meet Lucy, Janie, and Kyle."

Sarah Jennifer recognized Janie and Kyle from the side street encounter. "Good to see you two are okay," she told them sincerely. "You had me worried out there."

Kyle giggled. "Lady, I thought you were gonna *eat* us." He squinted at Sarah Jennifer, considering her for a moment. "You don't look so scary now."

Sarah Jennifer rubbed her stomach. "I don't know, I could eat," she teased, drawing more giggles from Kyle. She wasn't prepared for the boy dashing over and wrapping his arms around her waist.

"Thank you for saving us," he told her in a tight voice.

Janie nodded and offered a small smile, more reserved than her brother. "Yeah, thank you."

Sarah Jennifer shook her head. "You don't need to thank me. I'm here because my pack is going to put an end to that prison."

She waved her hands for quiet when the children

moved in, all asking questions at once. "Please. I don't have all the answers yet. One thing I can say for sure is that it's not safe for you to stay here any longer. I want you all to come with me to Salem, where you'll be taken care of until we can reunite you with your parents."

Sarah Jennifer waited anxiously for an answer. She expected some resistance. After all, they had put so much effort into their home here, and would they want to leave with strangers?

"Why do you think everyone is so busy?" Lucy asked with a grin. "Brutus told us Salem would be safer for us. We'll be ready to go by tomorrow morning."

Sarah Jennifer pulled Brutus aside as the children left to return to their preparations. "What did you say to them earlier today? I wasn't expecting them to just agree to change their location."

Brutus put a steady hand on Sarah Jennifer's shoulder. "I told them the truth. That we won't stop until everyone behind bars is free. I promised we would make the leeches pay for what they've done. I reminded them what it is to be taken care of, like they should be. Of having food and shelter provided, and adults to turn to when they need something. A few of the older ones argued for being part of the fight. I told them if they still think they can contribute after seeing the pack in action, they're welcome to join the training and prove they deserve a place there."

Sarah Jennifer patted his shoulder in return, grateful for his good heart and level head. "Well, thank you. We should get some rest soon. We have...how many kids to supervise on the hike?"

"Almost forty," Brutus replied. "I can't see it's going to be a challenge. They're good kids."

Sarah Jennifer gave Brutus a knowing smile as she walked past him to investigate what was cooking in the food preparation area. "Let's see if you're still saying that this time tomorrow."

CHAPTER TWENTY

<u>**Lowell, MA**</u>

Twenty-four hours after they'd left Harvard, Brutus was eating his words.

He muttered to himself while he searched the forest for the team of older kids Sarah Jennifer had sent for firewood. He silently cursed his naïveté as he followed the trail left by their crashing progress toward the water.

He found them by the river, unharmed but naked, having decided to abandon their haul of firewood to go skinny-dipping in the moonlight.

Brutus wasn't the type to lose his temper. He picked his way carefully over to where the teens had abandoned their clothing and gathered up every item before extracting himself with the same care and making his way back to camp.

He made a beeline for the fifth and smallest lean-to and crouched to get eye-to-eye with Sarah Jennifer. "I've got something to show you."

Sarah Jennifer raised an eyebrow when Brutus dropped

the pile of jeans and sweaters at her feet. "Dereliction of duty, I see." She winked at Brutus' grin. "I can give them a break this once."

Brutus smirked and nodded. "Doesn't mean I'm not going to give them shit about it. This time they're not in any danger, but they can't think it's safe for them to run around in the wilderness without a thought."

Sarah Jennifer dipped her head. "True. They're all okay?"

Brutus nodded. "They'll be back soon enough."

Forty-five minutes later, six sorry-looking wolves loped into camp. Every one of them had their tail between their legs while they walked up to retrieve their clothing from Brutus.

"Be quick getting dressed," Brutus ordered as they skulked back to the trees to change. "We need to have a conversation."

The teens returned in human form a few minutes later, looking no less sheepish than they had coming into camp.

"Don't look at me like that," Brutus told them. "I'm not here to punish you kids for having fun. Stupid punishes itself, which is what would have happened if one of you had gotten hurt out there and died. What are we supposed to tell your parents? 'Sorry, we saved you, but your kid died dicking around in a river at night.' You see the problem with that, right?"

The teens looked at each other and found no argument with Brutus' chastisement. They apologized for worrying him and Sarah Jennifer and headed for their respective shelters.

Sarah Jennifer settled in by the fire to take first watch

once the children were asleep. Brutus dropped a blanket on the ground beside the log she was using as a seat and lay down facing her. "I take back everything that I said about kids being easy," he told her, keeping his voice low. "Even the good ones are a handful."

Sarah Jennifer chuckled, looking up at the stars. "Sleep. We have a long day ahead tomorrow."

Brutus wriggled to get his feet a bit closer to the fire. "And the day after that, and on and on."

The major chuckled. "My grandfather told me that when Bethany Anne stepped up, her people swore to follow her for eternity. How does that sound?"

"Like I should have taken my chances in New York with my mom," Brutus shot back, deadpan.

Sarah Jennifer poked him with her foot. "Asshole."

Brutus grinned. "What's that? Ms. 'I Don't Tolerate Poor Language' is lowering her standards?"

Sarah Jennifer snorted softly. "What can I say? There's something about the company I've been keeping that leaves me no choice but to find a way to let off steam."

Brutus was quiet for a moment. "What's next, SJ?"

"We deliver the kids to Salem and get ready to hit the prison," Sarah Jennifer replied.

"I don't mean *next*," Brutus told her. "I mean, when we've freed the Weres and stopped the Madness. We might not have eternity since we're not fancy-ass vamps, but we have hundreds of years ahead of us, and you're not the sitting still type."

Sarah Jennifer ruminated on the question for a moment. "I haven't thought that far ahead," she answered eventually. "Would the pack follow me to space? I don't know if I could take them away from everything they know. I don't think I could force that choice on anyone, least of all you."

Brutus half-sat up and punched Sarah Jennifer in the leg. "Who's a dumbass now? We're family. Where you go, I go. As for the pack, I can't see you forcing a choice on anyone. If we're meant to go to space, then that's where we'll end up. Together."

Salem, MA

Esme was woken up by an acute sense of something being out of place. She sat up in bed as she realized it was the barrier hex alerting her to impending danger. Her connection was only triggered by one thing.

Unsanctioned nanocytes traveling toward the nanocytes blanketing the town.

While her recent modifications had allowed her to extend both the range and the sensitivity of the barrier, Esme knew there was no time to waste speculating about whether it was another Were pack, leeches, or worse.

She closed her eyes and reached out with her mind. *Lilith, are you there?*

Lilith's voice came through faint but stable. *It is as we feared,* she began without preamble. *The infected have made it over the land bridge from Siberia. They followed the coast down from Canada, infecting every living being along the way.*

Where are they now? Esme asked. *No, wait. Why am I only just hearing about this? Why didn't you contact me sooner?*

I expended too much of my energy reserve activating Sarah

Jennifer's nanocytes to make a connection to you, Lilith admitted.

Are you in danger? Esme asked immediately, concerned.

No. My power source will replenish itself over time, but I cannot risk being shut down. Lilith paused. *My concern is that it might be too late to prevent the spread of the Madness.*

Then we need to make this quick, Esme told her, hastily moving the pieces on her mental chessboard as she spoke. *I know just maintaining the connection is taking some juice. Where are the Mad? How many?*

I cannot say how many, Lilith replied, *but I can sense a mass traveling toward Salem from the north.*

Maine, then. I'll be in touch. Reserve your energy. Esme got out of bed and dressed in a hurry, wishing she could speak mind-to-mind with Sarah Jennifer and warn her.

They were lucky to have avoided the Madness for this long. Everything at the top of the world was gone, buried under the meters-thick ice shelf. The route from Eurasia was not easy, but it was there.

For now. When this was over, she intended to get the more troublesome witches out of her hair and give them a dose of reality at the same time. Sarah Jennifer would likely be amenable to sending a unit of Weres with them for protection. She wasn't the only one with troublemakers in the ranks.

Esme left her house, where she found Annie and Sarai about to enter the front gate. "Good. You're here. Saves me the bother of coming to find you."

Annie's red ringlets were in disarray. "Esme! You felt it too?" She pulled her long coat tighter around her body to cover her nightdress when the wind whipped through. "I didn't even stop to get dressed, just grabbed Tom's coat and my shoes."

Esme nodded, shooing them along the road toward the town common. "I couldn't miss it. There's something big coming."

"Did you ask Lilith what it is?" Sarai asked.

"The Mad," Esme stated. "That's who's coming. Lilith was able to tell me they've made it as close as Maine."

Annie wrung her hands, hustling to keep up with Esme. "We need to gather the rest of the council and wake the pack."

Esme didn't pause in her stride. "We can do that on the way to the lookout. There's still an opportunity to halt the spread, even if we can't wipe it out completely."

"What do you mean?" Sarai asked. "How can we stop them?"

Esme quit walking and grasped Sarai's arm. "By using the gifts we were blessed with. It's going to take everything we have, but Lilith told me they're sticking to the coast. It gives us a chance."

Lenore walked out of the shadow of her house. "A chance?"

Esme filled Lenore in as the four women walked together with determination to the common, where they came across Ozzie making preparations for the next day's training.

"What's going on?" he asked as the women walked by. He cursed on hearing their reason for being out in the middle of the night, then apologized for cursing as he fumbled his radio.

"What are your orders for the pack, ma'am?" he asked Esme.

Esme frowned. "What do you mean?"

"The major and Brutus aren't here," he replied. "That leaves you in charge of the Defense Force, ma'am."

"You can start by getting everyone with magic up to the lookout," Esme told him. "The rest of you stay on alert, but don't leave the safety of the barrier. The pack can't confront the Mad. We don't know what the corruption would do to your nanocytes."

Lenore volunteered to stay with Ozzie and get the Defense Force ready for battle, promising to send the magic users to the lookout. "My mind magic won't be any help against the mindless." She steered Ozzie toward the town hall while Esme, Annie, and Sarai continued on.

They climbed the hill to the stone circle, passing around the cold, rocky fingers on their way to the magic-made ridge that looked out over the land to the north of Salem.

Sarai was quiet until they reached the trees. "If it's as bad as Lilith says, it's going to require a serious amount of magic to take them out."

Esme led them through the oaks and up the grassy incline to where they could see the land open out beneath the ridge. "It won't be the first time we've shaped the land to protect ourselves."

The moon was thin, and the sky was blanketed with snow clouds desperate to shed their load. Nevertheless, they saw a faint red light moving in the far distance.

Annie scoffed, recalling the gargantuan effort of raising the land to put the town on high ground. "We did this slowly, and we were out of it for days afterward. Look out there, Esme. We have hours at the most before they reach New Hampshire, then they have a straight shot to Salem."

Esme closed her eyes and wished there was another way. Any other way. "We have time, but not much. We have to act swiftly and with mercy for the living. Diverting the Mad from Salem isn't our concern. The barrier will deflect them. We have to take whatever measures are necessary to prevent them from dispersing inland and spreading the Madness."

"What about the people?" Sarai whispered. "We can't just…"

"We might have to. If we can't stop the Mad, the people are as good as dead anyway." Esme looked out into the night, rubbing her suddenly slick palms against her coat. The sweat was warm, like the blood she would have on her hands before the night was done. There was no way to save everyone. "Don't despair just yet. Maine is lost, but we might be able to save New Hampshire."

Sarai swallowed, too afraid to speak as she lost track of the red light moving along the beach, miles away across the wastes and in the abandoned town to the north. Her heart sank when she realized that the breaks in the lights were caused by the Mad being hidden by tracts of forest.

"The Mad are coming," Annie whispered, taking her daughter's hand. "It's really happening. But we are witches, and we are equal to this, my love."

Sarai's jaw clenched as she lifted her chin, letting her anger wash out her fear. "Let them come. We're ready."

"Yes, we are," Esme agreed. "Ladies, we have work to do."

The horizon paled as they prepared for what was to come. Esme wished for it to remain dark so tracking the speed of the Mad would be as simple as following the light of their eyes. However, she wasn't about to let a little thing like not being able to see the approaching horde stop her.

"Where is that woman?" Esme grumbled, thinking about Sarah Jennifer as she knelt to place her hands on the loose dirt near the edge. She knelt and asked the earth to open to her. "Ready?"

Thunder rumbled overhead at Annie's command. "You bet your ass I am."

Sarai nodded, plunging her hands into the earth beside Esme. The three women connected to the nanocytes that saturated everything and reached toward the Mad.

Esme sent her awareness out over the miles, past Sarai's thorn wall, past the surrounding towns until she felt the land recoiling at the contamination of the Mad. She felt Sarai's efforts to turn the plants and trees into snares and nets to slow the advancing horde, but it wasn't going to be enough.

Annie scrunched her nose in disapproval. "Let's see what we can do about blocking them." She released the energy overhead, and the heavens opened.

Esme drew back and opened her awareness to encompass the coast from Portsmouth to Portland. All the people living there were at risk of being lost if they couldn't step it up and do something to halt the Mad.

Annie concentrated the weather system she'd created on the forest, pounding the trees with lightning to destroy the paths the Mad were on. "If I burn it all, it will take half a century to recover," she fretted.

Esme nodded. "I think we can do better than that." She clenched her hands in the dirt, then opened them again, visualizing lower Maine being washed clean. "Hold on, this is going to get shaky!"

The reaction along the coastline was too large for the women to take in at once. The ocean was sucked back and the seabed shifted, throwing up miles of cliffs as lava spewed out of the cracks that formed by the sudden shift in the Earth's crust.

The ridge shook while the land heaved to fulfill Esme's wish.

Esme wondered for a moment if she'd gone too far, but it was too late to do anything except look down from high ground she'd created with her own hands and watch the low ground drown in a flood of her making.

"That salt is going to be a nightmare to get out of the dirt," Annie complained, watching the tops of the trees reappear as the water receded.

Esme shook her head. "It's not enough. We're going to lose it all."

"What do you mean?" Sarai asked. "We can restore the land. We don't have to lose the forest."

Esme swept a hand out over the ridge at the glow in the distance. It was reduced by some, but not much. "The flood wasn't enough. Thousands of them were aware enough to grab a tree. We can't save everyone."

Sarai moaned when she looked out and saw there were still thousands of Mad coming their way. She reaffirmed her connection to the land and screwed her eyes closed, beseeching the plants to crush the Mad.

Lenore returned to the lookout with the magic users as

the sun painted a thin line on the horizon. Those with enhanced vision viewed the progression of the Mad into New Hampshire with varying levels of fear and anger.

"Where are they?" David asked, squinting into the murky mist.

"Don't worry," Annie told him. "They're there."

David knelt and placed his hand in the earth. His connection to the stone buried beneath its surface told him everything he needed to know. "Oh."

Esme shook her head. "Now's no time for thinking, David. Start shifting rock and stop the Mad however you can."

CHAPTER TWENTY-ONE

<u>**Lynwood, MA**</u>

Sarah Jennifer returned to camp with the unwieldy stag balanced on her shoulders just as the sun began to appear. While normally she couldn't spit in the forest at dawn or dusk without hitting a deer, they'd been scarce this morning. She hated to take a breeding male, but needs must when she had so many hungry mouths to feed.

Brutus nodded and continued stripping sharpened sticks to use as skewers.

"I hope you have coffee ready," Sarah Jennifer whispered.

Brutus handed her a steaming cup with a smile. "I'm not ready for the kids to wake up until I'm caffeinated," he replied quietly.

Sarah Jennifer put the deer down and accepted the cup. She inhaled the nutty aroma and took a grateful sip. "Normally I'd say tea was better, but somehow coffee is essential when you're camping."

She got to work dividing the deer into manageable

portions, which Brutus impaled on the sharpened sticks and stuck into the ground over the fire to cook.

The children's keen noses kicked into action as soon as the aroma of cooking meat made its way to the shelters.

Sarah Jennifer smiled as they emerged, rubbing their sleepy-but-hopeful eyes. "Breakfast will be a little while yet," she told them, pointing downstream with her knife. "Wash away from our drinking water, and stay in groups. Nobody goes anywhere alone."

"Ew," one of the girls complained. "What if we need to go to the bathroom?"

Sarah Jennifer waved her knife in a circle to indicate the wilderness surrounding them. "I don't see any bathrooms around here, Hallie. Stick together, and call if you need us."

"I'll keep my eye on them," Brutus offered, a twinkle in his eye.

Sarah Jennifer nodded with a knowing smile. "Have fun playing."

Brutus grinned. "I don't know what you mean," he called over his shoulder as he ran after the giggling children.

Sarah Jennifer filled the makeshift rack over the fire with strips of deer meat while the children—including the fifty-something-year-old one—splashed around in the icy stream.

The novelty of playing soon wore off, and they returned to dismantle the camp.

"Is breakfast ready?" Kyle begged, practically salivating at the smell of rendered deer fat.

Sarah Jennifer nodded as she removed the first stick

from the fire and handed it to the boy, who dashed off with his prize. "There's enough for everyone," she told the waiting children.

She was impressed to see that the teens didn't need any direction from her when it came to taking care of each other. They had already organized the younger children away from the fire and were happy to ensure they had food before taking a stick from the fire for themselves.

Brutus took his portion with a smile. "I can't tell you how much I'm looking forward to getting back to Salem," he told Sarah Jennifer between bites. "I want these kids back with their families."

"I'm hoping Jim has gotten the bus operational so we can get a move on with taking the prison out of the equation," Sarah Jennifer replied.

Brutus agreed fully. "We've got a few miles to go, and then you'll find out." He finished eating and wiped his hands on his shirt. "I'll be glad of hot water and clean clothes."

Sarah Jennifer chuckled. "Look at you, getting all attached to civilization."

Brutus wrinkled his nose. "You could do with a shower yourse—" He paused when he caught an odd scent on the wind. His heart flipped as his lizard brain screamed they were in danger. "What the fuck is that?"

The children giggled at his use of language.

Sarah Jennifer picked up the scent and changed her mind about castigating Brutus for his slip. She got to her feet and clapped for the attention of everyone in camp. "Kids, we have a situation. Everything will be okay, but I need you all to get ready to run."

The children stopped chattering and obeyed, slipping on the harnesses Sarah Jennifer had shown them how to rig before waiting in silence for her next instruction.

The sudden stillness allowed Sarah Jennifer to hear something blundering toward their location. She did a quick headcount of the children. "Good. Now, follow Brutus and don't get left behind."

"What about you?" Brutus asked.

Sarah Jennifer gazed into the trees, tracking the sound of the approaching threat. "I'm going to make sure you all get to Salem in one piece, starting with clearing your route."

She slipped into the forest as Brutus led the children away, her hackles well and truly up. The scent of wrongness was faint, but it grew stronger with every step she took.

Sarah Jennifer drew her knife and her pistol as the crashing got closer. She heard hoofbeats just before the foliage parted and a deer barreled through in a flash of tawny fur. The doe's ears were back, her eyes red with stress. Sarah Jennifer recognized fear when she saw it. She also knew that the doe wasn't responsible for the smell of rotting meat on the wind.

The trees grew closer together, their trunks and the ground strangled with aggressive ivy. Sarah Jennifer didn't have a clear view of what was ahead, but the stench was becoming unbearable. She advanced cautiously toward the source of the smell, ready to shoot anything that moved in a way that didn't please her.

Sarah Jennifer almost stepped on the Mad when she walked into the space between the trees where he was eating the fawn. Her cry of surprise was covered by the report from her pistol.

The enraged Mad's eyes burned with red light as he skittered back from the fawn in an unnatural crab-walk, escaping the bullet that would have torn through his brain. He twisted to his feet and came at Sarah Jennifer with his teeth bared.

Sarah Jennifer was less than keen on allowing the rotting man anywhere near her. She kicked him back and raised her pistol, noting when he flinched that the infected still had some intelligence. That gave her hope that the corruption could be reversed, as Lilith had told her.

Nevertheless, she put her next bullet between his eyes before he took a step.

Saving the living had to be the first priority.

She watched until the light in his eyes had vanished and his body had ceased twitching, then she hung around a little while longer to ensure he wasn't going to get up again before heading after Brutus and the children.

Brutus was filled with relief when he heard Sarah Jennifer yell his name on the road behind them. He called for the children to stop and jogged to meet her out of their hearing range. "What did you find?"

"The Madness is here," Sarah Jennifer told him flatly. "I just killed an infected man. We need to get these kids behind the barrier hex before more turn up."

Salem, MA

Ozzie and Bruiser were standing close to the edge of the ridge, tracking the destruction the magic wrought as they kept guard over the witches. The red glow was getting ever closer, distinct groups of Mad becoming visible on the beaches and in the few places the land rose to break through the trees.

Their number had swelled again, the Mad adding to their ranks with every living human and animal they came across and infected. Everyone with an ability to use in the effort to halt the Mad was lost in their element, unleashing the weather, the trees and plants, the very earth against the oncoming rush.

Lenore opened her eyes, releasing the birds whose vision she'd been borrowing. "They're into New Hampshire."

Esme sensed Sarah Jennifer's and Brutus' proximity to the barrier at the same time she sensed a small group of Mad veer around the barrier blocking the north road. She released her hold on the land and sat back on her folded legs when she also sensed a large number of Weres a short distance from their location. "The Mad are a lot closer than New Hampshire. I have to go."

"What is it?" Annie asked.

"Sarah Jennifer is back. Can you take care of this?" Esme got to her feet, cleaning the dirt off her hands with a flash of Etheric energy. "She's in trouble."

"Go," Annie urged, looking up. Her eyes captured the early morning light, shining with her power. "Just make sure Sarah Jennifer and Brutus are okay. We need them."

Esme hurried down from the lookout, picking up speed as she got out of sight of the others. She broke into a run, calling with her mind to tell Sarah Jennifer she was coming as she crossed the boundary hex at the north road. Not knowing if she could be heard, Esme feared she would be too late.

A few minutes later, she saw someone approaching and stopped to access her magic, not knowing at first whether they were friend or foe. Her answer was given when the runner came into sight and she recognized the blonde hair whipping around her head.

Sarah Jennifer pelted toward Esme. "Mad," she panted, coming to a rough halt and bending to support herself with her hands on her thighs. "They're here."

"I know," Esme told her. "They've made their way down from the north. We're fighting them off."

"No, *here*," Sarah Jennifer clarified, pointing at the ground. She lifted her hand to point back the way she'd come and set off back down the road. "I have to go back. Brutus has the children."

"Children?" Esme asked, breaking into a run to keep up with her. The pack she'd sensed were just children? It threw her for a moment. "We didn't need any more bad news. There's a mass of people infected with the Madness heading for town."

"Now isn't the best time to use your gift for understatement," Sarah Jennifer told her tartly. "How many? What's their position?"

Esme filled her in on the situation to the north while they ran to meet up with Brutus. They found him and the children stopped by the side of the road near the campsite where Linus and Reg had been kidnapped.

Brutus came over with an apologetic shrug. "The younger ones are tired. They're not used to the pace. I had to stop and let them rest."

Sarah Jennifer nodded her agreement. "You did great. You too, kids. Okay, let's get everyone inside the ruin and find a place to rest. We're leaving in half an hour, so make the most of it."

The children dropped their packs inside the remains of a house consisting of two and a half degraded walls that were only standing because gravity hadn't gotten around to noticing them yet.

Sarah Jennifer grimaced at the thought they might not be safe where they were if there were any more Mad in the immediate area, but she couldn't smell anything out of place, and Brutus was right. The youngest were exhausted from the forced march.

She saw that Kyle had already fallen asleep against one of the crumbling walls and took off her jacket to cover him against the cold.

"They need to eat," Esme commented. "But I don't like the idea of staying here for too long."

"Not a problem," Brutus told her, shucking two of the three packs he was carrying. He opened the second and handed out strips of deer meat, which the children gratefully accepted.

Lucy and Janie sat close to Sarah Jennifer while they ate.

"We're nearly there, right?" Lucy asked.

Sarah Jennifer nodded. "We've got a few miles to go, but yes."

"It seems silly to stop now, then," Janie commented.

"Are you going to carry Kyle the rest of the way?" Lucy shot back with a strained grin.

"I can carry Kyle if it comes to it," Brutus assured Janie,

whose face had paled somewhat at the memory of carrying her brother out of their family home at her mother's tearful insistence when the leeches raided their town.

The older girls told Brutus how strong and brave he was.

Sarah Jennifer and Esme laughed when Brutus went beet-red and looked down, unsure how to react to the full force of eight teenage crushes at once.

"Everyone needs to rest, even me," Sarah Jennifer told the children. "Settle down, now."

"Tell us about Salem," Luke asked.

The other children caught on immediately, begging for Brutus to tell them about the town and its people.

Sarah Jennifer lowered her voice to talk to Esme while Brutus entertained the children with stories about how things worked in Salem. "This has come before we were ready. I wanted the town and the pack at full strength before the Madness made it here from Europe. We haven't even started on figuring out how I'm going to get across the Atlantic."

Esme nodded in understanding. "I know, Duckie, but we'll have to cross that bridge when we come to it. The barrier hex will keep the Mad out of Salem, and everyone up on the ridge is working on removing the threat. The prison break won't be compromised."

"That's the first priority—rescuing the Weres and getting them safely inside Salem." Sarah Jennifer thanked the deity her grandfather was so fond of invoking for small mercies as she got to her feet. "Brutus, time to go."

Brutus shepherded the children out of the ruin while Sarah Jennifer and Esme walked ahead. The children's mood rose as they followed the north road. He cautioned them to keep the noise down when Esme announced the turn to Salem was in sight and their speculative chatter caused a flock of birds to take flight as they passed.

Esme nudged Sarah Jennifer, drawing her attention to a corresponding flock that burst from the trees just north of the turning. "That's not good."

The major's heart dropped. "No. It's not." She did a one-eighty and headed for the children. They were walking in a straggly line, bunched in little groups. "Pick up the pace," she told them. "If you can carry one of the younger kids, do so. Then go, and don't stop until you've made the turn and passed the standing stones."

Brutus picked up Kyle and another small child and led the way.

Sarah Jennifer took a knee and helped the two youngest girls climb into her arms. "Hold on tight, okay? There's danger ahead, and I might need my hands to shoot."

The girls buried their faces in her neck, squeezing tightly as they shook with fear.

"It's okay," she assured them. "We'll be safe in no time, just wait and see."

Benjamin hovered nearby, clearly frustrated about being unable to help his sisters. Sarah Jennifer indicated her pack with a nod. "Grab that and run. I've got Sunshine and Flower."

She matched her pace to the slowest child as they hurried the last few hundred meters to safety, her senses peeled for the progress of the Mad heading to intersect them.

Esme kept her hands free as they ran. She was on the

wrong side of the barrier to be able to track the Mad, but that didn't mean she couldn't be ready to react when they appeared.

Just as the first few children were about to make the turn, a Mad burst out of the trees opposite and lunged for them. The children screamed and dashed back to the group.

The Mad was followed by another, and another, then three more burst from the foliage a few feet to their left.

Three echoing reports from Sarah Jennifer's pistol left the first three Mad face-down in the road before they'd taken a step toward the children.

Esme winced at the noise. She gathered Etheric energy as the foliage shook with more Mad arriving, giving Sarah Jennifer a worried glance. "Well, if they didn't know where we were before, they do now."

CHAPTER TWENTY-TWO

"Get back!" Esme cried, releasing the formless energy at the tree line opposite the turn as around a dozen Mad crashed out of the foliage and charged at them.

Sarah Jennifer and Brutus instinctually put themselves between the children and the incoming threat. The children panicked, freezing in a tight huddle in the middle of the road behind the adults.

Confusion reigned for a moment when the attack did not come.

Across from the turning, the Mad were also frozen to the spot. Sarah Jennifer realized that their predicament was entirely Esme's doing and edged toward the Mad cautiously. "Nice work, Esme," she praised.

Brutus didn't drop his guard for a second. "What did you do to them?"

Esme inspected her hold on the Mad, finding her mental control of them surprising since she had never heard or read of the ability.

She snickered softly. The way the Mad were posed mid-shuffle would have been comical if not for their rotting flesh, bared teeth, and glowing red death-glares. "I don't know. I didn't have time to do more than decide that I had to get control of the situation."

Sarah Jennifer indulged her curiosity and prodded one of the Mad with the point of her knife. "Is it safe to take the children past?"

The Mad's eyes bulged with fury, but it couldn't move. Sarah Jennifer leaned in, her Were senses beyond offended by the smell of the corruption. "Would you look at that! You've paralyzed them?"

Esme nodded. "They can't do a thing I don't want them to. Go on, children. It's safe, I promise."

The children remained rooted to the spot, afraid to walk past the decaying monsters. They had no reference for this, no experience to tell them what the monster was. Esme's heart hurt to see them full of fear. It gave her the urge to do something to give them back a sense of control.

Her first reaction had been to find humor in their situation. She knew what she had to do as though another voice had whispered the idea in her ear.

Esme flashed a mischievous smile at the children when inspiration hit. "Watch, I'll show you. They're my puppets. Would you like to see them dance?" She flourished her hands at the Mad for effect, breaking into an upbeat hum as she willed them to move in sync with her thoughts. "*Da-da-da* daa daaa... *Da-da-da...*"

The children gasped when the living dead responded as one to Esme's gesture.

"It's okay, see? Esme reassured them, readying her hands as seriously as any choreographer. "The Mad are dangerous, yes, but they're not so scary when you know how to handle them."

Esme resumed her humming and the Mad went up on their tiptoes in time to her tune, lifting their hands to shoulder height as they turned to the left and leaned back. They held the pose for a beat, then pivoted to the right, swinging their arms in a smooth motion before repeating a mirror of the first maneuver.

Sarah Jennifer gaped at the Mad as they followed with a butt wiggle and a little kick. "Are they… Are you seriously making them *dance*?"

Esme snickered, jiggling her shoulders. "Just making light of the situation." The children giggled along when a flick of her fingers made the Mad shimmy three steps to the left and move their hands from side to side in an exaggerated manner. "The ultimate flash mob. Your grandparents would find this hilarious. Ah, well."

She snapped her fingers as she willed the Mad to continue dancing. "Take the children into town, Brutus. Sarah Jennifer and I have work to do."

"Wait a minute," Sarah Jennifer told Esme, heading after Brutus and the children.

She gave Brutus his instructions while she walked to the boundary hex with him and the children. "Light a fire under our chief engineer once you've seen the children safely to the town hall."

Brutus nodded, his eyes on the children. "You've got it."

Esme still held the Mad in her mental grip when Sarah Jennifer returned. "You took your time."

Sarah Jennifer severed the brain stem of the nearest Mad with a practiced thrust and kicked him away to remove his skull from her knife. "I told him to go to the forge and make sure the bus is ready to leave."

Esme nodded, her concentration on holding the Mad still while Sarah Jennifer dispatched them one by one. "Don't get that blood on you," she warned.

"Wasn't intending to." Sarah Jennifer released the next body and moved onto another Mad. "I know how blood and nanocytes are connected."

Esme destroyed the corpses with a steady stream of burning Etheric energy when Sarah Jennifer had finished with the messy part. They made sure all that was left of the Mad were charred bones, then made their way to the lookout, where they found all the magic users slumped on the ground near the edge of the ridge.

"They're just sleeping," Esme told Sarah Jennifer after examining Annie and Sarai.

"Yeah, Magnus, too," Sarah Jennifer confirmed, glancing at David when he let out a little snore. "Same over here. Everyone looks to be fine."

Esme wandered to the very edge and halted when she got to the view from the ridge. "Oh, my. I know why they're asleep."

Sarah Jennifer joined Esme, sitting down heavily beside her in the disturbed earth when she laid eyes on the devastation below. The previously flat land was rippled all along the coast, and the peaceful greens and grays of the distant forest had been burned, drowned, and ripped apart.

Her brain refused to accept the evidence of her own eyes. A crude tear split the land in two from the lake systems in the north all the way to the sea, forming jagged cliffs that dropped into a raw gorge widened further by rockfalls in the rapids of the new river thundering toward the coast. Plum Island was gone, replaced by towering cliffs whose faces glittered with cataracts, the many waterfalls fed by runoff from the magically-induced storm and groundwater released by the formation of the miles-deep wound in the Earth's crust.

"That's not possible," Sarah Jennifer whispered, awed by the scale of the change that had been wrought across the previously pristine land.

"Of course it's possible," Esme chided gently, her voice tight with emotion as the weight of their actions made itself felt. "This coast is riddled with fault lines. So many lives lost."

"How far does that canyon stretch?" Sarah Jennifer asked quietly.

"From here to Meredith, Maine," Esme replied. "David and Magnus have the ability to manipulate earth and stone. They drained the lakes to wash the Mad away."

Where there had been a beautiful beach, there was only evidence of the landslide that had occurred as a result of the gorge's creation. The debris ended in a churning trap where the river met the sea. Sarah Jennifer pointed out the corpses caught up among the smashed trees and rocks clogging the mouth of the river. "What about that?"

Esme pursed her lips. "The land wanted to drop there. Newbury was abandoned, so there's no loss of life there."

Sarah Jennifer was well aware that there would have been no survivors wherever the Mad had walked. She just hoped that none of Mad trapped in the blockage were still conscious. "That's going to be a problem. Can you do something to take care of it?"

Esme stared for a moment, contemplating the water building slowly against the unintentional dam. "I'm too drained for anything spectacular. We need to get closer."

"What about everyone up here?" Sarah Jennifer asked, glancing at Esme as she walked away from the edge.

Esme waved off her concern as they headed back down the slope. "They redirected the Mad, so let them sleep it off. They'll wake up in a few hours feeling hungry as Weres."

"I'd like to know where Bruiser and Ozzie got to." Sarah Jennifer picked up her pace, intending to take strip off the two sergeants for abandoning their post when she saw them next. "That's a hell of a lot of bodies down there, Esme."

"I'd put a jug of my homebrew on them running back to town when Brutus got in with the kids," Esme guessed. "Keep your eyes peeled for any survivors."

The terrain became increasingly rougher as they neared the dam. Sarah Jennifer sucked up the pain in her knee caused by trekking rugged miles as she scrambled down loose scree and around protrusions of disturbed rock.

"Have you still not managed to fix your knee?" Esme asked in surprise.

Sarah Jennifer sighed with exasperation as the pressure of her step tweaked her knee again. "I hadn't thought about it until it started playing up a couple of miles ago when the land started to dip. Any other environment would have been easier than downhill, but it's only pain. It will pass."

Esme abandoned her grip on a tree root to get down to the strip of loose ground Sarah Jennifer was on. "We haven't got the luxury of not having you at your best. I'd hoped you would work on activating your ability to heal at will, but I don't want you hobbling around in pain."

She passed a hand over Sarah Jennifer's knee, and golden light glowed for a moment. "That should do it for now, but only you can fix it permanently."

Sarah Jennifer felt the pain ebb and a strong heat in her knee joint that faded after a few seconds, leaving it feeling good as new. She rubbed her knee, wondering for the first time if maybe Sylvia and Esme were right about her holding onto the injury.

"All good?" Esme asked.

"Better than good," Sarah Jennifer told her with a grin. "Let's go bust this dam open so I can take my pack to kick some leech ass in celebration."

"Nothing would make me happier," Esme replied, sliding down the scree ahead of her. "I can hear water. Come on, we're almost there."

Sarah Jennifer pulled Esme back before she fell in when they reached a drop-off above the waterline without warning.

Esme recovered and joined Sarah Jennifer in her examination of the uprooted trees and bodies jammed in with the rockslide blocking the river's progress.

"Close enough?" Sarah Jennifer asked.

"I can take it out from here," Esme confirmed, forming a ball of glowing energy over her hand. "We'd better get it right. I haven't got another energy ball in me tonight."

Sarah Jennifer scanned the dam for a likely weak spot. She spotted a place in the rocks where a tree had gotten lodged between two large rocks and was supporting the buildup of detritus in its branches. "There." She pointed it out to Esme. "Take out the tree, and that whole section should collapse."

Esme flung the energy ball at the tree, which exploded in a spray of smoking splinters, leaving a gap for the water to surge through. The pressure washed the rocks away with the remains of the tree and the corpses, as per Sarah Jennifer's prediction.

"Nice shot," Sarah Jennifer told Esme, watching the dam crumble. She saw a lot more bodies being washed out to sea than she'd estimated there were from above. "It looks like more of the Mad got taken out than I thought. Maybe the prison rescue won't be compromised."

Esme winked at Sarah Jennifer and turned to head back up the slope. "What did I tell you? Have faith. And less chatting, more walking. We've got a hell of a trek back to Salem, and I want to get your opinion on expanding our defenses."

CHAPTER TWENTY-THREE

The sun had set by the time Sarah Jennifer and Esme turned onto the dirt road leading to the forge, still deep in conversation about Esme's plan to send a group north.

"You haven't been there," Sarah Jennifer reiterated. "We have no way of knowing what we'd be sending them into." She'd balked at Esme's suggestion that the land bridge could be blocked using magic, imagining the thousand and one ways the expedition party would die before reaching the harrowing subarctic climate of the ice shelf. "That's not even considering the danger from the Mad. If they've found a route, you can bet more will be following soon enough."

"All the more reason to cut them off before the numbers get too great to handle," Esme argued. "We only had to deal with a few thousand this time. Sarah Jennifer, there are millions of people in Europe. We are at risk from any band of migratory Mad that finds a route across the ice."

"We're at risk from everything else going on as well,"

Sarah Jennifer reminded her. "One step at a time. We break the insurmountable problem down into smaller, more manageable chunks, and we'll come out of this on top. Jumping ahead before we've got the resources to handle the Mad is only going to result in us all developing a hankering for brains come chowtime. We need to take care of the problems on our doorstep before we tackle the end of the world."

"So, you're saying you won't approve the expedition?" Esme asked.

Sarah Jennifer shook her head. "Not until it's logistically possible. I see your reasoning, and I agree. But I won't roll the dice on people's lives to make it happen."

"We'll pick this up again after the prison break," Esme promised.

"It might be a possibility by then, who knows?" Sarah Jennifer blinked to adjust her vision as they left the dark path and entered the pool of light that marked the start of Jim's property.

Jim's homestead was, if anything, even more enchanting with the moon on the snow lending its ethereal light to the night. The trees around the meadow were hung with lanterns, their warm glow caught by glittering icicles on the branches.

They went in through the gate, hearing music playing nearby. Sarah Jennifer's stomach growled hopefully at the smell of barbecuing beef on the air.

Esme nudged Sarah Jennifer with an elbow. "Sounds like there's a celebration going on, and here we are, all field-fresh…" Her voice trailed off as she sniffed her sleeve. "How dignified."

Sarah Jennifer smiled, knowing there was only one reason Jim would down tools. "The bus must be ready." She set off at a jog, hoping the absence of the magic users at the lookout meant her sergeants had returned to collect them while she and Esme had been dealing with the dam. "Come on, maybe we'll get invited for dinner."

They followed the teasing aroma to the clearing between the back of the cabin and the barn, where they found most of the people Sarah Jennifer had gotten to know in the last year. Some of the pack were dancing around a makeshift stage with the magic users and civilian volunteers, while the rock ensemble onstage played their hearts out.

Sarah Jennifer smiled, spotting Jim regaling Carver, Geordie, and a few of the other young Weres with a story by the fire, and Brutus battling Maria for command of the grill. Having everyone together was good; they'd all been working day and night to prepare for the prison break. To see them kicking back for a change, happy and carefree, warmed her soul.

Brutus waved with his meat tongs. "Ladies! You made it just in time. Grub's almost ready."

Maria swatted him with her apron. "What have I told you about calling my good food 'grub?'" She eyed the meat with alarm. "Brutus, you have to do more than wave the meat over the flames. Are you trying to kill the humans?"

Sarah Jennifer laughed when Brutus stepped back, apologizing profusely for his high standards in meat preparation.

Brutus glanced at Sarah Jennifer, then took off his apron and handed it solemnly to Maria. "It's clear I wasn't meant to cook for a living." He huffed. "I guess I'll stick to being an officer."

Sarah Jennifer was still laughing when Brutus walked over. "Don't sweat it," she told him, looking around for the objects of her ire. The sergeants were nowhere to be seen.

"How was I supposed to know humans can't eat rare chicken?" Brutus retorted in response to Maria's continued verbal harassment. He rolled his eyes at Sarah Jennifer's amusement. "What?"

"Rare chicken isn't a thing, cousin mine," she told him with a sympathetic pat on the back. "Trust me when I tell you that e. coli isn't pretty."

Esme chuckled. "No, it is not. I once accidentally almost killed two star athletes with a chicken."

"Star athletes?" Brutus echoed. "E. coli?"

Sarah Jennifer folded her arms and threw Esme a skeptical look, having more context for the remark. "Seriously? How?"

"It's a true story." Esme nodded. "Sports were commercialized before WWDE. Athletes drew followings, and the best could become world-famous. One time, I cooked a chicken dinner for my friend and me before we went to one of the theaters in the city. We guessed the men sitting in front of us were famous by the way others were reacting to them but we had no clue who they were. My friend started feeling ill, so we left early. The next day, the news had a story about two of the city's premier soccer players being benched. I was mortified when they showed the photo of the men from the theater. I called my friend, but she'd been rushed to hospital in the night."

Brutus frowned. "Why weren't you sick?"

Esme shrugged. "I eat my own cooking all the time."

Sarah Jennifer wrinkled her nose. "You must have the stomach of a Were."

Jim noticed the three of them talking and extracted himself from his audience with the promise he would pick his story up again later.

Sarah Jennifer matched Jim's wide grin as he ambled over. She indicated the yard with a nod. "This is nice. Does all the festivity mean we have a suitable assault vehicle?"

Jim cracked his knuckles. "Follow me, Major. Old Bluebird, well, she's had something of a makeover while you and Brutus were away rescuing those kids. How are they?"

Sarah Jennifer lifted her hands. "I don't know. Esme and I just got here from the lookout."

Esme frowned. "I don't see Annie or anyone else who was fighting there. Did they make it back to town yet?"

"I haven't seen them," Brutus told her, concern casting a cloud over his features. He grabbed Carver and Geordie as they went by. "Guys, Annie and a few others haven't come back from the lookout."

Carver pulled his shirt off and tied the sleeves together to make a bundle for the rest of his clothing in preparation for shifting. "I'll run up there and take a look. Geordie can check in town."

Geordie nodded. "I'll need someone to show me where they all live."

"I'll come with you," Esme offered. "But there had better be some food left when I get back."

"That good with you, Major?" Geordie asked.

Sarah Jennifer nodded her permission. She relaxed, guessing that Carver would find Annie and the others at home, sleeping off the massive energy expenditure it had taken to alter the landscape so drastically. "You didn't get around to telling us how the children are doing."

"The kids are settled in at the town hall," Brutus told her, his smile returning. "I stayed while they got comfortable and promised we'd see them as soon as we got back from saving their parents."

"You did a good thing," Jim told them. His demeanor shifted to total seriousness as they rounded the corner of the barn. "Look. I'm going to just say it straight. Some of those kids, well, they might not have parents coming back to them. I want to say that if any of them needs a home or wants to learn a trade so they can live independently, I'd be happy to help out."

Sarah Jennifer smiled. "I know you would. But stay positive, okay? We assume everyone is alive unless we learn differently."

Jim nodded. "You've got it." He left them for a moment to turn the patio lights on, chatting the whole time he was out of sight.

Sarah Jennifer threw up an arm to shield her eyes when the patio was flooded with strong white light. "Damn, that's bright!"

Jim laughed. "Yeah, I took a minute to wire the barn up to one of those power packs so I can have all the light I want at night."

When Sarah Jennifer's vision adjusted, she saw Bluebird in all her glory, surrounded by empty crates. Her previously yellow exterior was gone. The bus was flat-black, the original exterior hidden behind spiked metal cladding. Jim had replaced the front bumper with a pair of snowplow blades welded together to form a pointed ram. It gave the bus a wolfish look, helped by the sharp-fanged grin painted on the sides.

Sarah Jennifer walked around Bluebird, then stepped back to get a better look at the addition to the roof. Her mouth fell open when she spotted the barrel poking out of the squat cylinder at the rear of the bus. "Is that what I think it is?"

"If you think it's a Mk 19 grenade launcher, then yes," he replied with a grin. "You've got the scavenger crew to thank for that. The roof of the turret is separate from the walls, so the operator has three-sixty reach."

Brutus let out a low whistle. "I have no idea what you just said, but a shiver just went up my spine."

"You won't believe it until you've seen it in action," Jim told him amiably. "I had to test it before we designed the mount. I took Carver and Geordie out to the old dairy in the ATV. We set up on the far side of the field and sprayed the wall. Next thing, the grenades go off, right? Just, *bangbangbang*, one after the other."

He demonstrated with animated hand gestures as he spoke. "We drove over to check out the damage, and just like that, the dairy was gone."

"Sounds like we won't have any problem breaching the prison's walls," Brutus remarked.

Sarah Jennifer was only half-listening. She continued her inspection of the exterior armor, impressed by the attention to detail. She saw the use for the line of hatches along each side immediately and wondered how Jim had managed to fabricate everything in the few weeks he'd had.

"Did you have issues with any of the modifications I requested?"

Jim mopped his forehead with his bandana. "Not once I went through everything you brought back. Big Ace was a huge help. The boys did most of the labor while I worked on building the engine and yelled instructions at them from my workshop."

Sarah Jennifer chuckled as a raucous laugh went up at the party. "They do their best work when you get the tone of the yelling *just* right."

Brutus snorted, his eyes glued to the bus. "You would know. What about the weight of the armor? Won't it slow the bus down?"

Jim shook his head. "Funnily enough, I had the opposite problem. See, the engine components the major brought back aren't for ground vehicles." He lifted the hood and showed them the new engine. "Looks more like it belongs to a spaceship, right?"

Sarah Jennifer slapped her forehead. "They're airship components. I'd thought the problem would be converting the bus to run with the new engine, but it's the amount of power the new engine puts out, right? Please tell me she's not going to bunny-hop and wheelspin all the way to the prison."

Jim shook his head. "That's not going to happen, Major. I figured in a bunch of resistors to step the power down so she'll run smoothly, don't you worry." He closed the hood, giving her a sideways grin as he led them to the bus's door. "I shouldn't be surprised you know your way around a vehicle, what with your military background."

Sarah Jennifer "It's not my first rodeo, but I won't lie.

I'm kicking myself for missing the opportunity for an airship."

Jim snorted. "Sure, Major. I'll get right on that."

Sarah Jennifer smiled and patted the bus fondly. "Very funny. I'm going to want some time to get to know her quirks before we leave."

"No quirks," Jim promised. He opened the door and waved for them to follow him. "Ready to see the inside?"

"By all means," Sarah Jennifer told him before stepping into the bus. She made a similar sound of awe a second later when she got her first look at the inside. "Okay, *now* we have a tactical assault vehicle."

"You like?" Jim asked with a chuckle.

Sarah Jennifer raised an eyebrow. "You're kidding, right? I can't even take it all in, it's so...well, *practical.* You've done wonders, Lieutenant. Give me a minute to look it all over."

She was drawn to the hatches running down the sides of the bus. Opening one to look out, she noted there was a wire to pull the hatch back up again.

"Those are so the boys can shoot from inside the bus," Jim told her. "They've been training hard with the rifles you brought back, and they had a lot of input to how the bus was laid out."

Further inspection revealed individual boards on the inside that gave the person looking out somewhere to rest their elbow. Sarah Jennifer nodded in appreciation and closed the hatch. "I figured as much. Nice touch."

The fixtures were utilitarian and without much in the way of comfort, but perfectly designed to transport and defend the pack and a good many others in a pinch. The seats had been stripped out and replaced with two rows of storage lockers topped with benches that ran three quarters the length of the bus, leaving an aisle in the center for moving around.

Jim made his way to the rear while Sarah Jennifer examined the fixtures. "I'll hazard a guess that I'm not the only one whose favorite part is this baby," he enthused, patting the ladder leading to the loft above the larger lockers at the end of the bus.

Brutus rushed onto the bus, crashing into Sarah Jennifer.

Sarah Jennifer grabbed one of the straps hanging from the wire storage racks above the benches and managed to avoid an impromptu close inspection of the floor. "I know it's exciting to get a new toy—"

"Sorry," Brutus cut in, his eyes on the gun loft. "But there's a freaking *grenade launcher* on top of the bus. How could I be anything but excited? This operation is going to be a success."

"That's not all," Jim informed them, opening the lockers beneath the loft. "Between the weapons you brought back from Ms. Sylvia's and what Little Ace's crew found working with old Billy—"

"Who?" Brutus asked.

"He is Little Ace's historian," Sarah Jennifer guessed.

Jim nodded. "Oh, yeah. He's a historian, all right. Anyway, he had the idea that there were a group of people pre-WWDE who knew the apocalypse was coming and got themselves ready for it."

Sarah Jennifer nodded in surprise. "Preppers? Little Ace mentioned something about a possible weapons stash. This is the first I'm hearing about preppers. I always thought they were a myth."

Jim shook his head. "Not according to Billy, and we have the weapons to prove it."

Brutus slipped around Sarah Jennifer and picked up a piece of tubular equipment the length of his arm. "What's this do?" he asked, settling it onto his shoulder so he could look through the sight.

"It fires rockets," Sarah Jennifer told him, her mouth curling with amusement.

Brutus almost dropped the launcher in his hurry to put it back into the locker. "For real? What were these preppers expecting to defend themselves against?"

"Aliens, vampires, the government, liberals. My grandparents had differing views on their motivations." Sarah Jennifer shrugged. "From what I was told as a child, I'm not sure whether they were visionaries who were unappreciated in their own time or a bunch of lucky lunatics, but they sure liked to spend money on guns."

Jim guffawed, slapping his leg. "That they did, which makes *us* the lucky ones. Did I mention these people lived to stockpile? I mean, it makes sense if you knew what was coming."

Sarah Jennifer threw up her hands. "That's the question. Did they?"

Brutus opened another locker and found neatly racked semiautomatic rifles. "Damn straight, it does." He looked at Sarah Jennifer seriously. "I'm going to say those preppers were unappreciated in their time because I'm sure as hell appreciating them now."

Sarah Jennifer sighed as she climbed up to the loft.

"That's not how it works, dumbass. They didn't know—or at least, I don't think they did."

Brutus opened his arms wide and looked up at the loft. "If they're getting the appreciation, then it's working! Who's the dumbass now?" He winced as Jim sucked in a breath. "I mean…"

Sarah Jennifer poked her head out and fixed Brutus with a hard look. "Do I need to come down there?"

Brutus' bottom lip stuck out two inches more than usual. "No, Major. Sorry, I spoke out of turn."

Sarah Jennifer rolled her eyes and hauled herself to her feet. She dropped into the bucket seat and spun it all the way around. The curved space was a perfect fit for the circular platform the chair and the grenade launcher mount were fixed to. She peered at the levers set into the platform curiously. "Talk to me, Jim. What am I seeing here?"

Jim clapped in delight. "I'll assume you can figure out the grenade launcher just fine," he called. "Those levers by the chair are connected to projectile launchers at the front and rear."

Sarah Jennifer thought for a moment, but she couldn't remember seeing crates containing anything useful. "What load did you make for them?"

Jim grinned at the speculative look from Brutus. "Those crates you brought back were packed with treats. We have a case of smoke bombs, another of teargas, and another of explosives."

Sarah Jennifer left the loft with the plan coming together in her mind. She clapped Jim on the back as she strode past. "I've seen enough. We're ready."

Brutus and Jim exchanged glances, then shrugged at each other and followed her off the bus.

The pack called and whistled when they returned to the clearing. Rory came over with drinks for the three of them before dancing away, singing along with the band.

Jim raised his cup to the trio on the makeshift stage and meandered into the crowd.

Sarah Jennifer caught sight of Dinny sitting alone to the side. She plucked the cup from Brutus' hand before he could take a sip. "Burdens of command, what can I say? Dinny needs this more than you do."

Brutus followed her glance to the solitary Were and nodded. "He's been so focused since he recovered from the attack. See if you can get him to lighten up."

Dinny looked up as Sarah Jennifer joined him under the trees. "Hey, Major. Is everything okay?"

"I was going to ask you the same question." Sarah Jennifer handed Dinny the cup and got herself settled cross-legged next to him on the ground. "Brutus tells me you've been pushing yourself pretty hard. I thought you'd be cutting loose with everyone else tonight."

Dinny accepted the cup with a sigh. "I'm done cutting loose. It didn't get me anywhere before, and it's not going to get Linus and Reg out of that prison."

Sarah Jennifer put her cup down and leaned back against the tree. She scrutinized him for a long moment, seeing a very different person from the Were who had looked to Linus for approval for everything. "I get it."

Dinny looked at her in surprise. "You do?"

Sarah Jennifer nodded. "How can you relax knowing people you care about are depending on you?" She gave him a sympathetic smile, seeing she'd struck a nerve. "It's always worse when it's someone you know. You, Linus, and Reg might have been assholes to everyone, but you were there for each other."

It was Dinny's turn for reflective silence. When he spoke, it was hesitant. "I know we'll save them. But what if…" His voice trailed off in embarrassment. "I'm not the guy they knew. Becoming someone who can save them? Well, it made me different in here." He tapped his temple with a finger. "I can't see Linus taking too well to the new me."

Sarah Jennifer didn't know how to answer that. "I suppose you'll find out tomorrow. Either they'll accept this new you, or they won't. The question is, will you keep making decisions you can live with now that you know better? That's up to you."

Dinny's spine stiffened. "I won't go back to what I was. I saw the light when I woke up in the back of that wagon and you told me we were going to get them back. They don't deserve it, but you're too honorable to leave anyone behind. My duty is to make sure Linus and Reg have the same choice I did. If they don't want to get behind saving the world, it puts us on different paths. I'll be sad if it comes to that, but I'll go forward with my conscience clear."

He got to his feet and knocked his drink back. "Thank you, Major. I don't know how you always manage to say the right thing, but I feel a ton better for getting that off my chest."

"Just call me 'Major Therapy,'" Sarah Jennifer told him with a chuckle. "Now, I want to see your best attempt to get drunk as a skunk, and that's an order, Private. Do you hear me?"

Dinny saluted. "Yes, ma'am," he replied with a grin before heading for the bar.

Sarah Jennifer stayed where she was to savor the peaceful moment. She watched Dinny enter the party with spirit, finding herself suddenly reticent to throw these young men into a situation they might not survive.

A tingle at the back of her mind distracted her from the weight of leadership. That was new, but she somehow knew what it was. She rested her hands on her knees and closed her eyes, focusing on tuning out the sounds of celebration. "Lilith?"

Lilith's voice filled Sarah Jennifer's mind. *I sensed you needed me. You may speak with just your mind. I'll hear you.*

Sarah Jennifer was taken aback by the concern in the Kurtherian's mental voice. She opened her mouth to speak out of habit before making the effort to think her reply. *I'm having second thoughts about involving all these people in a war. I'd want to protect them, but doing that would mean saving them at the expense of everyone else.*

Lilith made a soothing sound. *You have learned to care for them. Your burden will not grow less as time passes. Everyone who follows you into battle is doing so by choice, and your army will grow with every new group of people you discover.*

Sarah Jennifer chuckled. *Did you contact me just to give me the same talk I just gave Dinny?*

This is the eve of battle, Lilith chided gently. *Is it not customary at these moments for a friend to offer last-minute counsel to the intrepid leader?*

Intrepid, huh? Then why do people keep mistaking me for the solution to their problems? I'm not exactly a social butterfly. Sarah Jennifer shivered when warmth passed through her mind as Lilith laughed. *Okay, then. Hit me with the wisdom.*

For someone who claims poor social skills, you've managed to unite a lot of people who were at each other's throats. Lilith's tone held no reproach, only admiration. *You worked with what you knew to bring those Weres back from the brink. I don't think there's anything I can tell you about running a battle, but I see glimpses through your eyes every day, and I can tell you that your people believe in you. Thanks to the training you've given them, they are a formidable force to come up against.*

Sarah Jennifer wondered if doubt was contagious. *What if I get them killed, Lilith? They're trusting me.*

The pack trusted you to prepare them for this, and you have fulfilled your responsibility, Lilith countered. *Now it's your turn to trust* them.

Sarah Jennifer knew that already. She did trust them. All she'd done was show the Weres the way. The original unruly mob of twenty-five Weres had welcomed the additions to the pack and transformed themselves under her leadership into the well-oiled machine she'd drilled on the training field...was that only yesterday?

Time is a slippery thing, Lilith interjected. *Ours has come to an end for now. Good luck, Sarah Jennifer.*

Lilith was gone in the next instant, leaving Sarah Jennifer to wrap up her contemplation with the conclusion that people's decisions were outside her scope of duty unless they were negatively impacting others.

Her cup was empty. She left the haven beneath the branches and made her way to the bar by the stage. Lilith was right, she realized as she was stopped countless times along the way by people both excited and nervous about the prison break.

Sarah Jennifer exchanged a few words with each of them, giving encouragement and her absolute assurance that they were more than ready. She had a crowd around her by the time Brutus stepped in.

"Make some space," Brutus called, ushering Sarah Jennifer to the bar.

"Thanks," Sarah Jennifer told him as she refilled her empty cup with punch from the bowl. "I didn't want to sound ungrateful, but it's been a hell of a day, and as much as I'd like to party—"

Brutus snorted laughter. "Yeah, right. You shuddered just saying the word. But you should make a speech. It's, like, traditional."

Sarah Jennifer punched him in the arm. "Some leaders would make a speech. I hadn't considered it."

"*You're* 'some leaders,' Major," Dinny called. "We want to hear it! Speech!"

The band stopped playing when the pack took up the chant.

Sarah Jennifer shot Brutus a glare that promised revenge and got up onto the stage. "Like I said, I hadn't thought about a speech," she began, giving herself time to think. "They aren't my style. Just like everyone here, I'm a big believer in actions speaking louder than words. Tomorrow is a day for action. Tonight is about reminding ourselves *why* we fight."

A disturbance at the back of the cabin forestalled Sarah Jennifer's next words. Everyone relaxed again when Carver and Geordie walked into the clearing with Ozzie, Bruiser, and the witches.

Sarah Jennifer extended an arm toward Annie and the others. "You all saved a lot of lives today. Let's give a huge hand to the returning heroes." She raised her voice to be heard above the applause. "For those of you who aren't aware, they diverted an attack on the entire coast."

Annie and Sarai made their way over with Esme. This wasn't the time to get onto the subject of the Mad. "Can we get food and drinks for them?" Sarah Jennifer asked, heading for the edge of the stage to greet the three women.

Just as she thought she'd gotten away with it, the attention of everyone in the clearing turned back to her.

"You have to finish your speech," Jim called mischievously. "You were just getting going."

Sarah Jennifer smiled wryly, pausing on the steps. "Oh, no. That was it. I told you, I'm not one for speeches. But I'll tell you this. Every single person here should be proud of themselves. The world is about to fall to pieces yet again, and it would be easy for everyone to just run and hide from it. But not you. You're not taking it lying down. You have worked your rear ends off to prepare, to train, to learn. You have put aside your differences and reached for empathy and understanding. Without *you*, none of what we're going to do tomorrow would be possible."

The belief and determination on her people's faces brought warmth to Sarah Jennifer's insides and a smile to her face. "My grandfather always said that none of us are as smart as all of us. I say that's true. I also say that none of us are as *strong* as all of us and that by coming together, we are unstoppable. Refitting that vehicle in the short window we had was nothing short of a miracle."

Sarah Jennifer waited for the cheers to fade before continuing, "The leeches are not long for this world. We have right on our side, and a hell of a lot of weaponry to assist us in making our point clear. The people inside that prison have no clue what's coming for them, but *I* know."

She raised her cup to everyone there. "The *best*."

CHAPTER TWENTY-FOUR

The difference in stamina for the party life between the enhanced and unenhanced was evident the next morning. Sarah Jennifer woke everyone up an hour after dawn to prepare for departure.

There were plenty of grumbles from those nursing hangovers, while the Weres emerged chipper and ready to go. Bacon, sausage, and hash browns fixed the aching heads and queasy stomachs. Mostly.

Sarah Jennifer walked around, making final checks after breakfast, starting with getting Brutus' breakdown of the morning reports.

The lieutenant ran through everything he'd been told by the sergeants while the pack suited up. "A bunch of humans and a couple of the magic users drank too much last night, trying to keep up with the pack. Someone needs to remind them that's not possible since alcohol doesn't affect us. Esme wants to see you in her tent. Did you say Geordie and Carver could call dibs on the grenade launcher?"

Sarah Jennifer nodded, her attention on watching the Weres help each other with the body armor from Little Ace's haul. Right now, they looked like a bunch of kids getting ready for their first day of ninja school, half-dressed in their all-black gear with scarves tied around their faces to conceal their identities. "They earned it." She smiled at his look of disappointment. "You can use the rocket launcher."

Brutus quit pouting and punched the air. "*Yesss!*"

Sarah Jennifer snickered. "Does that make you feel better?"

Brutus fixed her with a serene smile. "You know, it really does."

"Go gear up, man-child." Sarah Jennifer shook her head fondly and left for the meadow to find Esme's tent.

When she got there, three people were waiting outside. Sarah Jennifer went into the tent and found a fourth person being treated by Esme for an aching head and the misconception that the ground was rolling beneath his feet.

Esme shooed her patient out. "I'm glad you got my message before you left. I think you need to take someone with you who can do magic."

Sarah Jennifer scoffed. "Who needs magic when I have explosives?"

Esme shook a finger at her. "Stop and think about it before saying no just because you'd prefer I stayed here in Salem."

"I'm not taking you into a battle zone," Sarah Jennifer stated. "I'm going to run the pack through some drills this morning, and we'll be departing at noon.

"What if you come up against something explosives can't solve?" Esme returned.

Sarah Jennifer shook her head. "I said no, and I meant it. There won't be a problem we can't solve without the use of magic. You're needed here, and everyone who fought at the lookout is depleted and has to rest—including you."

Esme sighed, knowing Sarah Jennifer was being logical. "Fine. Just don't get yourself killed, okay?"

Sarah Jennifer placed a hand on Esme's shoulder. "You've got it, and in return, try to make sure the place isn't on fire when we get back, yeah?"

Outside Lowell, MA (twenty-one hours later)

Sarah Jennifer nudged the bus along the highway, weighing whether she was more grateful for the plow-blade ram or the snow chains Jim had fixed to the tires.

The ram won out when they came to a degraded section of the road where nature had rolled right across the concrete, regardless of the abandoned vehicles.

Sarah Jennifer chuckled at Brutus' sigh as they slowed for yet another obstacle. "Did you think it would be a straight shot? Some of the roads around here haven't been touched since WWDE."

"I hadn't considered how clogged they'd be," Brutus admitted, steadying himself on the pole by the driver's seat. "Is it like this the whole way?"

"Why would you?" Sarah Jennifer asked. "You've never used the roads. But no. It clears up once we get past the turnoff for Harvard."

Brutus shuddered, remembering their time spent

observing the prison workers' families. "I hated that place. Those people gave me the chills."

Sarah Jennifer kept her eyes on the road, putting her foot down again as she got them past the foliage-strangled pileup. "Not our concern unless they decide to gatecrash." She indicated an upcoming fork in the road with a nod. "We'll be in sight soon."

It was another hour before they reached the turnoff for the prison. Sarah Jennifer pulled over, feeling the tension rise another notch as the way ahead cleared.

The pack eyed her nervously as she got out of the driver's seat and faced them.

"We are about to face our first real test," Sarah Jennifer told them solemnly. She walked down the bus, meeting each Were's gaze as she spoke. "I see some of you are unsure about your fitness to complete this mission successfully. Look to your left." She waited while they did as instructed. "Now look to your right. See the faces of the people who have your back, just like you have theirs. We are not alone in this."

She pointed in the general direction of the prison. "The guards in that prison do not have your training. They have not been laser-focused on drilling assault tactics into their minds and bodies. They are complacent, ignorant bullies who have only gotten away with locking Weres up and stealing their blood because no one has had the guts or the ability to stand up to them."

Dinny got to his feet, his hands clenched into tight fists. "Not anymore!"

Sarah Jennifer applauded him. "That's right." She flashed a hard grin at the Weres seated on the benches.

oing to let those scumbags get away with what
ıe?"

ıe pack retorted as one, their shouts reverber-
...e confines of the bus.

Sarah Jennifer raised her voice to match theirs. "Are
you going to allow those children to be separated from
their parents for another day?"

The pack drummed their feet on the floor. "No!" they
shouted, their blood rising.

Sarah Jennifer's grin resembled a snarl. "*Are we going to
allow them to take our own without retaliation?*" she yelled.

"NO!" they thundered, increasing the volume of their
drumming.

Sarah Jennifer whirled a hand around over her head
and dropped back into the driver's seat. "Then let's get this
show on the road!"

Everyone on the bus broke into howls. Brutus resumed
his place by Sarah Jennifer's side as she pulled the bus back
into the road. "That was awfully speech-y."

Sarah Jennifer put her foot down coming out of the
corner, and the bus responded with a throaty growl. "Perils
of leadership," she muttered.

Brutus leaned into the pole to steady himself against
the lurch of the wheels biting into the road, his entire
being focused on the fight ahead.

Sarah Jennifer sensed his impending brooding session
and let go of the wheel momentarily to punch him in the
arm. "Hey. Suck it up." She held the bus steady, her attention on the road ahead. "We're here to shut that place
down. It's no time for you to be gazing romantically into
the distance."

Brutus laughed, hearing the care behind the reprimand. "Love you too, cuz. Don't get killed in there, you hear me?"

It was Sarah Jennifer's turn to laugh. "Not likely. We have a foolproof plan, remember?" She nodded at the huge, walled-in building straight ahead. "There's no way they don't see us coming. You want to go grab your toy?"

Brutus grinned and pulled the rocket launcher out of the compartment behind the driver's seat. "As if I'd miss my chance." He fed his arm through the strap and got the launcher comfortable on his back, then hooked his arm around the pole to free up his hands and turned to face the rear of the bus.

He clapped for the pack's attention, raising his voice to be heard over the adrenaline-fueled shit talk going on along the benches. "Get your asses in gear! Those guards aren't going to die by divine intervention."

His words sparked a flurry of movement. The pack howled their war cries as they got into position at the hatches.

Sarah Jennifer's heart beat fast as they bore down on the prison gates in excess of sixty miles an hour. "Brace!" she yelled as they went past the point of no return.

Her perception of time stretched in the moment before the fourteen-ton bus hit the gates, and she remembered Ted's observation about mass times acceleration equaling one hell of a mess when applied to colliding objects in the real world.

The night was shattered by sirens and alarms when the bus hit the gates, and her uncle's theory was evidenced by chunks of the prison wall exploding into the yard as the bus smashed through them in a shower of sparks.

Searchlights slashed the air, coming to rest on the hurtling bus. The screams of injured guards added to the disharmony. It was possible that some of those guards were Weres under duress, but there was no time to take names in the urgency of the mission.

A steady rattle of bullets pinging off the bus joined the symphony as the guards in the watchtower on the wall snapped into action.

"Carver! Take out that tower!" Sarah Jennifer ordered.

The bus shook as the grenade launcher did its work. A sweeping line of holes appeared in the tower wall and the 40mm grenades detonated, reminding Sarah Jennifer for all the world of the time she and Sylvia had set off a string of firecrackers outside Magnus' house in revenge for some imagined slight and accidentally started a fire.

The tower collapsed in a smoking heap, providing the guards with an opportunity to dash inside the prison through a smaller door set into the wall beside the imposing double doors.

Sarah Jennifer applied the brakes, bringing the bus to a halt side-on to the doors to give them cover. She paused before pulling the door release. "Those cowards want to run and hide. Stick together, do I make myself clear?" The pack raised their fists and whooped, eager to get off the bus and face the guards hiding behind the prison walls. "Geordie, give us some more cover out there."

"On it, Major," came the reply from the turret.

There was a pop and a hiss as he deployed smoke bombs, then the prison yard was filled with a covering cloud. Sarah Jennifer opened the door the rest of the way, and the pack flowed off the bus and into the formation they'd practiced until they could fall into it in their sleep.

Little Ace stayed on the bus to relieve Sarah Jennifer of driver duty. "Kick ass," he encouraged as Sarah Jennifer and Brutus left the bus.

"That's a given on any day. Be safe, okay?" Sarah Jennifer gave Little Ace a stern look as he slipped into her vacated seat. "Don't take any stupid risks."

The younger Ace's face was set in a hard mask that did little to cover his determination to take his measure in blood for the injustice that had been done. "You've got the hard part, Major. All I have to do is drive around and give Carver and Geordie room to raise hell until the prisoners make it out here, right?"

"You've got it," Sarah Jennifer told him, patting his arm before she hefted her rifle and left the bus with Brutus shadowing her.

She glanced around, noting that nobody had come back out of the prison to fight. "I'm guessing they're feeling shy," she remarked to Brutus with a nod at the rocket launcher. "Make a door, hmm?"

Brutus shouldered the launcher with a gleam in his eye that had nothing to do with the way his inner wolf was howling for him to get with the destruction already. He glanced at Sarah Jennifer, his scar pulled tight by the serious lines of his expression. "You sure about this?"

Sarah Jennifer nodded. "Go for it."

Brutus took aim and fired and the doors exploded in flames, leaving a smoldering hole in their place. The dust choked the fire as it settled, giving them clear access to the corridor beyond. "You think they heard that?"

Sarah Jennifer pointed out the guards spilling into the far end of the corridor and gave the order to engage as her reply.

Forty-plus well-trained and pissed-off Weres armed with pre-WWDE rifles and a burning desire to wipe the blood trade from the face of the planet piled through the breach, with Sarah Jennifer at their head.

The guards responded recklessly, attempting to mob the pack with all the discipline of pigs at a trough. Their arc rods were a danger, but most went for their sidearms. They clearly hadn't been taught that lead was only good for annoying the Were about to rip your face off.

Sarah Jennifer's sensitive nose caught a familiar scent in the second before the shooting started. It was gone before she could pin it down, the heat of the moment pushing it from her immediate concerns. Right now, they had to clear their ingress to the prison, which meant breaking through the guards blocking their way.

Her shotguns took care of the guards smart enough to figure they were fighting Weres. Wherever she saw an arc rod spark, she dropped the guard holding it. She fired and reloaded, fired and reloaded, careful not to waste a single valuable slug on a miss. She had plenty of shells in her harness, but she didn't want to risk hitting any of her pack.

How many damn guards did they have? The pack was becoming frustrated, and Sarah Jennifer felt the rising need in them to take more direct action—like, the teeth-around-throats kind of action.

"*Do not shift,*" she ordered through gritted teeth. "Remember your training. Push them back and don't give them a damned inch!"

The pack tightened their formation and staggered their fire as they advanced. Within minutes, they'd cleared the narrow corridor at the entrance, forcing the guards back into the open room that had originally been a reception area and was now clearly a rec room.

Sarah Jennifer gave the tac teams the hand signals to spread out and take cover, suspecting that the guards would make an effort to get their acts together on their own turf.

She was right. There were more guards waiting inside.

The men blocking the way cleared at a barked instruction from behind them. They took hasty cover, ducking behind overturned furniture while the men inside the room peppered the entrance with automatic rifle fire to hold the pack at bay.

Sarah Jennifer noted they were still using a standard loadout and not the silver frangibles she'd be using in their place.

"What do we do?" Brutus asked.

Sarah Jennifer glanced over her shoulder at the pack waiting eagerly for her orders. She wasn't going to send them in to get shot up, even if they could shake it off. "Wait here for my signal."

Before Brutus could argue, she'd taken his rifle and was gone.

Sarah Jennifer ramped up her speed as she darted into the room. She felt time slow like it did when she was running free, a consequence of her nanocytes reacting to the situation. The increase in her ability to process everything around her gave her time to identify the guards' hiding places.

She could smell them—sweat and adrenaline. Sarah Jennifer emptied Brutus' AK into the bar as she crossed to climb the furniture barricade, blowing it to splinters and killing the three guards who crouched behind it.

She dropped the useless rifle when she was done since she was only carrying magazines for her AR-15, and leapt onto the remains of the barricade.

The guards scrambled to get their weapons on Sarah Jennifer, unaware it was too late for them. She pointed her AR-15 down and strafed them with it

"It's a bad day to be a scumbag," she murmured to the slumped corpses as she jumped off the barricade.

Sarah Jennifer picked up Brutus' rifle and walked over to the door. "That was the signal," she told him as she handed his weapon back.

Brutus raised an eyebrow. "What, you coming back covered in brains and blood?"

Sarah Jennifer shrugged. "Let's move. Spread out and find the door."

The pack spread out to look for a way into the main building as they crossed the room.

"I found a door," Rider called from the left-hand side of the ruined bar.

"Same here," Ozzie called from the right.

A quick investigation showed them that one door went into the cell blocks, and the other went into the administrative block of the prison.

"This is where we part ways for a while," Sarah Jennifer told the pack, wishing they had better radios, or telepathy, or *anything* that wouldn't mean she had to keep leaving her pack without communications ability.

"Remember your objective and your training. Rely on each other."

"Where are you going, Major?" Brutus asked, knowing the answer.

Sarah Jennifer indicated the admin block with a nod. "I'm going to introduce myself to the warden. I'll be back as soon as I find the bastard and give him a taste of my shotgun barrel. Free the prisoners, and treat anyone working here with extreme prejudice."

Brutus nodded. Nobody needed an explanation for that term.

CHAPTER TWENTY-FIVE

Cell Block B

Linus watched out of the corner of his eye as the guards stopped talking to listen to the message that came over their radios. Something about a vehicle approaching. Not all of them took it seriously. He didn't dare stop working, but he strained to hear their argument about who got to leave.

Two of them won the argument and left, and the others went back to complaining about getting stuck with their duty because the tech people couldn't prevent the shock collars from shorting out in the steamy laundry rooms.

Nobody in the laundry room knew how to react when an explosion went off close by. The power went down, and every alarm in the prison went off simultaneously. The guards dashed out of the room in the chaos that ensued, leaving the prisoners unsupervised and without their shock collars.

Linus knew an opportunity when he saw one, and they'd never get one as fortuitous as this if they lived a thousand lifetimes. He dropped the sheet he was folding and grabbed Reg's sleeve, pulling him over to the hot press he'd seen Katia working at earlier.

"What are you doing?" Katia hissed, shooing them away. "Get back to work before the guards come back!"

"What?" Linus spluttered. "No! Didn't you hear that message? They're distracted by an attack, and we're not wearing those fucking collars. We're getting out of here while we can."

Katia's eyes widened in disbelief. "What about everyone else? The pregnant women? You know damn well the guards won't think twice about hurting them to get us back under control. It's just like you to think of yourself."

"I thought of you, didn't I?" Linus shot back. "The guards aren't paying attention to us. They're too busy trying not to die. We need to get moving. Who knows how long this diversion will last?"

Katia scowled when the backup generator kicked in and the shadows were replaced by pallid blue emergency lighting. "Fine, but we're going to give everyone else a chance before we go."

Linus sighed and set off in the general direction of the main floor and the control room. "Of course we are. We just have to deactivate everyone's collars without getting ourselves killed in the process."

Reg rubbed his hands together as they walked, his eyes gleaming yellow in the low lights. "I hope we run into the doctors," he murmured. "Those bastards owe us big time."

"Forget revenge. It'll get you killed," Linus told him, wincing when another explosion caused the floor to shudder. "This has the feel of a planned attack. Think safety in numbers and concentrate on getting out of here. We need to head in the opposite direction of the fighting. The more of us who make a break for it, the more likely we'll succeed if we run into resistance."

Reg's eyes returned to their usual color. "You're right. Hey, what if this is our rescue, and we're running away from it?"

"Not likely," Katia blurted. She clapped her hand over her mouth when she saw the hurt she'd caused in Reg's slumped shoulders. "I'm sorry. I just don't see anyone being capable of taking this place down. The leeches have all the power."

Linus shook his head to counteract Katia's scorn, suddenly certain that Reg was right. "I can't think of anyone else crazy enough to come at this place head-on except the major. If we get everyone out of here and find out it's her and the pack smashing the shit out of this place, then it's what'd you call objective achieved. Job done."

He stopped talking when he saw their fellow prisoners amassing in the space between the cells and the control room wall.

Katia shook her head, her attention on the group of prisoners who were approaching them. "How are we going to get them out of here if everyone but us gets shocked every time we go past a checkpoint?"

"Get everyone moving. I'll handle it," Linus told her.

He waited while Katia and Reg persuaded everyone to follow them before approaching the control room and peering in. The view through the tiny window in the door was restricted, but he made out the lone guard easily.

Linus looked back over his shoulder. Satisfied he was

alone, he banged on the door of the control room and called to the guard in the same subservient tone he'd been using to curry favor for weeks. "Finally, I found someone. Mister, you've got to help. There's a bunch of prisoners escaping. They're going after the doctors."

The guard's voice was hesitant over the speaker. "What's going on out there? My radio is down."

"The prisoners are rioting," Linus lied smoothly, finding it uplifting to be using his skills as an all-around dirtball on the side of good for once. He counted down from ten, expecting the guard would open the door by the time he got to zero.

The wall adjoining the next cell block exploded when Linus got to three, tossing him against the control room wall like a ragdoll. He cried out as his head bounced off the solid concrete, more from the pain of seeing Katia, Reg, and the other prisoners being forced back into the cell block by a squad of guards.

Linus groaned as his plan to get everyone out alive crumbled to ashes.

"Get in your cells!" the control room guard screeched over the speaker. "Don't make me use those collars."

Linus must have hit his head harder than he thought. He struggled to shake off his concussion, wondering why he wasn't shifting to heal it faster. The pain of his clavicle forcing itself back together did much to refocus his mind, but he still could not bring himself to shift. "What the fuck?" he mumbled.

"Linus, get out of there!" Reg yelled.

Linus was lost as the certainty that he would never shift

again set in. He struggled to his feet just as the male prisoners dropped to their knees, clutching their throats.

"In. Your. Cells!" the guard shrieked. "Or I'll shock the women. Don't test me!"

The women clutched their bellies in fear, but the males submitted. The guards who had recaptured them used their arc rods to force the prisoners to move.

Katia cried out in pain when a guard jabbed her in the ribs with his arc rod. Reg lunged for the guard, the assault being the last straw for him. "Leave her alone!" he screamed as he grabbed the guard by the throat, shrugging off the electricity coursing through his body.

The other guards piled in, applying their batons and arc rods liberally.

Linus saw it all through the falling dust. His head felt fuzzy, but he knew Reg couldn't be allowed to die. They were all each other had in this world with Dinny dead and gone. He was about to make an attempt to save him when a cloud of opaque gas came out of nowhere, obscuring his view once again.

The gas stung his eyes, and he was blinded by tears as a mass of soldiers dressed in black came in through the breach with their semiautomatic rifles at the ready.

Linus wasn't alone. Nothing made sense in the next few moments. The prison guards weren't equipped to deal with the weapons of the intruders. Linus clamped his hands over his ears, curling up against the wall to make a smaller target of himself.

When the gunfire ceased, the guards were dead, and the control room was open.

Linus looked around blankly, his confusion complete as

the prisoners tore the collars from their necks and threw them away. One of the masked men approached him and held out a hand. Maybe that concussion hadn't fully healed yet because Linus could have sworn the masked soldier was saying his name.

He blinked in disbelief when the soldier pulled down the scarf covering his face. "Dinny? You're dead. This isn't happening."

Dinny took Linus by the elbow, frowning with concern. "I'm real enough. Come on, let's get you out of the way." He steered Linus over to Reg and Katia and the others while two of his team moved into the control room.

Linus slumped against the wall beside Reg and gazed at the soldiers in awe. Watching them take care of the prisoners, his addled brain finally figured out that the soldiers were his pack. "Hey, Reg. You were right.

"Never doubted the major," Reg murmured groggily.

"They've changed," Linus murmured, unable to believe that the seamless military unit was made up of the Weres he'd known for most of his life.

Reg nodded gingerly, still healing from the masses of shocks he'd taken.

Dinny handed Linus a flask of water. "Yeah, well, a lot's changed these last few weeks. We'll talk about it later. The main thing is that you guys are okay." He grinned at Katia. "*You're* an unexpected bonus. Good to see you, Kat."

Katia held up the flask she'd been given. "What can I say? I live to surprise, but I never expected their fantastic story of an Alpha who would come for them through Hell and high water to be anything *more* than a fantasy."

Linus scrambled to get to his feet. "Where is the major?"

he asked, remembering his inability to shift in the chaos. "I have to tell her..." His head swam in reaction to the sudden movement, forcing him back to the floor.

"I'm guessing that she's meeting with the warden right about now," Dinny told him. "You'll see her on the bus."

Linus thought his hearing might have been affected by the blast. "What bus? I need to see her *now*." He made another attempt to get up and walk, taking a couple of steps in the direction of the breach before he stumbled.

Katia caught him. "You're going nowhere fast, sunshine."

Linus sagged in her arms, tears of exhaustion running freely without him noticing. "You don't understand. I have to get to Sarah Jennifer. *I can't shift!*"

Administration Block

Sarah Jennifer left Brutus and the pack to take care of the prisoners and made her way into the labyrinthine corridors of the admin block. She had complete trust that the pack would take care of their part of the mission.

Her part would be slightly grimmer.

She found the warden's offices easily enough. What she didn't find was the warden or any of the other people who should have been there working at the abandoned desks. There was evidence everywhere she looked. The warden was apparently a stickler for pristine record-keeping if the cabinets filled with neatly alphabetized files for every Were in the prison were anything to judge by.

Sarah Jennifer pulled out a few interesting sheets of paper and tucked them into her armored vest. She searched the assistant's desk before going into the warden's office. Her nose wrinkled when she opened the door. The warden's scent was distinct, and there was that *other* scent again, the one she'd picked up a trace of in the initial attack.

It was stronger here, but Sarah Jennifer still couldn't place it. Where had she smelled it before? Whoever the scent belonged to had been here recently, and they weren't the only one. Sarah Jennifer picked out six distinct scents in total. Perhaps they had all been with the warden when the pack attacked.

She left the warden's office, her eyes glowing as she engaged her senses. Tracking the scent trails took Sarah Jennifer to a junction where the administration block connected with the cell blocks, where the layers upon layers of scents covered the tracks of the warden and his entourage.

Sarah Jennifer walked around, trying to pick up the trail again without any luck. An explosion shook the walls around her, cluing her in that Brutus was nearby. His nose was better than hers, not that she'd admit it to his face.

She shot out the mechanism on the barred gate partitioning the two blocks and jerked it almost off the rails in her haste to find Brutus before he moved on.

The center of the prison was deserted as Sarah Jennifer headed through the cell block at a light run. The sounds of the battle got louder as she got closer. Then her senses told her she had company.

Sarah Jennifer drew her pistol without slowing her pace and crouched as she turned the corner into the long corridor. Two guards came around the corner at the opposite end, forcing a prisoner to walk ahead of them. They ceased prodding the prisoner with their arc rods at the sight of Sarah Jennifer.

Sarah Jennifer shot the guard on the left, but the one on the right must have been having a lucky day because he threw himself out of the way of her second shot and scrambled back around the corner with a scream.

The prisoner could only stand there since the manacles around her ankles and wrists made it too difficult to run. She cringed as Sarah Jennifer approached, quivering with fear.

"Please don't kill me," the woman whispered, her face rosy-red. "My blood won't taste good to a vamp."

Sarah Jennifer realized that her eyes were still glowing and laughed as she returned them to their usual clear gray. "Don't worry, I'm not a vampire," she assured the Were woman as she rifled the dead guard's pockets for the keys to the chains. "Let's get you out of here."

The woman rubbed her wrists when they were free. "Thanks. My name is Lydia."

Sarah Jennifer looked up from unlocking Lydia's ankles. "Nice to meet you, Lydia. I'm Major Walton from Salem's Defense Force, and I'll be providing your rescue experience today." She got to her feet and stepped back. "I don't suppose you know where the warden might be hiding?" she asked without much hope of the former prisoner knowing the answer.

Lydia shook her head, her lip curling in disgust. "He and his gang wouldn't stick around for this. He has an airship on the roof, so he'll be long gone."

Sarah Jennifer set off running for the stairs, leaving

Lydia behind. "Thank you!" she called back. "Get to the yard. There's transport waiting to get you out of here."

She streaked through the prison, grabbing Brutus when she bumped into him, looking for her outside the food hall.

"Where are we in such a rush to get to?" Brutus asked, keeping pace with her as they made their way to the roof.

Sarah Jennifer pushed harder, feeling time trickling away. "The warden," she replied tersely. "Roof."

They came upon a locked door at the top of the stairs. Sarah Jennifer growled in frustration and drew her right shotgun.

Brutus clamped his hands over his ears. "Are you sure that's a goo—"

He was cut off by the report as the lock and a chunk of the doorframe disintegrated in the spray of hot metal. "Okay, then," he murmured as Sarah Jennifer jerked the door open and strode onto the roof in the nimbus of red light cast by her eyes.

Sarah Jennifer was relieved to see a dirigible moored to the roof, its balloon still slightly saggy. The warden was one of a group of six people preparing to board, and Lydia had identified him as male, which took it down to one of two.

Sarah Jennifer had no problem taking both men down and bagging herself a dirigible in the process.

"So, we're all walking, and this asshole has an *airship*?" Brutus bitched, drawing the attention of the guards.

The warden's guards were less than happy to see them. One ushered the warden and his female companions into the cabin of the ship while the rest advanced on Sarah Jennifer and Brutus with their arc rods sparking.

The other man paused at the cabin door and turned to look at Sarah Jennifer and Brutus. Sarah Jennifer suddenly understood why she hadn't remembered *who* the scent belonged to. She'd last seen the man running from Salem after his faction had attempted to block the pack's entry into the town. She wasn't picking up his scent.

She was smelling his magic.

"You won't get away a second time," Sarah Jennifer yelled over the rising wind the man was whipping up.

The man flashed an evil grin and vanished into the cabin, yelling for the guards to cut the dirigible loose.

Sarah Jennifer readied herself to shoot her way through the guards. There was no way she was getting through this without getting hurt, but what the guards didn't know was that she didn't care about the pain from their shock rods.

The dirigible strained at its moorings as a pair of guards worked to free the ropes. Sarah Jennifer wondered if the rogue witch was the real boss. Whether it was the witch or the warden, her only goal was to get her hands on him and find out who he worked for before she tore his head clean off his body for what he'd done to the Weres.

Brutus unslung the missile launcher from his back, catching sight of the guns some of the guards had pointed at them. He fired at the dirigible, refusing to let the perpetrators escape.

Sarah Jennifer noticed what he was doing a moment too late. "No!"

The rocket hit the dirigible in the next moment, and everyone was thrown off the roof in the explosion when the hydrogen inside the balloon ignited.

CHAPTER TWENTY-SIX

A bolt of searing pain struck Sarah Jennifer. One moment she was somehow released from the strictures of gravity, the next she landed in a tangled heap in the prison yard and everything went black.

Sarah Jennifer hissed as she came around to fire raining down from above her, burning scraps of silk and chunks of wicker and wood cladding falling all around the prison yard as the remains of the dirigible came back down to Earth.

Moving to avoid the smoldering embers, Sarah Jennifer came to the realization that both her legs were broken, and that they were healing already. She wished Esme were there because the other alternative was going to make the top ten of the most painful experiences of her life.

Brutus groaned somewhere nearby.

"You alive?" she called, wincing as her burns healed.

"I'm still figuring that out," Brutus replied. "You okay?"

Sarah Jennifer ground her teeth, grunting despite her

resolve not to show weakness as she pulled herself to a sitting position. "I won't lie. I've been better."

Brutus extracted himself from the shrubbery that had broken his fall and limped over to Sarah Jennifer. "That bad, huh?" he teased. His smile dropped away when he saw the mess the landing had made of her legs. "Shit. You're going to have to let me—"

Sarah Jennifer waved him on, pulling one of her harness straps loose to bite down on. "I know. Go ahead. Just get it over with before you have to rebreak the bones."

"Brace yourself." Brutus took Sarah Jennifer's left foot in his hands. "Ready?"

Sarah Jennifer nodded and bit down on the leather, which did little to muffle her screams as Brutus pulled to align her bones while her nanocytes worked to rejoin the breaks. "Thanks," she told Brutus after the pain ebbed to a dull roar. "Even though it's the least you can do after blowing up the airship. That could have been our ticket to Europe."

Brutus looked up at the smoking wreck on the roof. "Nah, you don't want one of those. Just look what an idiot with a rocket launcher can do."

Sarah Jennifer fixed him with a stern look. "You want to help instead of digging yourself deeper?"

Brutus bent to pick Sarah Jennifer up and carried her over to the bus. "You're healing already, aren't you?"

She nodded. "I can't see that I'll be able to walk this one off for a few hours, at least."

"You'll ride on the bus," Brutus told her. "I won't hear any arguments."

"Wasn't planning on arguing," Sarah Jennifer replied as

tiredness stole over her. "What I need is a half a cow medium-rare and a thirty-six-hour nap."

The pack and the rescued Weres who could walk under their own power were crowded around the bus when they got to the yard. The pregnant women and the injured Weres on the bus reacted with shock when Brutus went sideways up the steps and squeezed through them to get Sarah Jennifer to a bench.

One of the rescued Weres got up to make space, grabbing one of the hanging straps to support himself on his one leg. "Ma'am, are you going to be okay?" he asked, sparking a flurry of questions from the others.

Sarah Jennifer winced as Brutus set her down. "I'll be fine, but it looks like I won't be driving for a while," she joked in response to the concerns.

Brutus did a double-take at the woman next to Sarah Jennifer. "Katia?"

Sarah Jennifer grinned, taking in the wiry, fair-haired woman. "I've heard a lot about you."

"Nothing good, I hope," Katia replied. She smiled tiredly at Brutus and ruffled his hair. "Hey, squirt. Good to see you."

Brutus wrapped his long-lost Alpha in a hug. "It's been twenty years. I can't believe how tough you are."

Katia returned his embrace with feeling. "I can't believe you got us out of there." She released Brutus and shifted on the bench to face Sarah Jennifer. "I didn't believe you were coming for us. I'm sorry for doubting you."

Sarah Jennifer leaned back and closed her eyes, too emotional to speak as everyone on the bus broke into cheers, applauding their freedom. She smiled, knowing there were going to be a whole lot of happy children when they got back to Salem.

Brutus grabbed a blanket from the storage locker and draped it over Sarah Jennifer's legs, smiling when she cracked an eyelid. "We won. You did it."

Sarah Jennifer was as comfortable as she was going to get. She pulled the blanket up and banged the driver's partition with all the enthusiasm she felt despite her pain. "Let's go home!"

North Road, MA

The convoy hit the north road just after the sun reached its zenith on the second day. The going had been slower on the way back to Salem than the outward journey had been, as expected. Sarah Jennifer had Brutus call regular stops for rest and food along the way, since many of the Weres were on foot and weak from the regular blood loss they'd been subjected to.

On the bus, the injured were resting while their nanocytes worked on healing them. Sarah Jennifer's legs had healed well enough for her to get up into the turret, where she had an unobstructed view of the road ahead. The gentle rocking of the bucket seat on its mount kept lulling her to sleep as they crept down the road at a walking pace.

Her eyes snapped open when she felt Esme's mind brush hers. She concentrated on opening her mind to the connection, needing to be just Sarah Jennifer for a minute. Not the major, or anyone's Alpha, just a woman who'd had a hard day talking to her friend. *Esme? Can you hear me?*

The sensation remained just that. Sarah Jennifer screwed her eyes shut and gripped the armrests, clenching every muscle in her body as she willed the connection to open.

Duckie, you did it! Esme enthused.

Sarah Jennifer's frustration melted instantly at the sound of Esme's mental voice. *Esme? It's so good to hear you. We're almost at Salem, and we have upwards of two hundred Weres in need of food, shelter, and medical assistance.*

We're ready and waiting for you, Esme assured her. Her voice gained the sharp edge Sarah Jennifer was more used to. *You're in pain. What did it take to get them out of the prison?*

Sarah Jennifer gave Esme a quick rundown of the operation and its outcome.

It looks like we know why Darren's faction was against you, Esme interjected bitterly when Sarah Jennifer described the man she'd seen on the prison roof. *You just described Stuart Banning.*

Sarah Jennifer nodded to herself. *I recognized the scent of magic. I didn't get a real look at his face that day on the road.* A thought hit Sarah Jennifer. *Wait...if the leeches and the rogue witches are working together, does that mean we can track them to their location?*

And by we, you mean me? Esme inquired dryly. *Honestly, I won't know until I try.*

Someone climbing up to the turret distracted Sarah Jennifer. *I have to go. We'll be there soon.*

The someone was Linus. He moved like he was bruised all over, his face swollen and crisscrossed with healed lacerations. He nevertheless broke into a smile when he met Sarah Jennifer's questioning expression.

It was the unhappiest smile she'd ever seen. Sarah Jennifer waved him up and indicated he crouch in the space Geordie used to man the projectile launchers. "What can I do for you, Linus?"

Linus crouched in the nook. "Sorry to intrude, Major."

Sarah Jennifer watched him fidget while he sought the words. "I'm going to guess you didn't come up here to thank me for breaking your behind out of that prison."

Linus sighed. "No, Major. I mean, yeah, I'm grateful you came for Reg and me and the others. But something happened to me in there. Something...*bad*."

Sarah Jennifer scrutinized Linus, wondering if he was up to his old tricks. The hopelessness she saw in his eyes assured her he believed everything he was about to spill. "I can't help if you don't talk." Her tone was soft but brooked no disobedience. "Tell me what the problem is."

Linus squirmed under her clear gray stare. "I can't shift. I've lost my wolf."

Sarah Jennifer sat up in alarm. "What do you mean, you can't feel it?"

Linus shook his head in desolation. "No. Not since I tried to shift during the breakout."

Sarah Jennifer knew better than to panic. She called for Brutus.

Brutus climbed halfway into the turret. "What's up?"

"Call a halt," Sarah Jennifer ordered. "I need to know if anyone has had any trouble shifting."

Brutus glanced at Linus, his eyes widening with concern as he put his old rival's hangdog look together with Sarah Jennifer's order and came up with, "Oh, shit."

He vanished, and the bus came to a halt. Sarah Jennifer

climbed down from the turret, dismissing the offers of help with a scornful shake of her head.

"I can walk by myself, thank you," she told Brutus. "Pick me up at your peril, and don't say I didn't warn you."

Brutus backed off, holding up his hands in defeat. "Fine, hobble around all you like. I just hope your bones are as hard as your skull because it's going to take longer to heal if you insist on walking around."

Twenty steps. That was all she had to walk. "Did you find anyone?" Sarah Jennifer asked tersely, ignoring the shooting pains that wracked her legs as she crossed the vast distance from the back of the bus to the door.

Brutus hovered, ready to catch her. "Nobody on the bus. There's a man name of Harris who wants to talk to you."

Sarah Jennifer gave in and used the overhead support straps to take her weight and expedite her progress. She let go of the last strap when she reached the steps and sighed when her knee chimed in with the grinding ache in her left femur.

She grabbed the pole and gritted her teeth. "I need to figure out instant healing. This blows a whole herd of goats."

Brutus slipped around Sarah Jennifer and hopped down the first step. "Lean on me. You can owe me a favor later if it makes you feel better."

Sarah Jennifer shook her head. "It's not that. I'm the Alpha. I have to be strong."

Brutus raised an eyebrow. "You're walking around on two broken legs. That's pretty fucking strong. Now, Major. Do I need to tell you to suck it up?"

His smirk set Sarah Jennifer chuckling. "You can, but then you might find me standing over your bed one morning with a hose in one hand and a camera in the other."

Brutus' smirk morphed into a full-on grin. "We don't have camera tech."

Sarah Jennifer smiled sweetly. "For this, I'd reinvent it. Let's go. Where's Harris?"

Sarah Jennifer allowed Brutus to steady her down the steps, holding on for a moment to make sure her legs were going to work once they reached solid ground. Satisfied she wasn't going to embarrass herself, she looked for the man who wanted to speak to her.

"The major will see you now," Brutus told a sandy-haired man who was accompanied by a female wolf.

"You had trouble shifting?" Sarah Jennifer asked. "Harris, is it?"

Harris stepped forward, his eyes lowered in respect. "Not me, Major Walton. It's my wife. She hasn't shifted since we got those collars off. I didn't think anything of it until you asked. I think she's trapped."

Sarah Jennifer knelt at the wolf's eye level. "What's her name?"

"Dakota," Harris replied.

Sarah Jennifer looked into Dakota's eyes and wasn't sure if she was relieved or horrified to see intelligence beyond that of a canid in them. "Dakota, can you understand me?"

The wolf nodded.

Horrified, definitely. There was no way around it; this

woman was trapped. "Have you tried to shift back?" Sarah Jennifer asked, already knowing the answer.

Dakota shook her head and whined softly.

Sarah Jennifer covered her eyes with her hand, packing down the despair that threatened to overwhelm her ability to reason. It would be too easy to give in to the temptation to wallow in yet another problem on top of everything else. That wasn't her way. It wasn't the Walton way, and it definitely wasn't the way to overcome.

She had to act immediately and decisively.

Sarah Jennifer dropped her hand and stood up with some difficulty, leaning on Brutus for support. "Separate Linus and Dakota from the pack," she told Brutus. "When we get to Salem take them to…" She thought fast. "Darren's house. He's not using it."

"Got it." Brutus didn't say what they were both thinking. If this were infectious like the Madness, it would wipe out Werekind in a matter of years.

"Can I stay with her?" Harris requested.

Sarah Jennifer nodded. "Yes. When we get to Salem, you will be quarantined and taken care of. We'll figure this out, but first, we have to make sure everyone stays safe."

She turned to face the Weres, her pack, steadied herself, and let go of Brutus.

"Listen up." She didn't hesitate or hold back on the seriousness of the situation. "Right now, we have a pack member stuck in human form, and another stuck in wolf form. I don't know if their affliction can be transmitted. As your Alpha, my duty is to protect the pack. I have no choice but to ban shifting until further notice."

The news stunned the already traumatized Weres. Sarah Jennifer searched for words that would give them hope. As much as she hated to speak anything less than the truth, this wasn't the time for a history lesson on the UnknownWorld.

Esme was going to have a field day with this when Brutus told her about it. Maybe it was a good thing camera technology no longer existed.

Sarah Jennifer lifted her hands to quell the disquiet. "It's a temporary solution. We're just a few miles from Salem, where food, medical attention, and safe homes are waiting. There are people there who have abilities that are comparable to magic. They will do everything they can to fix this."

The reactions from the pack were mixed. "Why would they do that?" a man called. "They don't know us."

"They took in our kids," another man argued. "They sound like good people to me. I'm willing to give them a chance."

Katia stepped out of the crowd. "We're supposed to believe in magic?"

"You will see it for yourselves soon enough," Sarah Jennifer replied. "While there is a deeper explanation, yes, magic exists. You will meet people who call themselves witches, and you will respect their belief system. Do I make myself clear?"

The Weres murmured their assent.

"What are your concerns?" Sarah Jennifer asked. She gave them space to talk it out for a few minutes. While she was within her rights as Alpha to demand obedience and get on with her day, she wasn't that kind of leader. She wanted these people to be able to learn to trust again. She wanted them to feel like they had a home and a pack, an Alpha who cared about their welfare. Eventually, she hoped they would want to fight for humanity, and that started with reminding them what it was to be treated like humans.

She listened to their worries, their hopes, and their fears, and took them all on board. More than a few were worried about conscription, while others wanted to enlist in the Defense Force immediately. Some were concerned about being accepted in Salem due to the size of the pack. Who had the resources to take in so many in these harsh times?

When the discussion petered out, Sarah Jennifer addressed them again. "I want to make a few things clear before we get back on the road. The UnknownWorld has been hounded by the leeches, and you have suffered unspeakably at their hands. But they are not the biggest threat. We are on the brink of a new age, an age where fantastic, incredible things will be part of everyday life. Salem is a haven for the UnknownWorld, protected and hidden by magic. There is enough to feed everyone indefinitely, again, because of magic."

Her eyes glowed as the reasons for her strictures came to the forefront of her mind. "There is a dark side to every silver lining. An affliction has infected mankind, a Madness that cannot be diverted by any means. It has overtaken much of the world already, and now it's on our shores. Salem is the only place that will be safe in the years ahead. I don't want to scare you with stories of what is coming. I want to inspire you to make the choice that will mean you live through it. You are free to choose your own path, but understand that returning to your former homes is not an option. Your children will be safe in Salem, and you will not be required to join the Defense Force unless you want to. You are my pack, and Salem will be your home for as long as you want it. In the meantime, I need you all to take my orders seriously. Do. Not. Shift."

She made her way back onto the bus, one painful step at a time.

Little Ace grinned at her from the driver's seat. "I think you got through to them, Major."

"I hope so," Sarah Jennifer replied. "Let's get moving."

CHAPTER TWENTY-SEVEN

Harris and Dakota were sitting on the roof of the bus a short distance from Linus and Reg, as ordered by Brutus, when the turnoff for Salem came into sight, raising a ragged cheer from the convoy.

Linus nudged Reg when the cheers went up. "What's everyone so excited about?"

Reg frowned, pointing out the standing stones. "We're almost there. Can't you see the road?"

Linus shook his head, drawing his knees to his chest. "What's wrong with me, Reg?"

Reg patted his back. "Those witches will figure it out. Don't worry."

Sarah Jennifer's voice came from the turret. "Listen to Reg."

"Do you know what's wrong?" Linus asked.

"Not in enough depth to understand how to fix it," Sarah Jennifer replied. "But Esme will, and if she doesn't, she won't stop until she does."

The town boundary came into sight, forestalling

further conjecture. Sarah Jennifer wasn't expecting a welcoming committee, but the people of Salem had come out in force, with Annie and Sarai at the forefront. The side of the road was lined with probably every cart in Salem, which was to say there were enough to take the pack the rest of the way if half of them didn't mind waiting for a ride.

The convoy slowed, then stopped as the two groups met, and the pack was given blankets and soup and sugary pastries to give them an energy boost for the last leg of their journey.

Brutus commandeered a cart and climbed into the bed to find the parents of the children they'd rescued from Harvard. None of the children had been old enough to know their home as anything *but* home when their parents had been taken. He settled for calling out each child's name and giving a general description if more than one family responded.

He had trouble locating Sunshine's and Flower's parents until he called their brother's name. A woman came forward hesitantly. "Can you tell me how old they are?" she asked in a near -whisper.

Brutus checked the list the children had given him with every detail they could remember about themselves. "Benjamin is ten years old. Sunshine and Flower are both—"

"Six?" the woman cut in, her eyes bright with tears.

Brutus nodded, smiling as he offered the woman his hand. "Yes, ma'am. Hop on up here, and we'll get you reunited."

The woman stared at Brutus' hand for a moment, then burst into tears when she realized the lengths her son must have gone to to keep his infant sisters alive after the leeches had killed their father and taken her from them. "I thought they were dead. This is a miracle."

The other parents gathered her into their huddle on the cart while Brutus gave the driver instructions to take them to the town hall.

Sarah Jennifer exited the bus stiffly as the first cart rumbled off, her legs still complaining about her weight. She waved Annie over. "Hold a small cart back. We have a situation."

Annie took the news about Linus and Dakota with less shock than Sarah Jennifer had expected. Sarah Jennifer swallowed her sinking feeling. "Please don't tell me the same thing has happened in Salem?"

Annie clasped her hands together and shook her head sadly. "I'm afraid I can't. We've set up a shielded area within the boundary hex for now. Esme is working on finding the cause."

That gave everyone on the roof hope. Sarai came over, leading Cordy by the reins. "I thought you'd want to go straight to the quarantine zone," she told Sarah Jennifer. "Esme is waiting for you there."

Sarah Jennifer took the reins. "Thank you. Where are we headed?"

"Just outside town," Annie told her. "Go past the park, and you'll see a marker stone. Turn there and follow the track. We decided to convert Darren's house into a hospital."

"Great minds think alike," Sarah Jennifer commented dryly. She mounted Cordy and looked up at everyone on top of the bus. "You heard the lady. Everyone down."

Leaving Brutus in charge of getting everyone else to where they needed to be, Sarah Jennifer escorted the group of four to the out-of-the-way cottage Annie had directed her to, with Kalder at the reins of the cart.

Everyone felt the shift in atmosphere when they made the turn at the marker stone. The chat dried up as a sense of foreboding settled over them.

Sarah Jennifer, already at the bottom of her well, just sighed and pressed on, leading them toward the source of their discomfort.

Esme had clearly constructed this barrier to keep *everyone* out. The horses shied away from the gate, even Cordy, who was usually easygoing. Sarah Jennifer directed Kalder to pull the cart up along the road before the gate, choosing a nearby tree to tether Cordy to. "Wait. Esme will know we're here."

Sarah Jennifer felt a presence at the gate. "Speak of the devil."

Esme folded her arms. "You're just sore because you're on the wrong side of the barrier. I told you it wasn't a pleasant experience for the uninvited."

Sarah Jennifer matched Esme's posture. "Are you going to keep us standing out here? I bet you haven't even got the kettle on."

Esme opened the barrier at the gate, giving them all a hard stare as they entered the garden. "Just shows what you know. You'll all be bathing before I allow you to sit at my table, wolf included."

Sarah Jennifer conceded that was fair since they were all covered in road dust and grime from the prison break. "Bathing" was pushing it. Darren's idea of modern plumbing had been an outdoor shower fed by a hand pump connected to the cottage's water collection system.

Esme made good on her hint that food would be available to the freshly-washed. She also provided clean clothing for the travelers and told them to help themselves to the urn of tea she had made. "It's hot," she warned.

Sarah Jennifer was a firm convert to Esme's Scottish tea, hot, strong, milky, and loaded with sugar. She searched the kitchen for the largest mug she could find and fixed herself some sweet, caffeinated goodness before going to talk to the other Weres who'd been hit with the malady.

It was disheartening to find that on the surface, there were no correlating circumstances connecting their inability to shift. Sarah Jennifer hoped it wasn't connected to the Madness, but she had to be realistic and consider that the two nanocyte malfunctions had arrived at pretty much the same time.

If only she had a contact in Europe apart from Lilith. Someone who had seen the early days of the Madness there. She needed something better than shortwave radio, but the only thing close to that was the device in Sylvia's house, and it wouldn't help her reach the other side of the world.

Sarah Jennifer searched out Esme after she'd eaten, finding her friend curled in a chair in the study. "Can we get the council out here for a meeting?"

"There's one scheduled at the town hall tonight," Esme informed her without looking up from the book she was engrossed in.

Sarah Jennifer nodded, wandering over to the bookshelves set into the wall. "I've been thinking about your idea to send some people north." She perused the titles while she waited for Esme's reply.

Esme chuckled. "I knew you'd catch up eventually. It's the logical decision. If we do nothing to block the land bridge, we'll be overrun with Mad."

"There's still the matter of transportation," Sarah Jennifer reminded her. "The bus would have been an option if the coast was intact. The warden's dirigible would have been perfect if Brutus hadn't blown it up. How do you expect to get our people there?"

Esme shook her head. "Sarah Jennifer Walton, you are thinking too *small*. What do you need?"

Sarah Jennifer laughed. "I need a military transport plane with a top speed of 'hold onto your cookies' that has room for the whole pack and our vehicles. I can't imagine there are many of those lying around."

Esme cracked up. "Even if there are, they won't be anywhere we could find."

Sarah Jennifer saw where Esme was going. "But we could locate private hangars relatively easily with local knowledge. What about pilots? How will we train them without pre-WWDE technology?"

Esme's laughter tapered off. "Not with magic, if that's what you're thinking. Let's focus on finding a plane before you start grilling me about technology."

Salem, MA

Sarah Jennifer and Esme arrived at the town hall just as the winter moon made its appearance over Salem. Brutus and Katia were talking on the steps outside, paying no attention to the people heading inside for the meeting.

Esme put a hand to her mouth when they turned as one, sensing Sarah Jennifer's proximity. "Is that a werewolf thing?" she whispered.

"You know we can hear you?" Brutus called.

Esme clicked her tongue. "It's polite to pretend you can't," she chastised.

Sarah Jennifer nudged the witch. "Give me a minute."

Esme nodded and went inside, swatting Brutus with her carpetbag as he ran down the steps to meet Sarah Jennifer.

Katia followed him at a more circumspect pace, her attention caught by Esme's departure. "Looks like it's getting ready to start. I'll get out of your way."

Sarah Jennifer put out an arm to stop her from leaving. "You should be at the meeting."

"Why?" Katia asked incredulously. "I'm not a part of this town. Did you see the way David looked at me?"

"You're a part of this pack," Sarah Jennifer told her. "Inside. No arguments." She left to catch up with Esme without giving Katia a chance to refuse.

Katia simmered with frustration at being told what to do, combined with the deep-seated need to please the Alpha. "This fucking sucks. I hate people at the best of times, but here? Salem? It's a special kind of hell. You know David has it in for me."

"You did kill his brother," Brutus murmured, steering her to the steps.

"Yeah, because the sick fuck was demanding we pay a

blood tithe to live here," Katia spat, digging her heels in at the door.

"It's not like that now," Brutus promised. "I swear. Sarah Jennifer is dead-set against the blood trade. She and Esme kicked a bunch of witches out of Salem when we arrived. I didn't say anything at the time, but I recognized their faces, Kat. There are no links to the blood trade here anymore. Salem is the home we dreamed of back in Boston."

Katia's shoulders lost some of their tightness. "I doubt that. You kids thought the streets ran with gold, you built it up so much. Let's just get this over with so I can go find a rock to hide under."

Brutus didn't know what to say to lift her mood, so he just nodded and opened the door. He was quiet as they made their way to the meeting room, his thoughts on the changes in Katia's personality. He was wondering what he could do to support the Weres who'd been in the prison for years as they adjusted to life outside its walls when he bumped into Sarai, knocking the basket of fruit she was carrying out of her hands.

"Sorry," he mumbled, bending to pick up the spilled apples. "I was miles away."

Sarai smiled before turning to retrieve an errant apple that had rolled under the table by the door. "You were. Care to share?"

Katia took one look at the dazed expression Brutus gave Sarai in return and snorted. "I'm going to find Esme. She's about the only one around here who isn't crazy."

Sarai watched her go before dissolving into giggles. "That's what she thinks. Esme is batty." She hugged her basket to her hip. "You were going to tell me what had you so occupied you didn't see me coming."

Brutus handed her the last apple. "I, uh…" He rubbed the back of his neck with a hand, lost for words. "We should get in there and take our seats before they start without us."

Sarai graced him with another smile and went into the meeting room in a flash of swishing skirts.

Brutus remained glued to the spot for a moment, unsure of what just passed between them. Sarai was… intriguing, but she wasn't pack, and he wasn't in the market for a distraction. He shook it off and went into the meeting room, taking his seat beside Sarah Jennifer.

"You okay?" Sarah Jennifer asked, raising a curious eyebrow at the flush in Brutus' cheeks.

Brutus resisted the urge to glance at Sarai and nodded. "Yeah. Just wondering how this is going to go down."

The town council looked a lot different this time around. Representation for all would do that. In addition to the witches, Brutus, and Katia, she'd requested that Big Ace, Jim Johnson, and a couple other Defense Force division heads be present.

Sarah Jennifer had already decided how it was going to go down. "Everyone will comport themselves with dignity and respect for their fellow human beings," she told Brutus loudly enough for everyone in the room to hear. "We will listen to Esme list the current agenda, then we will discuss each problem and its solutions. Everyone will be heard. Decisions will be reached by consensus, and if that fails, they will be made by Esme and me."

"What gives you the right to make decisions on our behalf?" David cut in angrily.

"The impending destruction of the human race," Sarah Jennifer stated coldly. "My pack, my military, standing between you and said destruction."

Esme banged her gavel for silence. "Sit down before you hurt yourself, David. The one thing we *don't* have is time for this to devolve into politics." She waved down the rest. "Everyone. We have a lot to get through if you want to get home tonight."

The tension level dropped as Esme's declaration of an all-night session took the wind out of David's sails. She put her gavel down and laced her fingers together, resting her hands on the table while she waited for everyone to get settled. "That's more like it. The major has my full support in everything she just said, and anyone who doesn't like it doesn't need to stick around. It's time to get real. We have a total of two hundred and sixty-eight people in need of permanent homes, jobs, healthcare, and education for their children. Civilization has not fallen as long as we uphold our duty as human beings to take care of each other. That brings us to item one, housing for the expanded pack."

Annie waved a sheaf of paper. "I have lists, and one is of housing needs."

"What do they need?" Magnus asked.

Annie listed the various accommodation needs the pack had, which included family housing for those with children, communal living space for the majority of the childless Weres, and isolation for the few who wanted to live apart after so long in a cell.

"Family housing isn't an issue," David told them

after Annie was done. "We have a number of recently vacated houses. Darren's is being used as a hospital, but that leaves five others in the vicinity of Durent Street."

"I'll give up my house for a family," Esme decided. "I can camp out in the DF office."

"I have room for a small family," Lenore offered. "I'll move out to my workshop."

Jim reiterated his offer to take in anyone who needed a home and a trade. "I have a few cabins in different places that will do for those looking for some space. I'm teaching woodworking as well as tinkering."

Sarah Jennifer just shook her head at Jim's humble description of his diverse skill set.

Katia leaned over to Jim. "Can I take you up on one of those cabins?"

Jim nodded. "Sure thing, Ms. Katia, if you'll take care of the traps and cut wood for the town."

Katia stuck out a hand. "You've got yourself a deal."

"Suggestions for group housing?" Esme asked.

"We'd need somewhere with a lot of space," Tom commented. "When I was feeding everyone at dinner, I heard most of those guys saying they want to join the Defense Force, so it can't be too far outside of town unless the major wants to set up another base."

"We'll get to that," Sarah Jennifer told him. "When we spread out, it will be with trained soldiers. For now, it sounds like we need a barracks as close to the town hall as we can get it."

The consensus was to add another floor to the town hall to provide barracks since those who wanted to live together were also the group that was most vocal about enlisting.

Sarah Jennifer nodded. "Agreed. That takes care of the families and the Defense Force recruits. What about the civilians? Not everyone will want to fight."

"I can have the reclamation crews focus on construction materials," Little Ace offered. "We'll need materials for the town hall extension anyway, so it's no problem to add a little more to the list."

Izzy raised her hand. "If the earth witches will help with the shells, we can get housing built a lot faster." She smiled at Katia. "I'm sure people would be happy to provide labor and put their own touches on their homes."

Katia's instinctual scowl melted away. "That's really thoughtful," she conceded.

"It might help with getting over being locked away for so long," Brutus interjected, looking at Sarah Jennifer hopefully. "What do you say?"

Sarah Jennifer nodded. "I like it. What's your status as a division?" she asked Little Ace. "You had three crews working last time I checked."

"Still three crews," Little Ace confirmed. "But that could change once I start recruiting from the pack." He paused. "I can do that, right?"

Sarah Jennifer smiled. "Double what you're working with for now. Same for you, Quartermaster. I want to see plans for procedures to help you cope with the growth of your divisions before the week is out."

Big Ace nodded, scribbling in his ledger. "I run a tight ship, Major," he murmured. "My brother will have to filter out the volunteers who are there thinking to get first dibs on salvage."

"Are we all happy the housing issue is resolved for the moment?" Esme asked. She banged her gavel when she got all-round agreements. "Okay, then. Next item for discussion is Defense Force transport. Sarah Jennifer?"

Sarah Jennifer had considered Esme's rebuke and had to concede she was right about at least surveying the land bridge to find out if it could be blocked. "It's a little bit more complicated than that. The efforts in northern Mass and beyond to stop the Mad were nothing short of heroic, but the work is not done. As long as the route from Siberia into the Americas remains open, the Mad have free passage from the rest of the world. Esme believes we can block the land bridge, and I'm inclined to agree after seeing the scope of what magic can achieve. Our only issue is in getting there."

"The bus is great," Brutus commented. "But you're not talking a couple of days' drive to a city where there are roads. You're talking about going farther than Canada. It would take months to get there and back."

"Which is why we're going to focus on getting ourselves airborne," Sarah Jennifer told him. "We're going to find a pre-WWDE plane, and Engineering is going to convert it to an airship."

Jim's mouth fell open. "You want us to build a *what*, now?"

"An airship," Sarah Jennifer repeated.

"That's not possible." Jim looked around the room for support. He found expectant stares from everyone who had gathered in the town hall for the meeting. "I don't know anything about building airships! Except that they need hydrogen, and producing enough to keep it fueled will take more lives than this cat has left."

Sarah Jennifer shook her head. "I didn't say anything about a dirigible. I need something more durable than a bag of air and a few gravitic thrusters. I'm talking full-on TQB-spec antigravity. I don't expect it to happen tomorrow, but I want to be able to get to the other side of the world in twenty-four hours before the Madness hits here for real."

"Impossible!" Jim protested. "Nothing has gone that fast since before WWDE."

"Not true," Sarah Jennifer told him. "There were still Kurtherian Pods zipping around less than a hundred years ago."

"Besides," Brutus added, getting on board with the idea instantly. "I'm going to find you an appropriate workspace. You'll have everything you need."

Esme interrupted before Jim could protest further. "What's your real issue, Jim? I know you're not refusing the challenge of a lifetime and the opportunity to work with the old technology."

Jim folded his hands on the table, his head bowed in deep thought. "That's just it. I haven't *got* a lifetime, and this could take longer than I have left on the Earth to accomplish."

Sarah Jennifer patted his hand. "There will be time, and we have options if it comes to that before you're ready. The other thing I want you to do is continue sharing what you know."

"You mean, continue with classes?" Jim asked. "I can't

see how I'll find the time if I'm shifting my specialty. I'll be studying as I go."

"Which is just fine," Sarah Jennifer agreed. "But you have time to teach the basics to a select few, like Geordie and Carver. They will be the ones teaching the classes, and that will give you a pool to recruit engineers from when we're ready to build."

The council murmured their agreement. Lenore spoke up. "Preserving human knowledge is vital, especially in troubled times when it can slip away without warning. I will work with you."

Jim's face reddened at her shy smile. "Thank you, Ms. Lenore," he mumbled.

Sarah Jennifer smiled, seeing the spark between them. She pushed her chair back. "If that's everything, we can break to eat."

"There's just one thing." David's tone drew pained sighs from everyone else. "Have the Weres all submitted to pack law? Including Katia?"

"Get over it," Magnus told him shortly. "They've just been rescued from the leeches, and you're already creating drama."

Sarah Jennifer shook her head at David's continued mistrust. She flashed an apologetic look at Katia. "I get that some people are too small-minded to see the world in any terms other than them and us. I can even understand it. What I won't do is tolerate that mindset being aimed at any living human being."

She sat back, her voice cool. "I'll remind you that there's only one distinction that matters anymore. You fought on that ridge. You know what's coming. Feel free to leave

Salem and take your chances with the nomads if you're not happy being part of the effort to save us all."

David dropped his gaze. "Forgive me for trying to protect us."

Brutus closed his eyes and counted to five slowly.

Sarah Jennifer was out of patience. "David, you're going to need protection from me if you keep on this subject. We need to discuss finding the airplane."

Katia observed the exchange with little interest. "He's not the first human to pass judgment without knowing me. He won't be the last. I'd have to give a shit for it to matter."

Sarah Jennifer glared David into silence. "If anyone has anything *relevant*."

"Why is this murderess dictating our actions?" David cut in, gesturing at Katia. "Have you all forgotten she killed my brother? Does his memory mean nothing to you?"

Brutus got to his feet, unable to see Katia take his insults a moment longer. "The only memory I have of your brother is of him telling us we could stay here as long as we paid for it with our blood. When Katia refused, he tried to snatch Carver and Bard, which was why he found himself missing his windpipe."

David's mouth worked a moment before he sat back. "I had no idea."

"I did," Magnus admitted. He bowed his head.

Sarah Jennifer grabbed Esme's gavel and banged it on the table. "Whatever anyone did before, whatever they believed in, it's gone. Over with. Done. This is a committee meeting, not a remediation session. The *only* thing that matters is the Madness. Can we for the love of sleep's sake get back on track?"

Little Ace suddenly clapped a hand on the table, sending his pen rolling. He recovered it and jotted a quick sketch of the area he was thinking of on his notepad. "I remember seeing a bunch of hangars near the prepper place. There's a museum or something nearby, too."

"Define 'near,'" Sarah Jennifer told him, examining the sketch with curiosity. "And what can we do about getting our hands on some biofuel for the vehicles?"

Little Ace grinned. "I'm sure we can figure something out, Major."

CHAPTER TWENTY-EIGHT

<u>Boston, MA (one week later)</u>

The museum had escaped notice by looters post WWDE. Much like the university, its status as an educational institution made it unattractive to scavengers looking for food, clothing, and weapons.

The museum was a side mission. Sarah Jennifer wasn't expecting to find much in there besides decommissioned display pieces and memorabilia. Still, there was always the chance there were good tools to be found, so she'd added the museum to their list.

Sarah Jennifer led Tac Team One around abandoned cars and trucks in the parking lot, keeping an ear on the progress of Teams Two to Four over the comm.

Little Ace and Carver finished their sweep of the parking lot and returned to Sarah Jennifer. "All clear, Major," Carver reported. "The lieutenant says he won't have a problem with the generator."

Sarah Jennifer nodded, glad she'd thought to bring Jim along. "That's what I like to hear. Hopefully the others have had the same luck, and we can get to finding out what we have here."

She lifted a hand to halt her team and clicked the button on her radio twice to let the others know her entry was clear, then waited while Brutus, Bruiser, and Ozzie double-clicked to confirm their teams hadn't encountered anything unexpected.

"Everyone has eyes on their ingress? Over." Sarah Jennifer received three double-clicks again. "Good. Move in, and keep your eyes and ears open."

Katia remained a short distance from the pack. She folded her arms, put out that she'd been told to stay back. Half of her wanted to be part of the pack again, seeing what they had become under the leadership of Sarah Jennifer. She'd been a good Alpha, but the major was something else entirely.

They had grown so much in the time she'd been locked up. She remembered how afraid they had all been leaving Boston for the forest. How she'd sucked up her own fear and found the strength to lead them to Salem, then dug deeper when they'd been forced to make their home away from the town.

She muttered to herself, more out of habit than unhappiness at the way things were. "Take my pack and leave me sitting here with my thumb up my ass while you all play soldiers."

Sarah Jennifer fixed her with a stern look from across the parking lot. "Don't think I can't hear you," she called. "We'll talk about this later. Come on, we're headed inside."

Katia hissed at being caught. She jumped down from

the car she was using as a lookout post and darted through the parking lot. "Okay, I'm here."

Sarah Jennifer pointed to the team. "Stay in the middle until we've cleared the building."

Katia snorted. "Why bother with all this?" she asked, indicating the formation they'd assumed with a wave of her hand.

Sarah Jennifer bit back her retort, seeing that Katia was still unused to the stoic discipline the pack showed these days. "This is how we avoid getting killed or worse. As my grandfather used to say, proper preparation prevents piss-poor performance. We won't be taken by surprise."

Katia eyed their surroundings as they entered the museum. "That sounds like bullshit to me."

Sarah Jennifer chuckled dryly. "It does? Let's see if you think that way when it saves your life. How long have you been around?"

Katia shrugged. "A century, give or take."

Sarah Jennifer guessed take was more likely. "So, you were still a kid when you took responsibility for the pack. I can't believe how hard you all had it. No one should have to raise themselves. Everyone deserves a family, I know I'd be a different person without mine to keep me in line growing up."

Katia looked at her long and hard. "That's why you're so self-assured. You had people who gave a shit. Look, I'm not going to challenge you for the pack. But I'm not going to stick around if you're thinking to make me part of your military. It's not in me to follow orders, and I had them rammed down my throat in that hellhole for so long that all I want is a quiet place to live by myself in peace."

Sarah Jennifer tucked the information away for later. She offered the worn woman a smile. "Don't we all? You're free to live however you want. Just remember that you're a member of my pack. You have people who give a shit."

She spoke into the radio as she led her team to the main entrance. "Move it or lose it, buckoes. Last Were inside that building gets to cook for everyone tonight."

The teams moved in. Sarah Jennifer waited for Carver to get the door open and went inside ahead of the team.

It didn't take long for the teams to clear the building and meet in the main gallery. Katia extracted herself from her bodyguards and indicated the displays with a grin. "What is all this stuff?"

"Records of the past," Sarah Jennifer told her, looking up at the four fighter planes suspended from the ceiling. "This place has plenty of potential. They had to have equipment to maintain the displays."

Brutus joined them, stopping to read the plaque below a suspended WWII fighter plane. "We'll keep looking until we find it."

Sarah Jennifer smiled. "We have other places to search, don't forget. Tell Bruiser the teams are to stay on stripping the museum and then meet us out front. Jim, Ace, Ace, Ozzie, Katia, Geordie, and Carver. You seven are with me. Let's go find us a hangar."

Little Ace led the exploration of the area immediately around the museum grounds, uncovering an overgrown airfield and a short runway with twin hangars at the near end a mile or so out from the museum.

Brutus radioed Bruiser with their position and instructed him to keep up the good work loading everything of value from the museum into the bus, the truck, and the SUV.

Sarah Jennifer grinned as Geordie and Carver whooped and congratulated Little Ace. "Don't get too excited just yet, boys. We don't know what's inside."

"It's gotta be something big, Major," Little Ace insisted with a hopeful expression. "Look at the size of the hangar." He examined the locking system while Jim circumvented it with the help of a portable power source and frowned at Sarah Jennifer. "It looks like it's sealed pretty well. My experience from reclamation is intact buildings like this protect whatever's inside to a degree."

Sarah Jennifer's experience was the same, but she held onto her hope for the moment. The hangar could contain a crop duster or nothing at all. Worse would be finding something like the pre-WWDE military used for transporting troops and equipment in such disrepair they couldn't reclaim it. Her grandfather had told her some of those behemoth planes could carry tanks—multiples thereof, no less. "There's only one way to find out. Brutus, Ozzie, crack those doors."

Jim stepped aside and Brutus and Ozzie hauled the sliding doors open, giving them their first look at the long body and curved wings of the Boeing 787 Dreamliner inside.

Sarah Jennifer walked into the hangar and stopped with her hands on her hips. She didn't know whether to be pleased they'd found something large enough to transport the entire pack with some modifications or crushed by the amount of work it would take to get the Dreamliner up and running.

Brutus whistled. "That looks *fancy*."

Sarah Jennifer smiled despite herself. "Fancy's the right word for it, but I'm not sure a private jet was on the acquisitions list." She looked back into the airfield. "Lieutenant Johnson!"

Jim strode into the hangar, rubbing his hands together with glee when he saw the Dreamliner. "We couldn't have wished for this," he exclaimed. "What a beauty!"

"Come back down to Earth for a moment, Lieutenant," Sarah Jennifer told him. "I need a realistic answer. Converting this vehicle if I get you someone who understands antigravity technology. Can it be done?"

Jim had a shine in his eyes. "She's not a warplane yet, but give me a few months, and I'll have her refitted. As for the engines, all it will take is time and the right components if there's someone who understands the technology well enough."

Sarah Jennifer wondered how Sylvia was going to take the news she was going to be a part of the race to save humanity after all. "We can get the components," she told him, wondering if the trip to Chicago had been inevitable this whole time. She hoped there would be a friendly face there, but she wouldn't be going alone.

"Can we take a look inside?" Brutus asked hopefully, staring at the curved wings in awe. "I can't believe something this big could fly."

"Please?" Ozzie begged. "I've never seen anything so majestic."

"Not outside of books," Jim agreed. "She's going to be a wonder once we get her airborne."

Sarah Jennifer broke into a smile, unable to resist the

boyishness the plane brought out in the others as they filtered through the door. "Can you open it?" she asked Jim.

Jim lifted his hands. "I don't know why not. Let me see what I can do. Boys, grab your tools and follow me."

Carver and Geordie jumped to it while Sarah Jennifer made her way back to the museum to get the rest of the pack. The Ace brothers followed at a brisk trot, talking through the logistical effort that would have to be organized.

Big Ace waved his ledger. "We're gonna have to make a lot of trips to get what we strip out of here back to Salem, and even with the bus to tow the plane, I reckon the cost in time and labor to repair and widen the roads is going to be a thorn in the side of the project.

"There's no shortage of weapons," Little Ace chipped in. "I reckon we'll have enough guns to fit a whole fleet of airships once we've stripped that museum."

"If we find an airplane," Bruiser grumbled as they walked into the museum lobby. "All we found in here is pieces of them."

"And the tools," Katia consoled, shifting the weight of the crate she was carrying. "It's gearhead heaven down in the basement."

Sarah Jennifer grinned. "That's a bonus. We'll be flying in style soon enough, don't worry, Sergeant."

Bruiser tilted his head in curiosity.

"What do you mean?" Katia asked with a look of apprehension.

Sarah Jennifer stalled the question with a finger. "Wait a minute," she told him, activating the radio. "Everyone, make your way to the second hangar on the airfield northeast of the museum. I have a surprise."

The pack gathered at the hangar as instructed. Sarah Jennifer had them wait for Carver and Geordie to open the sliding doors, anticipating their reaction to the jet. She wasn't disappointed.

Katia chuckled when every male there burst into excited chatter. They stormed the hangar, mobbing Carver and Geordie with questions.

Sarah Jennifer indicated Katia follow her to the mobile staircase by one of the jet's emergency doors. "Come on. It looks like Jim got her open."

Brutus and Jim met them at the top of the stairs.

"You have to see it in there," Brutus told Sarah Jennifer, pulling her by the arm into the lounge. "Can you believe people lived in luxury like this?"

Sarah Jennifer sucked in a breath as her feet sank into the carpet. "You think you'll be okay living here? It beats your old place in Lynnwood by a long shot."

Brutus laughed, dropping into one of the plush chairs. He spun it around, stretching his legs as he let out a moan of pleasure. "This airplane is designed for a few people to travel in comfort. The owner must have been as rich as hell."

"Likely," Sarah Jennifer agreed, bending to look inside the bar cabinet. She straightened up. "I want all of this stripped out," she told Jim.

Jim nodded and waved his notebook. "The interior changes are going to be the easy part. Tell me what you want, and I'll tell you what's doable."

"You can't be serious?" Brutus exclaimed. "Why would you want to change any of this?"

Sarah Jennifer ignored his protest, making her way out of the lounge to inspect the cabins. "I'll need to do a full walkthrough before I decide the details, but if this is our ride, I want it to take the whole pack, plus whatever equipment we need, to wherever the Mad are. How many cabins can you fit in without it getting uncomfortable?"

Jim stopped scribbling and scrutinized the guest cabin. "I don't know just yet. I'll have the boys strip it back to the bare bones, and then we'll know what square footage we're working with. There could be manuals or something that will help in the office out there."

Sarah Jennifer nodded, heading back into the lobby. "I'd rather take time to make sure it's fitted to our needs. Go and check the office, the way our luck's running there will be a step-by-step guide to converting this plane to run on power packs."

Jim chuckled as he left. "Sure, and I'll come across a cure for the Madness while I'm in there. We can sprinkle it over Europe and be home this time next Tuesday."

Katia came out of another door in the lobby. "I found the master cabin."

Sarah Jennifer went into the room Katia had just exited. This was the plushest place on the plane, possibly the whole planet, if she only counted the inhabited spaces. Her earlier joking came back to her when she realized that this cabin was the same size as Brutus' old home. It had more amenities, too, although the electronics were useless for the moment. She gave the kitchen area a miss and walked past the mahogany desk and the curved couch to find out what was through the door between them.

"No way." Sarah Jennifer almost didn't dare test the king-sized mattress on the four-poster bed. Almost. She sat down on the edge and sighed as she dropped back. "I want to keep you," she told the bed. "Really, I do. But you're too *big.*"

Brutus opened the door to the suite and called her name.

"Through here," Sarah Jennifer yelled back, reluctantly getting up from the bed to meet him in the living area.

Brutus was poking around the drawers in the sideboard when she walked in. "There you are. I just got back from looking around the storage space. There's a freaking *boat* down there! This was a good find, SJ. I can't believe our luck."

Sarah Jennifer smiled. "You and Jim both. Don't get too excited. We have a lot of work ahead of us before we're anything like secure. But yeah, we lucked out as long as Jim's crew can figure out how to plug gravitic engines into this thing."

Brutus clapped her on the back. "Then I guess we're going to make engineers of the pack. How long do you reckon it's going to take if we're all working together?" He grinned. "We'll be chasing our tails around Europe in no time. You wait and see."

Sarah Jennifer chuckled at her cousin's optimistic outlook.

"Just one thing's bothering me," Brutus continued. "How do we get the giant-ass airplane back to Salem?"

That was the question that had been going through

Sarah Jennifer's mind while she'd been exploring. "We're not," she decided. "We need to expand our defenses, and we have the Werepower to do it. I've been thinking...well, Esme has been talking about expanding a lot recently."

"You're thinking about the land bridge?" Brutus guessed.

Sarah Jennifer nodded. "We're vulnerable, and not just from the land bridge. The leeches aren't going to just shut up shop. We're at risk all along the coast, and anywhere the blood trade still has roots. If we reach out and build garrisons in a couple of the coastal towns between here and Salem, we'll have eyes on the sea. The north is a problem, but the pack is hundreds strong, thanks to our efforts at the prison."

Brutus listened intently, the seed of worry that had worked its way into his gut suddenly blooming at the thought of Linus. "You mean, after we've figured out what's affecting the Weres."

Sarah Jennifer shook her head. "We can't put people on lockdown unless we get proof it's contagious. I'm not certain. If it was, like, a flu, then everyone from the prison would be having the same issue with shifting. We can only act on an individual basis." She grimaced when Brutus nodded. "It's a tragedy. I've only had my wolf a short time, but I can't imagine losing the ability to run on four paws with the wind in my face and my senses on fire."

"It would kill me to lose half of what I am," Brutus admitted, looking at the floor. "Linus is devastated. They all are."

"Of course they are," Sarah Jennifer retorted without malice. "You went out to the quarantine house?"

Brutus nodded. "I went out two days ago. He was still pretty shaken, but he said he remembered a moment when he knew that if he shifted, he wasn't coming back from it. I think he's traumatized by his experiences, and he's blocking himself from shifting."

Sarah Jennifer looked at him in surprise. "You're a psychologist now?"

"What?" Brutus asked. "Sarai gave me a few books about helping people get past trauma. You're not the only one treading virgin ground. I want to do right by my pack."

"I can see that," Sarah Jennifer conceded with a thoughtful smile. She liked her cousin and Annie's daughter as a match, but only time would tell. "Part of helping people heal is giving them a purpose."

"You can just say I'm right," Brutus teased. He waved a finger to indicate the mischievous grin making his eyes twinkle. "Look how it makes me smile."

Sarah Jennifer punched him, then wrapped her arm around him and pulled him in for a brief hug. "You're an ass, Brutus Timmons, but the care you have for everyone is the most admirable quality I can think of."

Brutus took the backhanded compliment for the high praise it was and returned Sarah Jennifer's embrace. "Thanks, I think."

Sarah Jennifer shoved him away with a laugh. "Don't worry about Linus and the others. Esme will know what to do by the time we get back."

CHAPTER TWENTY-NINE

<u>Salem, MA</u>

Sarah Jennifer was sitting in her study with a pot of tea and one of Tom's fruitcakes on the table between her and Esme, waiting for Esme's prognosis. Linus, Dakota, and the two town Weres had been joined by another pack member who had gotten stuck in wolf form while she had been away, a teenage boy. They were being cared for by his mother and Dakota's husband, as well as Esme and Lenore.

"It's not in their heads," Esme confirmed.

"Brutus had his heart in the right place," Sarah Jennifer replied. "But I already figured it was unlikely that they're all suffering from the same psychological disorder. I have to consider that this *could* be connected to the Madness, and if it is, how do I stop it spreading through the pack without locking everyone down?"

She sighed, voicing her deepest fear. "What if the final stage turns Weres into flesh-hungry Pricolicis and I have to kill my pack?"

"Not at all likely, and it doesn't bear thinking about,"

Esme chastised firmly. "So don't waste time imagining it. We have some time while the plane is being refitted, and you have to persuade your sister to help Jim with the engines. We'll work with Lilith to get to the bottom of what's happening." She shook her fist for emphasis. "What's that you like to say? No Were left behind? Well, we'll have to work to make sure of it."

Sarah Jennifer smiled despite her concern. "Just when we got all the pieces in place to make a real difference. Esme, we have to do something. Is there anything you can think of that will help my people regain their ability to shift?"

Esme was quiet as she poured the tea. She passed Sarah Jennifer a cup. "I have no way of knowing why they can't shift without equipment to analyze their blood and their nanocytes, but my best guess is that something happened to jam the 'switch' that makes the shift possible."

"Okay, so how do we unjam it?" Sarah Jennifer pressed, eager to act instead of sitting around talking. She sighed at the pointed look Esme gave her. "Right. Equipment we need to stop the apocalypse isn't going to be lying around where we can get to it two hundred years after the last apocalypse." She paused, snorting softly. "Is this how we measure the passage of time now? By apocalypses?"

Esme let Sarah Jennifer talk herself out. "There's a possibility the equipment in some labs survived. What we don't have is a way of finding the labs. Huh. I miss Google."

"Who's that?" Sarah Jennifer inquired.

"Not who, what," Esme corrected without explaining. "But we do have Lilith, and she might be able to help us track down somewhere I can do a full workup on the pack's blood. We have to assume that corruption in their nanocyte code is to blame, but we only know of one transmittable virus that affects Kurtherian technology, and the presenting symptoms don't match those we saw in the Mad."

Sarah Jennifer couldn't disagree, but she needed to be prepared for either eventuality. "Neither of us knows how the Madness affects the already-enhanced. I don't want to make an assumption and end up looking back on this as the moment where I failed to prevent the goat rope we end up with because I couldn't keep an open mind. So, we don't close ourselves off to the idea we're dealing with a separate issue. However, we also can't lose our focus on protecting this country from the threat we know is there."

"I'm going to start planning the expedition north in the next few days," Esme told her. "We will raise mountains if that's what it takes to stop any more Mad finding their way from Siberia."

Another weight on Sarah Jennifer's shoulders made its presence known. "I feel like I should be going with you."

Esme laughed. "Not likely, unless you figured out how to be in two places at once." She put her fingers to her temples and exaggerated an expression of concentration. "I see many hours on the road for you before Jim gets the plane off the ground."

Sarah Jennifer pointed at Esme and smirked. "That's where you're wrong. Little Ace's crews will be spending their hours on the road. I'm going to be in the unfortunate position of riding a desk to keep everything running smoothly. I'll have my office moved to the airship when she's ready."

Esme sipped her tea. "Here's hoping that day isn't too far in the future."

Sarah Jennifer nodded. "I'll have to start the search for immunes as soon as the ship is operational. We have enough power packs for the conversion, and I sent Brutus to Sylvia with the message that we need her here. Have you seen Jim's plans for the layout of the airship? Your cabin is across from mine."

Esme shook her head, bristling at the news. "I can't leave Salem."

"I need you more than Salem does," Sarah Jennifer told her. "You're the only one who knows one machine from another. I can't perform the blood analysis on the Weres, and I wouldn't know what I was looking at, even if I could figure out how to access the Mad-infected nanocytes. Annie, Sarai, and the rest of the council will take care of the people. The pack will keep growing as word spreads and more Weres come from around the country to find a haven from the Madness."

Esme considered it for a moment. From Lilith's description, she suspected the expedition north would unveil an ice shelf that stretched from the Barents Sea to the Bering Sea, swallowing everything from Greenland to Hokkaido and beyond. The Arctic Ocean was definitely gone, and probably a good portion of the Atlantic as well. Sarah Jennifer was right; the long game was what mattered. "I suppose someone will have to make sure you don't get yourselves killed before you find the cure."

"Who else is going to make the Mad dance?" Sarah Jennifer teased. She was distracted from her next thought by a commotion outside.

She jumped to her feet and grabbed her gun belt as she darted to the open window. Seeing the townspeople running in the opposite direction of the beach, she dived out the window, landing feet-first in the shrubbery below.

"Go, Duckie," Esme told her. "I'll be right behind you."

Sarah Jennifer nodded and raced for the source of the disturbance. She ordered Bruiser and Ozzie as she passed to assemble the tac teams and follow her, reminding them not to shift.

Arriving at the beach, Sarah Jennifer was relieved to find the panic was just that. A valid panic, sure. Death had washed up with the high tide, and she couldn't blame civilians for being frightened by the scene that met her.

The teams hit the beach running, then slid to a confused stop when they saw the battle they were expecting had been won by the witches already. They surveyed the wreckage that littered the tide line, ready to act if any of the washed-up corpses of the Mad who had perished in the creation of the Maine gorge were still a danger.

Besides the twenty-four in the tac teams, many of the Defense Force recruits had also made their way down to the beach. They hung around the dunes a few hundred feet from the high tide line, watching Sarah Jennifer and the teams.

Sarah Jennifer paused by Bruiser and Ozzie. "I can't smell anything living in all of that. No corruption, either."

Ozzie tilted his head. "So, they die a second time, and their nanocytes stop working?"

Sarah Jennifer could only hope. "We'll wait to see if that's true." She swept the beach with a look of distaste—

splintered trees, bedraggled vegetation, and bodies everywhere. She saw lumber, parts of homes that had been destroyed in the battle to hold back the Mad. "I guess we should have considered this would happen."

Bruiser thought it would serve as a wake-up call for the reluctant. "Looks like we have the perfect opportunity to build some character in the recruits. What do you think, Major?"

Sarah Jennifer nodded. "Nice initiative, Sergeant. I want to see a cordon, then we scour the beach to make sure there are no threats remaining. Move the bodies out of sight. I need to find someone with fire magic."

Bruiser and Ozzie began barking orders at the pack. Tac Team One produced a few coils of rope and put up a long cordon to keep the civilians to the dunes as the sergeants instructed while the other teams began the arduous task of clearing the flotsam that had washed up along with the bodies.

Sarah Jennifer worked twice as hard as everyone else, as was her way when an example was needed. She dragged whole trees that had been torn from the ground, roots and all, to the designated spot to dry out, ready to form a pyre. Each body she carried respectfully to be placed with the others.

As the day went on, the townspeople who had run initially came back with others and gathered behind the cordon. The faces at the cordon changed as the hours passed. The people of Salem came out to offer their support, accepting Sarah Jennifer's refusal to allow them onto the sand until the contamination was clear.

The pack did not pause in their grim task until dusk

when the people behind the cordon began to sing. Just a few at first, people looking to pass the time and keep morale high. The song spread and the sound of many voices in harmony rose to lift the spirits of the Weres working on the sand.

Sarah Jennifer was reminded of Samhain again, except this time around, she didn't feel Lilith's presence.

Esme arrived with the witches just as the last pale streaks vanished from the horizon. They ignored Sarah Jennifer's cordon, and Little Ace's protests and marched onto the sand, carrying hampers stuffed with thick-cut meat sandwiches and flasks of soup and hot chocolate.

The beach was mostly cleared by that point, so Sarah Jennifer didn't order them back to the grassy dunes behind the cordon. She held up her hand when Esme offered her a wrapped sandwich and a flask. "Give me a minute."

She looked at the sea, which was still churning and grimy from all the mess from Maine, and settled for stripping off her overshirt and wiping what she could from her hands. "I wish I was in that beautiful bed on the plane, Esme."

Esme watched her efforts to clean her hands with amusement. "You can do that with Etheric energy."

Sarah Jennifer stared at Esme blankly, exhausted. "Huh?"

"Come here." Esme lifted her glowing hands and burned the dirt and grime away from Sarah Jennifer's face and hands. She fed Sarah Jennifer a boost of energy while they were connected, seeing her friend was at the limit of her physical endurance. "You have one more thing to do, then you can sleep."

Sarah Jennifer's gaze drifted along the beach, where her enhanced vision had no trouble making out the pile of bodies in the gathering dark. "I know."

"Not that." Esme put her hand on Sarah Jennifer's shoulder and turned her to look at the people behind the cordon. "Them. They're scared. They've seen for themselves what the Madness does to people's bodies. They want to know they aren't going to wake up like that."

Sarah Jennifer whipped her head around to stare at Esme. "I can't promise them that! I can tell them I'll fight it and shield them from it, but until we find our immune, nothing can stop the Madness."

"I know," Esme told Sarah Jennifer quietly, meeting her fiery expression with a comforting smile. "But you can give them *hope*. You are fighting, and that's what they need to hear."

Sarah Jennifer dropped her head. "Okay." She walked over to the cordon and looked the people in the eye. The words she needed to say came to her, clear as the starry night sky above. "You're scared. That's okay. This is something to be scared of. Esme thinks you need to hear that I'm going to fight for you, and rest assured that I'm going to fight."

She squared her shoulders. "What I want to hear is that *you're* going to fight. That you're going to do whatever it takes to keep humanity from extinction. I happen to believe in people empowering themselves. You have a right to be angry that your lives have been torn apart. Use that anger to focus. We are not fighting for our survival. We are fighting for the right for our children to live, and for their children to thrive. Surviving the Madness is going to take everything we have to give."

The people cheered, many of them calling out to offer their skills.

Sarah Jennifer smiled, seeing her words hit home with the people. Maybe it was going to be almost impossible, but that was a long way from the completely impossible she'd been working with just a few months ago when she'd started on this path.

She raised her hands. "Thank you all. Everyone has something they can offer that will increase our chances of winning. Your support today has meant a lot to everyone working here. But it's getting late. Go home, rest. Tomorrow is a new day. If you haven't already visited the town hall to add your name to the volunteer list, you can do so tomorrow."

Esme nodded in approval when Sarah Jennifer headed back over to where she was seated on a log. She held out a sandwich and a hot drink. "You're not half bad at this leadership malarkey," she commented, patting the log.

Sarah Jennifer sighed as she sat down beside Esme. "We've only just begun to tackle the obstacles. The more people we have, the better."

"Will Sylvia agree to come out here to help Jim?" Esme asked.

Sarah Jennifer paused before taking a bite of her sandwich. "I guess we'll find out when Brutus gets back into radio range. He should have gotten to Sylvie's house yesterday, so we'll find out soon enough."

EPILOGUE

Federation Space, Dren Cluster, Keeg Station, Spires Shipyard (one week earlier)

Felicity's heels echoed, announcing her arrival in the hall outside Ted's workshop. She found him gone to the world as always, lost in his work. "Plato, honey, can you tell Ted I'm here?"

Ted reluctantly deactivated the multiple windows he had running around the room and in his mind. He paused over a simulation he had running and decided he could leave that since it was near its conclusion.

Felicity touched his shoulder. Ted looked up, shocked as always by her beauty and comforted by the consistent love in her eyes.

"We have a call," she drawled, gracing him with her smile.

Ted's gaze drifted away from the shine of her red lipstick as he rapidly lost interest in the conversation. "We already had our scheduled call with the children this month."

His simulation was showing results.

Plato's voice intruded into Ted's mindspace. "Felicity asked me to inform you that it is Sylvia calling."

Ted disengaged from the sim. "Sylvie?"

Felicity nodded, no reproach in her smile for his momentary exit from reality. "Lita gave her the original IICS after we gave them personal IICS devices. She's saying Sarah Jennifer needs our help."

Ted's eyebrows lifted as he absorbed the information. His resounding memory of the twins as youths was of them raising hell. Sylvia was always more solitary than Sarah, who had always been full of questions more suited to Timmons or Shonna, or anyone but him.

It was an annoyance he'd felt the absence of for a while after she'd grown up and joined the FDG, but he'd adjusted once Felicity noticed he was struggling with the change in routine and began bringing him sandwiches to fill the time she'd left empty.

He had been thrown for a loop after Sarah vanished without a trace from her ranch, but he'd understood once Felicity had explained the emotional factors in relation to his own experiences of death. While he couldn't empathize, he *could* understand the logic of wanting to escape loss. He loved his children strongly enough to find a way to be present for them. Why shouldn't she seek to leave the world behind when denied hers?

Adjusting to the new order, he deduced that Sarah had come back from her self-imposed exile and gotten herself into a fight. The fight must be pretty big, or she wouldn't be….wait, no. Sylvie.

Sarah wasn't asking for help, Sylvia was asking on her

behalf, which meant Sarah thought she could win. That could mean anything. Sarah always thought she could win.

Still, he didn't see what any of that had to do with him.

Felicity saw he was drifting again. "Ted, there's a problem with the nanocytes on Earth. You're the only one who can help Sarah survive this crusade she's got her heart set on."

Felicity watched Ted's interest return at the mention of nanocytes. She slipped her arm through his and led him from the workshop. "I didn't see it coming either. I wonder what she's been doing all this time?"

Ted smiled. She'd catch up soon enough.

Pittsburgh, PA

Ted left the navigation to Plato while he ran through his mental checklist one last time. Felicity's voice drew him from his thoughts on Sarah's apparent certainty that she could reverse the zombie apocalypse with a little help from him.

"This is Pittsburgh?" Felicity looked away from the sprawling forest below. "Have we been away so long?"

Ted looked at Felicity a long moment. "Plato says we'll be landing in five minutes. I'm going to the cargo bay to check—"

"We're going to say hello to Sylvia and Brutus before we go on to Salem," Felicity told him gently but firmly.

Ted wondered if that was his punishment for zoning out earlier.

Felicity tilted her head to catch his sliding gaze. "Ted? Timmons having a grandson is a surprise, but unexpected family is always a blessing. I'm happy we have a chance to meet him."

Ted sighed. The things he did for love. "Fine. But if he's anything like his father, we're out of there."

Felicity's mouth curled up the way it did when she knew something he didn't. "Thank you."

Sylvia was waiting in the clearing behind her house when they reached the IICS coordinates. She waved with both arms, while Brutus stood to one side and stared open-mouthed as the ship touched down in silence.

Felicity descended the ramp with open arms. She enveloped Sylvia in a hug first, then Brutus. "Sylvia, darlin'! You're too thin, child. How wonderful to meet you, Brutus. Aren't you a handsome one? You must get your build from your momma's side of the family, but your eyes and nose are all your granddaddy's."

Brutus reddened under her scrutiny. "Well, ma'am, I, um… Thank you both for coming all this way to help."

Felicity swatted him with a hand. "I won't hear any of that nonsense from you. We're family. You can call me Felicity. Come on up to the ship. We can be in Salem in just a few minutes."

Ted eyed the muscled Timmons lookalike without acknowledging him. He did, however, accept Sylvia's hug as they boarded the ramp.

She squeezed his ribs with too much enthusiasm. "Hey, guess what? Sarah has a wolf form now, and she's friends with witches. Real ones, with magic."

Ted froze. "Magic doesn't exist."

Sylvia laughed. "Tell that to the witches."

• • •

<u>Salem, MA</u>

Sarah Jennifer was taking advantage of the relative quiet on the common to get some thinking done while she exercised to relieve the pressure sitting at her desk all day put on her knee. She was beginning to wonder if Sylvia had declined to come back to Salem with Brutus.

It had been eight days since he'd left to return her truck and pass along Sarah Jennifer's request, making her think Brutus was journeying back on foot. At least, he'd *better* be on foot. She was holding herself to the same stricture as she was holding the pack to, which meant no shifting for any Were under any circumstances.

Sarah Jennifer could admit she was feeling somewhat crabby after being cooped up for the last few days. While she'd been getting tenser about how long Brutus had been gone, she'd organized the upcoming training schedule for the Defense Force recruits, switched up the rota in preparation for beginning her version of officer training for suitable candidates. She was also working on expanding her abilities with the Etheric.

She'd come to terms with her connection to the Etheric. It didn't mean she was in agreement with the magic explanation, but she was starting to understand it was easier to let people believe what they needed to.

Working on the ability to create mental connections was at the top of her list. If she could figure a way to extend the ability to speak mind-to-mind with the pack, it would make them unstoppable. Increasing the reach of her compulsion was another thing she wanted to have better control of before they left for Europe, along with the healing capability Esme was so certain she had.

Sarah Jennifer forgot her troubles as she flowed through the stances, bringing her world down to her next footfall, the turn into the kick, *hold* for ten, the backward motion of her elbow as the ball of her foot touched down. She needed no weapons; she *was* the weapon.

Meditation was the key to inner stillness, which in turn was the door to accessing the potential locked in her nanocytes. Sarah Jennifer knew she could fix her knee. She just had to make it happen, and today felt like the day she was going to succeed.

Her mind clear, she focused on pushing the pain out of the ligament and cartilage as she moved. Her techniques were slow and deliberate at half-speed, holding each stance, working each part of her body as she focused on opening up the energy around her knee the way Esme did.

Sarah Jennifer felt the Etheric all around her, just out of reach. She believed if she closed her eyes, she could touch it. Eyes shut, she continued her movements, feeling a breeze spring up to cool her skin. She stepped and ducked, willing the pain to leave as she performed a series of blocks with her arms.

Recognizing that the reason she felt ready to heal her injury had much to do with the people she had taken responsibility for, Sarah Jennifer let go of the shame she'd felt since her grandfather had taken her down to instill some humility.

She wasn't so callow anymore, not since limping away from the family she'd loved and lost, then lost herself for too long before coming to Salem and finding this new purpose. She'd ended up exactly where she was supposed to be and been rewarded with finding family in Brutus and Esme.

Sarah Jennifer opened her eyes in shock when she felt a burst of warm energy flow outward from her body. Her eyes were glowing brighter than she'd yet seen them, casting red light wherever she looked, despite the brightness of the day.

"I'll be damned," a familiar, exasperated voice exclaimed from overhead.

Sarah Jennifer shook her head, releasing the energy when Ted's voice shattered the moment. She *couldn't* be hearing Ted.

"Told you," Sylvia's voice chipped in from the same place.

Sarah Jennifer looked up and saw a door hanging in the sky, filled by Brutus, Sylvia, and… "Felicity? Is that you?"

"In the flesh, darlin,'" Felicity called. "Ted's here too, but he just saw your little lightshow and ran off somewhere."

"Hopefully to land this thing." Brutus moaned, holding his stomach.

"Quit your bitching," Sylvia told him fondly. "This is the smoothest ride there is. What are you going to do on that jet plane of yours when it's all bouncing around with turbulence?"

Sarah Jennifer didn't register the bickering. Her mouth opened and closed as she tried and failed to process her shock at their sudden appearance. She stared as the door in the sky was joined by the rest of the ship it was attached to, then the ship landed in silence and Ted was walking down a ramp that appeared from…she wasn't quite sure where.

Ted pointed at Sarah Jennifer, then at the inside of his ship. "Pod-doc. Then we'll discuss your zombie problem."

Sarah Jennifer knew better than to correct him about the zombie thing.

A tune-up in a Pod-doc was just what she needed. Besides, giving Ted what he wanted without arguing would make him much more amenable to giving her pack some tweaks in there once he was done poking around in her nanocytes.

She smiled and boarded the ship with a spring in her step, calculating how many years this surprise visit was going to take off the war.

Almost impossible had just become completely doable.

Sarah Jennifer's story continues with *Walk The Line*, available now at Amazon and Kindle Unlimited.

Get your copy today!

AUTHOR NOTES - N D ROBERTS

APRIL 25, 2020

Hello! Thank you for joining me on the next step of Sarah Jennifer's journey, and thank you for continuing to these notes!

I'd like to thank everybody who has waited so patiently for this series from the bottom of my heart.

Thank you also to Lynne for her beautiful edit, to everyone in JIT and the Beta team for their input during development, and to Michael for putting up with answers like "accidental popcorn" to questions like "how is your book coming along?"

When I was asked to write something to answer the questions we all had, Sarah Jennifer was the natural choice as the lead character. The short story, *Sarah Jennifer's First Samhain* had already been published in the first volume of Kurtherian Gambit Fans Write For The Fans, and I had continued the story as writing practice with friends. (More fun times!)

That manuscript was 40k words, and many of the

elements from it made it into *Birth of Magic*. The story, however, did not. My practice was very separate from the rest of the KGU. I was careful not to use any of the star cast, and not to affect universe canon.

To quote Michael, "BWAHAHAHA!"

Sarah Jennifer grabbed my attention a long time ago, but her story has barely gotten started. Her life has been woven through the background of other character's stories, yet she's always been essential. The series has become a tapestry that pulls threads from all over the universe. Ted! I *love* Ted. I remember messaging Craig to thank him for writing an autistic character who was so real. Now here he is as a guest character in my book! It's the most beautiful thing.

If you haven't already read the short story that started this series and you'd like to read about what happened at the Samhain feast right before this book opens it's available here.

For writing updates, you can find me posting here whenever I come up for air:

https://www.facebook.com/NDRobertsBooks/

If this is the first time you're meeting Sarah Jennifer, you can find more of her backstory in the Terry Henry Walton Chronicles, and follow her into the Dark Messiah. Of course, if you're shiny and new, welcome! This is where you start to get the whole story.

All the books are available on Kindle Unlimited.

It's my great hope that you read this book and felt...if not at home, then close by.

Until we meet again in the author notes of book 2,
Good health and Happy Reading,

Nat

AUTHOR NOTES - MICHAEL ANDERLE

APRIL 30, 2020

THANK YOU for reading our story!

We have a few of these planned, but we don't know if we should continue writing and publishing without your input.

Options include leaving a review, reaching out on Facebook to let us know, and smoke signals.

Frankly, smoke signals might get misconstrued as low hanging clouds, so you might want to nix that idea...

If you're shiny and new, *welcome!*

We really appreciate you continuing our stories in the Kurtherian Gambit Universe and here, in the *Birth of Magic*!

I loved the comment above Nat shared in her *Author Notes*: 'If you are shiny and new, welcome!' It was a reminder to me that each new book, each new series catches someone's eye, and they start down this little path with one book.

And then another, and another and finally they realize they aren't just part of a series, but part of an age, and then a part of a huge universe of stories, authors, and friends they make because of the stories. It's just a wonderful huge time.

This story gives multiple hints as to what is going on with Earth and the nanocytes, which go a little…

Wrong.

And yet, while things go amiss, there are those on Earth who hold to the conviction of moving forward, no matter the challenges.

Or, sometimes, despite them.

In the end, we overcome and get to see the beauty of another sunrise!

So, if you happen to be "shiny and new" to the *Kurtherian Gambit,* we both welcome you and hope that this is just the start down a long and glorious new cast of characters you will call…

Friends.

Diary for April 26th- May 2, 2020

So, it's about six weeks into the stay-home phase, and there are mentions that states are going to slowly open up. A few words (well, a bunch) are slung all across the internet with opinions going both one way or the other.

Then I see a video about Anderson Cooper and the Las Vegas mayor. (Full disclosure, I live on the Strip and am not officially in the Las Vegas city limits but in Clark County. This is something I did not realize until this whole kerfuffle came about, and for some reason, I'm standing just a little bit straighter.)

Now, whether you knew this or not, I think it is interesting to note that the present mayor of Las Vegas is

Carolyn Goodman (in office 2012 to 2022 (likely term limit)), the wife of the previous mayor Oscar Goodman (in office 1999-2011 term-limited).

Further, she has been very industrious in the Las Vegas area, working for multiple organizations and leadership roles with the tourism industry, child welfare, and education. So, regardless of the state of the discussion on opening Las Vegas back up and using the citizens in this area (me included) as a science experiment (I'm rather against this notion), I find myself shocked to find out she has a lot of qualifications.

Amazing, I know.

Everyone who knows me through these *Author Notes* realizes I am cynical when it comes to government. In fact, before I reviewed more about the present mayor, I figured there had to be some shenanigans going on for the mayorship to go from spouse to spouse.

However, it seems I should have been paying more attention to the life of Mayor Goodman the First. He has a book (by him as author) published by Hachette titled *Being Oscar: From Mob Lawyer to Mayor of Las Vegas*.

I happen to know that there is a steakhouse he owns downtown at the top of the Plaza Hotel named... Guess? *Guess?*.... Oscar's!

He is a brand now.

I have to go.

I might be cynical, but steak covers a lot of cynicism.

I did a good thing...I think.

So my best friend and fellow author Craig Martelle lives in Alaska...inside the North Pole designation, and it costs him an arm and a leg to get decent internet up there in the frozen north.

I happened to ask him how come he loves it up there, and without a beat, he mentioned: "don't have to live near any politicians."

That's hardcore.

So, I received a marketing email from Skyroam about little internet pucks and sent the email to him. I have used Skyroam in the past for internet connectivity while traveling, so I knew how it worked. Apparently, it was working well enough to let him drop a line and save a few hundred bucks a month.

Then, I started looking at shotgunning his internet connections. I'm going to call and see if I can get him on the phone…

Hold on.

…. TALKING ….

I'm back. The short answer is no, it isn't working.

The longer answer is Craig spent an hour and a half playing with his Windows laptop, his Skyroam, and a phone that needed iTunes(??) to make it work. It hasn't so far, and I'm kinda bummed.

He was using some software (of which I can't remember the name), but I think there is just one major reason he is having this trouble.

Windows…He is using *Windows*. (This is complete and utter @#%@@! As it probably has nothing to do with Windows… But, he's on a PC, I'm a Mac guy… We have to carry the ribbing farther, even if I have to do it locked up in my condo thousands of miles away from him. Since Editor Lynne will be checking these author notes, I would not be surprised if she mentions something in here (she's a Windows person as well.)

(*Editor's Note: I shall nobly restrain myself, MacMan*)

I did the Brownstone Fries...

Short update to the Brownstone Fries idea with Jessie Rae's.

So, I had to speak with Mike Ross (Jessie Rae's BBQ) to explain my Brownstone Fries effort to help support their effort to make free lunches for those in the medical field.

Then, I left a message at their answering machine for call-in orders, but I was too late in the evening to get them to answer.

Bummer.

By the next morning, when I got a return call from Mike's mom, she already knew all about the Brownstone Fries, and it didn't confuse her at all.

Damn.

I was looking forward to explaining the "I need you to charge me for fries, but it's really a gift to help pay for people at the hospitals..." schtick I talked about in my last *Author Notes*.

Oh well, the gift went through, regardless.

Ad Aeternitatem,

Michael Anderle

They say that behind every great man is a great woman...but what if that woman is a Werewolf?

Available now at Amazon and through Kindle Unlimited.

This digital box set contains ALL 11 books of the best-selling Terry Henry Walton Chronicles series from Craig Martelle and Michael Anderle.

Nomad Found

Can Terry Henry Walton help bring humanity back to civilization?

He finds that he needs help and starts building his Force de Guerre, a paramilitary group that will secure this new world from those who would take and destroy.

When the enemies of peace appear before the FDG is

ready, Terry partners with a werewolf to fight a battle that he must win.

Nomad Redeemed

Sawyer Brown is no more, but he was just the minor opening act...

Terry Henry and Charumati (Char) have to deal with her Alpha coming back, the new refugees getting settled in the town and .. Beer!

With the FDG doubling in size, Terry Henry needs to bring about a little organizational structure to the group.While also deciding how to have that conversation with Char about her lineage...

Not sure how that is going to go, Terry Henry had better figure it out, or he is going to be up to his armpits in Werewolves and won't be sure if he can depend on his one ace-in-the-hole.

Or not.

Nomad Unleashed

The heat is unrelenting. The Wastelands are coming for New Boulder. Nature's a total bitch.

And then there's Werewolf heat.

Terry Henry Walton has to come to grips with the reality of his situation.

Civilization cannot return to humanity without help. More help than even an enhanced human can give. Terry and Char take their relationship to a new level before they head out to find a new home to save the people of New Boulder, to rally the survivors that the world is coming back...

And for themselves.

Nomad Supreme

Terry and Char cross the Wastelands returning to New Boulder carrying a message of hope. They'd found a better place. Could they move the whole town there, and would it be safer?

They have a lead on Terry's white whale, a secure military facility.

What will they find and can they break in?

Nomad's Fury

Settled into their new home of North Chicago, Terry and Char find more enemies than they suspected. Faced with their greatest threat, they put the FDG into action against a Forsaken who's surrounded himself with a small army of loyal humans. With Akio's aid, they go to war.

Nomad's Justice
Nomad Avenged
Nomad Mortis
Nomad's Fury
Nomad's Force
Nomad's Galaxy
Nomad's Journal

Available now at Amazon and through Kindle Unlimited.

BOOKS BY MICHAEL ANDERLE

For a complete list of books by Michael Anderle, please visit:

www.lmbpn.com/ma-books/

All LMBPN Audiobooks are Available at Audible.com and iTunes

To see all LMBPN audiobooks, including those written by Michael Anderle please visit:

www.lmbpn.com/audible

CONNECT WITH MICHAEL ANDERLE

Michael Anderle Social
   Website:
   http://www.lmbpn.com

Email List:
   http://lmbpn.com/email/

Facebook Here:
   www.facebook.com/TheKurtherianGambitBooks/